THE FURY

Alexander Gordon Smith

faber and faber

First published in 2012
by Faber and Faber Limited
Bloomsbury House, 74–77 Great Russell Street,
London WC1B 3DA

The right of Alexander Gordon Smith to be identified as author
of this work has been asserted in accordance with Section 77
of the Copyright, Designs and Patents Act 1988

A CIP record for this book
is available from the British Library

ISBN 978–0–571–27616–5

FSC
www.fsc.org
MIX
Paper from
responsible sources
FSC® C101712

10 9 8 7 6 5 4 3 2 1

This one's for Ariana Winter Edwards.
Thanks for making me an uncle!

Prologue

Thump-thump . . . Thump-thump . . . Thump-thump . . .

Wednesday

What are we but kings of dust and shadow? Lords of ruin,
Who watch empires rise and believe they will stand for all time;
Who tell each other that the end will never come,
That the night will never fall, that the abyss will stay forever closed.
What are we but mindless fools? For the end will come,
The night will fall, the abyss will open.
Soon or late the Fury will rise in all mankind;
And in its light the whole world will burn.

   Ancient Prophecy

Benny

It was an ordinary Wednesday afternoon in June when the world came to kill Benny Millston.

It was his birthday. His fifteenth. Not that anyone would have noticed. He sat quietly in the corner of the living room in the tiny box of a house that he'd called home ever since his parents had split up three years earlier. His mum lay on the sofa to his left, idly picking foam out of the gaping holes the dog had made in the ancient green fabric. She was staring at the telly over her huge stomach and between two sets of freshly painted toenails, her mouth open in an expression of awe and wonder, as if she were watching the Rapture, not *Deal or No Deal*.

On the other side of the room, slouched in a wicker bucket chair, sat his sister Claire. She had once been his baby sister, until his *actual* baby sister had arrived a year ago. The youngest Millston, Alison, squirmed in her high chair in the doorway between the living room and the kitchen, smacking the hell out of her dinner tray with a plastic spoon. Their dog, an elderly Jack Russell that he had named Crapper when he was a kid, sat under her, snapping half-heartedly at the spoon whenever it came close but too old and too lazy to make a proper effort.

Not one person had said happy birthday to him all day.

This wasn't what was bugging Benny, though. What was really starting to scare him was that nobody had even *spoken* to him all day.

And it wasn't just today, either. Strange things had been going on since last week. He couldn't put his finger on it, exactly; he just knew that something was wrong. People had been treating him differently. He wasn't the most popular kid at school, not by a long shot, but in the last couple of days even the guys he'd called friends – Adam, Ollie, Jamie – had been ignoring him. No, ignoring was the wrong word. They had talked to him, but it had almost been as if he wasn't really there, as if they were looking *through* him. And the stuff they said – *We don't need any more players, Benny. We're busy now, Benny. Goodbye, Benny* – had been downright hurtful. They'd been treating him like he'd taken an almighty dump in their mouth while they'd been sleeping. They'd been treating him like they *hated* him.

Things were no better at home, either. His mum's vocabulary was usually limited to about twenty words, of which 'do it now', 'don't argue with me' and 'I'm busy' were the most common. But this week he'd heard worse. Much worse. Yesterday she'd actually told him to piss off, which had come so far out of left-field that he'd almost burst into tears on the spot. Claire, too, was acting weird. She'd not said anything, but it was the way she glanced at him when she thought he wasn't watching, the way kids looked at strangers, at people they thought might be dangerous.

She was doing it right now, he realised, staring at him, her eyes dark, lined with suspicion, or maybe fear. As soon as he met them she turned back to the television, pulling her legs up beneath her, crossing her arms across her chest, curling into herself like a hedgehog being nuzzled by a dog. Benny felt goosebumps erupt on his arms, his cheeks hot but a cold current running through him.

What the hell was going on?

Benny reached up and rubbed his temples. His head was banging. It hadn't been right for a couple of days now, but what had started off as an irritating ringing in his ears now felt like somebody pounding the flesh of his brain with a meat tenderiser. And there was a definite rhythm to it, syncopated like a pulse:

Thump-thump . . .

Thump-thump . . .

Thump-thump . . .

Only it wasn't his pulse, it didn't match. If anything, it reminded him of somebody banging at a door, demanding to be let in. He'd taken a couple of paracetamol when he'd got home from school an hour ago, but they'd barely made a difference. It was literally doing his head in.

It was no wonder, though. He'd never been this stressed in his life.

No, not stressed. *Scared*.

He realised Claire was glaring at him again, and

the intensity in her eyes seemed to make the room shrink, the peeling floral-papered walls closing in. He pushed himself out of the armchair and his sister actually flinched, as if he'd been coming at her with a cricket bat. He opened his mouth to tell her it was okay, but nothing came out. The only sound in the room was that thumping pulse inside his head, like some giant turbine between his ears.

Benny walked towards the kitchen, Claire's eyes following him. His mum was watching him too, her head still pointing at the telly but her eyes swivelled so far round that the red-flecked whites resembled crescent moons. He turned his back on them, squeezing past Alison's high chair. His baby sister stopped banging her spoon, her face twisting up in alarm.

'Don't cry,' Benny whispered, reaching out to her, and the way she pushed back against her seat, her chubby fingers blanched with effort, broke his heart. She wasn't crying. She was too frightened to cry.

That's when he felt it, something in his head, an instinctive command that cut through the thunder of his migraine — *Get out of here* — surging up from a part of his brain that lay far beneath the surface. *Run.*

It was so powerful that he almost obeyed, his hand straying towards the back door. Then Crapper shuffled arthritically out from under Alison's high chair and limped over to him. The dog peered up with such kindness and such trust that Benny couldn't help but smile. He crouched down in order to brush a hand over his wiry fur, scratch him under the ear. Crapper's tongue lolled out, his claws chittering on the linoleum, his tiny tail beating with the speed of a hummingbird's wings.

'There you go, boy,' Benny said, tickling the dog under his belly. 'You don't hate me, do you?'

And all of a sudden the voice in his head was gone, even the pounding roar slightly muted. Nothing was wrong. He was just having a bad week, that was all. Claire was a teenager herself now, just turned thirteen, and their rivalry had definitely spiralled in the last few months. It was bound to, considering they were like toy soldiers packed tight into this vacuum-sealed house. And God only knew his mum was prone to fits of depression and unpleasantness, especially since Alison's dad – a tall, quiet guy called Rob who Benny had seen in the house two, maybe three times tops – had decided he wasn't coming back.

Benny poked Crapper tenderly on his wet nose then stood up, a head rush making the room cartwheel again. He opened up the crockery cabinet, searching the dusty shelf for a pint glass.

It wasn't like normal was even a good thing, he thought as he filled the glass with water. Normal sucked. He took a deep swig, letting his eyes wander. Something on top of one of the cupboards hooked them, a scrap of colour peeking out from the shadows. Benny frowned and placed the glass on the counter. He scraped a chair across the floor and hoisted himself up, coming face to face with a rectangular box in crimson giftwrap. A ribbon had been carefully tied round it, topped with a bow.

Benny's grin stretched so wide that his cheeks ached more than his head, and with a soft laugh he scooped up the package. It was big, and it was heavy. About the same kind of heavy as an Xbox might have been. And that's when the excitement really hit him, knotting up his guts. His mum had never, ever bought him a console – not a PlayStation, not a Wii, not even so much as a DS. But she'd always said he could have one when he was old enough. He'd never known just how old he'd have to be to be 'old enough', but now he did: fifteen!

He leapt down from the chair, bundling the box back through into the living room, almost knocking Alison out of her high chair in the process. So that's what this had all been about: his mum and his sister teasing him, pretending they'd forgotten his birthday, before surprising him with the sickest present ever, probably a 360 with Modern Warfare 3. They'd turn round, see him with the box, and their faces would dance into smiles. *Aw, you ruined it!* His sister would laugh. *We were gonna make you think we'd not got you anything.* And his mum would say, *Go on, open it, I s'pose I can miss a bit of Noel Edmonds while you set it up.*

'Thanks, Mum!' Benny yelled, thumping back down in his chair with the box on his lap. There was a gift card under the loop of the bow, and he fumbled with it, his fingers numb with excitement.

To Benny, at long last, maybe now you'll stop nagging us about it! Wishing you a really happy birthday. Lots and lots of love, Mum, Claire and Alison.

'This is so cool!' he said. 'I knew you were just kidding.'

His headache had gone too, he realised, that generator pulse now silent, obliterated by the unexpected turn the afternoon had taken. He tore at the thin paper, one rip causing it to slough to the floor. Beneath was a green and white box, the Xbox logo plastered all over it, like some beautiful butterfly emerging from its chrysalis. His mum had hefted her bulk from the sofa and was waddling towards him, arms out, and he waited for the hug, for the kisses he should have had that morning, preparing his mock protests – *Agh, Mum, gerroff, I'm fifteen, not five* – but yearning for it, so happy to be that kid again, if just for the day. Just *so* happy.

The slap made fireworks explode inside the living room, raging spots of colour that seemed to burn through his vision. He was rocked back into the chair, so shocked that the box tumbled off his lap, crunching onto the carpet.

You'll break it! was the first thought that rifled through his head. Then the pain caught up, a flash of heat as if he'd been standing too close to the fire. There was no time for anything else before the second slap caught him on the other cheek, setting off a high-pitched ringing in his ears and making it feel as though his whole face were alight. He looked up, tears turning the whole room liquid, like it was filled with water. His mum was there, at least a blurred silhouette the same shape as his mum, one arm held high, swooping down.

Crack! This time it wasn't a slap, it was a punch. Benny's mind went black, nothing there but the need to get away. He could taste something coppery and warm on his tongue, dripping down his throat, and he recognised it from the time he'd taken a football straight in the mouth.

Blood.

Panic catapulted him from the chair, and he pushed past his mum hard enough to shunt her backwards. She windmilled across the tiny patch of floor, striking the sofa, looking for a moment like she was about to do a *You've Been Framed*-style top-heavy tumble, only just managing to catch herself. She grunted, the kind of noise a startled boar might make, and Benny looked into her piggy black eyes and saw absolutely nothing human there at all.

'Mum,' he tried to say, but the word wouldn't fit in his throat. She teetered, her bare feet doing a weird, silent tap-dance until she found her balance, then she threw herself at him. The air was full of noise, the heavy, wet rasps of his mum's breathing and something else: a rising pitch, like a kettle coming to the boil. It took Benny a split second to understand that his sister Claire was screaming. She climbed out of the chair so fast that he couldn't get out of her way, her body flapping into his, skinny arms locked around his neck. Then his mum hit them both, her momentum knocking them to the floor like skittles.

Benny smacked his head on the carpet, his mum falling on top of him, cutting out the light. Her weight was impossible, pinning him to the floor, refusing to let him breathe. He was enveloped in her smell – body odour and shampoo and the stench of nail varnish. He lashed out, throwing everything at her, but he couldn't get any force behind his blows. And she was hitting him back, fleshy fists bouncing off his temple, his neck, his forehead.

Something white-hot burrowed into his shoulder but he couldn't turn his head to see what. This time the pain made him shriek, the cries muffled by the heft of his mother's chest. The agony increased, something wet gushing down the sleeve of his school jumper.

It isn't real it isn't real it isn't real.

But he knew it was; he could see sparks flashing in the edges of his vision as his oxygen-starved brain misfired. And worse, so much worse, he could sense death here, *his* death, somewhere in the dark recesses of the shape on top of him.

The thought gave him strength, so much adrenalin flooding his system that this time when he punched upwards he caught his mum in the jaw. Her head snapped back and she spat out a blood-soaked grunt, her body weight shifting to the side as she flopped off him. He pulled himself out like someone escaping quicksand, his nails gouging tracks in the carpet. Halfway out he saw that Claire's teeth were lodged in his upper arm, a scrap of flesh caught between them. Then he saw her eyes, so full of rage, and his fist flew automatically, catching her on the nose. With a cry she let go, tumbling away.

Somehow, Benny made it to his feet, careening wildly. He saw that Crapper's jaws were locked around his mum's ankles, aware even in the chaos that his dog was trying to save his life. His mum was rolling like a beached whale, her groans ugly, awful. She was trying to get up, he could see the determination in her eyes as they burned into him. She was trying to get up so she could finish the job.

Claire was already on her feet, lurching at him like a zombie. Benny stabbed both hands in her direction, pushing her into the wall. She bounced off, came at him again, and this time it was Crapper who stopped her, leaping over the floundering body of his mum and latching onto her thigh, bringing her down like a snapped sapling.

Benny crossed the living room in two strides, the kitchen door right ahead of him, the back door visible beyond that. He could make it, get out into the light. He *could* make it.

He sensed a shape at his side and turned to the window in time to see it implode. A hail of glass blasted into the room and he ducked to his knees, his arms rising to protect his face. Something crashed into him and he almost went over again, slamming a hand down onto the carpet to stop himself toppling. He pushed himself up, a sprinter's start, but a hand grabbed his ankle, yanking it hard, causing him to drop onto his face. He kicked out, turning to see his new attacker: a stranger dressed in jeans and a green Latitude T-shirt. He had both hands round Benny's leg, and his face –

bleeding heavily and flecked with sparkling shards of glass – was a mask of pure fury.

The man pulled again, reeling Benny in like a hooked fish. Claire had managed to prise Crapper loose and now the dog was running in circles howling, the whites of his eyes the brightest thing in the room. His mum was on her feet again. There was someone else clambering in through the window as well – their neighbour, Mr Porter, a man in his seventies, cataract-dulled eyes seething. His hands were balled into white-knuckled fists.

Benny tried to spin round, but the strange man was holding him too tight, his fingers like metal rods in his flesh. He hauled Benny closer, his fingers working their way up to his knees.

'Mum!' he screamed. 'Stop it! Stop it!'

They threw themselves onto him, all of them, so heavy and so dark that he felt like a body being lowered into a grave. He thrashed, but he couldn't move his legs and now something heavy was sitting on his back. Fat fingers were tight around his neck, squeezing his windpipe so hard that his throat whistled every time he managed to snatch a breath. He snapped his head round, trying to shake them loose, seeing two more people climbing through the shattered window, nothing but silhouettes against the sun. They crowded into the tiny room, trying to punch, claw, kick, bite, no sound but their hoarse, ragged breathing and tinny laughter from the television.

Something too hard to be a fist made contact with

the back of his head and a seed of darkness blossomed into full-blown night. He could still hear the sound of each blow, but he could no longer feel them. He closed his eyes, happy to let himself sink into this comforting numbness, happy to leave the pain and the confusion behind . . .

It stopped as suddenly as it had started. When he tried to breathe in he found that he couldn't. In the last seconds before his life ended, Benny heard the back door opening and the wet patter of footsteps leaving the house, the crunch of the wicker chair as his sister sat back down, a soft whine from the dog.

Then, incredibly, he heard the sound of his mum filling the kettle in the kitchen.

And it was that noise, so familiar, one that he had heard every single day of his life, which ushered him out of the world. Then that too was erased by the immense, unfathomable cloud of cold darkness which had settled inside his head.

His heart juddered, stalled, and he felt something burn up from inside him, a surge of cold, blue fire that burst free with a silent howl. Then Benny Millston died on his living-room carpet while his mum made the tea.

Thursday

Heav'n has no rage, like love to hatred turn'd
   William Congreve, *The Mourning Bride*

Cal

Everybody loved Callum Morrissey.

Captain of the lower-sixth football team. A gifted student but cool with it, not a try-hard. All-round nice guy. And he knew it, too. Right now he was belting up the right wing of the school pitch, the ball at his feet, running so fast that the roar of the wind almost drowned out the noise of the crowd. The opposition full-back, Truman – a beast of a stopper with a body like Shrek and a face to match – was dead ahead, big but slow. Cal feigned left, tapping the ball through the kid's tree-trunk legs before spinning to his right and cutting towards the goal.

In the eighteen-yard box were two of his best friends, Dan and Abdus, both of them with their hands in the air yelling out for a cross. Cal ducked round another defender, thought about trying to put it in the back of the net himself. But he wasn't greedy. He'd scored once already, a free kick taking the game to 3–1 in their favour. It was better when they all had something to celebrate after the match.

He took a deep breath, enjoying the way time seemed to slow down. Each second was drawn out, hanging lazily on the sunshine that painted the pitch gold. The clock mounted on the single stand of tiered

19

seats to his right – 'Sponsored by The Union Garage' stencilled over the face – read 2.32: thirteen minutes left, then it would be over, one step closer to the end-of-year Inter-form Cup. They'd be paraded through their classes like they were already champions, and maybe this time even Georgia would look up from her book for long enough to congratulate him. She couldn't ignore him forever, not when he was playing this well.

He drew back his foot, ready to launch a high, looping pass into the centre of the box. And that's when something ripped across his ankle.

He dropped to the floor, agonising heat biting into his leg. He blinked the tears away, gritting his teeth, rocking back and forth with his ankle between his hands until his vision cleared.

Incredibly, the game was still going on. Truman, the one who had tackled him, was back on his feet punting the ball down the pitch. Everyone else was chasing after it like Cal didn't even exist, including Mr Platt, the PE teacher, who was acting as referee.

'Hey!' he called out, lifting his hand to try and get the man's attention. It wasn't like he'd dived or anything – he could see the blood soaking through his sock, five lines raked over his ankle from Shrek's boot studs. He called out again, but there was nobody left in earshot.

Cal clambered to his feet, trying not to put any weight on his left leg. The pain was settling into an uncomfortable throb. It could have been worse, a tackle like that might have shattered the bone, knocked him out for the summer holidays, maybe longer. Truman was going to pay. He jogged towards the action at the other end of the field, ready to kick some ass. He'd get sent off, but who cared? With a handful of minutes left it wasn't like they were in danger of losing.

Up ahead the ball was at the feet of an opposition midfielder, a kid called Connor. Cal ignored the game, jogging towards Truman. The ogre had his hands on his knees, bent double, trying to get his breath back.

'Hey,' Cal said, increasing his speed, his whole body buzzing in anticipation. Truman turned in time to see Cal's fist heading for his cheek. There was a soft thud and the kid's head wobbled like a boxer's punch ball. It seemed for a moment like he was going down but he managed to stay on his feet, his pug ugly mug creased with annoyance.

No, it wasn't annoyance. The look he shot Cal was *way* beyond that. For a second Shrek's eyes seemed depthless, full of a hatred that Cal had never before encountered in his seventeen years. His face was so dark with anger that it seemed bloated, poisoned. It was the look of somebody who wanted to kill him.

He backed off instinctively, hearing the whistle blow again and again, its shrill pitch gaining volume as Mr Platt ran their way. Truman lunged, fists balled into boulders, his mouth hanging open like the village idiot's but his eyes set fast, furious.

Someone grabbed Cal from behind, arms locked around his chest. Someone else was at his side, shoving

21

him, shouting at him. In no more than a heartbeat he was being bulldozed by a crowd, their hands and arms like pistons, the sensation like being trapped inside an engine.

'Get off,' he yelled, feeling the fingers dig into his chest, the swell of chaos around him growing. One of the opposition team shoved him hard and he nearly fell, his legs tangled up in those of whoever stood behind him. Then the jowly face of Mr Platt rose into view, his cheeks an impossible shade of crimson as he blew into his whistle. The teacher reached out and grabbed Cal's shoulder, stopping him from toppling.

'That's enough!' he bellowed, his whistle dropping to his chest. 'I said stop that, right now.'

'Leave it out, Cal,' said a voice in his ear, and he recognised Joe McGowan, their right-winger, the kid who was holding him. 'Let it go, man.'

'Fine, it's over,' he said, his voice lost in the roar of the crowd. 'But look what that tosser did to my leg, almost took it clean off.' He reached into his sock, then held up fingers stained with blood, waving them at Shrek. 'See that?'

'I said enough!' Mr Platt barked, almost apoplectic. He blew his whistle again, waving everybody away and reaching into his pocket. He flashed the red card at Cal's face with the enthusiasm of a priest waving a crucifix at a vampire. 'You're off, Morrissey, and you're in trouble too. Get moving.'

Truman lunged again, but without conviction, happy to let his teammates hold him back. His face had softened and the expression it wore now was one of confusion, almost as though he couldn't quite remember where he was. Maybe Cal had punched him harder than he thought. Mr Platt turned to the ogre, the red card hovering at his side.

'Don't push it, Truman,' he said. 'Or you're off too. You're lucky I didn't see that tackle.'

Gradually the players were drifting away, a series of boos and jeers drifting down from the stands. Cal ran a hand down his football shirt, straightening the creases, and when he looked up Joe was staring at him, one eyebrow raised.

'You okay?' he asked. Cal nodded, and Joe's face broke into a grin. 'Almost knocked him clean on his rump; nice one.'

Joe's smile was contagious, and Cal found himself laughing. The adrenalin had dulled the pain in his ankle, and there were perks to missing out on the last ten minutes of the match – one in particular sitting in the front row of the stands. Joe held his hand out and Cal gripped it in a surfer's handshake.

'Stick one in for me, yeah?' he said.

'No probs,' Joe replied, running off. Mr Platt had put the ball down about ten yards from where Cal had thumped Truman, and once again he blew on his whistle, gesticulating wildly at Cal to get off the pitch.

'Yeah, yeah, I'm going,' Cal muttered, walking as slowly as he dared. He raised his hands to the crowd, shadow-boxing like Rocky, and milked a cheer from them which he rode all the way to the sidelines. He made his way over to his lower-sixth mates in the first line of folding seats, grateful to be in the shade of the stand. Eddie Ardagh clapped him on the back.

'Douchebag had it coming,' he said. 'Took you out like a lumberjack.'

'Shouldn't have hit him, Cal,' said Megan Rao, shaking her head. One of her crimson-dyed curls popped loose and she tucked it back behind her ear. 'He's gonna be after you for that. You know Truman's crazy.'

'Let him come,' Cal said, flopping down on the empty seat between Megan and Georgia. Georgia Cole. She had her perfectly petite snub nose in a novel, the way she always did, and when he lightly elbowed her she gave him the merest flicker of attention. Cal didn't press the matter – it didn't look good when you were the one doing the chasing. Instead he turned back to the daylight-drenched field as his team once again fought their way upfront. That hollow, rubbery *duff* of somebody kicking the ball had to be just about the best noise in existence, especially in summer. Everything sounded better in summer.

He saw Truman waddling around by himself outside the opposition eighteen-yard box, gently nursing his cheek. He'd never been scared of him, even though Truman was a year older and a hell of a lot bigger, even though he had a reputation for whaling on smaller kids. Cal didn't feel scared of anyone, not really. He'd studied Choy Li Fut kung fu since he was eight and although he'd never had to use it in a proper scrap, he knew he could if he needed to.

In his mind's eye he could still see Truman's face after he'd hit him, that primeval hate in his expression, a blood-boiling rage. He'd looked like a proper psycho, the kind you get in the movies. Megan was right, everyone knew that Truman was crazy. But this was the first time that Cal had thought that maybe he actually *was* crazy.

'Thirsty?' Eddie said, offering Cal a bottle of water with the label peeled off.

'You know I don't drink that stuff,' he said, pulling a can of Dr Pepper out of Megan's open rucksack. 'Water's bad for you.' He opened the can, taking a deep swig before unleashing a burp that almost blew his head off. 'DP. Pure rehydration.'

'Don't know how you're still alive,' muttered Eddie. 'Your insides must be glued together with sugar.'

'Go on!' Megan screamed, jumping about a metre into the air, and Cal saw that Ab had dribbled the ball into the box. He shot and the keeper dived for it, meeting it with about half a fingertip but enough to send it wide. Cal was on his feet, hands on his head.

'Man, that was close,' he said, collapsing back down hard enough to nudge Georgia's book. This time she looked up with a forced scowl, peering at him from beneath her blonde fringe. He grinned at her. 'Sorry, George, but this ain't no place for a nerd.'

'I was dragged here against my will,' she replied, and somehow her deepening glower made her look even more gorgeous, like one of those models who pouts on the front of a fashion magazine. Cal felt his stomach fold into itself, his whole body suddenly too heavy, like gravity had just doubled. And for a ridiculous moment – despite their victory, despite the rush of what had happened with Truman, despite the sun and the promise of an afternoon hanging out with his mates – he felt like he was going to burst into tears. He turned away, his eyes prickling, his whole body tingling, and after a single, ragged breath the feeling passed.

'Your leg okay?' Georgia asked, smiling coyly as if she knew what was running through his head. He glanced down, seeing those parallel red lines in his crumpled socks where Shrek's studs had raked through the skin. There was only a smudge of blood there, already clotted and drying.

'Dunno,' he said. 'Feels like it could be fatal. Might need some mouth to mouth resuscitation in a moment.'

'Ew!' Georgia protested, slapping him gently with her book. 'Get Eddie to do it.'

'*I'll* do it,' Megan chimed in, blowing Cal a kiss.

'Thank God,' muttered Eddie.

Cal laughed gently, lacing his hands behind his head and resting back in his seat. There was a worm of discomfort nuzzling at his temples, but that was nothing unusual after a match, especially one like this. It was part adrenalin hangover, part dehydration. He knew he should drink more water but he just hated the stuff. Dr Pepper, that was all the liquid he needed.

'That guy is a total donkey,' said Megan as Steven Abelard, their slowest midfielder, trotted up the pitch.

Cal tuned her out, tuned everything out, happy for a moment's peace. He took a deep breath, the pressure in his head softening. Then he exhaled and the pain returned, that and a faint pulse which seemed to echo around the front of his skull, no louder than the whisper of distant bird wings.

Thump-thump . . .

Thump-thump . . .

Thump-thump . . .

Daisy

'You're scaring me . . .'

Daisy Brien retreated, the ice-cold wall against her back making her jump. Her two best friends, Kim and Chloe, were moving towards her, their hair in identical braids, both wearing old-fashioned puffy dresses that hid their feet and made them look as though they were gliding. Their eyes were wide, unblinking. Ghost eyes.

'Guys, stop it!'

They had boxed her in, the overpacked clothes rails to her right and left like the walls of a hedge maze, too thick to escape through. There was only one door here, invisible in the gloom, but Daisy could make out the green emergency exit light with the little running stick man on it. It seemed a million miles away. Kim and Chloe were close enough to touch, and Kim reached out slowly with a hand draped in white lace. She ran a cool finger over Daisy's face.

'Stop it!'

'See how she leans her cheek upon my hand,' said Kim in a low, phantom groan. 'Oh that Fred were a glove upon my hand, that he might touch her cheek!'

Chloe raised both hands, fluttering them in front of Daisy's chest.

'One, two, and the third in your bosom,' she

28

moaned. 'Which is where Fred wants to be!'

'Oh Fredeo,' added Kim. 'Fredeo, wherefore artest thou, Fredeo!'

'Where fartest thou?' said Chloe. And that did it, the three of them cracking up in peals of laughter which filled the dressing room like sunlight. Daisy was giggling so hard that her sides were in danger of splitting. Chloe collapsed to her knees, the dress spilling out around her in countless folds, releasing the homely smell of dust and old fabric.

'I hate you,' Daisy said when her air-starved lungs began to function again. She slapped Kim playfully on her arm, the blow cushioned by an enormous shoulder pad. 'I told you, I don't like him!'

'But he's your Fredeo,' said Chloe, holding out her hands. Kim grabbed one and Daisy took the other, hauling her back onto her feet. 'Fredeo and Daisiet, the world's most romantic love story.'

'He's like so not interested in me,' she said. 'He's in Year 10 for heaven's sake.'

'The lady doth protest too much, methinks,' said Kim, wiping the tears from her eyes.

'Wrong play, dingbat,' Daisy shot back. She pushed past them, escaping the labyrinth of the theatre wardrobe and walking to the huge mirror on the left-hand side of the room. It was ringed by bulbs, just like in a Broadway dressing room, and they painted her reflection in sickly yellow light. Even so, she couldn't help but approve of the way she looked, with her long, brown hair trussed up in an elaborate plaited bun. The dress she wore was so white and so pretty that she could have been a bride, the high, narrow collar making her look taller and more slender than she actually was. It made her look older, too, maybe fifteen instead of almost thirteen.

Just about the right age for Fred . . .

She felt the heat in her cheeks and she was glad that she was already wearing her make-up, thick rouge concealing her embarrassment. She busied herself with her gloves, elbow-length strips of cobweb-thin silk that were a nightmare to put on. At first, three months or so ago, when they'd discovered their roles in the school play, she'd been mortified that the Romeo to her Juliet was going to be from Year 10. The idea was enough to make her scurry to the wings and hide in the shadows there until the whole thing was over.

But she'd bitten back her fear and soldiered on, the way her parents had taught her to. And despite her protests, she'd actually quite liked the attention. She had to keep telling herself that he was just acting, that this fifteen-year-old Adonis who already had a girl-friend wouldn't be interested in the real Daisy Brien in a million years.

'I still can't remember my lines,' said Chloe, her re-flection joining Daisy's, half a foot taller even though she was a month younger.

'You've only got about three,' laughed Daisy as she pulled the first glove on. Chloe was playing Lady Montague, Romeo's mum, and even though she appeared in only two scenes she always managed to get her words in a muddle. Kim was Tybalt, Juliet's cousin, who, their drama teacher had decided, was going to be a girl in this version of the play. She stood to the side, leaning against the make-up shelf, idly waving a cardboard sword back and forth.

'I wonder if you could actually kill anyone with this,' Kim said. 'Mrs Jackson, maybe.'

All three girls looked at the way the bent sword flopped back and forth and once again they were laughing. The moment was cut short by the snap and creak of the dressing-room door opening, a round, bespectacled face peering inside.

'Did I hear my name?' Mrs Jackson asked. 'Do you need me, girls?'

'It's okay, miss,' said Kim, jabbing the sword in the teacher's direction and breathing *die die die* in between her words. 'We were just practising our lines.'

'Good good,' Mrs Jackson said. 'Well, hurry up and get ready. Dress rehearsal starts in –' she checked her watch for what felt like an eternity, 'seven minutes.'

She hung on for a second more, as if waiting to be dismissed, then ducked back out of the dressing room.

'I can't be bothered with this,' said Daisy, feeling an unwelcome pressure in her chest. She knew it wasn't that she couldn't be bothered. It was nerves. She felt them every time they took to the stage, but it was definitely getting worse. Heaven only knew what she'd be like on the actual night. 'Does someone want to take my place?'

'And fake-snog Freddy? No way!' said Chloe. 'I'd

rather kiss Mrs Jackson.'

'Liar,' said Daisy with a smile. She'd finally managed to pull on her other glove, straightening out the silk around the crook of her elbow. 'Ready?'

She turned from the mirror to Kim. Her friend was still waving her sword back and forth, harder now, faster. It was difficult to tell with the glare of the bulbs behind her, but she seemed to be staring right back at Daisy, her eyes impossibly dark. And each time the tinfoil-coated blade swooshed through the quiet air her mouth breathed that same whispered word.

Die. Die. Die. Die. Die. Die. Die.

'Um . . . Kim?' Daisy said. Kim cut back and forth once more, then seemed to stir, as if emerging from a hypnotic trance. She blinked heavily a couple of times.

'Huh?' she said after a second or two.

'Nothing,' said Daisy, walking towards the door. 'Come on, let's get this over and done with.'

Brick

Brick Thomas hated everybody.

He hated his dad, he hated his stepmum, he hated his real mum too for dying when he was a ginger-haired sprat in nursery school; he hated his brother, who'd left home two years back to join the parachute regiment; he really hated his teachers, who had told him not to even bother turning up for his A levels, and he really, *really* hated the school counsellor who'd informed his dad he had behavioural difficulties; he hated his friends, if you could even call them that when they didn't bother talking to him any more; and if he was totally honest there were times when he hated his girlfriend – although he wasn't sure about this one because sometimes love and hate felt so similar he couldn't tell the difference between them.

He hated himself, too, his brain, the way it made him feel perfectly happy one minute then as miserable as a graveyard the next. He hated it for whispering things to him – *You're no good. You can't do that. You're too thick. No one likes you because you're a headcase* – not all the time or anything, but often enough for him to feel like there was something living up there, something that detested him. Most of all, though, he just hated the hate. It was exhausting.

He sat on the raised concrete footpath that looked down over the beach, idly tossing stones at the calm, quiet surf. The tide was out, but even so there was only about twenty metres of shore between the water and the massive dune behind him. On the other side of that lay Fursville, a vast shipwreck of shorn metal and rotting wood and rubbish and rat-droppings that had once been Norfolk's biggest and most popular theme park.

Back when Brick was a kid he'd come here all the time with his folks, patiently enduring the slow, boring drive through the country lanes from Norwich because the destination was well worth it. There had been a roller coaster, one of the old wooden ones, no loop the loop or anything but still pretty fast. Loads of arcades too, so many that their garbled, artificial birdsong was ingrained in his head, the clarion call of summer. They'd stretched all the way up from the plaza to a pier that had caught fire in 1999, on the eve of a massive Millennium celebration, and which was now a broken, skeletal limb all but buried by sand and surf.

His favourite thing about Fursville, though, had been the water flume, because you had to squeeze into this tiny little longboat which was ratcheted up Everest-high slopes before being slingshotted through freezing puddles of piss-yellow water. He'd liked it because it was the only time he'd ever got a hug from his dad. The old man didn't have a choice in the matter – you had to grab hold of the person in front of you or risk flying out of the boat on the downward bends. He'd loved that feeling of being held in place, the weight of those tattooed arms on his shoulders, like his dad and gravity were one and the same, stopping him from bouncing right off the planet into the cold, infinite darkness of space.

Not that he ever would have admitted to those feelings, even if he'd been able to put them into any kind of words back then. If nothing else, his pop would have thumped him. He was eighteen now, though, and he didn't care what his dad thought.

He glanced at the sky, a vast expanse of pale blue, the sun so bright that it made his retinas sting. There was no sound but the whisper of the knee-high waves as they cruised onto the stones, that and the distant chatter of gulls from Hemsby a mile or so south. A decade ago he'd loved it here because there were so many people, their constant motion and sound the exact opposite of the cold vacuum at home that his mum had once filled so effortlessly. Now he appreciated it precisely because of the quiet, the stillness. Here, in the mangled guts of Fursville, there was nobody to hate.

Brick's backside was getting numb and he stood up, lobbing a last fist-sized rock into the sea. His phone informed him it had just gone three. Lisa would be leaving school any second now and he'd told her he'd be waiting by the gates. Fat chance, it would take him half an hour or so to get back into the city and by that time he expected she'd be home, sending the first of a seemingly limitless supply of angry texts.

He groaned, feeling the delicate equilibrium of his

mood start to slide. He'd begun to feel like a tightrope walker, trying to keep his footing by using one of those long poles. Sometimes, when things were okay, his mood could balance perfectly on that thread. But it didn't take much to make it wobble. Anything could do it – somebody speaking out of turn to him, some aggro from his teachers, even a strange look. But he'd learned to deal with the wobbles: he just took a deep breath and let his mood stabilise again.

The problem was when more than one thing went wrong. The first would nudge his emotions like a breeze, perfectly manageable with a small adjustment, but the second would be like a crazed seagull full in the face, flapping and squawking, and suddenly his mood would drop like a ton of bricks and the world would go dark.

He closed his eyes, the spotlight sun leaving the faintest flutter of pain against his skull. One breath, then out, another, slowly, deeply, and when he opened his eyes again he felt calmer, his mood perfectly balanced.

He walked down the path, the back of his neck stinging where the sun had caught it. He tanned about as well as an albino vampire, his freckled skin veering wildly between extremes of milk white and tomato red throughout the year. His hair colour was to blame, about as bright a shade of orange as you could imagine.

A dozen metres from where he had been sitting was one of the many breaches in the Fursville fence. Most had been caused by nothing more than neglect, the metal simply rusting into oblivion. This one, though, he'd made himself about three years ago when he and a couple of mates had first explored the abandoned theme park. They'd brought a pair of wire cutters and a torch and a rucksack, and they'd spent the night looking for treasures – old soft toys and canned sweets from the crumbling games stands, cash out of the machines in the toilets, bottles left over from the bar where the adults had sheltered while their kids tore from attraction to attraction like banshees.

In the end they'd not found much apart from a couple of tubs of mouldy looking boiled sweets and a stack of plastic-wrapped urinal-disinfectant blocks which Brick's friend Douglas Frinton had claimed they could use to make their own vodka. But they'd had a hell of a night exploring the place. Although the outside areas of Fursville were derelict and dangerous, the inside – once you got past the chains and the locked doors – was in pretty decent shape. Brick had even spent the night there once after a massive dust-up with his dad, sleeping in the old restaurant, curled up under a couple of tablecloths that had been left behind.

He pushed his way in through the hole, making sure to tuck the fence back behind him and cover it with a massive square of plyboard. Not that he really needed to. Nobody ever came out this way any more, there were no lights on the walkway or in the park, and, like all places that had been abandoned, Fursville had its fair share of rumours about murderers and ghosts. He had visited enough times to know that none of those stories were true. Out here, there was only Brick.

It was always like running an assault course, getting from the beach into the central plaza, but he negotiated the rubble, the broken glass and the faded grins of the kids' mini roundabout characters with practised ease. His 50cc motorbike was where he'd left it, propped up against a fountain that was overflowing with algae, the front L-plate hanging at an angle where one of the magnetic catches had dropped off. He'd been riding it illegally for a year now and had no intention of ever going for his test. Not until he was rich enough for a Ducati, anyway.

He pulled the helmet on. It pinned his ears back uncomfortably but he didn't really mind. At least it hid his hair. Then he clambered on board, the bike far too small for his six-foot-five frame. It took six kicks before the lawnmower-size motor decided to wake up, the bike accelerating painfully slowly across the plaza. He ignored the signs for the exit – the front gates were boarded up and chain-bound, Alcatraz-style. Instead he cut towards the south-west quadrant of the park, the engine whining like a bloated fly. He followed his own burned tyre tracks round the corner and down past the medical shack – the words 'Boo Boo Station' just about still visible on the pebble-dashed wall. Right ahead was a gap in the fence, just the right size for his bike. He slowed as he squeezed through, gunning the engine to make sure it didn't stall, then edged between the two enormous laurel bushes that grew up right outside it.

He instinctively looked left and right, not wanting to give away his secret hideout. But there was no danger of anybody seeing him. The wide road beyond was deserted. On the other side of it was a car lot and showroom that had been forsaken for almost as long as the funfair. Past the empty expanse of concrete and dirt Brick could make out the smoking chimneys and blinking lights of the fertiliser factory which lay half a mile inland. That was the closest anyone really came to Fursville nowadays.

He paused for a minute, enjoying the stillness, the way time seemed to stop here. Even with the nasal whine of his bike it seemed quieter and more peaceful than back in the city. But Lisa was waiting, and the sad fact of it was that she was scary enough even when she wasn't screaming at him.

Sighing, Brick gunned the engine and took off for home.

Norwich, 3.57 p.m.

'So . . . It's Brick, right?'

Brick nodded, trying not to smile at the sight of Lisa's mum and dad staring out at him from the safety of their front porch. Mr Dawlish, who was in his early fifties but who looked twice that, was gripping the door with both hands as if he thought he might have to slam it shut at a moment's warning. His wife, who had all Lisa's bad qualities and none of her good ones, was on tiptoes peeking over his shoulder. Both weren't so much smiling as grimacing. He was used to it. Standing six five, and broad with it, people were naturally wary of him. And he had one of *those* faces, so he'd been told, whatever that meant. It was just his lot. Everybody hated Brick Thomas.

'She knows you're here,' said Mr Dawlish. 'I think she's coming down.'

He looked back at his wife and she shrugged.

'I think she is.' Mrs Dawlish peered at the helmet clasped in Brick's hands. 'I hope you're not planning to take her anywhere on that?'

'No, Mrs Dawlish,' Brick lied. Lisa always rode pillion. It wasn't like anything bad could happen to her – the bike's top speed was just shy of forty when there were two people on it. Despite his answer, Mrs Dawlish frowned. She opened her mouth to say something then obviously decided not to.

'Why Brick?' Mr Dawlish asked after an uncomfortable silence. 'I take it that isn't your given name.'

'Just another brick in the Thomas family wall, I guess,' Brick said. 'Like the song. My mum and dad have always called me it. It says John on my birth certificate.' That was a lie too, his real name was Harry, but he liked to see the look on people's faces when they thought his name was John Thomas. It took Mr Dawlish a second or two to get the joke, and when he did his forehead creased like an accordion. There were another few strokes of awkwardness before Brick heard footsteps from inside the house. Her parents both turned as Lisa appeared.

'Four o'clock?' she said, tapping the bare patch on her arm where a watch might have been. She was pretty, there was no doubt about that, but she did a good job of hiding it behind too much make-up and hair that was constantly straightened and dyed before being scraped back into a ponytail. She had a stud in her nose and a ring in her eyebrow – both of which her parents had blamed Brick for, even though he hated piercings. She looked at him now from behind false lashes that had been badly fixed.

'Sorry,' Brick said. 'I got caught up at work; there was a late delivery.'

'Trouble on site?' Mr Dawlish asked. Brick had told Lisa that he worked for the same scaffolding company as his dad. Which was true, strictly speaking, although he hadn't helped out for weeks now.

'Nothing we couldn't handle,' Brick replied. 'You just can't get the staff these days.'

For some reason that seemed to relax the old couple. Mr Dawlish nodded, a glimmer of a smile appearing in the folds of his face.

'You're not wrong there, son.' He turned to his daughter. 'Come on, love, are you going or not? You're letting all this heat in.'

Lisa locked eyes with Brick for a good seven seconds, then uttered a mini scream of frustration, barging past her parents and out the door.

'You better make this up to me, Brick,' she muttered, that expression demolishing the foot of height difference between them and making him feel like the smaller of the two. Out in the sunlight he noticed that she looked different, somehow, although he couldn't quite put a finger on why. Nothing so trivial as a new type of foundation or T-shirt. No, it was something in her eyes, in the way she looked at him. For some reason it made his skin crawl. She must have been *really* angry.

'Easy, tiger,' he said, holding his arms up in surrender. 'I will, I promise.'

'Have fun,' Mr Dawlish said as they walked down the path. Brick waved, hearing Mrs Dawlish's shrill cry follow them all the way to the gate.

'Be back by ten, please. And don't you go anywhere on that bike!'

He smiled, but it was short lived. He glanced at Lisa again, trying to work out what was making him so uneasy and wishing that he'd stayed on the beach.

Daisy

'Um, 'tis he, that villain Romeo,' said Kim without en-thusiasm, still thrusting her sword but this time at Fred.

'More venom, dear,' said Mrs Jackson from the wings, interrupting the same way she had done with pretty much every single line so far. 'You hate his guts.'

'I hate *your* guts, you old bag,' muttered Kim, the acoustics of the school hall carrying her voice further than she had intended. Daisy would have laughed ex-cept she was exhausted. They'd been here for three hours and they were still on Act I. At this rate they wouldn't be home till the weekend, even though they were only doing a cut-down version of the play.

''Tis *he*,' Kim spat, swiping her weapon, giving all the venom she could manage. 'That *villain*, Romeo!'

'Content thee, gentle cuz, leave him alone,' said Ethan, the fat kid from Daisy's year who was playing her dad. He was wearing a toga, and he'd drawn a goatee on himself with eyeliner which made him look ridiculous. 'I would not for all the wealth of all the . . . town, um, here in my house do him . . .'

'Disparagement, Ethan,' said Mrs Jackson without needing to look at the script in her hand.

'Yeah, disparagement. So be patient, take no note of him, it is my will.'

43

'It fits, when such a villain is a guest,' Kim went on. 'I'll not endure him.'

'You'll make a mutiny amongst my guests!' roared Ethan, shaking his fists. 'You will set cock-a-hoop!'

Everybody giggled — they always did at that line — the sound both echoed and muted by the huge, empty hall. Mrs Jackson shushed them.

'Romeo?' said Mrs Jackson. 'Romeo, wherefore art thou, Romeo?'

'Huh?' Fred said, obviously perplexed. He stood on the other side of a large canteen table, and he must have sensed Daisy looking because he glanced up, catching her eye. She twisted her head away so hard that something twanged in the back of her neck, her cheeks flaring once more beneath her make-up.

'It's your line, Fred dear.'

'Oh, er,' he put both hands on the table and stared at Daisy. This time she didn't turn away, trying to get herself into the mindset of a young girl with a crush on an older guy. It wasn't difficult. 'If I profane with my unworthiest hand this holy shrine, the gentle fine is this: my lips, two blushing pilgrims, ready stand to smooth that rough touch with a tender kiss.'

In the corner of her eye Daisy could see Kim cracking up, and it took all her strength to stop from joining her.

'Good pilgrim,' she said, her voice trembling.

'Too soft, dear, they won't be able to hear you at the back.'

Daisy cleared her throat, speaking louder, talking not

quite to Fred's eyes but to his chin. 'Good pilgrim, you do wrong your hand too much, which mannerly devotion shows in this; for saints have hands that pilgrims' hands do touch, and palm to palm is holy palmers' kiss.'

'Good, Daisy,' said Mrs Jackson, doing a perfect job of ruining the dramatic tension.

'Have not saints lips, and holy palmers too?' asked Fred.

'Ay pilgrim, lips that they must use in prayer.'

'O, then, dear saint, let lips do what hands do; they pray, grantest, lest love turn to, uh . . . despair?'

'Close enough,' said their drama teacher.

'Saints do not move, though grant for prayer's sake,' said Daisy. Her pulse was quickening, so fast she could feel it in her temples, so fast that it felt almost like a *double* pulse, running side by side. Three more lines, then it was her favourite – and least favourite – part of the whole play. She took a sideways step to her left, Fred mirroring her.

'Then move not, while my prayer's effect I take,' he said, using a fingernail to scratch a mark from the surface of the table. His cheeks were starting to glow as well. 'Thus from my lips, by yours, my sin is purged.'

They both took another step to the side, converging on the narrow end of the table – ground zero.

'Then have my slips the slin that they have took,' she said, her tongue not working properly. 'Sorry, *sin*.'

'Sin from thy lips?' Fred said, his voice a mumble, but for once Mrs Jackson didn't comment. He stepped round the side of the table and Daisy moved with him so that they were facing each other, almost touching. Daisy's head was pounding – not really painful, just a pressure there, like it might pop clean off. The theatre had never seemed so quiet, the gaps of silence between the words bottomless. Every single person was holding their breath. 'Oh, trespass sweetly urged, give me my sin again.'

Fred leant forward. Daisy craned up, standing on tiptoes, falling towards him as though some invisible hand was pushing her. Her head was screaming now, a kettle coming to boil between her temples. Daisy's eyes rose, she couldn't stop them – up from Fred's chin, past his lips, his nose, meeting his eyes as their lips converged.

She froze, suddenly breaking into a cold sweat, as if the temperature in the hall had dropped below zero. Fred's eyes were empty, the unseeing, unfeeling black beads of a doll that looked as if they might just roll out of their sockets as he angled in towards her. She recoiled, but Fred kept on coming, craning over her, his teeth clenched, grinding.

Then his mouth opened, and he spat in her face.

Daisy's heart stopped and for a moment she wondered if she'd died on stage. She could feel his warm saliva on her top lip – not much, just foam really, hot against her cool skin, but she couldn't seem to lift her arm to wipe it away. She couldn't move a single muscle.

Fred started to laugh, his lips pulled back over his teeth, those dead eyes still boring into her. Daisy staggered back, seeing Kim pointing at her and screeching with delight. The laughter was taken up by somebody else, and another, then another, until the hall reverberated with the sound of it.

'You kiss by the book,' said Mrs Jackson in between soft chuckles of her own.

'What?' Daisy asked, wiping her gloved forearm over her face.

'Your line, dear, you kiss by the book. You kiss by the book.' Mrs Jackson was tottering across the stage waving the script at her. 'By the book, Daisy.'

Daisy bumped into one of the Year 7 extras, almost sprawling on her backside. It was all too much, the hall starting to spin. She turned and ran, thumping down the wooden steps and barging through the double doors, Mrs Jackson's voice shrieking out behind her.

'By the book, Daisy, by the book, *by the book!*'

Cal

'Still can't believe we thrashed them,' said Abdus, breathless as he paddled past on his skateboard. He reached the steps that led to the small plaza outside the library, ollying down them but bailing before he hit the tiles. He recovered his balance, chasing after the rogue board before turning back to Cal. 'Three–one!'

Cal raised both hands in a rock-star salute. He was sitting at one of the three metal tables outside the milk-shake café that had become their favourite place to hang out, especially after a match. Called Udderz, it let you pick your favourite chocolate bar then blended it with ice cream and milk to make just about the best shakes on the planet. Cal was on his third of the afternoon, this one made up of Boost bars. It was making him feel a little queasy but he wouldn't let that stop him from finishing.

The place was mobbed. Sharing his table were Megan, Eddie, Dan and the keeper Jack, who was perched on the edge providing a nice bit of shade from the evening sun. The other two tables had been occupied by the rest of the team, all except Steven Abelard who lived out in the sticks and always had to leave early. Several other kids from his form were scattered around, including Georgia, who sat just inside the large front window, behind the huge stencilled 'e' of Ud-derz, absorbed in whatever it was she was reading.

Cal kept looking at her – he couldn't help himself, it was like his head and hers were connected by a string of invisible elastic. He could only stretch it away for so long before it snapped back. Whatever she was read-ing had to be good, though, because she'd not glanced up once. He didn't think there'd ever been anything so depressing, and so frustrating, as the side of that girl's head.

'Want another?' Dan asked, scraping back his metal chair and nodding at Cal's shake.

'I'm sorted,' Cal replied. 'Any more of these and I'll be blowing chunks all over the plaza.'

'Lightweight,' said Megan, her lips wrapped around her straw, cup gurgling. 'I'm already on numero five.'

'Yeah, and it's starting to show,' Cal said, grinning. 'That chair's about to break.'

'Shut up!' Megan said, reaching over the table and slapping Cal on the arm, her face full of mock outrage. Megan was five foot nothing in shoes, and twig thin. She couldn't have made that chair so much as wobble if she'd jumped up and down on it for a week.

Someone else flashed past on a board, a kid from the year below, Cal thought. He ollied onto the hand-rail that dropped down into the plaza, doing a sketchy grind then a trey flip, landing with nothing more than a wobble. He swooped round in an arc back to where a bunch of his Year 11 mates were looking up at the oc-cupied tables, like they were planning an invasion.

'So, fancy our chances tomorrow?' Eddie asked, pushing his glasses up onto his nose. Eddie was asthmatic, he had it pretty bad, which meant he couldn't play for the team. That was a shame, because whenever they kicked the ball about at lunch he was actually pretty decent.

'12H are tough,' said Jack without looking round. 'They won it last year. They got that tall kid, Nasim, the one everyone said was being scouted by Arsenal.'

Cal snorted, pretending to be unimpressed. Truth was that Nas, a midfielder, *was* good enough to be signed. Last time they'd been in a match together Nas had run rings around Cal. But Cal was a hell of a lot better on the pitch now.

'We'll take them,' he said. 'Nas or no Nas.'

'Well, if you can't outrun him you can always punch him in the face,' said Megan, and everyone laughed.

'Might not even get to play in the next game,' said Jack. 'If Platt has his way. Red card like that could get you shunted for a match or two.'

'Nah,' said Cal. 'Frosty got sent off in the first match and he played against us in week two, remember?'

'Oh yeah, slide tackled the keeper,' said Eddie, shaking his head. 'Stupid.'

One of the skateboarders took a tumble on the plaza, doing an impressive forward roll before lying flat and staring at the sky. Everybody cheered and clapped. Cal leant back in his chair, taking another sip of his supersweet shake. It was so warm here, and peaceful. The sounds of the plaza – the constant, liquid murmur of talk and laughter, the clack and roll of the boards – were almost dreamlike.

The only thing that was dragging on the mood was his stupid head, still pulsing. It didn't hurt, not the way a proper munter did. It was just uncomfortable – *thump-thump* . . . *thump-thump* . . . *thump-thump* – like there was something inside there, a dying bird slowly flapping broken wings, trying to lift off . . .

Christ, where had *that* come from? Cal shuddered, the image making his stomach churn even harder than before. Dan had reappeared, slamming back down into his seat and sucking on a brand–new shake. The gargling sound he was making seemed too loud, and it was a second or two before Cal realised that it was because the chatter in the plaza had softened. People were still talking, but in whispers. It was almost like one of those weird silences, the kind where everyone stops speaking because they think everyone else has, and they all look at each other for a minute wondering what's going on, then laugh and carry on.

Only nobody was laughing. The Year 11 kids below were still looking up at the café like they wanted the tables. The skaters had stopped and were all staring this way too. Cal felt something dance up his spine, his arms erupting into goosebumps.

'Creeeeeepy,' he said, doing his best to smile. Eddie was observing him with an expression of intense confusion, as if Cal had suddenly sprouted a pig snout or panda ears or something. It wasn't just Eddie, either. Megan was frowning his way, her nose wrinkled up.

Cal's head swung left and then right to see that pretty much everyone on the plaza seemed to be glowering at him. Even Georgia had finally looked up. It might have been the reflection of the evening light on the window, but Cal could swear her lips were pulled back, distorting her flawless face into a grimace.

He realised his heart was pounding so hard he could see each beat like a flash of light in his eyes. He scraped back his chair, getting uneasily to his feet, running a hand through his hair.

'Ha ha, very funny, guys,' he said, his lonely voice echoing across the plaza. 'Grow up, won't you?'

The three pints of milkshake he'd consumed that afternoon were now rioting in his stomach. Nobody replied, they were all just staring at him, their faces bent with the same stupefied expression. Cal pushed himself through the wide-eyed crowd, trying not to run as he made his way towards the steps. His throat tickled, the way it always did when he was about to hurl. The shake bar didn't have a toilet, but the library did.

He crossed the plaza in a dozen strides, dashing through the automatic doors. He stopped for long enough to look back, relief flooding through him when he saw that one of the skateboarders was moving again, that Eddie and Megan and the rest of his mates seemed to be back to normal, chatting away.

They've had you good and proper, he thought as he walked towards the toilets. They'd been taking the mick, something they'd probably conjured up that afternoon while he was getting changed. It was like the time they'd nicked Jack's school uniform after training, forcing him to spend the rest of the day in his goal-keeping kit. Or when they'd all told Megan that there was a teacher-training day one Thursday and she'd not come to school. They were always playing pranks on each other, and this was no different – *Psst, at quarter past seven tonight everyone stare at Cal, see if we can freak him out, pass it on.*

And the worst thing was it *had* freaked him out. He'd completely lost his cool.

He slammed open the outer door, pushed his way through the inner door and straight into the only empty cubicle. The second he opened the lid he thought his last shake was coming back, boiling up from his stomach. But after a couple of dry heaves he felt it settle. He stood hunched over the bowl for a minute more, just to be sure, then put the lid down and sat on it.

What was wrong with him? He was losing it. First the incident with Truman, the way that kid had glared at him. Now this. He'd always thought he was made of sterner stuff, but here he was in the toilet at the library ready to chuck his guts all because his mates had pulled some stupid prank.

Cal wiped a hand across his forehead, the skin damp, cold, then he walked out of the cubicle, splashing some water on his face and staring at his reflection in the graffitied mirror. He did look a little pale – *peaky*, as his mum always said. Maybe he was coming down with something. That would be his excuse, that he'd got swine flu, he wasn't feeling himself. His mates wouldn't buy it, of course, but he didn't care. He was still Cal Morrissey, and everybody loved Cal Morrissey.

Feeling a little steadier, Cal made his way out of the toilet. He'd suck it up, let his friends have their victory. Girls liked a guy who could laugh at himself. Georgia was always saying that he took things too seriously.

He walked over the plaza, keeping his head down in mock shame, dodging the skateboarders who criss-crossed the tiles, waiting for the catcalls, the whoops, the jeers. They didn't come, and it was only when Cal had jogged up the steps that he realised the kids who were sitting there weren't his mates at all. The Year 11s had occupied every single table, laughing and shouting at each other, a few of them eyeballing him warily.

What the hell? he said beneath his breath, scanning the inside of the café. Georgia had gone, *everyone* had gone. He swivelled, seeing no trace of them anywhere in the plaza or the two footpaths that led out towards the high street. He looked at the nearest kid, a girl with green hair and a Linkin Park T-shirt. 'You see where they all went?'

'No,' she spat, like it was the stupidest question in the world. She turned away from him and made a comment to her friend, causing them both to snort.

Cal scratched his head then snapped his hand back down, not wanting to look weak, confused. They were still here, somewhere, he was sure of it. Probably wetting themselves laughing. Jesus, this hadn't happened since he was eight years old and his three so-called best friends had run off, abandoning him in the middle of London Zoo. Well the hell with them, he wasn't going to stand around like an idiot waiting for them to show their faces. He moved away from the café, his head banging as he walked alone into the hot, heavy summer evening.

Brick

Fursville, 6.56 p.m.

By the time Brick arrived back at Fursville the sun was well on its way towards the white heat of the horizon. It was no cooler, though, the coast flattened by an invisible muggy fist. He was dripping with sweat, not helped by the fact that he'd been sandwiched between the bike's overworked engine and Lisa's limpet-like grip for the last thirty-five minutes.

'OMG, Brick, you've crippled me,' she said as she clambered off the pillion seat, nursing her backside with both hands. 'When are you gonna get a car?'

'When I can afford it,' he said, waiting for her to stand clear before swinging his leg over. His muscles put up a fight – that was nearly two hours he'd spent riding today, and another thirty minutes to go when he took Lisa home – but he ignored them. He stretched, hearing his spine pop, then he weaselled off his helmet. The pain of his pinned-back ears began to ebb, leaving the strains of an approaching headache. He recognised the discomfort, like the first rolls of thunder from a distant storm. It was nothing to worry about yet, but later that night he'd be lucky if he didn't have a full-blown hurricane between his temples.

Why on earth had he brought Lisa here?

It had been a spur-of-the-moment thing, a *stupid*

56

spur-of-the-moment thing. After he'd picked her up they'd ridden over to Riverside, the leisure complex, stopping at his house for a spare helmet. She'd demanded that he take her to the cinema to make up for being so late, and he'd reluctantly agreed, even when the only thing about to start had been some awful romantic comedy with Jennifer Aniston and some guy he half recognised from a comedy show on the telly. Brick hadn't laughed once during the whole thing except when Lisa had dropped her bucket of popcorn halfway through the big love scene while trying to fish her mobile out of her bag. And that laugh hadn't lasted long because she'd made him go and get her some more.

After the film, Brick had been so relieved to be out in the sunshine again that he'd had a sudden rush of euphoric happiness. The only other place he'd ever really been this happy was Fursville, and in some bizarre and flawed twist of neural logic he'd decided there and then to let Lisa in on his secret.

'You wanna see something cool?' he'd said as they made their way back to the car park. 'Come on, it won't take long.'

She'd protested and grumbled and moaned, and it only took about five minutes of riding out towards the coast with her voice in his ear for Brick's mood to plummet off its tightrope. He should have turned back, dropped her home, but for some reason he'd just kept his head down and roared east. Now here they were, in his haven, his hideaway, Lisa's nasal whine like some invading naval fleet.

'What the hell is this place?' she asked, pulling off her own helmet, smoothing out her ponytail. For a second, as she did so, she looked unbearably pretty to Brick. Then her face crumpled up into that all-too-familiar mask of misery and disappointment. 'Fursville? Didn't this used to be an amusement park or something?'

Duh, thought Brick, glancing up at the big wheel, or what remained of it. With only one of its gondolas still attached and its broken spokes bent out at all angles it resembled some leprous, anorexic giant.

'Please tell me you didn't drag me out to see *this* crapyard,' she spat. He didn't say anything. He didn't dare. He felt ridiculously protective of the place. Hearing her talk about it this way made his blood boil. He bit his tongue, looking away, his head pounding. He could hear his pulse ringing in his ears, probably from wearing the helmet for too long. 'Brick? Why the hell are we standing here?'

'Let's just get inside,' he said. 'Before anyone sees us. I don't want people to know I come here.'

'I'm not surprised. Why *do* you come here?' Lisa said as he wheeled the bike into the laurel hedge. It was cooler there, like he'd stepped into a fridge, and darker too. Just being out of the sun calmed him down a little. He could hear Lisa stepping after him, swearing as the laurel branches snagged her hair, as the fat, cool leaves brushed against her face. Then they were out, pinned between the shrubbery and the fence. The gap was dead ahead and he manoeuvred himself and the bike through it, hefting it over the rubble and the rubbish.

Home sweet home.

'Jesus, it smells like a dead dog in here,' said Lisa. 'There are probably vampires and stuff. Isn't it supposed to be haunted or something?'

'It's not haunted,' Brick said, feeling like a parent patiently trying to calm their annoying child. 'There are no vampires or dead dogs.'

'Killer vampires,' she persisted as they walked up the side of the Boo Boo Station. 'I bet my life on it. Come on, Brick, let's go. Hemsby's close to here, in't it? We can get candyfloss and play on the machines. Brick?'

'I hate Hemsby,' he said. 'You can't hear yourself think over there. It's full of chavs, no offence.'

'Shut up,' she said. They emerged out onto the plaza, the whole place drenched in silence. The big wheel stretched overhead, and behind it was the rotting wooden track of the roller coaster. A couple of seagulls were perched on the apex of the highest slope but they didn't call out, preening each other with their bright yellow beaks. There was barely an inch of ground that wasn't covered in ancient litter – old newspapers, empty cans that had lost their colour years ago, carrier bags pinned by rubble – and over to the left, by the main gates, was a Jenga stack of rusting dodgems that would have looked more at home in a junk yard.

'Bloody hell, Brick, you really know how to impress a lady, don't you.'

'You're no lady,' he said.

'Oi!' she tried to clip him round the head but he

dodged out of the way, jogging backwards as she came after him. 'You stand still and take your punishment, Brick Thomas.'

She charged again, and this time when he wheeled beneath her hand she was laughing. He turned, running to the left of the big wheel, past a boarded-up kiosk crowned with a huge plastic hot dog, making for the biggest building in the park. It was a squat, ugly box about the size of the hall back at his school, with a turquoise plastic façade that was supposed to make the roof look like rolling waves. A few of the three-metre high letters above the main door had fallen off, leaving the gap-toothed word PAV LIO . Lisa caught up with him under the decaying awning of the veranda, grabbing his elbow and spinning him round.

'I told you to take your punishment,' she grinned, then leant up and kissed him. He closed his eyes and opened his mouth, feeling her tongue flick against his. He didn't know how much later it was when she pulled away, and it took him a moment to remember where he was. The kiss had helped his headache too, that relentless *thump-thump* quieter now, like distant waves. Lisa stepped back, colour breaching the bottomless layers of foundation. 'Oh, now I see why you've brought me here,' she said, smiling. '*You're* a killer vampire!'

The smile was on Brick's face before he could stop it, even though it felt uncomfortable there in front of her.

'You wish,' he said, turning and walking along the side of the building. Lisa snuck up beside him, lacing her hand through his.

'You seriously come out here by yourself?' she asked as they turned the corner. The path here was cracked and uneven, the nine crazy-golf holes to the side overgrown almost beyond recognition. A giant squirrel with half its face missing watched them go from behind a thorned veil of brambles.

'All the time,' he said. 'The only place I can get any peace and quiet.'

'It's majorly creepy.'

Halfway down the pavilion's side wall was a fire exit, the two doors connected by a chain the size of a boa constrictor. Brick took hold of one and pulled, the doors opening a couple of feet before the chain stopped them. He ducked underneath it, squeezing into the darkness.

'No way, Brick, it's filthy in there,' Lisa said, her voice muted by the sheer weight of silence inside. Tendrils of light oozed down from algae-slicked skylights, barely enough to see by.

'It's fine, I promise,' he said, pushing the doors out as far as they would go. Eventually Lisa squatted down, worming through the gap, doing her best not to touch anything. She stood, looking around the gloomy corridor, brushing her palms over her jeans. 'Ew,' was all she could manage.

'It's pretty run down,' Brick explained, turning right towards the front of the building. Lisa was quick to follow, the click of her heels echoing into the swamp of shadows which stretched the length of the corridor.

'But the basement's still in decent shape.'

'The *basement*?' Lisa said, pulling herself closer to him.

Brick passed two doors on the left but opened the third. What lay beyond resembled a tar pit, so pitch black that it seemed to bleed darkness out into the corridor.

'You are *so* not serious,' she said, and the tone of her voice had changed, her anxiety now genuine. 'No way am I going in there, Brick.'

He reached in, fumbling in the shadows for the torch he'd left there. With a click it came to life, banishing the artificial night to reveal a staircase leading down towards a short corridor packed tight with junk. Even with the light it looked pretty sinister.

'Gets better down there,' he said. He held Lisa's hand tight, pulling her gently but insistently after him. 'Come on.'

She stumbled in his distorted shadow as he weaved through the junk and pushed open another door, leading her into the basement. He hadn't been lying, it *was* better down here. For some reason the smell of damp and rot which infested the entire park, especially the pavilion, was less potent below ground. He had cleared it out as well, the large, open space free of clutter. He propped the torch against the wall, its soft glow illuminating a moth-eaten pink sofa against the far wall, a coffee table in front of it. Other than a boiler which sat cold and quiet in the corner, and a bunch of electricity boxes on the walls, that was about it.

'Moved everything else upstairs,' he said, walking to

the table and picking up a box of matches. There were a couple of candles that he'd nicked from home and he lit them both, the shifting light on the walls making it feel like they were underwater. 'Kind of cosy down here, yeah?'

'I guess so,' she replied. 'If you're Dracula.'

'Shut up,' he said without malice. He let go of her hand, walking to the sofa and perching there. His laptop sat open on the coffee table and a pay-as-you-go internet dongle poked out of one of the USB ports, the tip flashing. He got a better signal upstairs, but he preferred it down here, especially in the evening, and it wasn't like he ever needed to hurry. That's what he loved about this place, there was no rush. Time just didn't seem to matter.

His headache was back with a vengeance and he used both hands to massage his temples, willing it away as Lisa sat down next to him.

'Okay, you've got me down here,' she said. 'Now what?'

She smiled, tilting her head and coyly chewing her bottom lip. The torchlight threw her face into sharp relief, picking out the woodchip-like spots beneath her make-up, but her eyes flashed with excitement and something else, too, something that made her just about the most desirable woman Brick had ever seen in his life. She leant in, and he met her, the world peeling away around them, forgotten.

Daisy

Daisy sat on the steps outside the school's main entrance, waiting for her mum to show up and trying not to think about what had happened back in the theatre. She was hurt and angry and sad, but the emotions were so evenly matched that all she really felt was numb. She couldn't believe that Fred had spat at her, that he'd *spat right in her face*. It wasn't that which had really stunned her, though, it was the laughter that had followed. It was like something from a nightmare, one of the ones where you've done something stupid and everyone turns on you and you can't understand why.

Except this was no nightmare. Everyone had turned on her, *everyone* had laughed.

She could still see Kim's face, twisted by some kind of sick glee. And Mrs Jackson too. She at least should have known better. Why hadn't she said anything? And Fred. There were words for him, words that she'd heard her mum use when she was really mad. Fred was all of those words and worse, if there was such a thing as worse. And if there wasn't then someone would have to invent a word for worse. She *hated* him.

A car pulled into the car park, circling the memorial flowerbed in its centre, and Daisy straightened. It was blue, though, not white, and she slumped back down, clamping her rucksack to her chest. She'd hoped her mum would arrive before everyone started to leave; she didn't want to see anyone else that night. She didn't want to see them ever again. She just wanted to go home and watch telly and draw and try to forget about everything.

The main door clicked behind her, making her jump. There was a thunder of footsteps, a gang of kids running down the steps. They looked at her curiously, as if they couldn't quite remember who she was. Better that than them still laughing, though. Daisy shrunk into her rucksack, peering over the top of it.

Come on, Mum, hurry up.

Click, more footsteps, and this time Daisy felt a hand on her shoulder. She looked up to see Chloe there. She'd taken off her costume and was wearing her school uniform again, her hair still done up in old-fashioned plaits.

'What happened to you?' she asked. Daisy's mouth dropped.

'What do you mean, what happened?' she asked, the anger quickening her tongue. 'You were there, I saw you laughing.'

'That thing with Fred?' Chloe said, sitting on the step next to her. More kids barrelled out, streaming into the car park. 'The *sneeze*?'

Daisy frowned, shaking her head. She quickly glanced over her shoulder to make sure the coast was clear before leaning in towards Chloe.

'What do you mean, "sneeze"? He spat in my face.'

Chloe grinned, but there was nothing nasty in it.

'He sneezed,' she said. 'Then you went running off before he could say sorry.'

Daisy was still shaking her head. It hadn't been a sneeze, no way. She could still see his eyes, devoid of anything nice, anything kind. He'd spat at her, and it had been deliberate.

Hadn't it?

'He said sorry?' she asked after a moment. Chloe pulled one of the bands from her hair, shaking out the braids. She seemed to think about it for a moment.

'No, not in so many words. He would have done, though, obvs, if you hadn't run off like your knickers were on fire.'

'You were all laughing,' Daisy said, quieter now, staring down the steps. 'I saw you.'

Chloe leant in, putting an arm round Daisy's shoulder.

'Sorry, but it *was* funny, you've got to admit that. Getting sneezed on by the boy you fancy? It's proper Oops TV stuff, that. I bet you anything you'd have been laughing if it was me.'

'Or me,' said a voice behind them. Kim jogged down the stairs, gave Daisy a quick hug from behind, then carried on, heading for the blue car. 'That's my dad. Sorry, Daisy, but it was quite funny. Don't be sad; I'm sure Fred still loves you.'

She clambered into the passenger seat, blowing Daisy a kiss through the window as they pulled away. Cars were spilling through the gates now, drivers doing their best not to run over the small army of pupils that had assembled at the foot of the steps.

'See, it's all fine,' said Chloe, giving Daisy a gentle nudge. 'You're coming to rehearsal tomorrow, right? The last one, you have to.'

Daisy didn't answer. Her shoulders felt a little lighter, her head clearer. Maybe Chloe was right. Maybe it had all been a misunderstanding. She was pretty tired. It had been an exhausting day. Suddenly another feeling broke through the numbness, this one worse than all the others: embarrassment. What if it *had* been an innocent sneeze and she'd stormed off like a kid? How stupid had she looked?

'That's me,' said Chloe, giving Daisy a hug. 'Love you.'

Daisy nodded, managing a ghost of a smile, then Chloe had gone, climbing into the back of her dad's four-wheel drive. It drove up to the gate, pulling out at the same time as a familiar battered white Spacewagon entered. Daisy got to her feet. She didn't think she'd ever been so relieved to see her mum. She ran to the car, opening the door so hard it bounced on its hinges, almost swinging closed again. She fought her way into the passenger seat, still clutching her rucksack to her chest like a life jacket.

'How'd it go?' her mum asked, tucking a wisp of white hair into her headscarf.

Daisy opened her mouth to answer, then froze. Mrs Jackson stood at the open door of the school, a lump of shadow. Her half-moon glasses seemed to burn across the car park, right into Daisy.

'Fine,' Daisy lied, shuddering. 'It went fine.'

Her mum drove through the gates. Behind them, Mrs Jackson stood in the doorway, unmoving, unblinking as she watched them go.

Brick

'Ow!'

Brick snapped his head back, almost leaving part of his bottom lip between Lisa's teeth. He sucked it into his mouth, feeling it start to swell. Pain pulsed out of it, crawling up the sides of his face and joining the grinding thump in his temples.

'What the hell, Lisa?' he said. 'That really hurt.'

Lisa didn't reply, she just stared at his mouth. Brick wasn't sure how long they'd been kissing for but it felt like forever – in a good way. The basement was still coming into focus around him, the real world slowly reassembling itself, like it hadn't existed at all for the last hour or so. He guessed it hadn't. Not really. The whole pavilion could have been burning to the ground over their heads and neither of them would have noticed.

'You gonna try and eat me again?' Brick asked, feeling his mood wobble. Lisa shook her head, looking as dazed as he felt. Her eyelids were heavy, half closed, and most of her make-up had rubbed off against his cheek, revealing the blush underneath. She had a red patch on her chin where his uneven, rust-coloured stubble had scraped against it. She leant towards him again and he wrapped his arms around her, pulling her close. Everything felt like it was in slow motion, the

69

silence more of a physical pressure in his ears than an absence of sound, and Brick once again had the absurd notion that they were underwater. He kissed her, their tongues dancing, reality spinning away once again.

More pain, this time so sudden that he saw it as a bright flash of light. He pushed Lisa back, putting his hand to his mouth. The tips of his fingers came away red. She'd bitten him in exactly the same place as before, a knot already forming beneath the skin of his lip.

'Jesus, Lisa, stop it.' He could taste blood against the words, coppery and sharp. 'I'm serious.'

Still she didn't speak, sitting back against the sofa and licking her lips. She seemed half asleep, and beneath her drooping lids her eyes were darkened with something that Brick couldn't quite identify. For the first time since he'd started hanging out here he wondered if it was safe, if maybe the candles were eating all the oxygen and spitting out carbon monoxide or something. It might not have had much of an effect on him but Lisa was about a foot shorter and half his weight.

'You okay?' he asked, grabbing her shoulder and giving her a gentle shake. 'Lisa?'

She seemed to stir, her eyes swimming into focus and her brow crinkling. She sat up straight, wiping the back of an arm across her face, taking a deep, uncertain breath. When she next looked at Brick it was almost as if she couldn't quite put a name to the face, squinting, the corners of her mouth drooping like they were being pulled by wires.

'Lisa? Baby?' He'd never called her 'baby' before, but she was seriously starting to freak him out. 'You want to go? Get some fresh air?'

After what felt like a solid minute she shook her head again. She reached out and grabbed Brick by the scruff of his shirt, reeling herself towards him with a wide-open mouth. Brick recoiled, his lip throbbing, but the thought of another kiss snuffed out everything else. He pushed his mouth against hers, working his hand back underneath her T-shirt where it had spent the last half an hour hovering with nervous impatience around her lower rib, uncertain about which direction to take so taking neither. Her skin was so hot she might have had a furnace under there. Brick's heart was like the beat-up engine on his bike, going so fast and so hard he was worried it might stall.

Lisa's hand was still wrapped around the collar of his shirt and she used it to push him back into the sofa, clambering onto his lap, their lips never parting. The change of position, his neck wedged at an awkward angle, made his headache worse, that pulse so loud now it was like a hand inside his skull, squeezing the flesh of his brain – *thump-thump . . . thump-thump . . . thump-thump* – not as fast as his own heartbeat but definitely more urgent. Talk about timing, the night he might finally get lucky with Lisa and it felt like his head was about to implode.

Lisa's kisses were furious now, so hard that their teeth were clashing. She banged her nose against his and he tried to tilt his head so it wouldn't happen again, a lance of discomfort spearing his neck. She didn't let up, bearing down on him, covering his mouth with her own so that he couldn't get a breath in, her tongue trying to worm down his windpipe.

He attempted to shove her away but she felt heavier than he would have believed possible. The angle his body was locked in – bent into the crook of the old sofa – made it impossible for him to find leverage. He pushed forward with his head and she moved with him, locked onto his lips like a leech. He did it again, butting her with more force. Her head swung back.

It wasn't Lisa.

It looked like her but there was something wrong with her face, like it had melted. All of her muscles had gone slack, reminding him of his nan when she'd had a stroke. It made her look years older, *decades* older. It made her look dead.

'Lisa? Lisa?' Brick said, the words half eaten by fear as he squirmed beneath her. 'What's wrong? Baby, tell me what's wrong.'

She came for him again, that sunken face closing in, her mouth so wide that Brick almost screamed at the sight of it. He grabbed her shoulders, keeping her at arm's length, trying to manoeuvre himself towards the edge of the sofa.

'Lisa, snap out of it, what's wrong?'

What if something happened to her out here. What if she *died*? And Brick realised with a sickening sense of shame that the first thought which flashed into his head – there and gone in a heartbeat – was that he'd have to leave her here and run, get the hell away before her parents found out. But no, of course he wouldn't, he could call for an ambulance, they'd be here in minutes, she'd be okay. She'd be okay.

He shook her, her head lolling back on her shoulders like a rag doll before snapping back, dropping towards him again.

'Brick,' she slurred, and he could see that the paper bag of her mouth was almost smiling.

'Lisa?' he said. 'You okay?'

And just like that the pounding in his head stopped, the pain vanishing with such speed that its absence was almost as frightening.

'No way,' he said. Lisa had stopped trying to kiss him, her head tucked into her chest, swaying gently. He still had her by the shoulders and he could feel the muscles beneath her T-shirt, small but tense. He wondered if maybe his headache and her weirdness were related. Maybe he shouldn't have lit the candles without proper ventilation. 'You okay, baby? Let's get—'

Lisa arched her back, her head twisting up to the ceiling, the tendons in her neck like steel cables. Then she screamed, the noise like nothing Brick had heard in his life. It was raw, it was savage, it was hate-filled, and it seemed to go on forever, threatening to bring the walls of the pavilion down. The scream died out with a hideous rattle, flecks of spit popping from her lips. Lisa lowered her head, her eyes so dark they looked black; insect eyes, fixed on Brick with a look of undiluted fury. He tried to call her name but he never got a chance.

She went for him, her head darting forward like a cobra's. Her teeth scraped down his forehead, locking onto the flesh of his eyebrow and biting hard. Brick found his voice, shrieking. Blood gushed into his eye, trickling into his mouth, choking him. She was chewing, working his face like a tough lump of lamb, her breath coming in short, meaty gasps. She was punching him too, he realised, the blows lost in the supernova of agony that burned in his face.

He shoved her as hard as he could. Her body snapped back but her teeth anchored her in place, threatening to tear off his forehead. He cried out again, adrenalin catapulting him off the sofa. Lisa clung on, wrapping her legs around his waist, her fists slapping against his shoulders, his ears, his throat.

Brick staggered, tripping on the coffee table, both of them toppling. She hit first, grunting as he crushed her, his weight rolling them both off the other side onto the floor. She landed on top of him, her teeth ripped from his eyebrow. She lunged again, going for his cheek, and he only just managed to get a hand up under her chin before her jaw snapped shut. He noticed she'd lost one of her teeth but she didn't seem to care. Her eyes blazed only hatred. She was rabid, feral.

And she was going to kill him.

He drew back his arm and punched her, catching her in the nose, showering himself with warm blood. Then he brought his knee into her ribs, twisting the same way so that she tumbled off him.

He grabbed the table, hauling himself to his feet. Lisa was quick, though, uncoiling like a snake and sinking her teeth into his heel. The pain almost sent him sprawling to the floor again. He wrenched his foot loose, limping towards the basement door. He could hear Lisa scrabbling and glanced over his shoulder to see her squirming on her back. Her ankle looked wrong, bent at a strange angle. She rolled, jerking up onto her feet like she didn't even notice her leg was broken, coming after him with long, clumsy strides.

Brick threw himself away, hearing her gaining, hearing that animal groan spilling from her lips. He careened into the door, falling through it face-first into the wall beyond. He thrashed in the darkness, turning, seeing Lisa tear towards him, foam spilling from her jaw, blood trailing out of her nose.

He kicked the door shut, and the whole corridor seemed to tremble as Lisa hit the other side. It started to open and he braced his back against the wall, keeping his legs tense, grateful for once to be six-five and tall enough to keep his feet against the metal fire plate. There was a patter of footsteps then another spine-snapping crunch, more like a rhino charging at the door than a sixteen-year-old girl.

More steps, another attempt. Brick didn't move, just kept his whole body rigid as the door bulged then clicked shut, bulged then clicked shut, some awful heartbeat as she charged again and again and again. Only now did he notice that he was bawling like a baby, his face wet with tears and blood and snot. But he couldn't stop, those sobs too big to be kept inside. He lay there crying, screaming into the boundless darkness of the corridor, while Lisa bayed for his blood.

The Other: I

Heed the breath of the Beast;
in death he rises,
and in our darkest days
he will devour us all.
    The Book of Hebron

Murdoch

Almost midnight, on one of the hottest, muggiest nights of the year, and here he was buried alive in the morgue at Scotland Yard.

And it wasn't even his shift.

Inspector Alan Murdoch traipsed down the last flight of stairs and along the green tiled corridor. There was nobody at the reception desk, which wasn't surprising given the time, but he knew the way all too well. The morgue was his second home, he spent more time in this crypt than he did at home with his wife and the baby he'd seen maybe a dozen times in twice as many days since it had been born. He could picture the room on the other side of that door – the chipped notice board with the 'Clean Hands Won't Contaminate Evidence: Wash Them Now!' poster, the upholstered benches against the walls, foam spilling out of them as if they were corpses too, the pocket of dust and lint in the corner around the fake cactus that the cleaner always seemed to miss – better than he could picture the face of his son.

Murdoch sighed, wiping a hand over the thick stubble he hadn't had a chance to shave since beginning his own shift twelve hours ago. Then he leant on the door, almost falling through it into the waiting area.

He was expecting it to be deserted as well – during the graveyard run people tended to avoid coming down here – but it wasn't. He did a quick head count: eight people crammed into the small room. His good friend and the force's chief pathologist, Dr Sven Jorgensen, was in the middle, a blond beanpole in a white surgical suit who towered over the similarly dressed assistants to his side. Even through the biohazard mask Murdoch saw that his face was creased into a deeper frown than usual. He caught sight of Murdoch and looked over, the reflection of the harsh halogen lights exploding in his visor.

'Good to see you, Alan,' he said, his voice muffled. He waved a hand and scattered his assistants as Murdoch walked over. 'You're not going to want to miss this.'

'Miss what?' Murdoch asked. 'Why the suit? Terrorists?'

The last time he'd seen the pathologist in a biohazard suit had been when the anti-terrorist squad had brought in three jihadis who'd poisoned themselves with the ricin they'd been planning to use on the Tube.

'Uh uh,' Jorgensen said, shaking his head. 'This is . . . This is something different. I can't explain it.'

Murdoch felt his pulse quicken. Jorgensen wasn't the kind of guy who scared easily. Murdoch had stood by the pathologist's side as he'd sliced open corpses of all shapes and sizes, kids and adults, men and women, burned, drowned, beaten, drained, punctured, flayed, cannibalised, starved, beheaded, disembowelled

– pretty much every method of dying possible. He'd never so much as seen the man tremble. But something had rattled him, that truth was in the waxy colour of his cheeks and a sheen of sweat on his forehead that had absolutely nothing to do with the close confines of the biohazard suit.

'Sorry to call you out so late,' Jorgensen went on. 'I wanted to show you. I don't know how much longer I'll have.'

'What?' Murdoch asked. 'Why?'

'I had to call this one in,' he said, brushing his gloved hands down his overalls. 'MI5. This is something new.'

'The security service?' Murdoch said, raising an eyebrow. 'Seriously?'

'You'll understand when you see it.' Jorgensen paused, and in that hesitation Murdoch understood that the man didn't want to go back inside the morgue. He felt a cold sweat of his own creep over his face and down his spine. Jorgensen not wanting to go to work was like a kid not wanting to go out to play – something was seriously wrong. The man seemed to snap out of his trance, turning a pair of bloodshot eyes towards the door. 'You'll need a mask.'

Murdoch looked up at the pathologist for a moment longer, then turned and walked to the steel lockers against the far wall of the waiting room. The one marked 'Hazardous' was already open, a couple of full-face masks left near the bottom. He slipped one over his head, switching it on and making sure the rubber seal was tight around his neck. He hated these things, the air inside them was like breathing from a dead man's lungs. Still, better this than inhaling whatever was inside the morgue, whatever had unsettled Jorgensen so much.

'This way,' said the pathologist, as if Murdoch hadn't been here a hundred times before. One of the morgue assistants held open the waiting-room door for them and Murdoch followed Jorgensen through, past the viewing window where loved ones had to stand and identify the remains of those they had once called mother or daughter or brother. The main entrance to the morgue was a few paces further down and yet more white-suited staff were clustered outside it. One of them pushed the door, holding it for them as they passed through.

'No change, sir,' the woman said. She had to shout over the rumble of the air conditioning units which were working overtime to cope with the heat. Even here, beneath the ground, Murdoch could feel it prickling his skin, making him itch all over.

Jorgensen nodded at her, leading the way across the huge room towards an area sectioned off with hospital-style privacy curtains. He stopped next to them.

'This is top secret, Alan, okay?' he said. 'Until we know what this is, nobody can find out about it. I brought you in because you're a friend, because I trust you. But nobody else can know. Okay?'

Murdoch nodded, trying to wipe a hand across his stubble again and knocking the mask. A bolt of pure, white adrenalin exploded in his gut and he took a couple of long, deep breaths which misted his visor. He was grateful to them, because they obscured his vision as Jorgensen reached out and pulled the curtain to one side.

He didn't want to see what lay in the corner of this room. He could hear it, though, a sound that rose up over the rattle and clank of the overworked air conditioners. It was a scream, a wretched, terrible, strangled scream gargled through a wet throat – not one thrown out but one clawed *in*, like a desperate asthmatic breath. He could almost feel that breath on his skin, breaking out a blanket of goosebumps that clung to him like a disease. It made him want to run from the room and throw himself into a bath of disinfectant, to hurl himself into the sun just so it could burn the touch from him.

The mist on his visor was clearing, and through the plastic he saw a naked body lying on a stainless steel surgical table. It was a young man. And it was a corpse. Of this there could be no doubt because its chest had been opened up like a birthday present, torn flaps of wrapping-paper-red skin pulled to the side to reveal a gift basket of withered organs. Its body was blackened on the underside where the blood had pooled in post-mortem lividity.

Don't look at its face, his brain told him. Yet he could no more turn away than he could sprout wings and fly out of the morgue. His eyes drifted up from the feast of its stomach, past its pulseless throat, to a face that was still alive.

No, not alive. Animated, yes – its mouth hung open, too wide, wide enough for Murdoch to get his whole fist into if he could ever bring himself to move again. It was this that was making the noise, that gurgling wheeze. It reminded Murdoch of the old VCR he used to have, the one his wife insisted they kept even though they didn't even make video tapes any more. If you hit the pause button the people on screen would freeze but they would still be moving, flickering, trembling, and the tape would emit a throbbing purr that would last until you pressed play again. This corpse was frozen in the same way, because even though it was dead, even though it wasn't moving, he could sense life inside it. It was as if something lay just beneath the surface of that parchment-thin skin, something writhing and twisting and breathing in that endless inverted scream.

It was its eyes, he realised. They were white marbles in puckered sockets, shrouded with death, and yet they could *still see*. He understood that instinctively, that these two pinprick pupils which stared at the tiled ceiling of the morgue were seeing something; they were watching.

'It's been like this for an hour now,' said Jorgensen from his side. 'Since the road patrol brought it in.'

Murdoch staggered, collapsing against the wall to his side. Jorgensen was looking at him, and he could see his own open-mouthed reflection in the pathologist's visor.

'There's no pulse, no blood pressure,' he went on. 'It's one hundred per cent dead.'

'It's not,' Murdoch spat. 'It's breathing.'

Jorgensen turned back to the corpse, shaking his head. 'Not quite,' he said. 'It's inhaling. But its lungs are flat, we opened them up to see where all that air was going.'

'Where is it going?' Murdoch asked, shouting over the same grating, unchanging, unending breath from that dislocated jaw.

Jorgensen shrugged.

'That's the weirdest thing,' he said, opening a bottle of talcum powder that was lying on the tray next to the table. He took out a pinch and flicked it over the corpse's mouth, watching as the dead man sucked it in like a vacuum cleaner. Murdoch managed a step forward, peering down into the gaping maw to see that the powder had vanished down the black pit of its throat. Jorgensen put the cap back on the bottle as he spoke. 'That's why I called MI5. That's what I don't understand. That air, it's not going anywhere; nowhere we can find, anyway.'

Behind them, one of the assistants appeared at the door.

'Sir,' he said. 'I think the government is here.'

'I'll be right there,' Jorgensen said. He turned to Murdoch. 'Whatever this thing is, wherever that air is going, it's not here.'

'Not here?' Murdoch asked. He looked at the corpse – its open chest gaping, its mouth inhaling, those pale eyes burning into the ceiling. 'Sven, what do you mean *not here*?'

Jorgensen sighed, a noise that sounded more like a sob.

'I mean exactly that,' he said. 'I mean it's going somewhere else.'

Friday

Turning and turning in the widening gyre
The falcon cannot hear the falconer;
Things fall apart; the centre cannot hold;
Mere anarchy is loosed upon the world,
The blood-dimmed tide is loosed, and everywhere
The ceremony of innocence is drowned
   W. B. Yeats, 'The Second Coming'

Brick

Brick sat at the top of the basement steps, his head in his hands, flinching every time he thought he heard a noise from below.

He felt empty, completely and utterly drained. It had taken all his strength just to make it up the stairs. Shortly after getting out of the basement he'd found a steel rod in the pavilion – it looked like one of the electrical poles from a dodgem – and had managed to wedge it tight between the door and the wall. He'd packed everything he could find around it to lock it in place, praying that it would hold up against the on-slaught from the other side. It had, so far. Lisa had spent the best part of three hours battering the door, each attempt growing weaker and feebler until the sound of her body hitting the wood and metal was no louder than a gentle slap.

It was the noises *in between* the crunches that had turned his stomach, though, that had made him think he was going to go insane sitting there in the darkness. Brittle snaps, something wet that accompanied her steps, shuffling flaps that he imagined were her falling and trying to get up again, some of which went on for ten, fifteen minutes at a time.

And worst of all were the groans and snarls, noises

89

that could have come from a wounded animal in a trap if it wasn't for the half-words buried in the mess. The only one he could recognise was his name, spat out again and again in panting, wretched screams until he had to clamp his hands over his ears and blot them out with cries of his own.

At 10.53 the attack on the door had stopped. Brick had pressed his ear against it, hearing jagged, even breathing. Lisa was asleep, or unconscious. That's when he'd made his way up the stairs. He knew that was the exact time because he'd had his crappy Nokia on his lap ever since, 999 thumbed into it but the call button unpressed. He'd been on the verge of ringing for an ambulance about a hundred times, but something had stopped him – the thought of what the paramedics would say when they got here, them and the cops. They'd see a girl beaten half to death, a broken nose, a snapped ankle and God only knew what else; a girl who'd almost killed herself trying to break out of a locked basement in an abandoned theme park. And when Brick showed them his single injury, the teeth marks in his eyebrow, they'd just say she'd done it in self-defence.

And, of course, Brick had one of *those* faces. Everybody hated him.

But that alone hadn't stopped him calling for help. After all, if the police arrived and Lisa was still going mental then they'd know for sure this wasn't his fault. No, it was a voice in his head, a good voice for once, saying *She's going to be fine, she just went a bit crazy, that's all; give her a few hours and she'll be better*, over and over, too convincing to ignore. The voice had to be right; give her some time and she'd be okay.

Something else in his head started to argue but he drowned it out, pushing deeper into his hands. His eyebrow was burning – he'd actually had to pick Lisa's missing tooth out of his flesh, the incisor still gripped in his palm – and he could barely open his swollen right eye.

He looked down into the pool of liquid darkness that sat at the bottom of the steps. There was a fine silver gauze hanging from the skylights but it didn't have the guts to go anywhere near the basement. He could just about make out the crack of candlelight under the door, unbroken ever since Lisa had stopped moving. He'd thought about going back down, seeing if she was okay, but his body had mutinied, refusing to obey a single command from his brain.

What *was* his plan? He didn't know. He just wanted to curl up and sleep, to wake the next morning in his own bed with a text from Lisa saying *soz, wnt hpen agn*. But he was too wired to sleep, his body aching all over from the fight, the adrenalin now a spiked ball in his stomach and lead weights in his arms.

There was a soft noise from below. Brick cocked his head, his heart once again in overdrive. At first he thought he'd imagined it, but sure enough there was another sliding sound, then a scrape that could have been fingernails on wood.

She was awake.

Brick didn't move, afraid that if he so much as breathed too loudly it might set her off again. The stripe of golden light split into two, then into four, then disappeared altogether as Lisa pressed herself against the door. He could hear breathing now, wheezed, desperate. There was a rattle as she tried the handle, the metal pole holding.

'Brick.'

Her voice was an old woman's, his name misshapen, the 'B' barely there and the 'r' now a 'w'. It was spoken not with malice but with fear.

'Hel . . . hel me.'

His stomach dropped into his feet, his heart following. He stood, swaying.

'Help me.'

'Lisa?' he said, his own voice high and broken. The shuffling noises grew louder. He could hear her scraping the door.

'Let me go, Brick,' she said. 'Please, I'm hurt. I just want to go home. Let me go, I'll do anything. Please.'

Brick ran a hand through his hair, feeling the tears coming again, echoing Lisa's which rose from the basement. He took a step down, gripping the railing like he was descending Everest.

'Please, Brick,' Lisa cried. 'I'm scared, why are you doing this?'

'I'm not,' he croaked, taking another step. 'You attacked me, you *bit* me.'

'I didn't,' came her reply, choked almost beyond recognition. 'I didn't do anything, just let me go, Brick.

I won't tell anyone, I promise.'

Tell anyone *what*? What did she think had happened? What if she didn't remember? What if she honestly believed he'd attacked her? He realised he was halfway to the next step, his leg hovering. He pulled it back.

'Brick!' she screamed, rattling the handle harder now. 'I'm bleeding!'

That did it, breaking through his need for self-preservation. What if she was bleeding badly? What if she was *dying*? So what if he got arrested, questioned? He hadn't attacked her, they'd do lie-detector tests or something and find that out. It was Lisa, he couldn't just stand here and let her bleed to death in the basement of Fursville's derelict PAV LIO .

'Okay, I'm coming, just hang on,' he said as he walked unsteadily down the steps. He dropped into the darkness, careful not to trip. Lisa's sobs grew louder as he neared, the scrape of her nails on the door setting his teeth on edge.

'Hurry,' she said. 'Bleed . . . hel . . .'

He reached the corridor below, crouching down to try and locate the metal brace. From behind the door Lisa's words were getting weaker and he imagined her lying in a pool of blood, trying and failing to get up on her broken leg. There was a grunt, a desperate breath.

'Brick . . . let . . . e . . . o . . .'

'Hang on,' he said, grabbing hold of the bar with both hands. 'I'll be there in a minute.'

Her words were now meaningless clumps of sound pinned between pig-like snorts. Brick paused, angling his head again. That short delay probably saved his life.

Lisa threw herself at the door, so hard that the top corner pinged open a crack despite the bar. She screamed, then again, pounding relentlessly, driving Brick up the stairs on all fours. This time he didn't stop at the top. He ran blind down the pavilion corridor, her banshee-like shrieks giving chase.

Cal

Cal was woken by his phone, the machine-gun sound effect calling him up from a dream about Georgia and prison cells. It spun apart before he could catch hold of it, dissolving into the warm morning light. He reached out groggily, fishing on his bedside table until he found it. The text was from Megan.

What happened 2 u yesterday?!?!?!

It took him a second to remember yesterday, and when he did he sat up in bed frowning. They'd left him, all of them, run off and deserted him at the library. He'd ended up walking home, even though it took about forty-five minutes rather than ten on the bus, getting more and more annoyed with them the later it got. By the time he'd stormed in the front door, ignoring his mum and going straight to his room, he'd been properly pissed off.

He yawned, then wiped the sleep from his eyes, blinking the phone back into focus.

You all left me, he started writing, then after a moment's consideration he wiped the screen clear and replaced it with, *Got bored, went home*. He wouldn't let them have the satisfaction of knowing they'd got to him.

He dropped the phone onto the table, folding

himself back under the duvet. He couldn't be arsed with the thought of school today. There was the next Inter-form Cup match at lunch but he knew he'd have to spend it listening to the jeers of his mates. *Poor Callum, did we scare you off? Aw, diddums, did Mummy make it all okay?* No, better let them sweat it out, make them think that maybe he'd decided not to play any more. Let's see them win 3–1 against 12H without their star midfielder.

His mum would let him skive, no problem. She was a big softie, all he had to do was give her his best puppy-dog expression and she'd give in to him. His dad – the only potential obstacle to his plan – was away on one of his endless business trips in Spain.

To be honest he wasn't actually feeling all that well anyway. His head was weird, like it was stuffed with cotton wool, that faint *thump-thump* of a headache still breathing against his skull.

He rolled over, stretching his legs and looking at the window. The light that seeped in past his curtains was thick and honey-coloured and he could already feel the heat of the morning pressing in from outside. It was going to be another flawless day. Too good to spend in bed, he decided, headache or no headache. Better to stockpile his sick-day points, use them later in the year when it was hammering it down outside and the streets were ice rinks.

Besides, he had his weekly kung fu class this evening and he really didn't want to miss that. He was going for his advanced-level Choy Li Fut grading in a few weeks and he still hadn't mastered everything he needed to.

He checked his phone again to make sure Megan hadn't texted back, then clambered out of bed. There was an *Inbetweeners* episode he'd only managed to get halfway through last night and he flicked it back on, listening to it as he brushed his teeth in the sink in his room. He got changed then opened the curtains, a shaft of pure sunlight bathing him like he was Bruce Almighty or something, being embraced by the finger of God. Man, he *loved* summer.

Cal headed downstairs, making a brief detour to the bathroom before strolling into the kitchen.

'Morning, Mum,' he said, yawning again, slumping down on one of the stools around the breakfast bar. His mum stood in the corner by their huge double range, a pan bubbling on the hob. She made him an egg every morning whether he wanted it or not. This morning was a definite 'not', the milkshakes from last night still somewhere down there playing tag in his intestines.

'I said morning, *Mother*.'

She didn't reply. Cal left her to her cooking, turning to the paper on the table and idly scanning the TV guide. Behind him, the pan rattled and clanked like an old car.

The machine-gun noise went again from inside his pocket and he whipped the phone out. Megan again: *A-hole, we didn't no where ud gone.*

What was she playing at? They were the ones who had left. And if they'd really not known where he'd gone then why hadn't they texted him while he was walking home? He punched the phone back into his pocket, feeling the hangover from his mood last night start to grow.

Something popped from the stove and the smell of burning filled the kitchen. Cal got up, walking over.

'Earth to Mum,' he said. 'You're burning the house down.'

The pan on the stove had boiled dry, two eggs inside oozing out of their blackening shells, the whole thing shaking so much it looked ready to take off. Cal grabbed the handle and lifted it from the gas, slamming it down onto another hob.

'What the hell are you doing, Mum?' he asked, turning to her. She still hadn't moved, her bleach-blonde hair concealing her face. And she smelled funny, older somehow. *Oh Jesus, she's had a stroke*, was Cal's first, heart-stopping thought. He reached out, pulling her hair back so he could see her face, and the touch made her jump – not just flinch, she literally jolted so hard her whole body came off the floor, like she'd had an electric shock.

'Mum?' Cal asked. 'What's wrong?'

She turned her head, slowly, her eyes taking a moment to find him. They were bloodshot and streaked with yellow. They weren't his mum's eyes. Cal took a step back, suddenly cold, his hand sliding along the kitchen counter, knocking a half-block of butter to the floor. The sound of it landing seemed to snap her back to attention. She tilted her head, her brow furrowing, her eyes swimming back into focus, once again her own.

'Mum?' Cal asked.

'Yes?' she said. A phantom smile danced over her lips.

'Nothing,' Cal said, bending down and picking up the butter but never looking away from her. 'Are you okay?'

She nodded like a puppet on a string. Then she seemed to remember where she was, picking up the saucepan with the eggs in it and giving it a shake.

'Oh, these are no good, shall I make you another?'

The way Cal's stomach was churning he didn't think he'd ever eat again.

'I'm okay,' he said, retreating towards the kitchen door. For some reason he didn't want to turn his back on her. 'I'll get something at school.'

'Your lunchbox is on the table,' she said, opening the metal bin and hammering the upside-down saucepan against it like she was chopping firewood. The noise was deafening.

Cal grabbed the Tupperware container, almost tripping over his feet in his hurry to get out of the room. His mum watched him go, beating the pan against the bin in purposeful, even strokes that he could hear long after he'd closed the front door behind him.

Brick

Brick woke beneath a blanket of sunshine, and it was only when he tried to move – a hundred tiny blades worrying into his muscles – that he remembered where he was. He sat up, Fursville shimmering into focus around him, drenched in fresh morning light. He was lying next to the Boo Boo Station, a stone's throw from his bike, a patch of thick sea grass for a mattress and his T-shirt for a pillow. He leant back against the wood, brushing ants from his face and neck, knowing there was a reason he felt so sore –

Lisa, we had a fight, she tried to kill me, she's still down there.

That thought sucked all the warmth from the day, leaving the park as dark and as cold as December. Brick shivered and pulled his T-shirt back on, wrapping his hands round his knees and hugging them tight against his chest. He rocked gently back and forth.

He'd made it this far last night after Lisa had started hammering on the door again. With nowhere else to go, and unable to leave her, despite the fact she'd turned into a raging psycho, he'd collapsed on the spot and drifted into an uneasy sleep. His dreams that night had been full of Lisa's screams and he wondered if they'd been real, if they'd cut up from the basement full of fury, searching for him.

He dug his phone from his pocket. There were no missed calls. Lisa's mum and dad must have been absolutely bricking it. Literally *Bricking* it, he thought with a bitter snort of laughter. He'd promised to get her home by ten at the latest. They'd be out there looking for him, the police too by now. Luckily they didn't have his number: his phone was a cheap prepaid one from the garage.

And nobody, apart from him and now Lisa, knew about this place.

He froze. *Lisa* had a phone. What if *she* called the police? That would look even worse; it would make it seem like he really *was* keeping her prisoner.

But wait, no, if she'd been able to use her phone then she'd have done it by now. The place would be crawling and Brick would be inside a cell at Norwich station, cops pounding him with questions. Maybe she was too far gone to remember how to work it. Maybe she'd messed up her hands so badly trying to get out that she couldn't press the buttons. Or maybe she couldn't get a signal down there. That would be it. Not all networks worked this far out of the city.

Brick started to rock again, feeling guilty at the relief that soothed his knotted stomach. *Great, your girlfriend can't make emergency calls from where you locked her up last night, that calls for a celebration!* And he wondered, not for the first time since the previous evening, whether *he* was the one who had actually gone nuts. Maybe he'd flipped. His moods had got worse and worse this past year, what if his brain had just reached meltdown and he'd taken out a lifetime's worth of anger and frustration on her.

He saw Lisa's face, those eyes boiling out of their sockets as she bit into him, smelling her heavy, blood-soaked breath, hearing that gargled, dying rabbit scream as she turned on him for no reason. No, that memory was real. It would be with him for the rest of his life.

So what could he do? Calling for help was no longer an option. It was too late. If the ambulance got here and she'd already . . . already . . .

He couldn't bring himself to think it. But if *that* had happened then he'd be done for murder: cold-blooded, first degree, front-page, crazy-guy-slaughters-girlfriend-in-creepy-abandoned-theme-park murder. Any defence he might have had if he'd called the police straight away was now long gone.

He could just go, leave her here, claim to her parents that he'd dropped her off down her street – that he didn't walk her to the door because he didn't want them to see her on the bike. Yes, that was good, it seemed plausible. His dad would give him an alibi, say he came home. His dad was good like that. They might never find her.

No, he screamed in his head, the noise spilling up his throat as a low, horrid groan. He couldn't do that. He wasn't like that. He couldn't leave anyone to die alone in a basement, let alone Lisa. The fact that the thought had even crossed his mind made him sick, made him feel like a monster. He slapped his forehead, twice, three times, opening up the wound in his eyebrow, feeling the tears start to swell again. What the hell was he going to do?

His dad. Maybe he should just tell his dad everything. He'd probably get a slap for it, but his dad would know what to do. If they went to the police together then it mightn't look so bad. His dad was a waste of space, no doubt about it, but at least he was an adult; they'd listen to him, they'd believe him.

Brick pushed himself up the wall of the Boo Boo Station. He'd never felt so weak in all his life, his whole body trembling, hollow. Over the caved-in roof of the ticket gate to his left he could see the highest peak of the log flume, not quite as tall as the roller coaster or the big wheel but still pretty impressive. He closed his eyes, the world moving like a spinning top that's almost out of momentum. He could see himself in the plastic canoe, racing downhill, his dad's arms rooting him in place. Gravity.

His mind made up, Brick walked to his bike, flipped up the kickstand and climbed onto the saddle. His helmet made his face sting but it did a good job of covering the wound. It took even longer than usual to get the bike going, seven or eight attempts before the engine buzzed to life, and he was out through the fence. He had fought his way through the laurel before he noticed that his petrol gauge was in the red. *Dammit*, he'd meant to fill up on the way over – two people on the back made the bike guzzle fuel – but he'd decided not to because he couldn't face the thought of stopping long enough for Lisa to start moaning at him again.

It was okay. There was a garage about a mile west. He'd fill up and be back in Norwich by nine. His dad would be at work but Brick knew which site he was on, the same one he'd been on for eighteen months – the massive housing development next to the old paper mill. He checked both ways, the coast clear, then he wobbled left, accelerating down the road and taking the first right towards the fertiliser factory.

It felt good to be moving, even though something in him baulked at the idea of leaving Lisa behind. The thought of running, of never coming back, ghosted at the back of his head but it vanished almost as soon as it had appeared. He kept at a steady forty, not wanting to draw attention to himself even though he felt as if he had a giant arrow over his head, labelled GIRLFRIEND KILLER.

But she isn't dead, he kept telling himself. *She's going to be okay.*

He turned off the main road onto the garage forecourt, pulling up at the nearest pump and cutting the engine. There was a fiver and shrapnel in his wallet and that would get him back to the city.

Through the window of the shop he could make out the cashier. He'd dealt with him dozens of times before on the way out to Hemmingway, a right miserable old git. But the way he was looking at Brick now was different. He felt his cheeks light up and lowered his head.

What if he'd been on the news or something? Pictures of him in the local paper. No, surely not, Lisa had only been gone for a night. The man probably just thought he was going to skip as soon as he'd fuelled up.

He looked again and the cashier had gone. He glanced at the pump – £3.31, £3.37. Maybe he needed to find a hideout that was closer to home, he thought, before realising that he might never be able to go back to Fursville. Strangely, that thought filled him with more grief than anything else.

There was a squeal of tyres behind him and he turned in time to see a small red hatchback slam into the back of a battered taxi on the road by the garage. The cars rocked together, steaming, then lay still.

Least I'm not the only one having a bad day, he thought. The driver of the taxi was getting out. He looked mega pissed. The woman behind the wheel of the car was opening her door too, her hair a mess, her face white from where her airbag had deployed. From the look of it they were about to have an almighty slagging match.

£4.01, £4.09.

A bell rang from the other direction and the garage door opened. The cashier walked through it, probably to make sure everyone was alright. But there was still something wrong with the man's face, it was twisted up into a kind of snarl, his eyes burning –

He looks like Lisa, exactly *like her*, Brick thought, and another bell began to ring, this one in the centre of his brain, some kind of instinctive alarm. The cashier was coming right at him, walking fast, grunting with each step.

'I'm going to pay,' said Brick, his voice broken into a thousand pieces.

The cashier didn't seem to care, his pace quickening. There were noises from the other direction, too, a ragged shriek. Brick swung round to see the taxi driver coming across the street, breaking into a run, heading for the forecourt. The woman was right behind him, her face so bent by fury that it looked painted on. She was the one who was screaming.

Brick ripped out the nozzle, throwing it to the floor. He jumped back onto the bike, fear turning his bones to liquid. He slammed his foot on the starter, the bike wheezing then falling silent. The cashier had reached the pumps, his old face mottled, jowls swinging. He was a small man, too fat and too old to ever have scared Brick. But that expression . . . There was nothing in it but murder.

'What?' he said, almost shrieking himself now. He tried again, his foot slipping off the pedal, then again. It was too late. The cashier threw himself at Brick and unleashed a punch. Brick ducked, the bike almost toppling between his legs and bringing him down with it. Only adrenalin kept him upright. The man grabbed hold of his helmet, wrenching his head down.

Footsteps behind him, more howls from the woman. Brick lashed out, all the time feeling like his head was about to be ripped off. The cashier wasn't budging.

'No!' the word forced up past the chokehold on his neck. 'No!'

He let go of the bike, unclipping the helmet and freeing it. The cashier stumbled backwards, hitting the kerb around the pump and falling on his backside, the helmet still grasped in his hands. Brick didn't look back, just leapt onto the starter pedal again, throwing all his weight down on it.

The engine wheezed, popped, then sparked on. He revved, the bike moving impossibly slowly. Something grabbed the back of his T-shirt, pinching his flesh, and he shunted himself forward on the seat. He caught sight of his reflection in the shop window, an ecstasy of terror, white-eyed and open mouthed, the taxi driver and the woman bearing down on him.

He wrenched the accelerator so hard the rubber grip tore, the bike guttering, on the verge of stalling. He swept round between the pumps and the shop, his feet on the ground propelling the bike forward, skidding on the oil-slicked tarmac, the woman still clutching his T-shirt. There were more people on the street now, swarming from their cars, all of them glaring – *Just like Lisa, they're just like Lisa* – all of them running towards him, a stampede. He recovered his balance, accelerating out of the garage, the woman's hand ripping loose, taking some fabric with it. He ducked beneath the arms of a man on the pavement, thumping into another woman hard enough to send her sprawling. Someone in a car veered towards him, clipping his rear wheel. But he clung on for his life, weaving left, right, the swelling crowd surging after him like rats after the piper as he fled into the sun.

Daisy

Daisy was late, *really* late. School had started an hour ago and she was only just now scrambling out of her pyjamas, trying to find a clean polo and socks while staring in disbelief at the clock by her bed.

Why hadn't her parents woken her up? They pulled her kicking and screaming out of bed every morning without fail, which is why she never bothered to set her alarm any more.

She took a ball of socks from her drawer, doing her best to put them on while walking, almost tripping herself up. She stopped, taking a deep breath. What was it her dad always said? Haste makes waste or something like that. By the time she'd decided that the phrase was meaningless she'd managed to wrestle both socks on, walking briskly down the landing towards the stairs.

She had clattered down the first four when she heard something moving in her parents' bedroom. She stopped, cocking her head over her shoulder. In the silence she became aware that her head was aching, a pulse – not hers – swelling and ebbing in her ears, the same as it had been yesterday but worse now.

Thump-thump . . .
Thump-thump . . .
Thump-thump . . .

Frowning, Daisy made her way slowly back onto the landing.

'Mum?' she called out. 'Dad?'

She walked to the door, only now noticing that it was closed. Her parents never closed their door, even at night. When she was much younger Daisy had demanded it was always left open, and it had stayed that way ever since, even though she was nearly thirteen now and knew things she hadn't back then and would almost *prefer* it if they kept it shut. She reached out, her knuckles hovering next to the wood but not making contact.

What was she scared of?

She knew exactly what she was scared of. She was scared of walking in and seeing her mum puking into the washing-up bowl, her hair coming out in clumps, her skin the colour of dishwater. She was scared of having to go through it all again, even though they'd told her that the chances of it reappearing in her brain were extremely low. She was scared of other things, too, worse things, but she'd trained herself to stop thinking about them because just having those things in your head might make them come true.

She swallowed, even though her mouth was as dry as sandpaper. Then she knocked.

There was another thump from inside. Then a thin, reedy voice. Daisy couldn't make out what it said, so she knocked again, her ear almost touching the wood. That voice again. Was it calling her name?

Her heart lodged in her throat, Daisy twisted the

handle and pushed the door open. Darkness and a dusty, almost sour smell seeped out into the hallway. The curtains had been pulled shut – thick, double-lined velvet ones that her dad had hung so that her mum could sleep when she'd been really ill. It looked like 3 a.m. in there.

'Hello?' she said, the room swallowing her voice. 'Daisy?'

She took a step inside, her eyes needing a moment to adjust. Her parents were two lumps beneath the duvet, their upper bodies black smudges on the cushioned headboard. For some reason the sight made her think of gravestones side by side in a cemetery, and she actually heard herself gasp.

She saw her dad move, leaning forward then throwing himself back, making the headboard crunch against the wall.

'Dad, what's wrong?' she asked, walking towards the bed, trying not to breathe in. The air was thick with the stench of old people – not old like her mum and dad, but *old* old.

'Come here,' said her mum, her voice like a breeze kicking leaves down the street. Daisy waited for the '*we need to talk*' but it never came, the only sound the click of her dad's throat as he breathed. She walked round her mum's side of the bed, her hand on the footboard to steady herself. She wanted to rip the curtains open, the window too, but she didn't dare. She didn't want to find out who was lying in that bed.

My parents, obviously, she told herself. *Who else could*

it be?

The wolf, something in her brain said. *It's the wolf, and it's dressed like your mum and dad. Look closely and you'll see it, Daisy. And you'd better, because if you don't then the wolf will get you.*

Shut up, she shouted to her brain. It always played tricks on her when she was scared. As if to prove to it that she was brave, Daisy sat on the edge of the mattress, her hand smoothing the duvet until it found her mum's. She clasped it, holding it tight.

'Are you okay?' she asked. Her mother's fingers were damp stalks. They made no effort to tighten around Daisy's. 'What's wrong?'

'Nothing,' said her mum. A little light was trickling in from the hall, tentatively exploring her parents' faces. It hung in their eyes as a bright spark, but it wasn't strong enough to illuminate their expressions. She was pretty sure she could make out her dad's teeth, though, clenched together between pulled-back lips. He sat slowly forward then lurched back again, the thump making the whole bed tremble. For the first time it occurred to her that she might be dreaming. Her mum turned her head until those sparks found Daisy. 'Come, lie with us.'

Don't, said her brain. But once again she shushed it. She climbed onto the bed, trying to avoid trampling her mum as she wedged herself into the middle. It was the safest place she could ever imagine being, sandwiched between her mum and dad in their room. It was the place she'd weathered a thousand nightmares.

111

And yet she didn't tuck her legs beneath the duvet.

'What's wrong?' she said, looking from her mum to her dad and back. 'Are you ill again?'

Her mum's head slid round, her body completely motionless. In the gloom the smile she gave Daisy belonged to a china doll.

'I'm fine,' she said. 'I'm as right as rain.'

'Right as rain,' said her dad, making Daisy jump. She looked at him and he stared back. He smiled too, but it slid off his face like water from a raincoat. There was a clack as he snapped his teeth closed.

'We just wanted a cuddle,' said her mum.

'A hug,' added her dad.

They moved together, their bodies shifting, their arms rising – too long, too spindly in the dark. Her mum looped both hands over her shoulders, pulling her close, nuzzling her lips against Daisy's hair. Her dad's followed, wrapping around them both, his chest against her back. They were breathing perfectly in time, and when they inhaled Daisy felt her bones creak as the space between them shrank. She tried to shift her arms to return the hug but there was no room.

'We love you, Daisy,' said her mum. 'Whatever happens, never forget that.'

Daisy couldn't twist her head round to see her mum, the kisses on her forehead were too fierce. They were battering her, like hail, making her headache sing.

'What do you mean?' she asked. 'What's going to happen?'

No answer, her parents tightening their grip, ratcheting her in like a snake with its prey. The smell seemed worse here and a tickle of fear crept into Daisy's stomach. Once again she could hear that voice in her head: *They're not who you think they are, it's the wolf and it's wearing your parents for pyjamas*. It was such a ridiculous, terrifying image that she couldn't decide whether to laugh or scream.

'What's going to happen?' she asked again. 'I don't want anything to happen.'

'Everything will be okay,' said her mum, her words muffled by Daisy's hair. 'We love you so much. Nothing will hurt you. *We* won't hurt you.'

Hurt her? What was that supposed to mean? She began to squirm, the tickle fast blossoming into full-blown panic. But they weren't letting her go, their grip so tight now that it was twisting her neck.

'Mum, it hurts.'

She could see her legs kicking on the bed, pushing the duvet down in rumpled folds. The old people smell was like something solid over her mouth.

'Mum!'

The hug began to loosen, her dad's arms relaxing as he rolled onto his back. Her mum unlocked her wrists, letting Daisy push herself up. She massaged her neck, looking at her parents, only just managing to keep the tears from flowing. Her mum smiled at her, using cool fingers to brush a strand of hair from Daisy's face. Her eyes were dark, but that firefly of light buzzed freely in them. It made her look happy, but far away. She stroked her hand down Daisy's cheek, gently holding her head.

'Whatever happens, whatever happens, always always remember that we do love you. Always remember. We love you so much, Daisy.'

'I love you too,' Daisy said. Then she threw herself at her mum, hugging her with the same force that she had been held by, pressing her forehead against her mum's cheek so hard she could see spots of colour bloom in her vision. 'I love you more than anything.'

Her mum breathed in, the noise almost a snort, and Daisy could feel her body tense up. She let go, worried that she was hurting her.

'You're late for school,' her mum said, the warmth stripped from her words. She was facing forward again, her arms by her side. 'You should go.'

'But Mum, I don't want to le—'

'*Go!*' The word shot from her mum's mouth like a bullet.

Daisy crawled off the duvet, feeling like something was about to explode from her chest. She stood at the foot of the bed for a moment, looking at the dark lumps of shadow there, then she retreated through the bedroom door.

Her mum called out after her, her voice as flat as a recording.

'We'll see you soon.'

But somehow, Daisy knew that was a lie. Somehow, so deep down that she wasn't even aware of it, she understood that they would never see her again.

Brick

Brick sat on the wooden steps that led up to the log flume in Fursville, shaking so much that his elbows kept slipping off his knees. He'd ridden straight back to the park after the incident at the garage – *they tried to kill me, they* all *wanted to kill me* – almost taking himself clean out by turning off the main road at sixty-three miles per hour, coming within a hair's width of decorating the smiley-faced 'Welcome to Hemmingway, Please Drive Carefully!' sign with his brains.

The crowd had followed him down the road, their faces twisted and contorted in his single rear-view mirror, their eyes angry white blisters. They'd actually *trampled* each other trying to get to him. The car that had almost knocked him off his bike had tried to come after him too, but it had veered off the road into a garden after a dozen yards or so, the driver kicking his way out of the broken windscreen and pursuing on foot.

By the time they faded out of sight there had been twenty people there, men, women, kids, grandparents. Brick had seen all this with absolute clarity – every bared tooth, every clenched jaw, every snatching, greedy finger – the kind of eagle-eyed, slow-motion action replay focus you only got when your life was

115

hanging by a thread.

He was paying the price for it now, though. His body felt like it had used up every last resource. Used up or wasted – he'd chucked his guts the moment he came through the hedge, last night's popcorn nothing but a milky foam. Now he felt the same way he did when he was really ill, the light too bright, his whole body trembling like it had once upon a time on the wacky walkway that was almost visible from where he was sitting.

The worst of it was that somewhere en route he'd lost his phone and his wallet. They had probably slipped from his pocket when he'd almost come off the bike, or maybe it had happened during the attack in the garage. The phone he didn't mind so much, but dropping his wallet could be bad – it meant the police would know he'd been in Hemmingway. From there it didn't take a genius to think of searching the old theme park. With any luck it had fallen into a bush, or down a rabbit hole. But luck wasn't the sort of thing that came willingly to Brick Thomas.

His elbow slipped off his leg again, jolting his head. He replaced it, shivering, his chattering teeth like hail on a tin roof, the loudest thing in the park. He was shaking so much he felt like a pneumatic drill, like he was about to hammer himself into the ground, and he pushed himself to his feet, pacing.

What the hell was going on?

There was an explanation banging on the door of his head, yelling at him, but he was refusing to pay it any attention. He was refusing because it was stupid, even though he'd seen stuff like this in a million movies – people turning feral, ripping into their loved ones. Usually it happened when the dead came back to life, but not always. Sometimes it was a virus or something, like in that film Lisa loved, *28 Days Later*.

Zombies, great thinking, Brick, you're a genius.

But that was exactly it: zombies were something from the telly, from video games. They didn't exist in real life, they *couldn't* exist, it was impossible.

Then what was it? What had turned Lisa against him and then invited the whole goddamned world to take a shot? Yeah, he had one of *those* faces, but it wasn't that bad. It wasn't *Frankenstein's monster* bad, bad enough to rile the mob.

As far as he could tell, there were three ways of finding out. First, he could call his dad, ask him what was going on, see if it was happening in the city too. Of course that was no longer an option because his mobile was gone and the nearest payphone was – *Ha-ha, Brick, try not to laugh at the irony* – back in the garage he'd just fled from. Second, he could clean the puke from his saddle, get back on his bike and head somewhere else, back into Norwich maybe. This wasn't really an attractive option either, because if a garageful of people had almost managed to kill him, then a whole cityful would certainly succeed. It felt a bit like diving into a shark-infested ocean to see whether there was a Great White hiding beneath your boat.

That left door number three: the *basement* door. His

laptop was in there. It had been on the table when he and Lisa had cartwheeled over it, so he didn't even know if it was still okay – the fact that she obviously hadn't used it to email anyone for help wasn't a great sign. But maybe she just hadn't thought of it. Or maybe the dongle had come loose and she couldn't get it to work again.

Either way, if he could get in and snatch his computer then he'd be able to search the news sites, see what was going on. He had a store of food and drink in there too; not much, but enough to keep him going for a day or two.

The thought of opening that door, of seeing what was inside, made him shudder harder and he had to sit back down on the steps. The wooden frame of the flume creaked overhead, expanding in the fierce midday heat. The sun was behind the big wheel, painting the park in a cobweb of fine, dancing shadows, so fierce that Brick had to close his eyes to stop the itch of light on his retinas. For a wonderful, mesmerising instant when he opened them again Fursville looked just like it had a decade ago, the haze shimmering from the cracked earth giving the illusion of movement, of people. It was so strong that Brick could even hear the song of the arcade machines from the pier, remarkably loud as they travelled on the warm summer breeze.

Then he remembered Lisa, throwing herself at the door so hard that he had heard the snap of wood – or bone – from the top of the stairs, even with his hands over his ears, even past his wretched sobs. The illusion vanished, leaving him alone.

Brick stood again, his twitching body unable to stay still. If he was going to do this, he had to do it now.

He set off towards the pavilion, both hands clenched in his tangled hair like he was a prisoner being marched at gunpoint. He reached the fire door, thinking *Please God, don't let this be the last time I see the sun* as he squeezed under the chain. He didn't let himself stop, knowing that if he paused for so much as a second he'd never get moving again. He'd end up like one of the plastic statues outside, the grinning squirrels in the crazy golf, frozen until the end of time.

He jogged to the door at the top of the basement staircase and peered down into that throat of darkness. The bottom corner of the lower door had been bent out from the wall, but it was still closed, the metal bar firmly in place. No light crept through it now. He couldn't hear anything, but it didn't stop him wanting to put his fingers in his ears and hum a tune at full volume as he stepped softly downwards. If he couldn't hear her, then maybe it would all be okay.

He put his ear to the door, his breath locked tight, feeling like he was about to throw up again – not food, this time, but his heart, which was so far up in his throat he could taste each beat like copper on his tongue. It was silent in there, as if he had his ear against a coffin lid.

Lisa? he said, realising only after a moment or two that he hadn't spoken out loud. He struggled to unblock his windpipe. 'Lisa?' He barked the word out this time, making himself jump. It sounded like it had been loud enough to bring the roof down. He held his breath again, listening.

There was movement inside the basement; a noise like something heavy being dragged across the ground. *A torso,* Brick thought. *It sounds like somebody moving a corpse.* There was a quiet cry, a kitten's mewl, followed by silence.

At least she was still alive. The knowledge filled Brick with equal amounts of relief and terror. Alive but weak, perhaps. He might be able to open the door, run in, grab what he needed and get out before she even really noticed he was there.

He went to call her name again, then thought better of it. In his head he counted down, *three . . . two . . .* and without waiting for *one* he kicked out at the bar, sending it clattering to the floor. He wrenched open the door, uttering a short, desperate cry of his own. Then, fists clenched so hard his nails were like scalpels in his palms, he stepped into the basement.

Cal

Cal crouched on the grass, the sun trying to peel open his head, the heat drumming on his skull – *thump-thump . . . thump-thump . . . thump-thump . . .* – wondering why the pain had gotten so bad in the space of a couple of hours. He really did feel like he was about to puke, not just the too-much-milkshake nausea he'd had last night but something else. It was like he needed to purge something poisonous from his body, to vomit it up from every cell. He felt that if he could do that then maybe the turbine that was roaring in his head would finally stop.

The shrill call of the whistle made him wince, and he squinted up to see Mr Lyons jogging onto the pitch. Both teams were waiting for the game to start, eye-balling each other over the halfway line. Cal had gone to the changing rooms as normal, wondering if anyone would mention what had happened yesterday on the plaza. Nobody had, but the way his mates wouldn't meet his eye, gazing at the floor as they walked outside, was evidence enough that they were ashamed or embarrassed.

Cal reached down and grabbed the bottle of Dr Pepper by his foot, finished it off and tossed it to the nearby sideline. Behind it was the pitch's only stand, and it was

121

packed – 200 kids waiting for the match to begin. The usual suspects were once again in the front row, Eddie sitting in between Megan and Georgia. For once, Georgia didn't have her book with her and was joining in with the chants. The noise was exhilarating.

He looked at the clock. 12.00. Chris did a few keepy-uppies before placing the ball on the centre spot. Lyons blew for the game to start and Cal charged into the opposition side of the pitch. It didn't take long for the ball to find him, a clever volley from Steven. Cal controlled it, knocking it ahead and chasing, feeling like he was running at the speed of sound. He heard someone yell 'man on' and stopped abruptly, trapping the ball as the defender flew past. Then he turned and scanned the pitch for white shirts, lobbing the ball in towards the box.

It wasn't his best pass, granted, and one of the other team intercepted, heading it clear. Still, it was pretty obvious that it was going to be a good game. An *easy* game.

The other team were pressing forward and Cal jogged after them, happy to let the defence handle it. Jack, the keeper, caught a shot and booted the ball upfield. The crowd was less noisy now, nothing more than a handful of chants and insults hurled onto the pitch. They were probably saving their breath for the goals. Cal glanced over as he ran, waving at Eddie and Megan and Georgia. They were looking right at him but none of them returned the gesture.

Actually, *everyone* in the stands seemed to be looking

right at him. They were facing the sun, so their eyes were narrow slits in their faces, but even so he could feel their gaze crawling over his skin like fingers, the sensation making him cold despite the heat. He shivered, more pain detonating right behind his forehead. *Of course they're looking at me*, he thought as he turned away. *Everybody loves Callum Morrissey.*

Up the other end of the pitch Nas was closing in on the goal, Jack trying to make himself as big as possible to stop the shot. His two centre-backs, Sam and Sprout, should have been chasing but they were just standing there, like they didn't quite know what to do with themselves.

They were both staring at Cal.

Thump-thump . . .

Thump-thump . . .

Thump-thump . . .

Confusion was making the engine in his head rev even harder, battering against the soft flesh of his brain.

'Go on,' he yelled. 'Tackle him!'

More of the players were turning to face him now. Nas had actually frozen outside the six-yard box even though it was just him and the keeper, even though nothing was stopping him taking the shot. The kid's head was twisted round too far as he fixed his eyes on Cal. Even Mr Lyons was looking his way, his whistle clamped between his teeth. It was quiet enough in the stands for Cal to be able to hear the whistle warble softly every time the teacher exhaled.

Jack took a couple of steps towards the ball then

stumbled to a halt, as if his batteries had just run out. He raised his head, his eyes dark despite the sunlight on his face. Jack was the last. Now every single person was looking at Cal. The only sound was the soft whisper of the whistle, almost lost behind the hammer blows inside his head.

'What?' he asked, his voice ridiculously loud against the unnatural canvas of silence. He turned to the crowd. People were standing, pushing themselves out of their seats. The way they moved reminded Cal of a flock of birds, how they all seemed to do the same thing at the same time without being told. Two hundred or so people swayed as one, their gaze so intense it seemed to push Cal down into the warm soil.

It's a reality TV show, he thought as he scanned the pitch, the players like statues. No, like *gargoyles*, their lips pulled back, their teeth clenched, their eyes bulging, so full of anger and madness. *I'm being filmed, right now. This is all a set-up,* Jackass *or something like that. Just be cool, Cal, you don't want to look like a loser.*

And it *had* to be that, didn't it? How could it be anything else?

But something in his head, something buried deeper than the ache, was screaming at him. It was just about the oldest, simplest, most instinctive message the body was capable of sending.

Run.

And Cal would have, too, if the pulse of agony in his head hadn't vanished – *thump-thump . . . thump-thump . . . thump* – gone so suddenly that it was as if somebody had thrown a switch. He'd had the headache for so long that for a second or two its absence was almost worse, like not having it meant there was something missing in his brain. But there was no denying the relief.

'It's gone,' he said, wondering if, when they watched this episode of whatever prank show he was starring in, they'd be able to spot the exact moment when the razor wire was pulled from his brain. 'Hey, guys, it's . . .'

His words dried up as Mr Lyons starting running towards him – not jogging, *sprinting* – his face knuckled into a fist of rage. Others followed, as if the teacher pulled them behind him. A peal of thunder rose up from the other direction and Cal swung round to see the crowd surging from the stands, a tidal wave that crashed and spat down the aisles, spilling over the seats. There was so much movement that the ground was shaking.

He managed one more empty smile. It lasted no more than a second, enough time for Cal to realise there were no cameras, there had been no cue for everybody to start running; enough time for him to hear that voice inside him, that raging, desperate animal cry which screamed, *RUN! RUN! RUN!*

Enough time for him to understand with absolute clarity that if he didn't obey that voice then he was going to die.

He lurched so hard that he almost tripped on his own feet, bolting up the middle of the pitch as the crowd surged onto it. He saw a couple of kids from the front row fall beneath the weight of the crowd, a wet, red explosion erupting briefly then lost in the surging mass of feet.

He ran faster than he thought possible, the adrenalin in his veins like nitrous oxide in a car, a shot of pure fuel, his arms and legs pistoning him across the school field. Cal risked a look over his shoulder to see Nas right behind him, spit hanging from his too-wide mouth, his eyes two hate-filled sores in his face as he gained ground. Behind him churned the crowd, a tsunami of flesh.

Cal put his head down, trying to speed up even though his lungs were already burning. He was fast, but he couldn't manage an all-out sprint for long.

The main school building was in sight. If he could just get inside then somebody would stop this, one of the teachers or the headmaster. But even as the thought crossed his mind he saw a group of kids sitting outside the doors lift their heads, sniffing the air like lions scenting a gazelle. As one they scrambled to their feet, charging towards him, that same look of lunatic rage turning their faces into crude Halloween masks.

Cal angled off to the left, towards the bike sheds, his mind a hissing mess of white noise. There were more kids converging on him from the school doors. One of them screamed, a brittle shriek that was picked up by somebody in the crowd behind him, and Cal only realised how quiet they had been when they all started to cry out, the sound deafening, almost a physical force against his ears. It was all he could do not to collapse right there, clamp his hands over his head and just pray that it would be quick.

He heard rasping, jagged breaths right behind him, then something brushed his shoulder. Cal forced himself to think. He'd been studying martial arts for years now but every single thing he'd learned had somehow been sucked from his brain, dissolved by terror.

Nas reached again, and this time he snagged Cal's shirt, yanking him so hard that he missed his footing. Cal fell, skidding on his knees, almost managing to push himself back up again before Nas thumped into him, sending them both sprawling. Nas pinned him and threw a punch that glanced off Cal's jaw, not hard enough to hurt. He could hear the relentless pounding of feet, those banshee screams rising to a hideous crescendo.

Think! screamed his brain, his body unable to draw breath. Flashing spots appeared in his vision, leaving charred black scars when they faded. *Do something or they're going to kill you!*

He bent and spread his legs beneath Nas's weight, planting his feet firmly on the ground. Then he punched up with both arms, knocking Nas's hands loose and trapping them beneath his own. At the same time he rolled his hip, pushing up with a grunt. Nas tumbled off, the murder never leaving his eyes. Cal lashed out, hitting him square in the throat as he jumped up.

Someone else was right there, reaching out for him,

and Cal shoved the kid as hard as he could. He ducked under another pair of hands, plunged into shade as the crowd tried to surround him. It was like running into a forest of limbs: root-like feet tripped him, torsos like trunks blocked his way.

Cal threw himself at the only shard of sunlight that remained, breaking free, his whole body numb as he started to run again. He was right next to the school building now. One of the windows exploded outwards, a bloodied face squirming through teeth of broken glass. Cal scrambled past the bike sheds and up the narrow path along the side of the school. Straight ahead were the gates, and past them Rochester Street with its cars and its crowds. There was nothing but death that way.

To his side was a fence, and past that a strip of woodland. The trees there were spindly, too few to provide any cover. But what choice did he have?

He leaped at the fence, grateful that there was no barbed wire as he flopped clumsily over the top. Through the mesh he could see the crowd flood the passageway, a thrashing river that pushed itself against the wire, causing the posts to bend into the woodland. Megan was there, or something demonic that had once been Megan, her hands twisted into talons, straining for him.

Cal gulped down air, slipping and tripping over the rough ground. Somehow he ran, using the trees to push himself on until he hit the fence that backed onto Rochester Street. He climbed, slipped, climbed again, rolling head-first over it.

Hands reached through the wire, pinching his shirt, his flesh, driving him to his feet again. He heard an engine gun, looked up in time to see a car veer across the street straight at him. Through the sunlight-dazzled windscreen he could make out a face identical to the ones behind him, and it was the sight of this warped mask rather than two solid tons of silver SUV that made him dive to the side.

The car slammed into the fence, piling right through it into the crowd. Cal knew this because of the sounds, a song of muffled snaps. He looked back to see that people were pulling themselves over a mound of ruined bodies, twitching limbs, their eyes still blazing. One girl was crawling after him even though her left arm was no longer properly attached. She pulled it behind her like a baby dragging a toy.

Cal scanned the street as he limped onwards, his brain running in double-time, his body filled with lead. People were streaming from the Tesco supermarket opposite the school. More cars were accelerating up the hill, veering wildly from side to side. One smashed into a lamp-post, bending it at a forty-five degree angle. The driver, a middle-aged man, had opened the door and was stumble-running across the road, shrieking.

The car. It was his only chance.

Cal threw himself towards the man, waiting until he was close enough before unleashing a powerful Choy Li Fut kick. His football studs sank into the man's face, almost making him do a full backwards flip. Cal raced for the car, throwing himself into the driver's seat and closing the door just as the first of the Tesco shoppers reached him.

The engine had stalled. Cal pushed in the clutch and twisted the key the way he'd been taught in his driving lessons, and the engine roared to life. A woman was swinging her basket at the window, the glass already cracking. More shapes threw themselves at the doors and Cal engaged the central locking just in time. Someone had climbed onto the bonnet and was kicking at the windscreen.

Cal tried to wrestle the gear stick into reverse. It wouldn't go. He felt it with both hands, finding a ring on the shift, pulling it up and allowing the stick to slot into place. He revved and let the clutch rise.

The engine stuttered, then cut out. The passenger window exploded, hands reaching in. There was no sunlight left inside the car, three more people now on the bonnet, so many on the roof that it was bowing inwards, the metal creaking. He turned the key again, forgetting to push in the clutch. The car juddered, people falling from it into the crowd.

Cal swore, pushing in the clutch, trying the ignition, revving it hard with his right foot. The whole car was rocking now as the people outside attempted to roll it over.

He let the clutch rise slowly. It bit, groaned, then the car jolted backwards. It didn't get far, the sea of bodies behind it blocking the way. Cal stomped on the accelerator, shunting his way through them. The car growled, flattening anything behind it as it gained speed.

Cal slammed on the brakes, remembering to push in the clutch as well. He wrestled it into first, spinning the wheel all the way round as he pulled away, not caring that people were bouncing off the bumper, not caring that he drove right into a kid that he'd played football against yesterday, not caring that the car was bucking wildly because of the countless squirming bodies beneath the wheels.

He just drove down the hill as fast as he could, screaming silently through the sun-drenched, ruby-red stained glass of his windscreen.

Brick

The torch lay just inside the door, on its side. Brick turned it on and it spat out a weak light, hardly enough to illuminate the gloom.

The first thing he saw was his computer, lying face down on the floor, its screen throwing out a ghostly aura. He scanned the room, waiting for a shape to come flying at him, for teeth to lock into his face, his throat. But it was strangely still in here, like he'd stepped into a painting, the quiet broken only by the soft whirr of his laptop and the thrashing beat of his pulse.

Then a portion of the darkness moved, smoke against shadow near the far wall. From here it looked like a burlap sack, a lump of cloth bundled into itself. A groan escaped it, followed by a soft sob and a clump of unintelligible words.

Don't just stand there, get the laptop! his brain commanded, but the sight of Lisa there, so hurt, so *damaged*, was too much. He wanted to go to her, to help her, to carry her out of this place and take her to hospital. He wanted her to be like she had been before last night, annoying and selfish and bossy, yes, but also funny and kind and sexy as hell when she chose to be. It wasn't too late.

The lump shifted again, a long limb flopping out and hitting the floor with a sound like a foot stepping in a puddle. Another followed, making Brick think of a spider caught in running water, unfolding itself before scuttling off. But this thing — *It's not a thing, it's Lisa!* — wasn't going anywhere. She giggled, the laugh like cut glass, becoming another low, choked groan.

'Lisa?' he asked. He couldn't stop himself.

She raised her head, her eyes pockets of darkness in the flesh of her face. A bruise fanned out from her nose and her mouth was a ragged hole that opened and closed in a bandana of blood.

Lisa observed him, tilting her head first one way, then the other. She attempted to crawl towards him, but her left wrist was bent back at an impossible angle, the tips of her fingers almost lodged in the crook of her elbow. It couldn't hold her weight, and she crashed down.

The basement went dark, and for a second Brick thought he was going to faint. Lisa had done this trying to hurt him. She had *broken* herself. Even now she was trying to get to him, using her legs to shunt herself forward, her face sliding wetly. It was this that spurred Brick on. The longer he stayed here, the more damage she'd do to herself.

He walked towards the table, never taking his eyes off her for more than a moment. He picked up the laptop, folding it closed, feeling for the dongle and finding it in the USB port. Lisa had raised her head again, studying him. The change of angle meant that he could see her eyes. One of them was completely red, swimming in blood. In spite of her injuries they burned. She looked possessed.

Brick walked to the corner, to the pile of bags that sat there. They had been emptied over the floor, a bottle of water half drunk and lying on its side and three or four packets of sweets. Still keeping his eyes on Lisa, and one hand on the wall, he edged around the room, crouching down and loading the sweets back into a carrier bag. There were five bottles of water left in the multipack and he snatched them too, then changed his mind and pulled three of the bottles from the cardboard, leaving them. He could always drink from the taps in the kitchen, and he didn't know how long Lisa would be down here.

He put everything, even the laptop, into the bag, holding it in one clenched fist as he retreated towards the door. Lisa watched him move for as long as she could hold her head up, then it dropped once more. She uttered another moan, full of frustration, full of confusion, and it almost snapped Brick's heart clean in two. He waited until the open door was at his back before speaking.

'I'm sorry, Lisa, I don't . . . I don't know what to do. There's water, and I left you some sweets.' The sound of his voice was making her lurch, a hand sliding towards him. He noticed that one of her fingernails was hanging loose. He took a step back, stumbling over the junk in the corridor, hitting the wall hard enough to have his breath snatched away. He clutched the carrier bag to his chest. 'I'll find a way to help you,' he said. 'I promise, you'll be okay. I *promise.*'

She made one last effort to look at him, her eyes inkwell black. There was nothing in that face, it was a half-melted mask that seemed to be sliding loose. Her mouth fell open, something bubbling from it, but Brick reached out and slammed the door shut before he could hear what it was, shouting out one last time:

'I'm sorry!'

☹

He secured the metal pole between the door and the wall again, not that he thought Lisa would be going anywhere. Then he walked up the stairs and turned left, heading down the corridor away from the fire door. He reached a double door on which a peeling sticker read: *To all Pavilion staff. Remember to SMILE!* And for some reason he obeyed that advice as he pushed his way through, his mouth peeling open into a corpse-like grin.

Yeah, no doubt about it, he was going nuts.

He was in the front foyer of the pavilion, the box office a small window in the wall to his right, and past that the main doors, sealed tight with more chains. On the other side of the room were the toilets, the stairs to the floor above the gift shop, and next to them – past a diorama of plastic jungle plants and a life-size stuffed leopard toy which looked as though it had come from one of the games stalls outside – were the doors to the theatre. A banner reading 'Jurassic Farce!' drooped from the wall like a creeper.

He collapsed against the wall amongst the plants, next to the glass-eyed leopard, taking one of the water bottles from his bag and quenching a thirst that had raged unnoticed until now.

He pulled out his laptop, expecting to see the screen cracked and useless. When the machine warmed up, however, he saw that it was just as he had left it apart from a dark, inky blotch on the top right corner of the screen. The battery sat at a little under half full, which was worrying because out here there was no power. A little box told him that he had been logged out because of inactivity, and he quickly typed his password back in, clicking the 'Connect' button.

The little blue light on the dongle flashed furiously as the screen reported *waiting for network . . . connecting . . . authenticating . . . You are online!* Then the box disappeared, leaving the browser window. He typed BBC News into the Google bar, the page loading up faster than it would have downstairs but still painfully slow.

'Come on,' he said. 'Come on come on come on.'

He bent forward, his face practically up against the screen. What was he expecting? A headline reading 'Zombie outbreak across the country as people turn on each other' followed by advice on how to cope. *Stay inside, do NOT go out because random strangers WILL try to kill you. Be especially careful not to make out with your girlfriend as she may bite your face off.* Or maybe there wouldn't be anything at all. Maybe the BBC News site would be down. Maybe the whole internet would be down.

The logo flashed up, the page loading below it. Brick scanned the text as it appeared. 'North Korea Nuclear Tests Condemned'. 'Royal Divorce to Go Ahead'. And a whole raft of things about the Olympics. Not a single mention of savage mob attacks or unprovoked violence. Brick frowned. Maybe it was a local thing. He typed 'Eastern Daily Press' into Google and was directed to a front page full of reports about broken council pledges and a bit about some guy who collected pillar boxes. He found the date and time of the latest article. It had been posted eight minutes ago. The events at the garage had been, what, three hours before? Surely a riot in a quiet Norfolk town was more newsworthy than the fact that some saddo had a rare South African mailbox.

This didn't make any sense. Brick rested his head against the wall, chewing on his thoughts. When an old lady was so much as knocked over in the street the *EDP* gave it a six-page feature, how the hell could it have missed this? That garage must have been swarming with cops and paramedics all morning, juicy photos of bloody tarmac and shattered windscreens just begging to be taken. He typed 'Garage, Hemmingway' into Google, finding nothing but an address for the petrol station and a load of stuff about the writer, even though the names were spelled differently.

Something hit the main doors hard enough to make

the chain rattle. A white shape bounced up past the filthy glass, squawking, another one joining it. Two seagulls. There was a flash of yellow as the birds fought. One flew off, the other in pursuit. Brick tried to swallow his heart back down into his chest, waiting for his hands to stop shaking before hitting the keys again.

'Why does everyone hate me?' he typed, scanning the list of results on the Google page. They were all from Q&A and self-help sites. He clicked the top one, Yahoo Answers, reading a few lines about some kid who didn't have any friends.

'I'm sorry to hear that,' Brick said as he clicked the 'Back' button. 'But I think my problem is worse than yours.'

He deleted the last request, entering 'Why is everyone trying to kill me?' A couple of entries down, he saw it: 'Everyone is trying to kill me!' He clicked, only to see a video game site loaded up. 'Everyone in Thieves Landing is trying to kill me, what did I do?'

'Dammit,' he said, going back to the search page, scanning about a hundred entries before realising it was pointless. He was frowning, and it hurt his face – the bite wound in his eyebrow was pounding. He should probably have washed it or something; if it got infected he'd be truly screwed. He opened a fresh bottle of water, splashing some in his palm and then over the ragged tear. It felt like there was a hot coal stitched beneath his skin.

He wiped his hands on his jeans then tapped the keys gently, trying to decide what to do next. After a minute or two he loaded up the Yahoo Answers page again, logging in with his ID. He chose the 'Ask' option, typing in 'Why Is Everybody Trying to Kill Me'. Then he filled in the next box:

> This isn't a joke. My girlfriend just tried to kill me, for no reason. REALLY tried, she bit my face. Then I went to fill up my motorbike at the garage and suddenly there was a crowd of people coming after me. Someone tried to run me over and they would honestly have killed me. They chased me up the road. I'm serious. This ISN'T a wind-up, I'm really scared. Has anyone else had the same thing happen? If you have, please answer.

He read it through, making sure it didn't give anything away about his location. He couldn't do much about his identity – he had to use his Yahoo ID to post the question. But as long as nobody knew *where* he was, it would probably be okay. He selected the 'Post' option, waiting for the new page to load up. Looking over it again, the question looked absurd, so ridiculous that it made him doubt the whole thing. Had that *really* happened to him? Had he *really* been attacked?

His face burned, his body shook, his stomach churned on itself again and again and again. Yes, it had happened.

He closed the laptop to conserve the battery, folding his legs up to his chest and resting his head on his knees. All he could do now was wait.

Daisy

Daisy stared at the poster on the door of the school theatre, a lump in her throat the size of a house. It was the advert for the play, and where her name had once proudly stood was now a big black smudge. Underneath it somebody had scribbled 'Emily Horton as Juliet'.

For a moment, Daisy decided she was just going to go home. After what had happened with Fred yesterday this was too much. Mrs Jackson and the rest of the drama club could throw themselves off a bridge for all she cared. It might have been a mistake, but more likely it was a joke, somebody taking the mickey. If they wanted their precious Emily Horton they could have her. The stupid girl was supposed to be Daisy's understudy, and she hadn't even known what that meant. She'd skimmed through the entire play looking for a character called Juliet's Understudy before somebody had explained it to her.

Yes, she'd go home and forget about the whole thing. She'd be lying if she said she wasn't slightly relieved at the thought of not having to perform to a hall full of people. But that relief was poisoned by something else, something that sat inside her stomach like too much food. She tried to tell herself it was disappointment. And she *was* disappointed, there was no doubt about it. There were other things down there too, though. Anger, definitely. Hurt. And fear. There was a great deal of fear.

Because she didn't really want to go home. She didn't want to have to explain to her parents that she'd been bumped from the lead role in the play. She didn't want to see them hide their disappointment. She didn't want them to order Chinese as a treat because they thought it would make her feel better.

It was more than that, though. She didn't want to walk in through the front door and find her parents still in bed.

Daisy rubbed her temples, that same *thump-thump* drumming inside her skull. Then she walked into the theatre, a couple of lanky sixth-formers nearly bowling her over on their way out. Hoisting her rucksack onto her shoulder, she made her way down the short corridor that led to the second set of doors. She pushed through them into a maelstrom of movement and noise, a hundred or more kids running round the auditorium, leaping over the folding chairs, throwing balls of paper at each other. On the stage were a couple of girls from her class who'd been appointed scenery managers. They were trying to move a wooden picnic bench – Juliet's balcony – into the wings.

Emily Horton was there too. She was on the other side of the boards, chatting with Kim and Fred. And she was wearing the Juliet dress. *Her* dress.

Daisy hesitated, the theatre suddenly huge, the stage

boundless. In her whole life she didn't think she'd ever felt so small. She walked up the steps towards the back of the stage, stepping through the curtain. In the sudden dark and dusty quiet the tears began, too many of them to stop. She wrapped the heavy curtain around her, the same way she sometimes did with her duvet, pressing her face against it and sobbing gently.

Why was everyone being so horrible? Was it just the stress of the play? Had she done something to upset them all? She waited until the moment had passed then wiped her eyes, hoping they weren't too red. She didn't want to look like a silly crybaby. Then she inhaled deeply and marched across the stage until she was standing next to Emily. The girl was taller than her by about half a foot. So was Kim. Fred towered over them all, looking at Emily and smiling. Daisy didn't think she'd ever seen him smile like that before.

'Excuse me,' Daisy said. Nothing. She reached out, grabbing Emily's collar. Emily looked down. They all looked down, their smiles vanishing like mice beneath a hawk's shadow. Daisy's voice was a whisper: 'Um, I'm playing Juliet.'

Emily's eyes seemed to swell, bulging, then she turned away, carrying on her conversation. Fred and Kim both laughed at something she said but Daisy couldn't catch it. Her blood was hammering in her ears, like there was a giant machine between her temples.

'There's been a mistake,' she said, her eyes burning. *Don't cry, not again, be strong.* 'I . . . You're still the understudy.'

She glanced at Fred, hoping that maybe he'd say something, stick up for her. She knew he didn't fancy her or anything but they'd spent three months pretending to be lovers, they'd had some awkward laughs about it. That had to count for something, right?

Wrong. Fred was standing there checking his nails, as if he couldn't bring himself to look at her. This was all *his* fault. Everybody had seen what had happened yesterday, when he'd spat in her face, and now they all thought she was a total loser, not even worth talking to. Daisy turned back to Emily, a hot, fat tear worming down her cheek.

'But you don't even know the lines,' she said, brushing it away furiously. 'You haven't been to rehearsals.'

Emily still didn't reply, grabbing the sleeves of her dress – too short, the ruffles only reaching the middle of her forearm – and tugging hard to try and make them longer. Daisy shook her head, tasting salt as the tears flowed freely again. That dress had been made for her, her mum had taken in the sleeves especially, and she'd hemmed it too so that it fell right to her ankles and wouldn't trip her up. Emily was too big for it, packed in like a sausage in a casing. One sudden move and the dress would split.

'You'll rip it,' she tried, but the three of them were laughing again, Fred practically in stitches at something Emily had said. Why did he find her so funny? She was being really rude, really cruel.

There was a call from behind the curtain, the whole thing billowing before Mrs Jackson's face popped out.

She saw the turmoil in the stands and trotted onto the stage, calling to the kids who rioted there.

'Right. Right! Everybody, this is no way to behave in a theatre. I want you all to take your seats, straight away please. Anyone who doesn't want to be here had better leave right now.'

Gradually the noise levels ebbed as the audience took their seats, a few people drifting out the back.

Mrs Jackson looked at Emily. 'Are you ready?' Emily nodded. 'Good girl, now off the stage so we can get started. You too, Fred, Kimberly.'

'Mrs Jackson,' said Daisy. 'What about me?'

Mrs Jackson had already vanished back into the dressing room.

Daisy stood there, hugging her backpack strap with both hands. Fred, Kim and Emily were strolling into the wings, still giggling. The audience were whispering in soft tones, occasional paper missiles still hurtling from row to row. Daisy had the terrifying idea that she was actually dead, that she had choked in her sleep or something. How else could she explain what was going on? She felt like screaming out to the crowd just to prove that she existed.

There was a crunch and the lights in the hall went out, the stage spotlights blazing overhead, blasting away Daisy's shadow and making her feel even more like a phantom. Once again the curtain opened, Mrs Jackson reappearing. She walked to the centre of the stage, about three metres from where Daisy was standing, and held out her hands.

'Thank you all for coming,' she said, her voice trembling with nerves. 'It's lovely to see so many of you here. Um, as you all know this is technically a dress rehearsal, not a finished performance, so please forgive any slips of the tongue or prompts from myself or occasional retakes.'

Daisy didn't move, couldn't move, her cheeks burning more fiercely than the lights.

'Please, please, please remember to turn off your mobile phones, children,' Mrs Jackson continued. 'And, yes, just enjoy the show. Ladies and Gentlemen, I give you *Romeo and Juliet*, a tragedy by William Shakespeare.'

Mrs Jackson turned around to go, and Daisy managed to break her paralysis, waving her arms at the teacher.

'Please, Mrs Jackson,' she whispered as softly as she could, sensing the weight of the audience in the shadows. 'I need to talk to you.'

'You shouldn't be on the stage,' Mrs Jackson replied. The harsh lighting turned her face into a leather mask. 'Get off.'

'But—'

'You're going to ruin it,' Mrs Jackson snapped, waving at Daisy like she was a fly on her dinner. 'Now shoo.'

Daisy stood there, in the middle of the stage, her mouth hanging open in disbelief. The crowd was silent, an audience of glass-eyed dolls.

'Get off,' said Mrs Jackson, and this time she took a

step towards Daisy. The heat from the bulbs overhead was too much, an island of light in the middle of an ocean of darkness. Daisy stumbled, looking for the stairs. She saw them too late, missed her footing and tumbled down. Pain grabbed her left leg like a clawed fist as she landed on her hands and knees, her heavy rucksack swinging over her shoulder. She waited for the laughter, the screams of delight, the insults, but the theatre was deathly quiet.

Daisy struggled to her feet. From here, out of the glare, she could see the kids in the crowd. Nobody was looking at her. On stage Mrs Jackson was holding the curtain open, ushering out the girl who was playing the narrator. She gave her a thumbs–up then sank into the black depths. The girl took her position then started to speak.

'Er, two households, both alike in dignity . . .'

Daisy backed away, heading for the doors, wishing that everybody *was* laughing at her. This was worse, so much worse. This was like something from a nightmare. By the time she was at the doors she was running, bursting through them, barrelling out the main exit into the sun, her mind screaming *this isn't happening, this isn't happening, this isn't happening* over and over again as she tore across the car park. Eventually she crashed against the hedge, snatching breaths in between fits of sobs.

Only when she felt like she had wrung out every last tear did she look up, using her sleeve to clean her face. Compared with what had just happened, home seemed like the best possible thing she could imagine – even if her parents were tucked up in bed, even if her mum, God forbid, was getting ill again. At least they still acknowledged she was there.

Her mum was supposed to collect her again tonight at the usual time, but her house was only a ten-minute bus ride away. Daisy hurried up the path, swerving round the packs of pupils that loitered near the gates, wishing that one person – just *one*, a pupil or the teacher on duty or the policewoman who always stood outside at home time – would notice her. But she may as well have been invisible.

There were three buses lined up on the road. She climbed on board the middle one just as it was leaving. She didn't have a bus pass, but after standing at the driver's side for a minute or so waiting to pay, trying to stay upright as he accelerated down the road, she slinked off to a window seat at the front. From there she watched the world flash by, rubbing her throbbing temples, thinking that if she was a ghost then surely she wouldn't have to keep wiping the glass to clear away her breath.

The traffic was heavy, and it was more like fifteen minutes before her street came into view. Daisy pressed the button, getting out of her seat when the bus pulled to a stop. It wasn't a long way to her house but all the same she walked quickly, almost running, desperate to be inside, desperate to see her mum. If the tumour had come back, Daisy decided, then it didn't matter. She'd look after her, she'd make sure she was okay. Her mum had beaten it once before, she could do it again.

She reached her front gate, feeling a little better. So what if everyone at her school was a total jerk. She had more important things to worry about. Maybe that's why she'd had such a rubbish week – maybe life was preparing her for a tough few months, maybe it was trying to make the thought of staying at home and caring for her mother easier. Yes, that was it. For the first time in what seemed like the whole day she remembered to breathe in.

She was halfway down the path before she realised there was another piece of good news.

Somewhere between getting off the bus and arriving at her front door, her headache had gone.

Brick

He saw her too late, the copse of plastic greenery shielding her approach. It was only when she screamed – a wet shriek gargled through a throatful of blood – that Brick knew she was there.

Lisa threw herself at him, wedging him in the angle between the wall and the floor. Her body felt like a bag of bones and gristle, nothing in the right place, broken things poking through her skin. And yet she was heavy, too heavy, a dead weight that crushed him, which stopped him from getting up – even when her toothless maw stretched impossibly wide, closing over his mouth like a plunger, stealing the air from his lungs.

'I still love you, Brick,' she breathed a hot stew of words into him, the stump of her tongue flicking against his lips. 'Even though you did this to me. Even though you did this to me. Even though *YOU DID THIS TO ME!*'

Brick choked, crying out, swinging his fists. She dissolved, spinning apart like sugar in water, leaving only the coppery taste of her. He lurched awake, gasping, heaving, his hands at his throat as if he could somehow widen his airways. He sucked in oxygen, his cries weakening as the nightmare bled away. He was drenched in sweat, his T-shirt plastered to his chest and back, his eyes stinging from the salt. The stuffed leopard stared at him and he glared back.

'Great watchdog you turned out to be,' he muttered, reaching over to the laptop and sliding it towards him. He opened it up, waiting for the dongle to connect to the internet. He'd left his Yahoo Question page open, and he refreshed it, his heart kicking when he saw that somebody – PWN_U13 – had already left an answer. His excitement didn't last long.

> Dear weirdo
>
> Either you are a total nutjob who has imagined all this BS and needs to seek professional help for your brain problems, or you are a total nutjob who has p****d a lot of people off and done some crazy stuff and needs to seek professional help for your psycho problems. Hope this helps.

'Thanks a lot,' he said to PWN_U13, refreshing the page, then again just to make sure, before gently closing the laptop.

What if it *was* just him? What if he was the only person in the world this was happening to? He remembered somebody at school once telling him that people could be allergic to each other, to the oils in the skin or their saliva. Kissing or touching that person could bring them out in a rash, even send them into some kind of shock. Brick hadn't believed it at the time – the kid who'd told him this also told him that rhino horns were made of hair – but it could have been true. What if people were suddenly allergic to him? To his *one-of-those-faces* face. Would that make them want to kill him?

He considered going online again, Googling it, but he decided not to. Even if that's what was happening, looking at stuff on the internet wasn't going to help him. No. He'd wait it out. Sooner or later somebody had to give him a sensible answer, didn't they? Brick rested his head against the wall, his heart still drumming from the dream.

This time, he would stay awake.

Daisy

It was like opening a door into another universe, cool darkness spilling out, muting the sunshine and the heat. The change in light was so extreme that it took Daisy's eyes almost a minute to penetrate the shadows of her hallway, the gloom inside her house like a solid, living thing.

She stepped inside, pulling the Yale key free and wiping her feet on the big doormat. The silence was immense, as if it had wrapped itself around her head, pulling her in. In spite of the fact that her headache had gone – or maybe because of it – she felt weird. Lighter, somehow, as if part of her wasn't there.

The house was empty. She could always tell. A house without people had a different sort of atmosphere, as though it was waiting for something. It creeped her out, and she'd told her parents plenty of times that she didn't like being here by herself. *You're almost a teenager now*, her dad usually said. *Aren't you old enough to be alone in the house? Aren't you old enough now not to be spooked by shadows?* Yes, she was practically a teenager, but that didn't magically take away the fears that had lived inside you for all those years. A birthday didn't suddenly make you brave.

Daisy slung her rucksack on the floor beneath the coat stands, massaging her shoulder where the strap had dug in. It was brighter in here now that the imprint of the sun had ebbed from her retinas, but even so she flicked the hall light on, and the kitchen light too as she walked to the back of the house. Her dad would be at work – he was an accountant at a firm in Ipswich. Her mum hadn't gone back to her teaching job after her illness, but she often popped out for the shopping, or to see friends, or just to get a little fresh air.

Or maybe they're at the hospital? Daisy's brain suggested. *Needles plugged into mum's veins, her hair coming out in handfuls, her face a thousand years old, Dad pretending that his eyes are red raw because of the pollen, or the exhaustion.*

She shushed the thoughts, going to the sink and filling a glass from the filter tap. Their back garden, through the window, was a mess. It always had been, even though both her mum and her dad were out there all the time in spring and summer. The little box of grass was short, but the flowerbeds were a riot of colour, taking over the garden – *like a tumour* – a little more every day. Soon they wouldn't be able to get out the back door without being clawed to death by thorns and jaggies.

She finished the water and walked back through the kitchen, heading for the living room. It would do her good to sit down and watch a little telly, it would help calm her. Already the events at school seemed like a million years ago, vague and distant as if she'd imagined them. It probably hadn't been as bad as it had seemed at the time. It wasn't as if this was the first time that people had ignored her.

She was through the kitchen door when she realised that something was wrong. She ducked back inside, looking at the key box over the radiator. She'd made that box in her last summer in middle school. There was a door which wouldn't close because she'd screwed the hinges in the wrong place, and inside it were nine hooks in rows of three for the family's keys. Hanging on those hooks were three sets — the spare one, her mum's and her dad's.

Daisy frowned, prodding them as if to make sure they were actually there. The little 'Best Mum Ever' and 'Dad's Taxi (and Cash Machine)' key fobs she'd bought them last Christmas jingled. That didn't make any sense. If the keys were here it meant — *They're still in the house, they're still upstairs, they're still in bed.*

Her skin went cold, goosebumps breaking out so fast that they stung. She nearly made a break for the front door, for the sun, before managing to calm herself down. It was no great shock that her parents were still in bed. She already knew — or as good as knew — that her mum was ill, so it made sense that she'd be up there, under the covers, resting, her dad keeping watch over her.

So why didn't she want to go and look?

Daisy stood by the kitchen door, unable to do anything else. Her fear was too huge to understand, it seemed to fill up her whole body. *You're just worried about seeing her looking so sick again*, she said to herself. *And all that stuff at school today, it's just made you a Nervous Nellie, that's all*. But it wasn't just that. It was the thought of her dad smashing his head against the bed, looking at her with that manic, bug-eyed face; of being cocooned forever in their too-long arms.

Daisy took a step forward, and another, her momentum building as she walked to the stairs. She was halfway up when she understood what had happened. It hit her like a fist to the gut, making her slump onto her hands and knees on the steps.

It was the smell. She knew it from the time a cat had been hit and killed by a taxi outside their house. None of the neighbours had known who it belonged to so her mum had brought it in and put it into a cardboard box in the garden shed. Daisy – she'd been seven or eight, she couldn't remember – had snuck in first thing in the morning, before her parents had woken up, hoping that it might have come back to life, that it would spring from the box and lick her hand and meow and purr, and that she could keep it and look after it and make sure nothing bad ever happened to it again.

Daisy had opened that box and the smell had clawed its way down her throat right to her stomach. It wasn't a rotten smell, not like when the bin needed emptying. It was hardly even there at all, yet somehow it was everywhere. And even though she was only seven or eight Daisy had known exactly what that smell was. It was death, plain and simple. It was the smell that death left behind when it had been inside your house.

It was here now. It clung to everything – the stairway carpet, the walls with the framed photographs on. It was on her skin, too, so pungent that she thought at first that *she* was the one who stank, that death had come for her.

Only it hadn't. It had been here, but it wasn't Daisy it had taken.

She forced herself to climb the last few steps. Hunched over, she crossed the landing to her parents' room. The door was closed, and on it was a sheet of paper on which her mum's haphazard script read: *Daisy, do not open this door. Call the police, darling. Please don't come in.*

She reached up, a puppet, unable to stop herself. The handle popped, the door creaked, and a fresh wave of the smell washed over her, settling into her nostrils. The stench was so strong that there could have been a dozen dead cats in boxes inside the room, two dozen, a hundred.

Or one mum, her mind suggested, a perverse rhyme from somewhere inside her brain. *One mum, dead in the bed, the cancer is back and it messed with her head.*

'Shut up!' she shouted, the tears flowing. She leaned on the door jamb, trying not to breathe, but the sobs kept emptying her lungs, forcing her to suck the smell into her mouth. The heavy curtains were still pulled tight and it seemed that there was no air in the dark room, just death.

There were two figures in the bed, the same as before. Only this time they didn't stir. They sat propped against the headboard, leaning on each other, two shadows that reminded Daisy of the pictures she'd seen at school of the victims of the nuclear bombs in Japan, their shapes burned onto the pavements by the heat of the explosion. She wanted to call out to them, but she didn't. She didn't want to fall into the silence where their response should have been.

Instead, she moved to the window, thinking that it was the lack of light which had her parents bound tight. Maybe if she let the sun in, the warmth, it would blast death away, clear his stench from the room.

She grabbed hold of the heavy velvet, yanking the right-hand curtain first, almost hard enough to jar the pole loose from its mounts. The light that flushed in from outside was less golden than umber, burned and sticky. She wrestled with the left, jigging it along. It got stuck halfway and she had to tuck the end behind the mirror on the sideboard. She stared into the glass, seeing her parents asleep on the bed – *They're asleep, that's all it is, it's obvious, look closely and you'll see them breathing.*

Only they weren't asleep. They weren't even her parents. There was something wrong with their faces, their muscles turned to jelly beneath their skin.

A barrage of sobs broke free from her chest and Daisy doubled over. She didn't fight them, she just let them come, knowing that whatever she saw when she turned around it would be better if all the tears were already gone. She didn't know how much later it was that the last of them dropped from her trembling lips. With a heaving, groaning sigh she walked to the bed and sat down on the edge of the mattress, the same place she had sat that very morning, a million, billion years ago.

She turned to face them. Her mum's head was resting on her dad's shoulder, and they looked more peaceful than she'd seen them in years. Their faces were pale, except for a spot of colour on each cheek. Their eyes were closed. They didn't look real. They looked like plastic models of her parents, like the waxwork people she'd seen once at Madam Tussaud's – so close to human and yet so obviously not.

But there was no denying the truth. These were her parents, her mum and dad, the people who had created her and brought her up, who had seen her every single day of her life, who had nursed her when she was ill and fed her when she was hungry and hugged her when she was sad and—

Daisy felt a scream building in her head, her mind reeling as if reality had slipped off the tracks and was now ploughing in a new and frightening direction. She no longer felt like crying, she wasn't entirely sure if she could remember how to. She looked at her mum's hand, cupped in her dad's, both of them as still as a photograph. Next to this was another sheet of paper, folded in half, her name printed on the front. Daisy reached over and lifted it, opening it up. It was her mum's handwriting – scratched and scribbled in big, frightening, insane letters – and there was a lot of it. She scanned the lines, unable to make sense of it, as if it had been written in a foreign language. Only the final paragraph was clear, inscribed in letters twice as big as the rest:

Please forgive me, Daisy. Didn't you feel it? Something is coming, sweetheart, something bad, and it would have made us hurt you. I felt it already, something inside me, something pleading with me to do terrible things to my little Daisy, to my sweet beautiful daughter. I don't think it's the disease. No, it's definitely NOT the disease. I have taken care of your father for you. I don't know for sure if he would have hurt you but I think so. We both would have. Be safe, be strong. We love you, Daisy, we had no choice. We couldn't bring ourselves to hurt you. We couldn't do anything to hurt you. We WOULD have hurt you.

That last 'would' was underlined so hard that the pen had been pushed through the paper. Daisy didn't read it again. She carefully folded it and laid it onto the bed. Her head was stuffed tight with cotton wool and packing chips, no thoughts allowed in or out. She stood, wanting nothing more than to get out of this room with its sickly orange light and its fat stench of death. She made her way calmly downstairs and back into the kitchen, pulling the cordless phone from its cradle and dialling 999. Somebody picked up on the third ring.

'Emergency, which service do you require?' said a woman.

'An ambulance, please,' said Daisy, like she was ordering a pizza. 'My parents are dead. My mum killed herself. She killed my dad too.'

There was a pause, then the woman said: 'Oh my saints.' It was, thought Daisy, a stupid thing to say.

'You hold on now.' There was a click, then Daisy was talking to somebody else, a man. She answered his questions without really thinking, just staring out into the garden, not seeing the flowers or the grass or the sky, not seeing anything at all.

'The ambulance will be with you real soon, okay?' the man said. 'I'm going to stay on the line with you until it arrives. Just a couple of minutes and we'll be there.'

Cal

Cal sat in his living room, waiting for images of himself to appear on the television, waiting to see his own screaming face as he ran from the hunt. The house was empty, as it always was at this time of day. His dad, a businessman who never liked to talk about what kind of business he did, was abroad and his mum volunteered at the charity shop round the corner in the afternoons, Tuesday to Friday. He was glad that they weren't here. As much as he wanted to talk to them, to hear them say that everything would be okay, he didn't know what would happen when they saw him – *They might come after you too, Cal. They might chase you and kick you and stamp you into the pavement just like everybody else wants to* – and he needed to find out what was going on before they came home. He needed to work out what to do.

His whole body shook. The last few hours didn't seem real, *couldn't be real*. Those kinds of things didn't happen, except in the movies. And yet ugly purple flowers were blossoming on his arms, his chest, his neck and his back where they had grabbed and beaten him. He had a bite mark on his hand which he couldn't even remember getting.

He almost hadn't made it home. The car had seemed

161

to pull people off the pavements like a magnet, random strangers throwing themselves at it, bouncing off like bags of meat, squirming in his rear-view mirror. He'd expected to see the police behind him, had *wanted* to see the police there just so they could make sense of it all. But there were no police, no ambulances, just an army trying to batter its way inside.

The crowds dwindled the further from school he had got, disappearing altogether when he reached his road fifteen minutes later. He'd parked the gore-encrusted car inside the double garage, so that nobody would see it, before staggering inside. He hadn't quite made it to the sofa, collapsing onto his knees beside the television where he still sat.

The 24-hour Sky News channel had pretty much run its headlines and there was nothing there about a savage mob attack on a seventeen-year-old boy in East London. He left the telly on, pushing himself up, forcing his numb legs to navigate across the living room to the computer desk by the French doors. He slumped in the chair, switching the machine on and closing his eyes while he waited for it to boot up.

Images flashed against the dark canvas of his eyelids: gaping mouths, blunt teeth snapping, fingernails stained with his blood, and a hundred pairs of eyes all brimming with hatred, overflowing with it, straining right out of their sockets.

They had meant to kill him, without reason and without question. But why? What the hell had he done to provoke them?

He opened up Internet Explorer, loading the Yahoo home page. He scanned the links down the left hand side, not quite knowing what to do. He was clicking on the News page when his pocket started to vibrate, making him jump so hard that his knees cracked against the bottom of the desk. He pulled out his phone. It was Megan. He stared at her pixelated name, laid over a photo of her with two pens in her mouth pretending to be a vampire, for what felt like hours. Then he answered.

Silence. His mouth felt too dry to form words.

'Cal?' she said eventually, and he was relieved at how far away her voice sounded. 'Did you hear the news?'

That you all tried to kill me? But all that came out was a grunt.

'Georgia's in hospital, she got trampled. Where did you go, Cal? We needed you.'

Cal lowered the phone, rubbing his eyes then looking at her picture again to make sure the call was real. He heard Megan shouting his name and he put it to his ear.

'Are you okay?' she asked. 'Things got a little weird at school. They think there was a problem with the stands, that the kids at the back thought it was collapsing or something. We almost had our own Hillsborough.'

'Megan,' he managed eventually. 'What are you talking about?'

'Today, during the match,' she said. 'You must have seen it. We thought that's why you'd run off. Thanks

163

very much for that, by the way, *my hero.*'

Did she not remember chasing him? Did she not see what happened outside the English block, then on the street? Maybe in the confusion she hadn't realised what was happening – *But she was there, you saw her in the pack, reaching for you through the fence, her face boiling* – had just got carried away in the heat of the moment, some kind of group hysteria or something. He'd heard about that sort of thing happening, loads of people fainting at the same time or going crazy. She was still talking, fast, the way she always did when she was emotional.

'You tried to kill me,' he interrupted. Megan must have said two-dozen more words before it sunk in.

'What?' she said after a moment's pause. 'Be serious, Cal, this isn't a joke. Georgia's got a broken leg and a fractured collarbone or something and I've . . . Well I sprained my finger, which isn't much but it still hurts, and it was scary, Cal, all those people.'

You think? he almost spat.

'Cal, please, will you meet us at the hospital? We're in the children's bit. Georgia didn't want to stay there, but they said she was too young for the adult wing. There's an Xbox. Please, Cal?'

There was no dishonesty in her voice, no sense that she was trying to lure him out so they could attack again. There was just Megan, scared and hurt but the same girl he'd known for nearly eleven years now, the same girl he'd once gone out with for two months when they were in Year 5, who'd made him a little heart out of multicoloured paper clips that still sat on the windowsill in his bedroom. Even though he could see her running after him, teeth clenched, her face a mask of pure fury, he couldn't work out how to be angry with her.

'I'll be there,' he said softly. It was a lie, but it seemed to calm her down. 'Just give me a little while, okay? And say hi to the others. I hope they can fix your finger.'

Megan laughed.

'Thanks Cal. Love you.'

He didn't reply, and after a second or two she hung up. He sat there with the phone against his ear, unable to make sense of the conversation. Why didn't she remember? Had she blocked it out from shock or something? It didn't make any kind of sense. He thought about dialling Georgia, to see whether she knew what had happened. Nas's number was floating around somewhere in his address book too. But what exactly could he say? *Hey, Nas, just calling to ask why you tried to strangle me to death on the school field*. It was crazy, and he threw the phone onto the desk with a grunt of frustration.

Think, Cal, he said to himself, rocking back on his chair. *What do you do?*

There were rules to surviving a natural disaster, he'd read about them. They were designed for earthquakes and volcanoes and hurricanes, stuff like that, but he guessed they'd work for this too. Rule one, find a safe place. He'd done that, he was safe here, for the moment anyway. Rule two was to check for injuries and do the utmost to ensure your own survival. Well, he was pretty beaten up but he wasn't going to die from bruises and bites. Rule three was to look for other survivors, to make sure nobody is trapped under the rubble or cut off by lava or stuck on the roof of their house. Rule three, essentially, was to find out whether anyone else was in the same situation.

Cal leant forward, clicking in the Yahoo search box. He paused for a moment, trying to work out the best way to phrase his question, then wrote:

'Why is everyone trying to kill me?'

Daisy

'How did it ever get in such a state?'

Daisy spoke the words beneath her breath as she brushed her mum's hair. It was easier than usual because her neck was really stiff, almost locked in place, which meant her head didn't jiggle. She worked it into a ponytail, trying not to notice how cold her mum's skin felt.

She crawled over the bed, looking at her. It was so easy to forget – *Don't say it, don't think it, it isn't true, the ambulance people will fix them* – that they wouldn't be waking up this time. That they wouldn't yawn and stretch, that her dad wouldn't pat her head and her mum kiss her on the lips, that they wouldn't order Chinese as a treat and eat it in front of the telly.

Daisy felt like she should be crying but she was still numb all over, inside and out. The only thing she could really feel was a great big pressure in her chest, like something was sitting on her. It made it hard to breathe, and she had to keep taking great big gulping swallows of that horrible boxed-cat smell so that the room would stop going spinny and weird. She knew, or at least she thought she knew, that she was in shock. Although she didn't actually feel shocked, like she'd got a fright or put her hand in the plug socket. It wasn't like that at all. It was more like a big nothingness.

The room was shifting, and Daisy looked up to see waves of thin blue light flicker across the window, like she was underwater. She went to kiss her mum on the cheek but froze halfway at the thought of that damp, waxy skin against her lips. Instead she blew one, climbing off the bed as much to hide her guilty expression as to look out of the window.

'They'll look after you,' she said, pulling back the net curtain to see an ambulance outside, parked right behind their car, two wheels on the pavement. One man in green overalls climbed out, arching his back. The other was inside. Daisy couldn't make out his face because of the glare of the sun on the windscreen. The blue lights flashed, and Daisy suddenly realised that these strange men would be taking her parents away inside that thing, away to be buried or burned.

That awful weight on her chest seemed to double and she had to rest her forehead against the cool glass to stop from keeling over. The man in the street looked up. He squinted into the sunshine, putting a hand up to shield his eyes. Then he smiled sadly and waved. Daisy waved back but she couldn't manage a smile. Her face felt as tough and plasticky as her mum's and dad's. He glanced back inside the ambulance then started walking towards the house, carrying a bag with him. He didn't seem in much of a hurry.

Daisy made her way to the top of the stairs. She'd left the front door off the latch so the ambulance people could come in, but the man rang the bell anyway, turning the handle as the chimes of Big Ben filled the house. From where she was standing she could only see the bottom of the door, a pair of black shoes trampling over the mat.

'Hello,' Daisy said. The man replied, but she couldn't quite make out what he'd said. It had started off like a word — *hello*, she thought — but by the time it had reached the *ll*s it was stretched out of shape, becoming more like a groan, a throaty purr that seemed to fill the hallway below. He took a lurching step forward, his legs coming into view, then snorted.

'Hello?' she said again, uncertainty turning the word into a question. Ambulance people were nice, weren't they? They were supposed to be friendly and helpful and heal you when you were really sick.

Then why was her tummy going funny?

Because they're here to take your mum and dad away, that's all, she told herself. *That would make anyone's tummy go funny*.

The man took another step, then another, his chest appearing and then his shoulders and then his . . .

It wasn't the same man. Somebody else had come into her house. No, not somebody but *something*, something wearing the man's clothes and his hair and carrying his bag but something that wasn't here to be friendly and helpful. This was something bad, something using the man's face as a mask, its mouth drooping open, like a horse's mouth, the teeth huge and blunt and yellow.

He lumbered up the steps, in more of a hurry now

than anyone Daisy had ever seen in her life, so fast that he tripped on one and banged his forehead on the wood. He didn't seem to notice, just crawled up them on all fours. The noise was deafening.

Daisy waited until he was halfway up before the part of her brain that was saying *Don't worry, he's here to help* was completely and utterly consumed by the part which screamed *GET OUT OF HERE! YOU HAVE TO RUN! HE'S A BAD MAN!* She backed away down the landing, unable to take her eyes off him. He reached the top of the steps, trails of foam hanging from his lips, the whites of his eyes blazing. He used the banister to pull himself up, wrenching it so hard that the rail splintered free from the post.

Daisy screamed, spinning round and running for the back room, the man's animal grunts right behind her. She made it, slamming the door closed and leaning against it. The man struck it a second later, the wood making a sound like a pistol shot. All the doors in the house had tiny privacy locks on, and she flicked it across just as the handle turned. The man threw himself at the door, a jagged tear running down the side. Daisy staggered back. This was the box room, barely big enough for the single bed against the wall and the piles of old clothes which slept on it, and by the time she'd taken three steps she'd hit the window.

The door crunched again, specks of plaster drifting down from the ceiling. She could hear more footsteps too, hammering down the hallway. Fists and feet pounded the door. Why were they doing this? Why were they so angry with her? Did they think she'd killed her parents?

'I didn't do it!' she shouted, her voice lost in the thunder. 'I didn't do it!'

The door flew open so hard it ripped a chunk out of the wall. The man seemed to take up the entire room, a giant whose braying horse's mouth looked big enough to swallow her whole. Daisy's legs gave out, but before she hit the floor his massive hands connected with her chest, shoving her through the window.

Glass exploded, the universe shattered into a thousand sparkling shards as Daisy fell. She hit the roof of the kitchen extension, pain like fire in every part of her body. She rolled, tumbling over the guttering, in mid-air once again until the rhododendron bush broke her fall.

Even past the agony, past the roar of blood in her ears, Daisy could hear the screams of the men above her. She sat up, seeing nothing but fizzing silver light for a second before the garden popped back into view. She rolled out of the flowerbed, not trusting her balance enough to stand up, crawling sideways down the garden like a crab. Only when she was past the sprawling bulk of the laurel hedge did she dare look back.

The box room window was empty.

The shed sat at the bottom of the garden. It wasn't locked because it was falling apart, the roof all but caved in. She wrenched open the door and tumbled into the far corner. A fog of damp wood and slushy grass from the mower washed over her but it was so much better than the stench in the house. She breathed it in, hearing the familiar squeak of the back door.

Don't find me, please don't find me, she thought, her heartbeat so loud that the whole street must have been able to hear it. Footsteps rose up from the other end of the garden. Daisy pulled her knees to her chest, trying to make herself as small as possible, even smaller than she actually was, as small as the woodlice that scuttled up her shoes. *Please God don't let them know where I am, I'm begging you.*

The noises grew quiet. Still Daisy didn't dare move, even though her skin burned and she could see a blade of glass glinting in her arm, even though her shoulder and ankle throbbed. She hunched herself into the silence, her eyes screwed shut, praying, praying, praying.

Voices. She could hear them, although not well enough to make out what they were saying. One of them she recognised. It was the old Scottish lady who lived next door, Mrs Baird. She always gave Daisy a little box of Quality Street at Christmas and a five-pound note for her birthday. The other voice was a man's, just a deep rumble. Incredibly, they were laughing.

She couldn't bear it any more, not knowing what was going on. She eased herself up from the corner, skirting round the walls of the shed, careful not to trip on any loose firewood. Taking a deep breath, she peered through the grime-covered window.

The ambulance men were there, both of them. Only the second one was a woman, not a man. They were standing next to the fence in a puddle of broken glass. Mrs Baird was leaning over from the other side, pointing up at the box-room window. The man shrugged, looking at the garden. Daisy ducked, but she couldn't stop herself from peeking out again.

The lady paramedic walked into the house through the back door. The man was shaking hands with Mrs Baird — *Those are the hands he pushed me out of the window with! The hands he tried to kill me with!* she wanted to scream — both of them laughing again. Then he followed the woman inside.

Daisy watched the door swing shut, half relieved that, for some reason she didn't understand, they seemed to have given up looking for her but half wishing that they would stay outside, because she knew that they were going to take her parents now, knew that they weren't going to let her say goodbye. She sat back down beneath the window, put her head in her hands and started to cry.

Brick

Refresh. No change. Refresh. No change. Refresh. No change.

Brick felt like taking the laptop out of Fursville and hurling it into the ocean. It was driving him crazy. He'd been sitting in the foyer for four hours now, and for the last forty-five minutes or so he'd had the computer on his lap repeatedly loading up his Yahoo page. Apart from the adverts there was nothing new every time the page displayed. Just his desperate question and some tosser's idea of a funny reply. Brick wished he could find PWN_U13 so he could throw him down in the basement with Lisa and watch her claw his throat out. Let's see who had *psycho problems* after that.

Refresh. No change. Refresh. No change. Refresh. No change.

'Come on, you piece of junk,' Brick shouted, grabbing the laptop by its screen and shaking it. The battery was dipping towards quarter full now. If it died . . . well, he didn't want to think about that. He should be conserving it, but the longer he sat here the more anxious and angry he got. He swore, ready to start tearing his hair out. 'Just work!'

Refresh. No change. Refresh. No change. Refresh. No change.

This time he actually smashed his fist down on the keys, writing *kjhhjuk* in the question box. He deleted it, replacing it with '*How would you like it if I smashed you on the floor and stamped on your stupid electronic guts?*' He poked return, unsurprised when Yahoo couldn't find him an answer. He clicked back onto his page. No change. Refresh. No change. Refresh. No change. Refresh. No change.

Even though it wasn't yet five o'clock it seemed to be growing darker in the foyer, colder too. The thought of that blanket of night unfolding across the planet, ready to bury him and Lisa together, was terrifying. In the dark he'd have no idea if she'd got out, if she was stalking the corridors, if she was standing right next to him . . .

His whole body shuddered and he pushed the image away. Something would happen before then. He'd work out what to do.

Refresh. No change. Refresh. No change. Refresh. No change.

His anger was like something living inside him, tendrils worming up his throat into his brain, making it scream. His temper had never been very stable, the short fuse inherited from his old man. His dad's moods could change like a light switch being flicked, one second happy and laughing and joking around and literally – *literally* – the next his eyes would go dark and that smile would run from his lips and his hand would be out. *Crack! Don't mess around, Brick. Act your age, Brick. Just eff off and mind your own business.*

Brick wasn't as bad as that, no way. But there had been times when he'd shouted at Lisa, when she'd got on his nerves so much that he'd almost lifted his hands to her. Almost. The closest it had ever come was when they'd been drinking cider at her house when her parents were out and he'd thrown his glass into the corner of her room. He couldn't even remember why he'd been so furious that day. Something to do with her ex. He'd seen white, the whole world burning phosphorous. And in the second or two it took that feeling to pass he could have done anything. Luckily, he hadn't hurt her. He honestly didn't think he could *hurt* her – except in self defence – he just wasn't that sort of guy.

As for hurting the laptop, though. He wouldn't have a problem with that if his temper reached a thousand degrees again.

Refresh. No change. Refresh. No change. Refresh. No—

He'd got so used to the routine that it took him a few seconds to realise that something *had* changed. There was another answer below the first, and the shot of adrenalin that rocked Brick's system almost meant that he couldn't read it. He took a deep, shuddering breath and closed his eyes for a second, feeling a little calmer when he opened them. The response was from somebody called CalMessiRonaldo.

wtf man? are you serious? this has jst happened to me too. i was at school and everybody attacked me for no reason, chased me onto the street and i had to steel a car

to get away. i think i ran some people over. why is it happening? what do i do?

Brick leant into the screen, reading the message
again, then again, then again, trying to work out if it
was real or if it was another idiot who thought he was
a comedian. There was nothing in it to suggest it was a
joke. Although it was hard to get a sense of somebody
through a written message, Brick got the feeling that
this guy – this *kid*, if he was attacked at school – was
scared.

He typed a response beneath the kid's answer.

Look, I'm not messing around, this really happened to me.
If you're being serious then I need to talk to you.

He paused, reading back over what he'd written and
then deleting it, starting again.

I need to talk to you. I'll start a forum. I'll call it

He stopped again, trying to think.

Hated, okay? It means we can talk where nobody will see
it. Be quick, though.

He posted it, checking the battery life of the laptop,
then set up a new forum.

Tell me what happened? Are you on your own? Has it
happened to anyone else? I don't know what to do.

He thought about writing more, telling the kid
about Lisa, but something was holding him back. This

might be a trick, the police's way of finding out where he was. It was unlikely, but there was no way of telling for sure. Not yet, anyway. He'd wait to find out who he was, wait to see if he thought he could trust him. But he couldn't stop that calming blue wave of relief from damping the fire in his gut at the thought that maybe he wasn't in this alone after all.

'Come on, CalMessiRonaldo,' he said. 'Don't keep me waiting.'

He looked at the clock on the screen. 4.42. Then he settled back against the wall.

Refresh. No change. Refresh. No change. Refresh. No change.

Cal

Cal pulled another jumper from the chaos of his wardrobe, stuffing it into the duffel bag on his bed. He'd already packed half a dozen T-shirts, all of his jeans and tracksuit trousers, and two more jumpers. He'd emptied his underwear drawers and wedged in a second pair of trainers. The little pack with his toothbrush and other stuff from the bathroom sat on his pillow along with his mobile phone charger.

Part of him still thought this was a stupid idea. But it was the same part of him which insisted that what had happened that afternoon was just a big misunderstanding, that there really had been a stampede from the stands and he'd simply got caught in the middle of it. It was the same part of him that claimed Nas hadn't meant to strangle him, that those people hadn't jumped on the car so they could kick the living crap out of him.

That part of him was wrong.

They *had* tried to kill him, his friends and his teachers and strangers off the street. And if they had tried, then it made some kind of horrible sense that other people might give it a shot too. Other people like his mum. If that happened, then he needed to be ready.

He pulled his coat from the hook on the back of

the door. It was summer, hotter than he could ever remember it being. But he didn't know how long he might be out there.

Out where? he asked himself as he laid it into the bag. *Where are you gonna go, Cal?* He didn't know, not yet. He'd think of something, though. He wouldn't be on his own. *No, because everybody loves Callum Morrissey, right? Everyone loves him so much they just want to hug him and hold him until he falls to pieces.*

And maybe he wouldn't have to go anywhere. Maybe his mum would come home like she always did and give him a big cuddle and tell him that it would be okay, she'd look after him. That's what mums did, right? But even she had been acting weird that morning. She'd been acting just like his friends had before they tried to kill him. Ignoring that fact might cost him his life.

He had a quick check inside the wardrobe to make sure he hadn't missed anything, then he hefted the bag from the bed – it weighed a ton – and out into the upstairs hallway. He walked into his parents' room, an instinctive sense of guilt gripping him as he entered their walk-in wardrobe. Tucked at the back of a bottom shelf was his dad's safe.

He got down onto his knees, pulling out the musty collection of old shirts and throwing them to the side. His dad didn't realise that Cal knew the combination. The fact was he'd known it for about three years now, and it had taken him almost that long to work it out. Pretty much every time his parents had gone out

Cal had been in here trying out different sequences of numbers – birthdays, memorable dates, telephone numbers, mathematical equations he'd learned at school. Nothing had worked, but he'd never given up. He hadn't even known what was in the safe. His dad – whenever he was around, which wasn't often – had refused to tell him. It had become like a secret mission, like he was a spy and the safety of the world depended on him eventually cracking the secret. He'd grown obsessed with it.

Eventually, when he was fourteen, Cal had worked it out. He'd been talking to his mum and dad over dinner one night. They'd both been in a great mood, better than he'd seen them in ages. And they'd been telling Cal about how they first met, at a party in the West End.

You were gorgeous, his dad had said, flashing his mum a look that Cal hadn't really understood back then but which he knew all too well now. *You were my very own perfect little 36, 24, 36*.

The numbers had been a mystery, but the next day when he'd got home from school he'd given them a go, unable to stop giggling when he'd heard the safe click and the small, solid door swung open.

It did so now, the memory powerful enough to loose an insane surge of laughter up his throat. He choked it off, glancing into the bedroom to make sure he wasn't being watched before turning his attention to the safe. Inside were the same things he'd first seen three years ago. On the right-hand side was a pile of money –

tens, twenties and fifties all bound together in neat little bricks. The amount changed every time Cal looked, but he'd counted it once and it had totted up to over a hundred grand – more than enough for Cal to steal a few hundred quid every now and again and not be found out. Next to that was a small, flat black box which contained his mum's most valuable jewellery. Resting on the box was a portable hard drive that he was pretty sure just had their family photos and things on – he'd never bothered investigating.

There was one more thing in the safe, and it was this that Cal reached for. It was heavy, so much heavier than it had any right to be, so much heavier than they ever looked in the films. The polished wooden grip fitted his damp palm perfectly, the dull silver barrel much longer than the toy Airsoft BB version Cal had in his bedside cabinet. He flicked out the chamber – six empty holes peering back at him – then shut it with a deft flick of his wrist. He cocked the hammer, the tendons in his hand biting with the effort, then he pulled the trigger. *Click*.

He'd played with this gun for three years, cocking it then firing in a thousand imaginary games. He'd even put bullets in it once, from the box marked .38s at the back of the safe, although he hadn't dared pull back the hammer on that occasion just in case he'd blown a hole in the wardrobe wall, or his own leg. Cal found it hard to imagine his dad – who was balding, wore glasses and was usually mild-mannered and gentle – with the gun in his hand. His mum always described him as a 'businessman', although it was a business that involved monthly trips to Spain and lots of dodgy characters turning up at the house after dark. Cal knew the truth in his heart, of course, although he never wanted to admit it. His dad was one of the bad guys.

Cal picked up two bundles of cash – a couple of grand, he reckoned – and the box of bullets. Then he elbowed the door closed and spun the dial back round, hearing it lock. He paused for only a second, doubt nagging at the back of his mind. If he got caught outside with a gun, a *real* gun, then he wasn't going to get a slap on the wrist and a lecture from the cops. He was looking at a long, long time behind bars.

But if he didn't take it . . .

He saw the mob, those clawed fingers pinching him, knuckles pounding his skin, fat hands clamped around his throat. If he didn't take the gun, sooner or later he would regret it.

'Let's see you come after me now,' he said softly, aiming the pistol into the bedroom. But the thought of firing it, of actually shooting somebody, made him queasy.

He carried his stolen treasure back into the hall, placing the gun carefully in the bag, burying it in a nest of his clothes. He put one of the wads of cash in with it, then zipped the bag up tight. He looked at the other one, rifling it like a flick-book, the Queen's unchanging face frowning back at him. Thoughts of new trainers or games for his Xbox bubbled up automatically to the surface of his brain but he snuffed them out.

If things were as bad as they looked then this was survival money – food, shelter, maybe even transport to get him the hell away from here until whatever was going on had stopped going on.

He stuffed the cash into the pocket of the tracksuit trousers he'd put on when he was packing, throwing the bag over one shoulder. He struggled downstairs, through the garden room into the short corridor that led to the garage, leaving it by the door. Then he doubled back to the main lounge, stopping in the kitchen for a bottle of Dr Pepper from the fridge. The computer was on, the Yahoo answers page up where he had left it. It had been the first thing to appear on Google when Cal had typed 'Why is everyone trying to kill me?' He took a swig from his drink, the sugar perking him up, then he clicked the refresh button.

There was a comment beneath his answer, and Cal felt a mixture of relief and panic as he read it. Relief because he wasn't on his own. Panic because if this had happened to somebody else as well it meant that things were *really* bad out there. He ran the mouse over the guy's screen name, Rick_B, then he clicked on the link to a private forum called Hated. The chances were that the man was nothing but an internet creep who was trying to get kids to talk to him. It didn't matter if he was, Cal had the gun now, he could defend himself.

And maybe, just maybe, it was genuine.

'Okay, Mr B,' he said as the forum loaded. 'Let's see what you've got to say for yourself.'

Brick

CalMessiRonaldo: it's like i said, i was at school playing
football and everyone started chasing me. not for a joke, i
thought thats what it was at first, then they tried to stragle
and punch me and they chased me right out the school
onto the street and others came after me too, like shoppers. i only got away cos of the car. they would have killed
me. what bout u?

Brick put another fizzy cola bottle into his mouth,
chewing slowly as he reread the post that had appeared
below his own. He swallowed, then reached out and
typed.

Rick_B: My girlfriend tried to kill me, she tried to bite my
face off. Then she pretty much battered herself senseless
trying to get to me through a door. I'm holed up somewhere safe, somewhere no one knows about, need to find
out what's going on. Any ideas?

He posted it, then took another sweet from the
Haribo packet. He adjusted his position on the hard
floor, wondering whether he should go upstairs to the
restaurant where there were comfy chairs and tables.
He didn't dare move, though, in case somehow he lost
the connection to the one person who might be able

185

to help him. He wanted to refresh the page right away, but he forced himself to wait for five minutes – actually counting slowly to 300 in his head, the immense quiet of the foyer almost sending him off to sleep again as he did so – before he clicked.

CalMessiRonaldo: no idea, scarin the sh!t out of me, tho. i'm at home, my mums gonna be bck any minute. you think shell attack metoo? where are you?

Brick reached for another sweet, but the seven or eight he'd already eaten were dissolving unpleasantly in his empty stomach. He belched acid, swallowing it back down with a grimace. What now? Should he tell him about Hemmingway, about Fursville, or would that be too risky? He honestly didn't think it was a cop – and even if it was there were rules against this sort of thing, weren't there? Entrapment or something. And surely the police would have a better grasp of English than this guy. He banged his head gently against the wall behind him, trying to knock a plan loose from his brain. He needed some kind of proof that the kid had been through the same thing.

Rick_B: What happened after?

He posted the question, thinking about the way that Lisa had seemed to snap out of her fury, go back to being herself, the way she had forgotten what she had done. The memory scratched and bit inside his head, her blood-soaked voice pleading with him to let her go. Then the sight of her slumped and broken against the wall, still trying to get to him. He coughed out a painful sob, refreshing the page to see two posts waiting.

CalMessiRonaldo: i sh!t myself, thats what happnd after. what do u mean?

CalMessiRonaldo: actually i got a call from my mate, one of the ones who attacked me if thats what you mean. she didnt remember what shed done. where are u?

There was no way the police could know that, right? They might have found out that he'd been attacked by reading his Yahoo question, but they couldn't know that Lisa had gone back to normal as soon as he was out of sight. He flexed his fingers, nodding to himself as he typed.

Rick_B: I'm on the coast, a place called

And that was as far as he got before another thought crossed his mind. This guy had been attacked in the same way as him. But did that mean he wouldn't attack Brick – or vice versa – when they came face to face? He'd kind of assumed that maybe they had something in common, that maybe they were immune to each other or something, but he knew absolutely nothing about what was going on here. He certainly didn't know the rules of how this thing worked. The last thing he needed was another crazy trying to kill him – he'd end up with a pavilion full of locked doors with psychos behind them. His very own Bedlam.

So what, then?

Brick deleted what he'd written, starting again.

Rick_B: I'm in Norfolk, on the coast. I can tell you where to meet me. We need to be sure we can trust each other, that we won't try and kill each other, okay? Where are you?

He posted it. They didn't have to meet at Fursville. Pretty much the whole of Hemmingway was a ghost town, just the fertiliser factory inland, then the Sainsbury's about three miles to the north on the road over to Winterton. There were a few houses up that way, old people in bungalows mainly, but he'd never encountered any of them close to the park. He just couldn't see a bunch of old grannies climbing over the fence to sit on the rotting wooden horses of the carousel. He refreshed the forum.

CalMessiRonaldo: london, oakminster. i can prob get to u in a few hours if i can get out thecity,. tell me where, i gotta get out here real soon

Crunch time. Yes or no. Brick's fingers hovered over the keys and he chewed his bottom lip like it was another sweet. He was better on his own, he always had been. He wasn't good with other people, they either picked on him or pissed him off. And this kid, with a name like CalMessiRonaldo, was probably some footballer or something. Pretty much number one on Brick's list of people he hated, and people who hated him. If he told him about Fursville then the chances were they'd end up killing each other anyway, even if they weren't affected by what was going on.

But the alternative was worse. The alternative was that he stayed here by himself, Lisa dying in the basement – *if she isn't already dead* – him slowly going crazy in the creaking, rusting remains of his childhood paradise.

Rick_B: You need to head north, right up the coast. There's a village called Hemmingway, Googlemap it, just up from Hemsby. It's deserted. About a quarter mile from the village sign there's a track going off to the right, to the beach. Loads of dunes and stuff. At the end of it is a car park, well overgrown, and an old toilet block that's boarded up. That's not where I'm staying, that's just a place we can meet without being seen. If you're leaving now you can get there for eight. If you're late, just wait there overnight and I'll try again tomorrow. DON'T BRING ANYONE ELSE. Okay? If you're not alone I won't even show myself.

He read it back through, feeling ridiculous, like he was doing a hostage negotiation or something. But it paid to be careful. He posted, read it through again, then typed something else into the text box.

Rick_B: Good luck.

He closed his eyes, letting his head drop. He felt exhausted, which wasn't a surprise considering what he'd been through. He didn't want to sleep, though. He didn't want to close his eyes now and wake up to find that darkness had fallen, that he was alone here with his nightmares.

He logged back on to Yahoo, wondering whether he should wipe his original question, at least until he found out what happened when he met this guy. He clicked onto it, the arrow hovering over the 'delete question' option, his thumb ready to tap the trackpad button, and he almost didn't notice them until it was too late.

He scrolled down the page, his eyes widening, his pulse quickening as he took in what he was seeing:

There are currently 8 answers to your question.

Cal

Cal sat in the driver's seat of his mum's Freelander convertible, the engine purring quietly and the nose nudged out of the right-hand garage door. He'd put it in neutral so that he could rest his foot off the clutch, and his leg jiggled with nervous impatience as he kept watch on the gate. To his left was the car he'd escaped in, the blood now dried into vein-like rivulets along its sides and shattered windscreen, its roof caved in like a fruit bowl.

His bag was on the back seat of the 4x4, along with three carrier bags stuffed with crisps, sweets and drink. With any luck he wouldn't need it. With any luck his mum would come through the gate, see him sitting in her car and have a massive bug-out – mad but not psycho mad. He shuffled in his seat, feeling like his insides were lodged in his throat. His right hand gripped the wheel so hard that he didn't think he could let go even if he wanted to, his left resting on the gear stick. They told the true story – he was pretty sure he'd have to make his getaway a quick one.

He didn't know yet what his plan was, if the worst came to the worst. The guy he'd talked to online, Rick_B, sounded weird. Cal hadn't got a good vibe from the few messages they'd exchanged. What kind of

191

person picked an old abandoned toilet in an old abandoned village to meet in? Yet his message had sounded pretty genuine.

And what option did he really have? He couldn't exactly head west into the most heavily populated city in Europe. East was Southend and the ports, twenty-four hour industrial hubbub. South were the endless queues into Dartford Tunnel. Sure there were a few quiet places around here – hundreds of fields within driving distance, plus the country park where he could shelter in the trees. But what was he supposed to do? Live like Stig of the Dump for the rest of his years? At least if he headed north he'd be moving away from the city into the ghostlands of East Anglia.

Somebody walked past the wheelie bin outside the gate and Cal jumped, his twitchy right foot revving the engine. It was an old man shuffling along holding a Waitrose bag that was almost as big as he was. Sunlight glinted off his specs. He didn't look in. On the other side of the street one of the neighbours was loading something into her car. The sound of the door slamming and her feet crunching across the gravel seemed to carry too far, too loud, on the heat.

Cal ducked down in the leather seat, keeping his head as low as possible. He turned on the radio to try to calm his nerves, flicking impatiently through the stations and settling on Kiss. Something trancy filled the car, making him want to floor the pedal right now and just get the hell out of there.

There was a thump. Cal's head jolted up to see the

wheelie bin lid open. It slammed shut to reveal his mum behind it. She grabbed the handle and pulled it into the drive, that hollow rumble the loudest thing in the world.

What if she attacked him — *She won't, she won't, she can't* — came at him like the others, tried to open the door and pull him out so she could stomp on his head with her Uggs? It was his mum, for Christ's sake, his *mum*. The closest she'd ever come to hurting him was a gentle slap when he was nine because he'd sworn at her. Even that had hurt for much longer than it should have. A slap from your own mum is like a sledgehammer to the face. They were powerful that way.

'Please be normal,' Cal whispered.

She was halfway down the path when she heard the mutter of the car engine. She stopped, putting her hand up over her face, peering at him through a mask of shadow. In her purple top and black jeans she looked a bit like Bat Girl. Cal gripped the wheel, the fake wood slick inside his sweat-drenched palm. His words dried up inside his mouth, his tongue suddenly like sandpaper.

A car drove past on the street outside and his mum peeked over her shoulder. When she turned back to Cal she lifted her hands, her bright red nail polish like rubies, and shrugged dramatically.

'Cal, what the hell are you doing?' she said, her voice muted. Cal let out a breath that he hadn't even realised he'd been holding. Suddenly the sun seemed twice as bright, the leaves on the trees and bushes a brilliant shade of green that hadn't even existed until now.

She was okay. She was normal.

His mum let go of the wheelie bin and it rocked back on its wheels, rattling. She took a step towards him.

'Turn that engine off right now, young man,' she said, walking towards the garage. Cal grinned at her, reaching for the key.

'It's okay,' he shouted, wondering how the hell he was going to get the gun back into his dad's safe without her noticing. 'I was just having a laugh.'

'You're going to be in big truuuu, yumman,' she said. Cal froze. His mum's face had come loose. One side of her mouth was drooping, her left eye too big, too red. She took another step, swaying this time. 'Get out the car, get out, Caaaaaaaa . . .'

His name stretched from her lips, horribly distorted, dripping out alongside strings of saliva. His mum lurched across the last ten metres of the drive, her face slipping even further like a mask that had been badly glued on. She hit the bonnet of the Freelander hard enough to jolt the car, her hands squeaking on the metal as she clawed her way towards his window, still groaning that guttural version of his name. This close, Cal could see that her eyes were like hot coals, full of darkness and yet blazing with heat.

'Mum?' Cal said. He shook his head, unwilling to believe what he was seeing, even though deep down he had known this is what would happen, even though there was nothing left of his mum in the thing that pounded on his window with small, brittle fists, coating it with spittle as her voice grew into a banshee scream. 'Mum, I'm sorry.'

He put the Freelander in gear and pulled away slowly, so as not to hurt her. She ran alongside, thumping the windows hard enough to leave smudges of orangey blood there. He pulled out onto the pavement, not looking where he was going. His eyes were on the rear-view mirror, on the figure that lumbered after him like a zombie, her face so familiar, and yet so alien. She lost her footing on the gravel and plunged from view, and it took everything he had not to stop the car and go to help her.

Goodbye, Cal tried to say. Then he floored the accelerator, lifted the clutch and roared up the street.

Brick

Brick couldn't believe what he was reading.

> This is happening to me 2, got attackjed by my brother.
> :(((((((need help as I canb't walk.

It was right at the bottom of the page, posted by somebody called EmoTwin3 literally two minutes ago. It was the twelfth answer. Above that was the eleventh, by JoeAbraham:

> don't call the police they tried to kill me I AM NOT
> JOKING. Happened last night, Only got away by jumping
> in a river. mum was one of them thought she was gonna
> strangle me. i'm at my dad's place cos he's away for the
> summer but there's people all over and I ain't going outside
> again unless I got somewheres safe. where u at bruv?

They'd both just appeared the last time he'd refreshed. Brick scrolled up the page, his hand trembling so much that he kept losing his place. He'd read the other entries over and over. Not all of them were serious; somebody had written 'You guys are massively weird' for answer number seven. But the rest were so similar that they could have been left there by the same person. He scanned through them for the billionth time, shaking his head as the same sentences leapt

196

out at him.

. . . she broke my arm, she was trying to pull it right off . . .

. . . they all just came after me like they hated me . . .

. . . I went to the hospital and it was the same there, one tried to scalpel me . . .

. . . please help me I don't know what to do . . .

They pretty much all ended along those lines, too – *please help* – like Brick was some messiah who could lead them all to salvation. The hell with that, though. He didn't even know what was going on himself.

He put the laptop on the floor so he could stretch out his legs. Pins and needles radiated from his backside. He could just switch the laptop off and ignore everything he'd read. He could delete his question and the answers would vanish alongside it. He might even be able to convince himself he'd never seen them.

No. He couldn't do that. He could no more leave a bunch of people to die than he could run over the ocean.

And they sounded so young too. That was why the messages had all seemed similar – the language, the spelling, the lack of grammar – they were written by kids. He couldn't be sure, of course. There was just something in those messages that made him fairly confident that they weren't adults.

The laptop sat open, the screen almost fully dark

to conserve the battery but those messages still visible, staring up at him, imploring.

'Okay, okay,' he muttered to them. 'But not before I know you're not all gonna go psycho on me, okay?'

That was the best solution. He'd go out and meet CalMessiRonaldo, and if they didn't end up tearing each other's throats out then maybe he'd send word to the rest of them. This other guy might have some better ideas too.

He checked the clock. It was only a twenty-minute walk to the car park from here but he could do with stretching his legs properly, getting some air that didn't smell of bird crap and rot. He pushed the lid closed with his foot, hearing it go to sleep. Then he set off back down the maintenance corridors, stopping at the top of the basement steps for no more than a second – *It's fine, it's quiet, no need to check, no need to go down there, she's fine* – before it felt like his heart was about to slip from his throat and plop down the stairs like a slinky. And *was* it quiet down there? Wasn't that a gentle scraping he could hear? Nailless fingers on wood? He almost ran the last few metres to the fire door, crawling and kicking through the chains like a man pulling himself from his grave.

Cal

This was bad.

Really bad.

And it had been going so well, a clear path out of Oakminster, the main road free of traffic despite the fact that everybody was leaving work. He'd had to stop once, at the set of lights they'd just put in for the giant new Asda, but nobody had crossed. The woman in the car behind him had started to get out, but the lights had changed before she could stagger over.

The satnav had offered him a choice of routes: via Ipswich or Norwich. Some inner voice had drawn him irresistibly to the second option. Now he was wishing he'd ignored it. He'd taken the back roads onto the M11, happy keeping the Freelander at seventy in the middle lane, passing people too quickly for them to see him or *sense* him or whatever it was that was going on. Traffic had been fast on the motorway, and it was only about an hour after setting off, when he finally let himself think that he might actually be okay, that luck took a massive crap right on his head.

The electronic boards were flashing a warning at him – accident, long delays between junctions 8 and 9 – and he could see the gridlocked traffic from half a mile away. The inside lane had been barricaded by a police van, its flashing blue lights multiplied a hundredfold in the windows of the cars that purred motionlessly alongside it. Further down he could see a pillar of smoke rising almost perfectly straight into the calm blue sky. He slowed, keeping to the middle lane as the cars started to converge around him.

'Take the next exit,' the satnav lady suddenly barked at him, making him jump.

'I'll try,' he replied. 'But it isn't going to be easy.'

The brake lights from the car in front blazed and he slowed from forty to twenty-five. Something big trundled by on his left, hydraulic brakes hissing, plunging him into shade. Behind him an old Mercedes was pulling up fast, the driver a hunched shadow behind the wheel.

This was really, *really* bad.

The car in front reached the back of the queue and stopped dead. Cal slammed on his brakes at the last minute, the Freelander rocking to a halt. Another lorry pulled up to his right, squealing, and it got even darker inside the car, the steep-walled containers on either side making him feel like he was inside a grave.

Stay calm, just stay calm, he told himself. *They don't know who you are, they're not going to come after you.*

Then why was the guy in front climbing out of his ugly green Fiat? It was a middle-aged man, dressed in sweats and trainers like he was going to the gym. He stopped with one leg in the car and one leg on the motorway, stooped over, frozen. The Mercedes behind was closer now, the driver gunning the engine. Was he *speeding up?*

The Fiat man seemed to remember what he was doing, dragging his left leg out of the car. Then he turned to Cal.

'Oh no,' Cal said as the man's face changed, his cheeks sagging like old cloth, his lower eyelids drooping to reveal the red-veined orbs of his eyes. He staggered forward like a marionette, throwing himself at the raised bonnet of the Freelander just as the Mercedes slammed into it from behind.

Cal's car lurched into the back of the Fiat, the man caught in a bear trap. There was a crack, a spurt of blood from his misshapen mouth, then he vanished between them. The impact threw Cal forward, his face hitting the centre of the wheel hard enough to honk the horn. He crashed back, wondering why the airbag hadn't gone off, trying to make sense of the world through the supernovas that detonated in his vision.

Fiat guy had to be dead, Mercedes guy wasn't moving. But Cal could make out other people climbing from their cars further down the queue. There were seven or eight of them making their way towards him, all with looks of concern, some with phones out, others beckoning urgently to the police van in the inside lane. One by one, as they stepped past an Argos lorry maybe twenty metres away, their expressions changed, their pace increasing as they lurched and stumbled towards his car.

Cal fumbled it into first gear, praying that the crash hadn't done any damage as he hit the gas. There was a deafening crunch, the squeal of metal against metal, but the Freelander didn't budge. He looked over his shoulder at the Mercedes crammed up against him, its bonnet crumpled and smoking. He was pinned tight between them. He swore, wrenching the stick into reverse, flooring the pedal and shunting the car back a metre or so.

A hand thumped his window, somebody trying the handle. Cal didn't look, just threw it into first again and rammed the back of the Fiat, freeing up another bit of space. Somebody was screaming, half-words buried in the noise as they battered the glass with their fists. One of the people from the queue – a teenage girl – was trying to climb onto the bonnet but Cal reversed again and sent her tumbling to the floor. He managed a little more momentum this time, knocking the Merc back far enough for him to break out.

He swung the wheel all the way to the left, nudging the wrecked Fiat out of the way. There was hardly any room between it and the lorry to his side but he didn't let up, squeezing through, serenaded by more shrieking metal. Somebody was on the back of the car trying to tear through the canvas roof, two black blisters of eyes boiling through the hole he'd made.

More people were surging up the aisles between traffic, and for a second Cal thought they had him, that there was no way out. Then he squeezed past the lorry to see that the car in front of it was a Smart car. He pulled hard to the left again and rammed it. He was only doing twenty but the weight of the Freelander pushed the tiny thing in front out of the way like it was a toy, rolling it onto its side and clearing a path onto the hard shoulder.

Cal accelerated onto it, passing the police van close enough to rip its bumper off, hitting fifty in five seconds. The man on his roof had gone. Up ahead he could see the source of the smoke he'd spotted earlier, a car that had come off the road, punched through the barrier and down the bank to the side. It sat in a field, surrounded by people, hundreds of them, swarming all over it the same way they had swarmed over him back at school. They didn't seem to care about the black clouds that billowed from the engine, they were just tearing and scratching and kicking and even biting at the metal like starving rats trying to get at the meat inside a bin.

He eased his foot onto the brake as he drew level, slowing to about twenty before realising what he was doing. Some of the people on the smoking car looked up, a couple of them tumbling free from the pack and starting to run up the slope towards the road. The crowd behind was catching up too, a tide of flesh filling his rear-view mirror.

Then he heard it. Although heard was the wrong word because this was nothing to do with his ears. There was something in his head, something that wasn't him, a voice that at the same time wasn't a voice. It seemed to grab time and pull it to a halt, the people all around him running in slow motion like those new hi-def cams they used for the football. The voice seemed to be the opposite of noise, a profound silence that cushioned the world and yet which still somehow communicated with him. And in that instant Cal knew exactly what was inside that car.

It was a person, somebody just like him.

And they needed help.

The world unspun like a clockwork toy that had been wound up tight, reality snapping back. The screams from outside were deafening now, more people pounding and scraping at the Freelander. Past faces ravaged by hate Cal could make out the car below, bodies squirming all over it. He accelerated hard, swinging to his left, grinding past flesh and bone as he headed for the broken barrier. He didn't know what he was going to do when he got to the wreck, but he had to do something.

The lightning came before the thunder. The car in the field erupted in a ball of white heat that sent charred corpses spiralling out in all directions. Cal had time to see a fist of smoke punch up towards the heavens – and something *inside* that smoke, an impossible shape of blue flame which opened its mouth and howled – before the shock wave hit the Freelander, peeling away the people outside and blowing in the passenger windows. He shielded his face, poisoned air clawing into his lungs, the 4x4 bouncing on its wheels so hard he expected it to roll over.

By the time he lifted his head the worst of the explosion had passed. Smoke still gushed skywards like liquid from the blazing car, but there was nothing in it except darkness. The engine had stalled and Cal turned the key to bring it back to life. He swung the wheel to the right, accelerating away from the carnage, away from the burning shapes that ran and howled and fell in his mirrors.

There was one police car on the hard shoulder but he passed it with plenty of room. The queue continued up the motorway, faces peering out of car windows at the smoke-darkened skies, but the exit was clear.

'Continue on the current road,' said the satnav. Cal wiped the ash from his stinging eyes, trying not to think about the people who had been on the car – twenty, thirty, maybe more, all dead; trying not to think about the person inside it, the wordless voice somehow begging him for help, which had vanished like a radio being turned off the moment the car had exploded; trying not to think about the shape in the smoke, that figure of flame which screamed as it rose.

He let the fresh air empty his head, and drove on.

Daisy

Daisy crawled through the garden like a lioness, the ones she enjoyed watching on the telly. They were so graceful, so quiet, and she tried to imitate them as best she could as she crept forward on all fours, making sure to always stay hidden in the overgrown bushes.

She hadn't seen anyone inside the house for ages. The horrid ambulance man had last appeared maybe half an hour ago. It might have been less. He'd gone back inside after smoking a cigarette, chatted to some police in the kitchen, then they'd all filed out and that was the last she'd seen of them. Of course they might still be inside, hiding in the shadows, ready to jump out at her . . .

The thought of it, of that ambulance man's horse face braying at her, his rough hands pushing her out the window, stopped her dead. She twisted her hand in the long grass, locking herself to it, smelling the roses and the rhododendrons and the buddleias. It reminded her of her mum. Her poor mum. It had come back and had been eating her brain, just like before. The tumour had made her act weird last time, but only twitches and tics and the occasional word that came out wrong. This was so much worse. She had killed Dad, she had killed herself.

It wasn't the cancer, though, Daisy thought, remembering the note. *She said it wasn't the disease. It was something else. She knew what was coming, that she was going to hurt you.*

The thoughts were painful and she pushed them away, untangling her hand and creeping towards the back door. There was a big, bald patch of lawn between the last bush and the house. If she crawled over that then anybody inside would be able to see her. She glanced right, the flowerbeds full of thorny things, and past them the passage up the side of the house. To the left, Mrs Baird's garden. The nice old lady's apple trees hung over the low fence, a pool of shadow beneath them.

Daisy skirted towards them, grateful when she plunged into the shade. She could hear something on the other side of the fence. It might have been Pudding and Wolfie, Mrs Baird's cats. She started forward again.

About ten metres or so from the bush where she'd landed after her fall from the box-room window, Daisy saw the first shard of glass – about the size and shape of one of the steak knives in the kitchen. It was nestled in the dirt, a line of blood down one side. Sunlight shone through it, painting the grass a vivid shade of red, making Daisy think of cathedral windows. She half thought about picking it up and putting it in her art box, it was so beautiful, until she remembered it was *her* blood.

She stood up, not wanting to cut her knees and elbows on the twinkling scalpels of glass between here and the house, squatting to stay below the fence. It was hard walking like this but there wasn't far to go. The noises to her left were louder now, but she could definitely hear the familiar 'briiiow' of the cats. It was the noise they made when Daisy snuck out some prawns or tuna for them after dinner, the noise they made when they were being fed.

But if *she* wasn't feeding them . . .

Daisy glanced over her shoulder to see a figure half hidden behind the knotted trunk of one of the apple trees. It was wearing an ancient brown dressing gown, and smoky puffs of thin white hair billowed out from the pink scalp beneath. One small, black eye peeked out from the shade, looking right at her.

'Mrs Baird?' Daisy asked, coming to a halt, still on her haunches. 'Is everything okay?'

The nice old lady was breathing hard, almost grunting. There was a clatter of wood and one of the cats – Daisy could never tell them apart as they were both black – jumped onto the fence. It wobbled, catching its balance, rubbing its head on Mrs Baird's sleeve and making the same 'I'm hungry' protest. Mrs Baird ignored it, still staring at her with that one dead eye.

Daisy straightened, taking a few steps towards the back door. And she'd just grabbed the handle when the old lady threw back her head and screamed. It was a horrible sound, like she was having a heart attack or something, and Daisy almost went to her, her first instinct to help.

With a phlegmy cry Mrs Baird hurled herself against the fence, the wooden panels bowing under her weight. She lost her grip, disappearing with a sickening snap. *That's a broken bone*, Daisy thought as her neighbour reappeared, her whole body trembling, great trails of saliva hanging from her pale lips. She was still grunting, the noise a pig might make. Daisy turned the handle, pushing the door, almost banging her head on it when it wouldn't open. She tried again, using both hands this time.

It was locked.

There was another gut-wrenching noise, then something thudded to the ground. Daisy looked to see that Mrs Baird had managed to flop over the fence and was now lying in a heap trying to get up. Her arms and legs wriggled in the air, like a beetle on its back, her dressing gown open to reveal the velour tracksuit underneath. One of her slippers was gone, and there was something wrong with that bare ankle. It was pointing the wrong way.

Daisy turned back to the door, wrenching the handle, kicking the bottom hard enough to make the glass rattle.

'Come on!' she screamed at it, suddenly wishing that the police were still inside, that *anybody* was still inside. Mrs Baird was no longer trying to get to her feet. She had flipped herself over and was scuttling across the garden on all fours the same way Daisy had been earlier, her wrinkled fingers pulling out clods of dirt as she clawed forward.

Daisy kicked the door once more then backed away, heading for the side passage that led to the street. Mrs

Baird was gaining, her sagging face filled with exhaustion but those piggy eyes more determined than Daisy had ever seen them. Her glistening mouth gaped wide, breathing in the same short, piercing double-shriek cries that might have been her name – *Day-seee, Day-see, Day-see* – broken and clogged with spit. She ploughed across the grass, her arms and legs moving too fast for an old woman, like there was a horrible clockwork machine under her skin.

Daisy turned and fled into the passage, not knowing where she was going, not caring about the voices she could hear from the street outside, just wanting to get away from the thing that crawled after her, that called her name with each wheezing breath.

Cal

'Turn around when it is safe to do so.'

Cal really wished he could take the satnav lady's advice. He wanted nothing more than to be able to swing the Freelander one-eighty, get the hell out of this weird little town and back on the dual carriageway.

Only he couldn't. Something had made him pull off the relatively empty A11 just after Mildenhall – that same weird voiceless voice inside his head, making him ignore the instructions from the console, flick his indicator on and pull the car off the high street down a narrow road packed with houses.

There were people here. A delivery driver was unpacking crates from an Iceland van a few cars down, and a bunch of teenage skateboarders were messing around on the corner, one riding on the back of another, all of them laughing. They could have been Cal and his mates outside the library back in Oakminster, not a care in the world other than the constant ever-shifting mystery of who fancies who and what to do about it. He thought about Georgia, about Megan and Eddie and the others. It felt like a million years since he'd last seen them.

The delivery driver started to sniff the air as Cal pulled closer. The crate tumbled from his hands and a plastic carton of milk burst. He ran at the Freelander and Cal pressed his foot down a little harder, accelerating. The skateboarders had caught wind of him too. With a row of parked cars on each side there wasn't any room to manoeuvre so Cal kept his speed at a constant twenty-five, hoping they'd get out of the way.

They didn't, the first kid meeting the 4x4 head-on like a charging bull, bouncing almost straight backwards. The others were bumped aside by the bonnet, knocked into the gaps between the cars. Cal didn't stop, even when the Freelander ran over something under its wheels, something big, something soft. He steered around the corner, guided by that strange radar in his head, a silence that seemed vast and unbroken even though he could hear the monkey-like shrieks from behind him, the sound of doors opening, the thunder of footsteps. There was a turning to the left and he took it, increasing his speed so that the little kids with the garden sale wouldn't sense him until it was too late.

The road went down a hill, curving to the right then rising steeply again. Whatever it was inside his head was louder now, but still utterly silent. It reminded him of being at the bottom of the swimming pool, a perfect, pitchless peace. Even though he could see the crowd running after him in his rear-view mirror, even though he had no idea what lay ahead, it made him feel safe. It made him feel that he was doing the right thing.

He swung round another corner, the Freelander clattering over a pushbike that had been abandoned in the road. There was movement up ahead, a man running away from Cal, towards a small mob clustered outside a house on the left. There were four or five of them, a mix of men and women and even a little boy who didn't look any older than five. The ones he could see wore the same expression of utter fury, so fierce that it turned their faces into demon masks. He sped up, somehow knowing the exact same thing that he had back on the motorway – that there was somebody close by who was just like him.

There was no time for a plan. Cal reached the mob in seconds and slammed on the brakes, the Freelander skidding into a low wall. A woman staggered towards him, howling as she tried to worm in through the broken passenger windows. Cal reached for his bag but couldn't get it, the woman's fingers pinching the flesh around his throat, her breath hot on his face. He grabbed the first thing he could find, a two-litre bottle of Dr Pepper, using it to batter her hands away. He opened his door and tumbled away from her onto the street.

What the hell am I doing?

Another woman reached for Cal with bloodied fingers. He swung the bottle like a baseball bat. It made a ridiculous boinging sound as it hit her head, spinning her onto the tarmac. The first woman was crawling out of the car and Cal slammed the door in her face, twice, then legged it around the back of the Freelander.

One of the adults in the garden charged at Cal, stumbling on the broken wall and giving him enough time to see that the others were clustered around a gated passage that led down the side of the house. Past the bars of the gate he could see a girl. She looked maybe eleven or twelve and she was screaming, but it was a different sound from the one the people on this side of the gate were making. It was filled not with hate but with terror.

He lifted the bottle over his shoulder, waiting until the man was almost on him before swinging hard again. It clipped his nose, a brittle crack echoing around the street. The man didn't seem to notice, grabbing Cal around the neck and squeezing, flecks of blood spraying from his face with each snorting breath.

Cal thrust the bottle into the soft spot beneath the man's chin, pushing up until the hands around his throat loosened. He swung the bottle at him. It hit, but exploded, the drink fizzing out like there were Mentos inside. The man gnashed at it, distracted, and Cal punched him in the face.

Something was biting him in the leg and he looked down to see the little boy there. He knocked him away as gently as he dared, kicking the woman who followed in the face. The last guy was big, but Cal remembered his Choy Li Fut training. He stepped behind him, locking his right leg around the man's knee then shunting hard. The guy tripped, dropping like a felled tree, his head cracking on the concrete path.

Cal glanced up the street to see people hammering down it. He had maybe thirty seconds before he was swamped. He ran to the gate, ignoring the fire that burned in his muscles and lungs. There were actually two people inside, the second a white-haired old lady with crooked fingers coiled around the girl's legs. The girl was kicking out at her, her face twisted by fear and blunted by shadow, her screams amplified by the narrow passageway. Cal tried the gate but the handle wouldn't budge.

'Hey!' he yelled. 'Let me in!'

The girl ignored him, her cries reaching a crescendo as the old woman sank her teeth into her leg. Cal glanced up the road again. Fifteen seconds. He swore, took a step back, then kicked out. A jarring pain tore up his leg and his back but the gate didn't budge. He paused, breathing in through his nose, taking up a guarding stance then kicking out again with every ounce of strength he had.

The rusted lock snapped, something metal clanging down the passageway as the gate swung open. Cal ran through it, booting the old lady like he was taking a penalty. He grabbed the girl under her arms, ignoring her screams and her punches.

'It's okay, trust me, I'm not going to hurt you,' he said, the words only half formed in his breathless panic. He clamped her to him as he sprinted out into the garden, dodging one of the mob who was back on her feet then tearing open the Freelander door. The woman who had climbed inside the car was unconscious – or dead – and Cal grabbed her by the hair and tried to pull her free. She wouldn't budge, her limbs locked between the seats. The hail of footsteps was deafening now, each panted breath audible.

'Don't run,' he said, putting the girl down and

grabbing the woman with both hands. Her body slid from the car like a bag of meat, slopping to the ground. The girl took a few steps away from him but stopped when she saw the crowd pounding down the street – maybe twenty people now, all howling. She looked up at him, her eyes so wide with shock they didn't look real.

'You can trust me, I promise,' he said. The kid at the head of the crowd – one of the skateboarders, Cal thought – had almost reached them. 'We need to go.'

He held out a hand and she took it, letting him help her into the driver's seat. He climbed in next to her, slamming the door just as the skateboarder drew level. Momentum carried the kid past and he slipped on the gravel, disappearing with a yelp. The girl shuffled into the passenger seat as Cal slung the car in gear and floored it, barrelling down the street, the chaos and the carnage once again safely contained in the cracked glass of his rear-view mirror.

The only one who spoke was the satnav lady, and even she seemed relieved to Cal as he happily followed her directions out of Boxwood St Mary back towards the A11. He didn't take his foot off the gas, finally remembering to breathe when he hit the slip road that led back onto the dual carriageway. Only when he was doing seventy in the outside lane did he notice that his entire body was as rigid as stone. He let himself relax,

216

tremors taking the place of the tension.

'Continue on the current road,' said the lady.

Cal glanced over at the girl. She was curled up in the passenger seat, making it look huge. Her face was ashen, like she'd been completely drained through the cuts on her arms and neck. Her long hair swayed like seaweed in the gale from the broken windows. She stared out of the windscreen through watery blue eyes, but Cal knew she wasn't seeing anything except maybe a replay of whatever it was she'd been through.

'That lady's name is Miss Naggy,' he said, his voice too loud despite the howl of the wind and the heavy thrum of tyres. It was a stupid thing to say, but Cal didn't have anything else. He glanced at the road then back at her. 'She lives in the car and tells me where to go.'

The girl didn't budge. At least she wasn't trying to attack him, that could only be a good thing. A car was coming up fast behind him and Cal braced himself, indicating left and sliding into the inside lane. The BMW wobbled a little as it blasted past but it didn't stop. Cal checked his mirrors then pulled out again to overtake a lorry. If he moved past people quickly enough they seemed to go back to normal before anything bad happened.

'When I go the wrong way she tells me off,' he went on. 'Well, she usually tells my mum off, that's why she called her Miss Naggy. It's her name, not mine.'

Smooth, Cal, he thought. *You're so great with kids.*

'What's your name?' he asked her. She didn't reply, didn't even seem to notice him. He thought about leaving her alone. Maybe she was in shock or something, and he wasn't sure what you were supposed to do with people like that. Wasn't there a rule about not letting them go to sleep? Or was that for something else. Constipation or something.

Concussion, idiot, his brain said, and he snorted a laugh. The noise made the girl jump. She snapped out of whatever trance she'd been in and gazed fearfully at Cal. He saw her fingers stray towards the door handle – *Christ, don't do that, kid, you'll be pâté on the motorway* – and he held up his left hand to show that he wasn't going to hurt her.

'It's okay, please don't be scared.' The road ahead looked clearer and he pulled back into the left-hand lane, slowing down so that the noise inside the car was more a summer storm than a full-blown hurricane. 'My name is Cal, you can trust me, I promise you.'

She shuffled further back into her seat, curled up like a hedgehog.

'Where are we going?' she said. Or at least that's what he thought she said, her voice was a whisper bound up and carried off by the wind.

'Somewhere safe,' he replied. 'At least, I think so. I'm not sure. But I'll look after you, don't worry, okay?'

There must have been something friendly in his face because the girl seemed to relax. She rested her chin on her knees, those huge eyes never blinking.

'Miss Naggy wants you to put on your seat belt,' Cal said, realising that neither of them was wearing one. He clipped on his own. 'She'll tell us off if you don't.'

The girl looked at him, then at the built-in console where the voice came from. She reached up and pulled the belt over her curled-up legs, clicking it into the socket. They'd driven another half mile before she spoke, her voice so soft and so full of sadness that Cal felt a lump rise inside his throat.

'Everyone hates me.'

'They don't,' he said before he'd thought about what he could follow it with. 'There's just, I don't know, something wrong with people. It's making them do things they don't want to. Like zombies, you know?'

She didn't respond.

'Everyone has been attacking me too. It started at school, all my friends, they tried to . . .' he faltered, the words scared of being heard. He coughed them out. 'They tried to kill me. Then people from the street, people I'd never seen before in my life.' He'd wiped a tear away before he even noticed he was crying. 'Then my mum.'

The girl looked back at him, her mouth hanging open, and a jarring blast of adrenalin tore through Cal as he thought she was about to throw herself over the seat and sink her teeth into his throat.

'Your mum tried to hurt you?' she said. Cal nodded. She stared at something a million miles away, deep in thought. There was a moment of revelation there, some awful understanding. Then she lowered her head to her raised knees and began to sob, great heaving cries. Cal's hand hovered over her for a second or two before landing on her shoulder. Her whole body jolted at the touch but other than that she didn't acknowledge it. He gently stroked his thumb back and forth, the way his mum had always done with him when he was upset.

'It's okay,' he said, keeping his voice low, soothing. 'It's all going to be okay, I promise. We'll find out what's going on and then we'll know how to stop it, we'll fix it, then our mums will be okay, they won't be angry with us any more. I promise.'

He was making a lot of promises for a guy who knew nothing about what was going on, but what else could he do? It didn't seem to be working anyway. If anything he'd made the girl cry even harder. He put his hand back on the wheel, seeing a huge green sign advertising Norwich in fifteen miles and Yarmouth in forty. The satnav said they'd be there within an hour. They would be late, but he was pretty sure Rick_B, whoever he was, would hang around.

He drove in silence for the next few minutes, the satnav lady chirping up and navigating him around a series of roundabouts. It was a while later that the girl stopped sobbing, her face rising from behind her kneecaps. Cal smiled at her as gently as he could, not wanting to say anything else in case he set her off again. But she seemed like she was cried out, wrung dry. She looked up at him, wiping her nose with the back of her hand.

'You really think there's a way to make things normal again?'

The look she gave him, suddenly so full of hope, of

trust, meant there was only one answer he could give.

'Yeah,' he nodded. 'I really do. Whatever this is, we'll work it out together. I promise.'

She wiped her nose again, sniffing. Cal leant over and popped the glove box, a half-empty pack of tissues inside. He gestured at them and she took one, patting her eyes dry then scrunching it up and tucking it in her sleeve. She took a deep, juddering breath that seemed to shake some colour back into her cheeks.

'Thanks,' she said, a ghost of a smile in her thin lips, her pale eyes. 'My name's Daisy.'

Brick

He was late.

Either that or he was dead. Where had he said he was coming from? London? If things were as bad as Brick thought, that was one hell of a journey – a gauntlet of ten million psychotic people trying to slaughter you on the street. Thinking about it that way, it would be a miracle if he made it here at all. That made his stomach crunch up, like he'd eaten something bad. As much as he hated to admit it, he really didn't want to be on his own.

He rested his head on the warm sand, enjoying the comforting touch of the evening sun – not too hot, not yet muffled by the evening chill. He was lying on the slope of one of the dunes that ran the length of the beach, one of the big ones that would have looked at home in the Sahara if it wasn't for the wavy sea grass comb-over. Ahead of him was the unbroken slate of the sea, almost perfectly waveless, so smooth that he half thought he could run right over it to Holland or Denmark or whatever lay beyond the horizon.

On the other side of the dune was a short stretch of pine forest, a bed of soft-needled trees into which the sun was slowly sinking. A dirt track led from them to a small concrete car park, the ugly square block of the toilets sticking up like an ulcer. There were boards over all the doors and windows, smeared with graffiti too windblown and rain-washed to read. The soft lap of the waves and the whispering pines made him feel inexplicably at peace.

Maybe the guy had decided not to come. Brick hadn't exactly been a charmer in his messages. He tried to think back to what he'd written, unable to recall a single word other than to come alone. That in itself had been a pretty stupid thing to say – if CalMessiRonaldo was like him then he wouldn't exactly be mobbed by friends right now. Why had he been such an asshole?

Blame it on stress, he thought, twisting a long strand of grass between his fingers. *Blame it on shock, on fear.* But the truth was much more simple than that. He *was* an asshole. He promised himself he'd make an effort to be nice as soon as the guy showed up.

If he showed up.

He wished he had a watch, or the phone he'd dropped when he was riding away from the garage. Norfolk was as flat as a pancake, which meant the day-light stretched right out into the evening, but once it hit ten it would get dark. Really dark. He'd have to be back at Fursville by then or he'd end up spending all night on the beach.

An ant struggled past right under his nose, its feet moving so fast they were just a blur as it attempted to negotiate the crumbling sand. He lowered a piece of grass in front of its nose, watching it climb on board before gently letting go. The ant scuttled off along it, vanishing into the tangled web.

'You're welcome,' he said, sitting up to stretch his spine, trying to shake the blood back into his legs. The knees of his jeans were wet. How did sand always manage to stay moist even on a day like today? He was brushing the blotchy stains with his hands when he heard a car, distant but unmistakable.

He ducked back down, peering through the mess of sea grass, his heartbeat rising along with the pitch of the engine. It seemed to take an eternity before it finally showed itself, the thing that trundled from the treeline not a car but one of those baby Land Rovers. There was something – *Blood?* – spattered all over the crumpled bonnet, as bright as paint. The passenger windows were wound down, or broken, and a massive crack stretched diagonally across the windscreen, making it difficult for him to see inside. The car limped over the concrete and pulled up next to the toilet block.

Nothing happened. Nobody got out.

'Come on,' Brick whispered. He worked his jaws, his ears feeling like they were blocked, the same way they did when he swam too deep. The strange silence clashed with the fear, making him feel weirdly seasick. The car was pointing straight at him and he got the feeling that whoever was inside was watching him, waiting for him to make his move. It was ridiculous, of course. Nobody would be able to spot him tucked behind the dune. Unless . . .

He looked to his left and right, scanning the beach.

What if the guy hadn't come alone? What if there was more than one of them? His friends might have spread out, flanking the car park, ready to attack him from all angles. He swore. Why hadn't he brought a weapon? Fursville was full of metal bars and old tools, there were even knives in the restaurant. All he had here were his own two fists.

It wasn't too late to retreat. If he slid down the dune he could walk back along the shore. They'd never be able to find him – *unless they follow your footsteps in the sand*. He swore again, his mind wheeling. He'd had hours to prepare for this, what the hell had he been doing all that time? Sunbathing and rescuing ants.

Calm down. You're panicking like an old woman. Keep it cool, it's going to be okay.

Was he supposed to make the first move? It was like one of those old spy films. He wiped a hand across his forehead, sand sticking to the sheen of sweat that had broken out there. He still felt that weird pressure in his head, a silence that was almost a sound. It was as though something was inside his brain, inside his thoughts, and he suddenly felt ridiculously exposed. He squinted, trying to make out the shape behind the steering wheel. There was definitely somebody there – *What did you expect, Brick, a ghost?* – but was that somebody in the passenger seat too?

The car horn blared and Brick almost screamed, his rasping cry lost in the flap of a dozen birds that took flight from the trees. Adrenalin was a white heat in his veins. Suddenly he was all too conscious of how uncomfortable he was, of the damp creeping into his clothes and the sand scratching in the crook of his elbows. The horn honked again, twice.

'Get out of the car,' he hissed into the dune. *I'm not showing myself until you do.*

His words were too quiet to carry, but they worked anyway. There was a loud clack, then the driver's door swung open with a painful squeal. Somebody clambered out, and Brick had to lean to the side to see him through a loop of sea grass. It was a kid dressed in grey tracksuit trousers and a T-shirt. The boy brushed a hand through his hair as he scanned the car park, looking maybe sixteen or seventeen.

'Hello?' the boy called out, the tremors audible in his voice even from where Brick was lying. More birds blasted from the trees and he spun round, his hand moving towards his lower back. There was something under there, Brick realised, a lump beneath his shirt. The kid had a weapon. Again that instinctive need to get away almost ripped him from the dune, numbed by the same weird, calm silence that sat like cotton wool inside his head.

'Is anyone there?' the boy called out, his words drifting effortlessly over the hot ground. 'Rick?'

Rick? Brick thought, before remembering his login name. He felt an answer surging up from inside him of its own accord when he heard the sound of the passenger door opening. He clamped his mouth shut as the boy shouted something at the car, gesturing at whoever was inside. Brick couldn't hear the reply but it didn't matter. The kid had broken the rules.

He began to retreat. This wasn't worth the risk. One teenage boy he could handle, but if there were two or maybe more in there then he was in trouble – especially if they started to attack him the same way as everyone else. The car was almost out of sight when the passenger climbed out. Brick paused, shuffling back to the top of the dune. The other person was a little girl, tiny next to the Land Rover, her face crumpled by anxiety. She was wearing black trousers and a burgundy polo with what might have been a school badge.

A boy and a kid, maybe brother and sister. Even if they did go crazy Brick thought he'd be able to handle them – so long as he took out the guy first he could easily outrun the girl.

I guess we're about to find out, he thought. Then he ran his hand over his forehead once more and got to his feet.

Cal

'There's nobody here,' Cal said to Daisy.

'Yes there is,' she replied, looking up at him. 'Don't you . . . don't you *feel* them?'

Cal shook his head, but there was something there, that same strange, ebbing sense of peace ringing round his skull. He swept his eyes over the car park again, nothing but cracked concrete and small drifts of sand. The toilets were boarded up, which was a definite re-lief. Some places were just plain creepy. The gun was tucked into the waistband of his trousers, and every time he nudged it back into place he worried he would set it off and blast away half of his backside. He should have left it in the car.

'See,' Daisy said. He followed her line of sight to the dunes that hid the sea from the car park. Somebody was walking down them, a tall man with hair so ginger that it glinted like copper in the fading sun. He was wearing jeans and a filthy white T-shirt, and his long, gangly arms were held out to his side, fingers spread.

'Is he going to hurt us?' Daisy asked, running to his side. Cal didn't reply, holding her tight with one hand. He felt the weight of the gun, cold and sharp against his back. *Please don't let me have to use it, please God let him be okay.*

The man – it was difficult to tell how old he was – stopped at the bottom of the dune, about ten or fifteen metres away. This close Cal could see the blood-stains on his T-shirt, looking more like chocolate in the growing pool of shadow. Dried blood pocked his face as well, an ugly looking wound above one eye. There was something about the guy that made Cal instantly suspicious, something in the bluntness of his cheekbones, the narrowness of his eyes. And yet there was something inside his head – more the absence of something, really – a feeling that was telling him it was okay, that the red-haired man was one of them.

All the same, for a good minute or so nobody moved, everybody wary of the same thing – that someone was about to start screaming, to charge across the car park fists flailing and teeth biting and eyes boiling. Those sixty-odd seconds seemed to stretch out forever, everything perfectly still, only the quiet lull of the unseen waves and the crack of the trees letting Cal know that time hadn't frozen.

Daisy was the first to stir. 'He isn't attacking us,' she whispered, looking up. The guy must have heard her because he snorted a laugh. His hands lowered to his sides, but he was still visibly tense.

'Are you Rick?' Cal asked.

The man squinted, holding up a hand to shield his eyes. The sun was over Cal's shoulders, nesting in the treetops, lighting the kid from the chest up. 'What do you think?' he said, his brow crinkling. 'I thought I told you to come alone.'

'Um, this is Daisy,' Cal said, feeling suddenly and overwhelmingly protective of the girl. 'I found her on the way. She's like—' he almost said *us*, but it was too soon for that. 'Like me, she got attacked too.'

Daisy lifted her hand and gave a flick of a wave.

'I'm Cal,' Cal went on. Then he ran out of things to say. The man watched warily, his eyes dodging back and forth between him and Daisy.

'CalMessiRonaldo,' he said. 'You like football, then?'

It was spoken more like an insult than a question so Cal didn't answer. He could feel his hackles rising. The gun slid further down the waistband of his trackies and he had to nudge it back. It was so heavy that if he wasn't careful he'd be standing here in a minute in nothing but his pants. The silence that followed was just about as awkward as silences could be.

'I'm Brick,' the guy said eventually.

'Brick?' asked Daisy. The man smiled, just a slight twitch of his lips but a smile nonetheless. It seemed to make his face more human.

'Because of my hair,' he said to her. 'It's the same colour as a brick.'

'No it's not,' she replied. 'Bricks are sort of pink and your hair is bright orange.'

Brick's smile grew, finally reaching his eyes. Cal could see that, despite his height, Brick wasn't much more than a boy himself.

'You can call me Carrot if you like,' he said. He looked back at Cal and the smile vanished. Seconds of silence ticked away, the gulls circling overhead like vultures. 'What's going on out there?'

'It's bad,' Cal said. 'You're the first person I've seen who hasn't tried to rip my head off, other than Daisy. It's like the whole world has gone insane.'

Brick nodded. He glanced to his right, then back at Cal.

'Yeah, it's really hit the fan alright.' He was chewing on something, and after a moment or two he spat it out. 'Gonna get dark soon. I've got a place, a safe place I think. It's about twenty minutes from here. No food or lights or anything—'

'We've got food,' interrupted Daisy. 'Got loads of stuff in the car. It's Cal's, not mine.'

'That's good,' Brick went on. 'It's not ideal but nobody knows about it. You can come if you want.'

Duh, thought Cal. *We just drove all this way to say hi but now we're gonna hit the road again. Of course we're coming.* But instead he said: 'Sure, okay, can we bring the car?'

Brick looked at the Freelander as if it was another unwelcome stranger. Cal shifted his weight, and as he did so he felt the heavy knuckle of metal slip from his waistband and down his legs. It hit the concrete with a crunch. Brick's eyes widened as he saw the gun there. Then, before Cal could say anything, he turned and ran.

'Wait!' Cal yelled. The guy was bolting with impressive speed, his arms and legs pistoning him back up the dune. 'Wait! It was just in case, I wasn't going to use it!'

Brick wasn't listening, practically vaulting over the dune in a shroud of kicked-up sand. Cal swore, then bent down and snatched the gun.

'Wait here!' he said to Daisy, legging it across the car park. He jumped onto the dune, his feet sinking as he charged upwards. He reached the top in time to see Brick sprinting down the beach.

'Brick, wait!' he shouted. The older boy didn't stop, didn't even slow. Cal started down the slope, making it four or five paces before realising that, as fast as he was, he was never going to catch up with him. Instead he lifted the gun, pointed it straight up and pulled the trigger.

The recoil juddered down his arm into his shoulder, ending up as a painful cramp beneath his ribs – so shocking that he almost dropped the revolver. His ear broke into a high-pitched song. It worked, though. Brick missed his footing and sprawled onto his face. He spun round, crawling backwards like a crab, the whites of his eyes visible even from where Cal was standing.

Cal kept the gun high, pointing towards the skies, half thinking that the bullet was going to come right back down and cave in his own head. He took a deep breath, gunpowder like firework smoke in his lungs.

'I'm not going to shoot you!' he yelled. 'I only brought the gun in case you were crazy. Look.' He lobbed the pistol towards Brick. It landed halfway between them, burrowing itself into the sand. Then he held his hands up, ignoring the part of his brain that was screaming at him – *You're an idiot, do you know what you've done? He's going to kill you now!* 'It's yours, take it, just don't leave us here, okay?'

Very slowly, Brick got to his feet. He was stooped over, hunched into himself like he was expecting another shot to come from somewhere else. He walked back through the craters of his own footsteps, picking up the gun by its barrel and holding it away from him. It reminded Cal of a kid carrying scissors.

There was a frantic puff of breath and Daisy appeared by Cal's side, grabbing his right hand with both of hers. They looked at Brick, who stood statue-like, the gun still held out before him, his shadow a huge lower-case 't' on the beach.

'Please don't leave us,' Daisy said. 'We weren't going to hurt you.'

It seemed to take an age for Brick to nod at her.

'We'd better go. The sound of that shot must have carried for miles.' He turned and walked slowly along the shore, keeping close to the water. 'Leave the car here. We don't want to leave tyre tracks. Just grab your stuff and follow me.'

Daisy

Daisy walked between the two boys, breaking into a trot every few seconds to keep up with their giant strides. She was exhausted, her legs aching from the sand and her hands from the two carrier bags she held, but she felt safe. Which was weird, really, considering she'd broken one of the most important rules, one of the things her mum and dad had drummed into her again and again and again. Never, *ever* talk to strangers. And *certainly never, ever, EVER* get into a strange boy's car and let him drive you across the country to meet another even stranger boy and then go with them both to a secret place that nobody else knows about.

She should have been more nervous, but that usual horrid feeling in her chest and stomach she got when she was scared – like there were living things crawling around inside her – just wasn't there. It might have still been the shock of what had happened. It might have been the fact that in the last few hours everything in her life, everything she knew about the world, had changed.

But there was something else, too.

'So, where are you from?' she heard Cal ask.

He was a few paces in front of her, a huge black duffel bag over his shoulder and the last carrier gripped

234

in one hand. The other boy was a few paces in front of him and he wasn't carrying anything except the gun. They were almost walking in line. The sea was still to their right, huge and shiny like a big bit of silver foil. The dunes rose to their left. The sun had dipped below them now, making the sand look more like wet cement. She jogged forward a few steps until she was by Cal's side again.

'Around here someplace?'

He's from the Larkman, Daisy thought idly. Which was weird because she'd never heard of the Larkman before.

'Norwich,' Brick grunted without looking back.

Oh, thought Daisy.

'A place called the Larkman, actually,' he went on. 'You won't have heard of it.'

'Cool,' said Cal. He smiled down at Daisy and she smiled back without having to think about it. Cal was nice, and she could trust him. Even if he hadn't saved her life she'd have known that. He wasn't from Norwich, he was from a place called Oak Minster or something. It made her think of a church made of wood. That little piece of knowledge floated in her brain like an ice cube in a glass of water, kind of see-through and almost invisible but definitely there. It made her head feel cold, not in a bad way.

'You okay?' Cal asked her. 'You want me to take those bags?'

'I'm okay,' she replied, not wanting to feel even more like a kid than she already did. With her parents not around any more – *Not gone, though; remember what Cal said, he could make things normal again* – she'd have to look after herself for a while. She couldn't expect these boys to, because everyone knew boys were a bit rubbish. She looked up at Brick's back. Even in the dark the bigger boy's hair seemed to glow orange. *He hates it*, she thought. *Not because of the colour, or because people tease him, but because it reminds him of his dad.* Her head was full of ice cubes, each one different, all of them clinking little bits of knowledge over her thoughts.

'Who did you say attacked you?' Cal asked. 'Your girlfriend, was it?'

Brick shot a look over his shoulder that was easy enough to read – *Don't go there* – but it softened after a moment. He bent down and picked up one of the little stones that littered the beach, lobbing it out into the sea. It went a long way. Daisy felt sorry for it, because it would be stuck in the cold, dark water for ages. Maybe forever.

'That's how it started, yeah,' he said as he walked. 'We were making out, y'know? Then she just went mental. She bit me.' He turned again and pointed at the wound above his eye. It looked dirty and horrible. 'Wasn't just that, though, she was proper psycho, tried to claw me to pieces. No reason, I didn't do anything. Then I went to the garage, to get help, and a load of people came after me. They wanted to kill me.'

He's not saying something, thought Daisy. And another ice cube floated by inside her mind, a dark corridor and some steps, a locked door at the bottom of them. This thought gave her a bad feeling, an unpleasant tickling in her stomach, and she pushed it away by focusing on the gulls that bobbed on the sea. They peered back at her, and their little eyes reminded her of the people who had attacked her – the ambulance man and Mrs Baird and all the neighbours and people she'd never seen before – because there was nothing at all in those eyes. They were hollow black marbles.

'You call the police or anything?' Cal asked.

Brick shook his head. 'They'd have come after me too. Don't know how I know that but I do.' He looked at Cal. 'You know it too.'

So did Daisy. Everyone would come after them, no matter where they went or what they did. Until they found a way to fix this, the whole world would have the fury. This wasn't another ice cube thought, this was a big flashing light in her head, impossible to ignore or push away.

'The fury,' said Brick, nodding as if Daisy had spoken it aloud. 'Question is why. Why us?'

The only answer to this was the sound of the sea as it lapped the beach with its foamy tongue, that and the gentle cries of the gulls settling into bed. Did they sleep on the water? That was odd. How did they not capsize in the middle of the night?

They walked in silence for a few more minutes, Daisy falling further and further behind as the soft, un-even ground took its toll on her legs. She tried to make sense of the other ice cubes. She could see one with a pretty girl reading a book. That was Cal's. There was another of a pier full of arcade machines that was too see-through to make any sense of. There were nasty ones, too: people screaming and biting and punching and kicking and chasing that belonged to both of the boys. Daisy surfed through them like someone channel flicking, not really understanding how these things could be in her head, unless she was imagining them.

After a while Brick moved off to the left, towards the dunes. Up ahead the beach narrowed, and she could make out a weird wooden thing – like a huge collapsed rope bridge – stretching over the sand into the sea. She jogged to catch up, almost stumbling. Cal waited for her at the bottom of the dune, Brick already halfway up.

'You sure you don't want me to take them?' he asked, hiking his bag up over his shoulder. 'I don't mind.'

'It's okay,' she said. 'I think we're almost there.'

How did she know that? She wasn't quite sure, she just did. Just like she knew she'd see a big wheel even before it rose over the top of the dune like a rusty metal sun. The ice cube image was almost exactly the same as the real one, laid over it and shimmering ever so slightly. Only in the ice cube the wheel was actually turning, people visible inside the rocking carriages. Could she smell doughnuts too? She blinked and the ice melted. The wheel was ancient, nothing like the big one in London she'd been on. Bits had even fallen off it, some of the metal poles in the middle and three or four carriages too. It looked like a giant that was missing some of its teeth.

Brick flapped gracelessly down the other side of the dune, towards a huge fence. Daisy saw that there wasn't just a Ferris wheel ahead but a whole theme park — there were two roller coasters, by the looks of things, and one of those rides that whizzed up and down and made you feel sick just looking at it, and a large square building with a roof like waves. Her heart lifted when she saw a carousel too, although she could only make out the painted, cone-shaped roof over the fence. She loved carousels! It was the closest she'd ever really come to riding a horse.

'It's a theme park,' she said.

Brick turned and somehow a smile managed to land on his sour face again.

'It used to be,' he said. 'Don't get excited, though. Nothing works any more. But it's safe, nobody ever comes here apart from me.'

It didn't matter if nothing worked, there still might be horses. In fact couldn't she see them now, like another one of those weird half-invisible thoughts that made her brain feel cold? She could see their kind eyes and their long noses and that horrible dark corridor and the steps going down and the locked door and something behind it that moaned.

Her skin went prickly and she ran to Cal, walking by his side as they followed Brick down the dune onto a concrete walkway. It ran alongside the fence, and about halfway down Brick squeezed through a gap and disappeared. He was waiting for them on the other side when they caught up.

'Watch you don't scratch yourself,' he said to Daisy. 'The wire is pretty sharp.'

Cal grabbed the fence and pulled it open and she looked at the gap. She searched inside herself, looking for warning signs, looking for those little electric currents that told her something bad might happen. But they weren't there. Other than that corridor and the locked door – *which might not even be real, which might just be in your head* – she felt absolutely one hundred per cent safe.

She crawled through the gap on her hands and knees, standing and dusting herself off as Cal followed. Brick shushed them out the way, grabbing a huge piece of wood on which she could make out the letters NDYFLOSS AN. He rested it over the fence, giving it a shove to make sure it was firmly in place. Even with the exit blocked Daisy couldn't feel the slightest trace of fear. In fact she couldn't remember ever being anywhere before where she'd felt quite as much like she was *supposed* to be.

Brick turned and stretched out his long, freckled arms. This time his smile was nervous, almost bashful.

'Cal, Daisy, welcome to Fursville.'

Cal

It could have been a romantic dinner, if it wasn't for the fact that he was eating a packet of prawn cocktail crisps and the person sitting opposite him, on the other side of the candlelit table, was an ugly ginger guy called Brick.

They were on the first floor of the pavilion, in the small restaurant called Waves. One side of the room was made up of floor-to-ceiling windows, but there was no sea view any more. They'd been boarded over from the outside, much of the glass cracked and stained so that the stuttering candle was reflected in it several times, making it seem like the room was alight. The whole place was an inch deep in dust and cobwebs, and the stench of sea rot hung in the air along with the smoke.

His discomfort must have shown because Brick snorted out another one of his not-quite-laughs.

'It's not the Four Seasons or anything,' he said.

'It's fine,' said Cal, funnelling the crumbs into his mouth then flattening the crisp packet against the mouldering tablecloth. Daisy lay on a small, damp chaise longue to their side. She'd climbed on it about five minutes ago and she was already fast asleep, her snores as soft as velvet. 'It's safe.'

'It's definitely safe. Nobody's ever here. Ever.'

That wasn't a surprise, from what they'd seen in the last half hour. Brick had given them a guided tour, acting like he worked here as he showed them the roller coaster and the log flume and the carousel and the dodgem track and the overgrown miniature golf course. What he really should have been doing, Cal thought, was showing them the emergency exits, the safest hideaways, the supplies, the weak points, the lookout areas. At the very least he could have pointed the way to the facilities. But no, he'd walked around muttering about arcade machines and doughnuts and which was the best seat to take on the flume if you didn't want to get wet – even though none of it even worked any more.

Cal hadn't said anything, though. It did seem quiet here, and from what he and Daisy had seen in the car on the drive up this part of the coast was as good as deserted. There would be plenty of time to shore the park up in case people came looking.

He sighed, hard enough to make the candlelight flutter. It was the first time he'd admitted to himself that this might not go away overnight. It might not go away at all.

'What?' Brick asked.

'Nothing. This whole thing, it doesn't seem real.'

'I know. Feels like another lifetime that I was riding out here with Lisa, that we were fine.'

Another lifetime, thought Cal. It really did. How long had it been since he was back at school playing football? Maybe ten hours. Ten hours for the rules of the universe to unravel around him, for everything he knew to turn to rot. It reminded him of a poem they'd done in English, but he couldn't remember how it went. Something about things falling apart. They sat in silence, both of them chewing their own thoughts as the candle guttered like a chesty breath, a death rattle.

'Your girlfriend,' said Cal. 'Lisa? What . . . I mean, er, is she—'

'You don't have to worry about her,' said Brick sharply, with a look that told Cal it would be better not to pursue the subject any further.

'You have any idea what might be causing this?' Cal asked, quickly changing tack. 'I mean I can't think of anything. Except genetics maybe.'

'Huh?' Brick grunted.

'Like cats. You know how some cats are, they just need to see another cat and they go for it. They fight to the death sometimes. Dogs too, I guess.'

Brick nodded, deep in thought.

'But something like that doesn't just happen,' he said eventually. 'You don't just flick a switch and everyone hates you.'

'It wasn't just that with me,' Cal said. Daisy stirred, snuffling and pressing her face into the chaise longue. He waited for her breathing to even out again before continuing. 'Things have been strange for a few days now. People were ignoring me, acting weird. I thought they were just playing games but . . .'

He didn't need to finish. Brick drew patterns in the

dust on the table, the nail on his forefinger a crescent moon of dirt and blood. When he lifted his arm Cal saw a circle with two x's for eyes, angry slanted eyebrows and a downturned mouth. A smiley without the smile. Somehow, without properly acknowledging the thought, he'd known that was what Brick was going to draw.

'The fury,' Brick mumbled, looking at his creation. 'Good name for it, right?'

'Certainly fits the bill,' Cal said. 'Why us, though? And why now?'

Brick's eyes met Cal's for a fraction of a second before bouncing off. He leant down and rummaged in a carrier bag – one that he'd picked up from the foyer as they were passing through. He hefted a laptop from it and laid it carefully on the table, covering up his dust drawing.

'I need to show you something,' he said as he opened the lid. Cal heard the whine of the hard drive coming to life, and the boy's face was suddenly bathed in a sickly white glow. Cal got up, wiping the dirt from his palms as he walked round the table. Brick was online, the browser showing the same Yahoo Answers page that Cal had seen back at home. He could see Rick_B's original message, and below that his own panicked response. Brick peered up, looking half his age from this angle. 'It's not just us,' he said.

'I know,' Cal replied, watching Brick's eyes widen. 'I saw it happen on the motorway, a ton of people on top of a car attacking somebody inside. It was someone like us. I'm not sure how, I just know it.'

He choked as the memory burned back, the flames from the explosion seeming to sear the flesh of his brain. Brick turned back to the screen. When he raised his dust-blackened finger to the trackpad it was shaking.

'It's not just that,' he said. 'You weren't the only person to reply. Look.'

He scrolled down the page slowly enough for Cal to read the eleven answers that followed his, all of them but two almost a carbon copy of his own. By the time he'd reached the last he felt like he'd run a marathon – that or been punched hard in the gut. He had to lean on the back of Brick's chair to stop his disco legs throwing him to the floor.

'That's from four hours ago,' Brick said, moving the pointer over the time of the last entry, 6.05 p.m. 'I haven't checked since then.'

He led the arrow up towards the refresh button and Cal almost screamed for him not to press it. He didn't want to see. He didn't want to know.

Brick clicked. The page loaded up painfully slowly. The Yahoo header, then the adverts, then the frame, then Brick's message. The answers followed, all together like they were being vomited onto the page.

All forty-eight of them.

'Jesus,' said Cal, and this time he had to sit on the chair to the left of Brick's. His whole body felt numb, cold. 'Please tell me they're not all real.'

Brick was scrolling down again, and his ghostly

pallor had nothing to do with the light from the screen. Cal watched the boy's face crumple into itself a little further with each new answer he read. It seemed like an age later when he finally turned his red, swimming eyes up. They looked at each other properly for the first time, and despite their differences they could have been mirror images.

'Brick?' Cal asked. 'What do they say?'

'The same thing,' he breathed, breaking away to the screen again. 'They're all exactly the same.'

'What do we do?' Brick didn't reply, the candlelight giving his skin a waxwork sheen. *Like he isn't real; like none of this is real*, Cal's brain insisted. *How can it be? How can this be happening?* 'Brick, what do we do?'

Brick looked up, and this time when their eyes met, Cal knew exactly what Brick was thinking.

'We tell them,' Cal said. 'We tell them about this place.'

'We have to,' Brick confirmed. 'I don't want to but we have to. Look, you and me, we haven't killed each other, or Daisy. If we're . . .'

'Different,' Cal said when he saw him struggling.

'If we're different, if there's something about us that's different from the others, from the Fury' – *He's given it a capital F*, Cal realised, *it's more than just a word now* – 'then we have to get together, as many of us as we can. It's the only way we can be safe, we can figure it out.'

'But you can't tell them where we are,' Cal said. 'Not on there, what if the others find us? Brick, we need to think about this.'

'We don't have time,' he replied, tapping his finger on the top of the screen. Cal noticed the battery icon there, red and flashing. 'It's about to shut down and there's no power here.'

Cal swore, loud enough to stir Daisy again. She wriggled over, opening her eyes and seeing him. By the time her distant, dreamer's smile had faded she was asleep again.

'Look,' said Brick quietly. 'I won't tell them about Fursville. There's a second-hand car showroom just over the road, it's empty. I'll tell them to go there and wait for someone to come to them. We can keep watch on the place, and if anything looks suspicious we just won't show ourselves. Yeah?'

Cal shook his head.

'Yeah?' Brick repeated.

'Okay,' Cal said, throwing his hands in the air. 'Okay, whatever.'

Brick was already typing:

You're not alone. We have a safe place, there's a few of us here and we're not attacking each other. If you can get to us, we're in a town called Hemmingway, in Norfolk, right on the beach, up from Hemsby. On the main coast road there's an abandoned car showroom, called Soapy's. Go there and wait, we'll check it at noon every day.

He stopped, running both hands through his hair.

'Will that do?' he asked. Cal didn't reply. Brick read it through once more, the pointer hovering over the Post Reply button. 'I guess it will have to.'

He clicked, and five seconds later the post appeared on the refreshed page.

'You know it's not gonna take a genius to work out that if we're not in the showroom we're gonna be in the bloody great big empty amusement park next door,' Cal said, slumping back. 'We should have met them at the car park.'

'It's too far away,' Brick said. 'We'd have to make that slog every day. It's not safe.'

'*This* isn't safe,' Cal snapped back. Brick closed the laptop, tapping his fingers on it. 'We need to make extra sure this place is secure,' Cal went on. 'Seal up the fence, have an emergency plan, just in case.'

It took Brick a moment to look up. He stared at Cal, but it seemed that he was peering through him, at something much deeper.

'Things fall apart,' he said, his voice as low as the guttering candle. Cal shook his head as the poem he couldn't remember, the one he'd learned at school, tumbled from Brick's lips. 'The centre cannot hold. Mere anarchy is loosed upon the world.'

Brick looked away, firelight burning in his eyes as he finished.

'The blood-dimmed tide is loosed. And goddamned everywhere the ceremony of innocence is drowned.'

The Other: II

In his presence the mountains quake,
and the hills melt away;
the earth trembles, and its people are destroyed.
Who can stand before his fierce anger?
Who can survive his burning fury?
His rage blazes forth like fire,
and the mountains crumble to dust in his presence.

Nahum 1:5–6

Murdoch

'Look, I just want to know what's going on.'

Detective Inspector Alan Murdoch had been speaking the same words to the same locked door for the better part of three hours. And it was nearly twenty-four hours now since he'd been bundled into a car along with Jorgensen and his assistants from the morgue and taken to the massive MI5 HQ by the Thames. He was being treated like a terrorist, as though somehow he was responsible for the freak corpse and its endless breath. When he'd first arrived they'd strapped him with diodes and sensors and asked him question after question, blatantly refusing to answer any of his. And after that he'd been thrown into this basement room to rot.

He hadn't even been allowed to call his wife. His mobile phone and police radio had been confiscated; so had his warrant card. He was supposed to have been home this time yesterday, she'd be worried sick. He felt something shift in his gut, the dread of never seeing her again, of never holding his baby boy.

You're being ridiculous. It's the exhaustion talking. Only he knew it wasn't. He'd seen it, this impossible thing, this living corpse which made a mockery out of everything he knew. Reality had begun to crumble,

251

and here he was with a front-row seat to the end of it all.

'I really am sorry,' said Jorgensen for what must have been the hundredth time that day. He sat on the other side of the small room – no, the *cell* – looking a hundred years old. 'I never should have called you in, Alan.'

No, you bloody well shouldn't have, Murdoch thought, saying: 'This isn't your fault, Sven. You were just doing your job.'

The pathologist gave him a weary smile then planted his head back in his hands. Murdoch slammed his fist against the door, hard enough to hurt.

'You've got no right to keep us in here, dammit,' he roared. They'd been given water and a sandwich each but that had been hours ago. Murdoch's hunger was lost behind the rage inside his gut. 'I'm a police officer, I have a right to know what's going on.'

Rights. Murdoch laughed bitterly. He had no rights, not here, not in the heart of the government's secret service. They could hold him forever and make sure nobody ever asked any questions. But *why*?

There was a metallic clang from outside the door, followed by footsteps. A key turned, then the door swung out to reveal a man and a woman in orderly uniforms. The man was holding a tray with more sandwiches and two bottles of water. He started to walk in but Murdoch barred his way.

'You can't keep us here,' he said. 'I demand to see your commanding officer.'

'I'm sorry, sir,' said the woman. 'I'm afraid nobody is

available to speak to you right now.'

'Please wait inside the room,' added the man, and there was a definite *or else* that he left unvoiced.

Murdoch bit his tongue, looking past the orderlies to see a long, windowless corridor. At the end of it was a reinforced metal door, guarded by armed men. Murdoch knew that's where it was, the living corpse. The thought of it there, so close, made him shudder. Even as he watched, the door opened and a group of people walked out. They wore a mix of uniforms – some military top brass, some white surgical coats – but they all wore the same expression of fear. They strode down the corridor and turned out of sight.

'Look,' said Murdoch, forcing himself to stay calm. 'I don't want to cause any trouble, I just want to go home. My wife, she doesn't know where I am. Can you at least tell me how long you're going to keep us here?'

The orderlies must have seen the desperation in his gaunt face, because their expressions softened.

'The truth is, we don't know,' said the woman. 'There's something . . . They're saying it's something bad, really bad. They're holding anyone who's had any contact with it. Did you see it?'

'Yeah,' said Murdoch, sighing. 'And they're right, it's bad.'

'Take this,' said the man, passing the tray to Murdoch. 'It might be over soon, they're bringing in some kind of expert. With any luck they'll be able to work out what's going on and get you guys out of here.'

'An expert?' said Jorgensen, walking over. 'What kind of expert?'

The man shrugged, saying, 'Just somebody who might know what this thing is.'

And what it wants, Murdoch's mind added.

The sound of voices rose up, a group of soldiers walking out of the same corridor the others had left by. They headed up towards the guarded door and Murdoch saw somebody else with them, somebody dressed in black robes. The orderly looked over her shoulder.

'That's him now,' she said.

'The *expert*?' Jorgensen asked. The man and woman nodded.

'No way,' Murdoch said, scarcely able to believe what he was seeing. The soldiers reached the door and the man turned, revealing the white collar around his neck, the heavy crucifix that hung over his chest. The expert wasn't a scientist or a doctor or a general.

He was a priest.

Saturday

The fiend in his own shape is less hideous than when he rages in the breast of men.

Nathaniel Hawthorne, 'Young Goodman Brown'

Rilke

'We shouldn't be doing this.'

Rilke Bastion ignored her brother the way she had learned to do through years of practice. He trotted along by her side as if he were a dog, not her fifteen-year-old twin, his sad little face turned up to her with those puppy-moist eyes. If Schiller had a tail, it would be permanently fixed between his legs.

'Rilke, please, mother will be angry.'

Their mother wouldn't even know. She was cocooned in the same musty, tea-stained sheets she spent half her life in. She spent the other half in the old-fashioned wooden bath chair that sat wheel-locked beside the huge windows in her bedroom suite, her eyes watching over the estate but her mind rotted, unthinking.

'Please, Rilke, I don't want to go.'

His canine whine was a knifepoint in her ears, making the headache she'd had for at least two days now infinitely worse. She stopped, spinning round and grabbing Schiller by the collar. Looking into his face was so like looking at her own reflection, and yet utterly different. She could see the same high cheekbones, the same sharp green eyes, the same narrow nose. And yet it was as though she were staring into a trick mirror, one of the ones that distorted your image, making her chin too weak, her jowls too loose, her eyes too watery. She glared at Schiller until he looked away, as he always did. Only then did she release him.

'Go on, then,' she said as he brushed his hands down his polo shirt, trying to get the creases out. 'Go home.'

Schiller peered down the street where the vast bulk of St Peter's Church sat like a mountain in the dark. A mile or so past that lay home, the crumbling manor house entombed in the shadows of its endless grounds.

'Go on,' she snapped. 'What are you waiting for? If you're going back then go. I'm finding this party with or without you.'

'But I don't feel too good,' Schiller replied, rubbing his left temple. His eyes darted up, meeting hers for a fraction of a second. The truth was that she wasn't feeling too good either, her head was pounding. But she ignored the throb, glaring at her brother until his hand dropped in submission. 'Okay, but I don't want to stay all night. Please, Rilke.'

Good boy, she thought. *Good dog.* She patted him on the head, hard enough to make him flinch. Then she turned and carried on down the street. She'd heard about the party from a cleaner called Millie who worked part-time at the estate. Not that Millie had told her to her face – none of the staff dared talk to Rilke. She'd overheard the girl chatting to one of her friends when they were dusting the library. An illegal rave, she'd called it, and they'd giggled at the word 'illegal'. *It'll be cool, just music and stuff, come along, it's not far out of town, you know the Logan farm up by the coast.*

'Not all night, though?' Schiller said to her back. 'Please?'

'All night, little brother,' she said. She always called him that, even though he was technically a few minutes older. 'Till the birds start singing.'

Farlen wasn't a big town. Some people didn't even call it a town at all, more like a village with an ego. It had grown up around their own house, centuries ago, back when the Bastion family was rich and influential. Over the last couple of generations the estate had crumbled under its own weight, the huge house disintegrating, rats gnawing at its foundations and pigeon droppings eating through its rafters. And the town seemed to be under the same curse.

Good riddance to it, Rilke thought as they reached the end of the high street and the boarded-up shops that sat there. The line of lights ended, a pool of bottomless black beyond looking like the edge of the world. The stars were out, the moon too, but the cool silver glow they emitted was reluctant.

A pang of something nestled uncomfortably in her stomach. She slowed, opening her arm and letting Schiller slide his own through the loop. He hugged it tight, and she could feel his gratitude ebbing off him in great, golden waves.

'I love you, little brother,' she said. 'You know I won't let anything happen to you.'

'I know,' he whispered as they stepped out of the light. Rilke slid the torch from her jacket pocket, flicking on the beam and carving a channel through the night like Moses with the Red Sea. She pulled Schiller closer, picking up the pace and practically dragging him along by her side.

'Come on,' she said. 'It's not far.'

☹

The music hit her at the same time as the stench of the ocean.

She hated that smell. What did they say? That in Britain you were never more than seventy miles from the sea. And every year it seemed to creep in a little closer, eroding the beach and the cliffs, rotting the land away a few metres at a time. It was the vast weight of it that scared her, not just its width – spanning the gulf between continents – but its unthinkable depth. There was just so much of it, and if one day it decided to swell, to spill its lightless guts onto the land, it could wipe the world clean without a second thought. A frightening thought, if not necessarily a bad one. There wasn't much in this world that made Rilke smile.

She breathed through her mouth, focusing on the glow ahead. Spotlights rose from a stubbled field maybe half a mile away, throwing light right back at the stars and the huge grinning face of the moon. The music was nothing more than a pulse that she could feel in her feet, as if the very ground were alive. The truth was she hated this kind of party, the people you got there, all high on something or drunk off their faces. All stupid, the same way most people were stupid. But it had to be better than another night of unrelenting boredom at home. Rilke had never been a big sleeper.

She shone her torch on the short, grassy bank then stumbled up it, Schiller's arm still limpet-tight around hers. It was tough going on the uneven ground but the earth was hard and she kept her pace steady, sticking to the same ploughed furrow. The heartbeat grew more powerful the closer they got, popping in her ears, brushing against her skin. It found an echo in the pain between her temples – *thump-thump . . . thump-thump . . . thump-thump* – like something was stuck inside her skull and trying to beat its way out. She picked up her pace, the rave pulling itself out of the distance like a cathedral of light.

They were halfway across the field when Schiller stopped, planting his feet into the dry earth like an anchor. She turned, shining the beam into his face.

'I don't want to go,' he moaned, squinting in the harsh light. 'I'm scared.'

'You're such a baby, Schill,' she replied, wrenching him forward. He dug in, fighting.

'Something bad is going to happen,' he went on.

'Don't be stupid.' And yet even as she said the words she felt something inside her, something in her gut, scream out – *He's right, he's right, he's right* – a wordless, instinctive jolt of adrenalin. The rave was close enough for her to see the ring of vans and cars that circled the party like wagons; and past them the heaving mass of flesh that seemed to breathe in and out with that bone-shaking heartbeat.

Rilke swallowed, suddenly cold. She almost retreated

right there, ready to lead the way back across the field towards home. But once again that stubborn streak stopped her in her tracks, made her bury that instinctive warning. The Bastion family had always been driven by its women. They were the ones to lead.

She clenched her arm, trapping Schiller's tight and pulling him across the field. *He needs a leash*, she thought. They walked for another minute or so, the crowd ahead coalescing into individuals – guys and girls in their teens and twenties pretty much all wearing glow sticks. Most were inside the ring of vehicles but others were loitering in the shadows around the party, talking or kissing or lost in their own private drug-induced dances. There was nothing to be scared of here. She'd stay for an hour or so, just to see what it was like, just to have had the experience, then they'd go. She'd pretend to be leaving for Schiller's sake, that way he would owe her.

He was resisting again. Rilke looked over her shoulder, not slowing. He said something, his words lost in the deafening bass thump that seemed to rise from the earth. *What?* she mouthed, shrugging her shoulders, waiting for him to start moaning again. But he wasn't.

'My head,' he yelled, leaning in close. 'It doesn't hurt any more.'

She was about to reply when she realised that the ache in her own brain had gone, so swiftly and so suddenly that she hadn't even noticed. She put a hand against the side of Schiller's head, stroking his temple with her thumb.

'See, little brother,' she shouted, smiling. 'What did I tell you? Everything is fine.'

He couldn't have heard what she said over the noise but he smiled back, the reflected spotlights making his eyes twinkle.

It didn't last.

She knew what he was looking at before she could even turn round, like she'd seen it with her own eyes – two people, a man and a teenage girl, stumbling towards them. And there was more – a flash of something else, something that smelled of rot, a girl and two boys asleep in an old restaurant, someone else walking through a forest, someone else driving a car, then a dozen more, two dozen maybe. The images were so strong that she was gripped by vertigo, as though she'd been wrenched out of her own body and thrown into a lightning-fast orbit.

Schiller called out her name and she spun round. The man and the girl were sprinting towards her, *fast*, uttering pig grunts as they gained ground. There were others too, the kids that had been loitering outside the party, charging across the field.

They all had the same expression, silhouetted against the lights but unmistakable. They were furious. These people meant to kill them both, Rilke understood – the knowledge absolute and unquestionable. They meant to trample them into the field, to make mud of them.

She gave Schiller a shove, yelling at him:

'Run!'

Brick

He swam up from an ocean of darkness, breaching it like a swimmer who has gone too deep, expecting to feel warmth and daylight on his face but instead rising into an endless, heatless night. He tried to take a breath, couldn't remember how, his lungs screaming at him.

He could see the new kid, Cal, right there, giving off his own weird light like some deep-sea jellyfish. The boy was struggling in the torrent of darkness, his eyes bulging, his mouth gasping like a fish. And behind him, visible over his shoulder, a tiny form that could only be Daisy, her twig-thin limbs clawing at the water, trying to find the surface.

He reached out, noticing that his own skin seemed to be glowing, as though he were radioactive. He stretched, trying to grab hold of Cal, willing the kid to grab hold of the girl, all of them kicking upwards.

Brick woke, his screams more like barks as he coughed up darkness. He pushed himself to his feet, his chair toppling over behind him. There was still no light, but he could feel the ground under him, could feel the pain in his cheek where he'd been sleeping on his laptop. There was something else, too, a ringing in his ears that was also profoundly silent, inverted cathedral bells whose peals were each a gaping absence inside his head.

Daisy cried out, her voice pinched by fear. Brick screwed his eyes shut, even though there was no light, trying to remember where she was.

'It's okay,' he called out, edging around the table, feeling for the matches. 'Don't worry, we're here.'

She began to cry even harder, and he heard a thump as she rolled off the chaise longue.

'Daisy don't move, you'll hurt yourself, just hang on.'

He found the candle, burned down to the stick, and beside it – *bingo*, a box of matches. He carefully pulled one out, striking it on the box, the tiny flame filling the huge restaurant with soft light. Daisy stood by the sofa, her arms out, her sobs muted as she studied the burning match.

'Here,' said another voice, and Brick turned to see Cal walking over from the far side of the room. He held a candle out and Brick lit it, placing it on the table. Daisy saw Cal and came running over, hugging him tight, her eyes still full of sleep. 'You okay?' Cal asked her. 'You have a bad dream?'

'We were drowning,' she said into his T-shirt. 'You were there, and the other boy too.'

'Brick,' reminded Brick. Cal looked at him, and when their eyes met Brick realised the boy had been locked inside exactly the same nightmare. Not only that, but he knew that if he'd waved in his dream, the others would have seen it. That ringing in his ears seemed to grow louder, and yet infinitely quieter, and he worked his jaw to try and unblock his ears. It was a second or two before he noticed that Cal was doing the same thing.

'You hear that too?' he asked.

'Bells,' Cal replied.

Daisy pulled her head from his chest and jammed a finger in her ear.

'They're too loud,' she said. 'But not loud. I can't really hear them. I don't like it.'

'I've had this before,' Cal said to Brick, his hand gently smoothing back Daisy's ruffled hair. 'My head was . . . I don't know, like full of sound but empty at the same time. It led me to Daisy.'

And just like that Brick knew exactly what he was hearing. They all did, a moment of understanding that passed between them as easily as the reflection of the candlelight in their eyes.

'It's one of us,' said Brick.

Cal nodded, saying, 'And they need help.'

Rilke

The first of the crowd, the man, was nearly on them. Rilke bent down, scrabbling on the field until her hand closed over a stone the size of a satsuma. She waited until he was close – his animal grimace a jagged, toothy chasm that split his face in two – then she lobbed the stone at him with every ounce of strength she had.

It struck his nose with the sound that a milk bottle makes when it's dropped on a stone floor, and the man fell. Rilke bent down, looking for another missile, but it was too late. The teenage girl slammed into her, sending them both tumbling over the field. Corn stalks dug into her arms and legs, the wind punched from her as the girl's elbow hit her solar plexus. By the time she'd worked out which way was up the girl was on her chest, knees gouging her ribs and claws raking down her cheeks.

Rilke shrieked, the gargled sound that spilled from her own lips somehow more terrifying than the assault. There was no pain, just the roar of her blood. She lashed out, thumping her attacker in the cheek then grabbing a handful of soil, rubbing it into the girl's eyes and forcing her back.

Another howl. Rilke looked up in time to see some dreadlocked guy about to take a punt at her head.

She rolled, the girl spilling from her, the man's foot swinging wide and sending him tumbling off balance. She scrambled to her feet, each breath a shriek. There were more people coming now, maybe ten or twenty of them.

'Schiller!' she yelled, ducking as another girl swung a punch. She kicked, her foot connecting with the girl's knee and unleashing a pistol crack. Where was he? There was only the crowd, tearing relentlessly forward. If she couldn't find him then they were both dead.

There, fifteen metres or so away, a bundle of shadow that had too many arms and legs. It had to be him.

Rilke ran, slipping on the loose soil and nearly going over. The tremors she felt beneath her feet were now nothing to do with the music that still played. She didn't look back, knowing that to do so would kill her. The only thing that mattered was reaching Schiller.

She could hear him now, his brittle cries. He was lying on the ground, a man sitting on his stomach choking him with fluorescent orange fingerless gloves. Schiller's eyes were the size of pickled eggs, looking like they were about to pop right out of his head, his own hands batting pathetically at his attacker.

'*GET OFF HIM!*' Rilke screamed. She was a dozen yards away now, her fist bunched and held over her head ready to cave the bastard's face in.

Someone behind her clipped her foot and she went flying, momentum flipping her body over in a clumsy somersault. A weight dropped on her back and this time there was pain, a buckle of white heat that burned up her spine. A fist connected with the back of her head, pushing her face into the dirt. Then another, like a sledgehammer. She tried to breathe but found only soil and wormstench. Somebody had hold of her right hand, bending it backwards.

She was going to die. They were going to kill her in this very field, a mile from where she lived. They would bury her here, and nobody would ever find her. It was an impossible thought, too crazy to be real. Too insane to believe.

They're going to kill Schiller too. Those screams of his will be the last thing you ever hear. And *that* wasn't impossible. *That* wasn't crazy. That was all too real. They would kill her brother, stomp him into the ground.

No. She wouldn't let them. They couldn't have him.

Rilke wrenched her head up so hard she thought her neck would snap. She reached behind with her left hand, grabbing a fistful of flesh and squeezing hard. There was another grunt, this one laced with pain. The weight on her back shifted – not much but enough for her to worm her way forward. Schiller was ahead, almost close enough to touch. There were four or five people over him now, each one different and yet each one wearing that same fury-filled expression. Their hands and feet rose and fell, rose and fell, like pistons, like some horrific machine. Yet Schiller was still alive. She could see him through the gaps in the crowd, a hand held out towards her.

If she could just reach him . . . *What? You can die here holding hands?* No, it was something more than that.

Something else.

A knuckled weight crunched down on her leg, another on her shoulder. She didn't stop, crawling forward with everything she had. She reached for Schiller, the distance between them mere centimetres now but at the same time a vast, abysmal chasm.

'Schill,' she spoke his name through blood, but he heard her, turning his red, disbelieving eyes her way.

'Rilke.' He stretched, his fingers crawling over the soil. She grasped for him, the gap shrinking from five centimetres to four, to three, to two.

Their fingertips touched and the world burst into cold, dark fire.

Daisy

'Did it work?' asked Cal.

'Did what work?' said Brick. 'Standing here like a bunch of idiots holding hands?'

They were doing exactly that, huddled in a circle in the flickering light of the restaurant. Daisy wasn't sure why. She couldn't remember whose idea it had been. It had just happened, the same instinct that makes you flinch when somebody throws a punch, that makes you seek shelter when you hear thunder.

'It worked,' said Daisy, freeing herself from Brick's huge, clammy palm. Brick pulled his other hand out of Cal's, both boys wiping their hands on their clothes as though they had poison on them. Cal held on to her for a moment longer, giving her a gentle squeeze before letting go.

'How do you know?' he asked.

'I just do,' she replied. And she did. She'd seen it in her head, inside one of those little ice cubes. Although *seen* was the wrong word. She hadn't really seen anything, she'd just felt it. But what exactly had she felt? Two people, or maybe just one, they were so similar she couldn't be sure. They'd been scared, they'd been in pain. They'd been about to die.

But then what?

271

Daisy didn't know for sure, but she understood that the three of them – her, Cal and Brick – had helped. They'd done *something*. She could still sense the person, or the two people – the *twins*, she realised with a sharp intake of breath. Only there was something different about them, something she couldn't quite put her finger on.

They were coming here, though. That much was clear. Daisy frowned, trying to remember more, trying to see inside those transparent, clinking movies that played inside her mind. There was something there that frightened her, something that burned, but she couldn't work out what it was.

'What now?' asked Brick. 'We light some joss sticks and sing "Kumbaya"?'

Daisy didn't reply, she just stared at the fire inside her head, trying to work out what was wrong, and why she felt so scared.

Rilke

Rilke's first thought was that she'd died.

The thought that followed was that she couldn't have died, because she was still thinking. Then came the realisation that she couldn't have died because she was in *pain*.

She opened her eyes, the lids sticky as if she'd been asleep for a week. The stars were moving, spiralling across the infinite black canvas of the sky. Her ears were humming. Her whole body seemed to be locked tight with a muted, throbbing ache. Smoke clawed its way into her nose. It filled her head too, draping heavy shadows over her thoughts, her memories.

Why was she here?

Schiller, her brain told her, and at once her paralysis snapped free. She sat up, a jet of milk-white vomit erupting from her mouth without warning. She held her stomach with one hand, wiping spit away with the other. Stars drifted down from the night, landing on her face and the field beside her, glowing fiercely. She held out her hand, letting one settle on it. The spark guttered then died. *We knocked the stars from the sky*, she thought. *Our fingers touched and we knocked loose the stars*.

Only they weren't stars. How could they be? They were ashes, like the flickering embers from a bonfire.

They filled the air, dancing on their own heat. She looked through them, the world gradually coming into focus. Schiller was there, lying next to her. His face was a mosaic of bruises, blood running freely from his nose and his mouth. But he was alive. Seeing him like that brought everything back, and Rilke staggered to her feet, ready to defend herself from another attack.

There was nobody there.

Not only was there nobody there, she didn't know exactly where 'there' was. They were in a field, a *different* field. This one had something growing in it – a carpet of fat leaves painted silver by the moon. There was a glow against the horizon, and it took her a minute to understand that she was looking at the party, the rave. The distant crowd danced in the weak glow as if nothing had happened. She looked back at her brother, her brain desperately trying to put the pieces together, trying to make some kind of sense of what had just happened.

'Schill?' she asked. 'Are you okay?'

He didn't reply, didn't show any sign that he'd heard her. Rilke crouched down beside him, pressing two fingers against his throat and feeling the pulse there, faint but steady. But he was cold, he was *freezing*. Touching him was like picking up a glass of ice water, and Rilke had to pull her hand away after a minute or so as the numbing chill crept into it.

'Schiller,' she said again, shaking the blood back down her arm. 'Talk to me. Please.'

He was in shock. He had to be. He'd taken a pretty

bad beating, they both had. But how had they got from over there, getting the life stamped out of them by a bunch of stoned strangers, to right here? *I fought them*, her brain argued, picking strands of logic from the confusion. She looked down at her hands, stained pink like she'd been cutting up beetroot. *I fought them, and we ran, and it was so terrifying that I've already blocked it out*. That had to be it, didn't it? She wished she had a watch, or a phone, so she could check the time.

And so you can call an ambulance, right?

No. She wasn't going to do that. There was no precise reason why not, only that she knew it would be the wrong thing to do. There was an image in her head, a picture, a memory that she had no actual memory of – a paramedic in his green overalls, his face somehow a horse's face as he threw himself at her, as he pushed her through a window.

Somebody cried out from the direction of the party, a word she couldn't make any sense of. She tapped her pocket, feeling for the torch but not finding it. It was probably better this way. If they saw the light then they might come after her again. They might be coming after her now, feet pounding through the darkness, fists clenched, that same depthless rage burning through their faces.

The Fury.

'We need to go,' she said, lifting one of her brother's arms and looping it around her shoulders. She braced herself, pushing up with her legs, his body rag-doll loose against hers. 'Schiller,' she snapped, his name seeming to echo against the night. 'Pull it together. We need to get out of here.'

His head lolled against his chest, swinging from side to side like a nodding dog on a car's parcel shelf. She looked over her shoulder to the party, trying to get her bearings in the dark. If she was where she thought she was then the road back into town was way off to her right. But that's not where she was headed.

'Fursville,' she whispered, the word ridiculous, meaningless, and yet the only thing she could think of. She caught a glimpse of a roller coaster, the wood rotting, a deserted restaurant. This was where she was supposed to go. And somehow she knew how to get there, too, something inside her head pulling at her, leading her.

You're crazy, her head told her. *Go to the hospital, get Schiller some help. He'll die if you don't.*

Only she wasn't crazy. This was something else. The swarm of ashes had calmed, but they were still falling, darting like fireflies. She held out her free hand and caught another one, a fragment of charred pink leather that flickered and died in her palm. Another followed, this one a burning scrap of fluorescent orange – *Like the man's gloves, those fingerless gloves around Schiller's throat, choking the life from him* – which took flight again after a second or two, rising back into the night.

Yes, this was definitely something else.

She hoisted Schiller up and started walking. He didn't give her any help but she hauled him after her step after step after step. The cold that was coming off him was unbelievable, like she was walking through the middle of a blizzard. This wasn't something a doctor could sling a bandage on or temper with antibiotics. Schiller didn't need a hospital, he needed whatever lay inside the place in her head, that abandoned theme park called Fursville.

Right?

She pushed the questions away, locking on to those instincts, to her absolute gut belief that what she was doing was okay. The sea wasn't far from here, and the little boat yard that belonged to the neighbouring village. She could hotwire one of the old roll-ups or dinghies. She'd done it before. It was a clear night, no wind, they could be there – wherever *there* was – before dawn. All she had to do was follow that feeling in her head, that guide rope tugging gently on her thoughts.

Shivering, her teeth chattering so hard she was worried the ravers might hear them, Rilke kicked her way through the ash and the dirt, heading for the sea, heading for Fursville, heading for answers.

Brick

Waking was easier this time, apart from the dull ache that sat in every muscle. Brick sat up, rubbing both hands through his hair and yawning so hard his jaw popped. Beads of light pearled through the cracks in the boards over the windows, hanging on the dust and revealing Daisy on the sofa, Cal lying on the floor beside her, both still fast asleep.

What had happened last night? They'd sensed something, or someone. It had been Daisy's idea to try and send them a message, a mental picture of Fursville. It had seemed like a good idea in the dead of night, but daylight had a habit of bringing reality with it, common sense. Brick felt his cheeks burn at the thought of the three of them standing hand in hand in the middle of the restaurant beaming psychic baloney out across time and space.

He made his way towards the door, careful not to nudge any of the chairs or tables. He increased his speed once he was out in the corridor, hurrying past the peeling menus and special-deal posters – *Upgrade to a large haddock or cod for an extra 30p!* – and down the steps into the foyer. The light here was brighter, making his eyes sting, and he was almost glad to be back in the service corridor that led towards the fire exit.

Until he reached the basement steps.

He stopped, his heart jackhammering in his throat. If Lisa was alive – *Of course she's alive, it's only been a day and she's got food and water and just don't think about her injuries, Brick, don't even think about them* – then this was about as close to her as he could get without her going nuts again. Without her getting the Fury.

He cleared his throat, then he called out her name. The word was a sigh, deafening to Brick but too soft to carry. He looked right and left, trying not to think about what might have happened if she'd got out, if she was loose inside the building. He imagined her hands reaching from the shadows, those broken finger-nails scraping down his face.

Something moved behind the oil-black darkness at the bottom of the steps, a shuffling thump.

'Brick?' Her faint voice almost knocked him to his knees. His eyes burned again, tears flowing before he even knew he was crying – *Thank God, thank God she's alive, she's okay* – and he put his hand against the wall, hoping that somehow his touch might travel down into the basement, warm against her cheek. 'Please let me out,' it sounded like she was speaking through a mouthful of toffee, but she seemed stronger than she had yesterday. 'Brick? It's not too late.'

'It's okay, Lisa,' he called back. 'There are more of us now, we'll think of something together, okay?'

'Please Brick, just let me out and we can talk about this, I'm not . . . I'm not angry at you.'

'I know,' he said. 'I know you're not. I know you

don't understand. I don't either, but . . .'

But what? But he'd find a way to fix it? *Because you're a scientist, yeah? Because you're really clever, because you can work all this out then put that genius head of yours into gear and make everything better? Right.* He slapped his hand against his forehead, knocking the voice away.

'I will,' he answered it. 'I will fix you, Lisa. I . . .'

I love you, the words were there, but his mouth didn't know how to shape them.

'I'll make it so things are like they were,' he went on, those three unspoken words burning a hole in his throat. 'I swear I will. Just hang on, remember to drink, I'm right here, I won't leave you.'

There was another thump, a crash this time, and at first Brick thought Lisa was throwing herself at the door again. He took a step back, trying to get out of her radar, or whatever it was that set off the Fury. It was only when he heard it again – a pounding, like fists on wood – that he realised it wasn't coming from the basement.

It was coming from outside.

It's the police, they've come for you.

He moved down the corridor towards the fire exit and crept under the chains, his whole body on alert, ready to bolt at the first sign of a flashing blue light. He was fast, he could outrun them. *Can you outrun the dogs, too? The helicopters?* But there were no sirens, no loudspeakered demands, no thunder of chopper blades. There was just that same rattling thump.

Brick swallowed, realising that his head was filled

with the same muted numbness as the previous night – that weird inverted silence. With that realisation the fear sloughed away. Whoever was out there, it wasn't the police. He started across the overgrown path, walking past the crazy golf and the one-eyed giant squirrel, heading for the seaward side of the park. By the time he'd reached the storage sheds that ran along the back of the pavilion he could hear a voice too. The sound of the sea disguised the words but he was pretty sure it was a girl.

'Hello?' he called out. Maybe he should go back, wake the others. He could get the gun, too, just in case. But despite his nagging worries he didn't feel in any danger. He walked alongside the nine-foot tall fence, boarded with the park's old ride signs and advertising hoardings. The one with the 'Hook-a-duck' picture on was rattling hard, and when he stopped beside it the girl's voice was clear.

'Is anyone there? Let us in.'

Us? Brick thought, wondering again about the gun.

'Hello?' he said. The pounding stopped, leaving the park eerily quiet. For some reason it was colder here too, like he was standing next to an open fridge. 'Who are you?'

'We need help,' the girl said. He could hear her shivering. 'My brother is hurt.'

The girl, whoever she was, hadn't gone rabid. She wasn't snarling at him through the fence. That had to be a good thing.

'There's a way in,' he said. 'Go left. About fifty metres

or so down there's a break in the fence. I'll meet you there.'

He set off without waiting for a reply, jogging until he reached the engineering workshops. He ducked down the alley between them, moving the NDYFLOSS AN board and squeezing past the wire. The sun was just lifting up over the horizon, already dazzling, and he capped a hand to his forehead, peering through the shadow to see two people walking down the beach. The girl was a little younger than him, dark-haired and pretty, her face so pale it was blue. A mosaic of bruises and blood coloured her face and neck. She was almost carrying a boy, his arm around her shoulder, and as they got closer he saw that they had the same face.

'You maybe want to help?' she snapped.

Brick grunted, trotting towards them. He was about a dozen yards away when the cold hit him, like he was running into a winter storm. Goosebumps broke out over his arms and he could see his own breath, ghost-like in front of him. He stopped, wrapping his arms around himself.

'What the . . .' Then he saw the dusting of ice that covered the boy's face, crystals hanging from his lips and his eyelashes. His skin was grey, and although his eyes were open they had been frosted over.

'Hurry up,' said the girl. Brick started forward again, slower this time. His whole body was shuddering, the cold actually burning him. He manoeuvred himself around the side of the boy, ducking under his free arm and taking his weight. It felt as though he'd just buried himself in a snowdrift. The girl eased herself out, standing away and rubbing flecks of ice from the side of her face. 'We need to get him inside,' she said.

'What's wrong with him?' Brick asked through his clacking teeth. The girl fixed him with a look as cold as her brother.

'That's exactly what you need to tell me. Because I want an explanation, and I want it now.'

Daisy

Daisy couldn't work out how the boy could be so cold and yet still be alive. Brick had carried him into the restaurant a few minutes ago, waking her. He'd shushed her off the sofa she'd spent the night on and laid the boy there, running off to find something to put over him.

'It's going to be okay, Schiller,' said the girl who had walked in with him. She knelt beside the boy. She was wearing just a short skirt and a top. No wonder she looked so frozen. Her face was very pretty, other than the bruises, but there was something in it that made Daisy feel uneasy. It was probably just because she was a stranger.

'I've found a couple more,' said Cal, walking over with a handful of candles. He placed them on the coffee table beside the sofa, lighting them from one that was already burning and using the wax to stick them to the wood. The flames seemed reluctant and Daisy didn't blame them – the air was so cold that even fire had to feel it. It would be easier to take the boards off the windows and let the sun in, but Brick had told them they couldn't do it in case people noticed and came snooping.

'Who are you people?' the girl asked.

'You were attacked, right?' Cal said. 'By complete strangers.'

The girl stared at Cal and even though half a dozen candles burned, her eyes stayed dark. Daisy felt some of those strange, translucent ice cube images clinking in her brain. She tried to get a better look at them but they bobbled just out of reach.

'Right?' Cal said when she didn't reply.

'And you saw our message online?' added Brick as he staggered back into the room, peering over a mountain of linen. He dumped it all at the head of the sofa and the girl began to sort through it, shaking out each tablecloth before layering them over the boy, tucking them under his motionless body. His cold had turned the damp inside the sofa to a sheen of ice which glittered like diamonds. Daisy blew out puffs of cotton wool breath, watching them dissolve into the air for the few minutes it took for the girl to finish.

'Schill, can you hear me?' she said, getting to her feet and blowing on her blue fingers. The boy didn't respond, his glazed, frozen eyes staring at the ceiling. He was wrapped up tight, like a mummy. She put her hand to his forehead, then turned and glared at Brick as if this was somehow his fault. 'Message?' she said after a moment.

Brick looked at Cal, then at Daisy, and when nobody else spoke he finally turned back to the girl.

'We left a message, online, saying for people to come to Hemmingway if they'd been attacked.' He floundered, running his hands through his hair. 'You didn't get it?'

More clinking ice cubes in her head. Daisy saw a

field, and the heavens falling – burning flecks of stars. The boy was there, the girl too. And she could sense *herself* in the picture, her voice weird, like she was listening to it on a badly tuned radio.

'You heard us,' she said. 'Last night, we told you to come here and you did.'

The girl looked down at her, scowling. She took a deep, shuddering breath that appeared like a thought bubble. Daisy could almost read it, the emotions there packed tight – fear and anger and a great deal of confusion. She felt sorry for her.

'Look,' said Cal. 'The truth is we don't know any more than you. I don't think so anyway. Let's go outside, get some air, some sunlight. We can talk about it there. Yeah?'

They all shivered through another moment of awkward silence, and in it Daisy saw an ice cube vision float through her brain, the same one she'd seen last night only now much clearer. This one was full of fire, so real that she felt like putting her hands to it, thawing them out on its heat. But there was something bad about it, something she didn't quite understand. The image shifted, melting, and Daisy thought she saw the park, Fursville, lost inside the flames. And the girl, too, in the centre of the inferno. Then the images split apart, fading into the guttering candlelight of the restaurant.

'Okay,' said the girl. She tucked the tablecloths around her brother's neck and whispered something into his ear before looking at Cal. 'Lead the way.'

Cal walked from the room, the girl following, then Brick. Daisy trotted after them, wondering if it was safe to leave the boy here swaddled in cloth next to half a dozen candles. It wasn't that which was making her uneasy, though. The ice cubes had gone but they'd left something unpleasant in her head, a feeling that she couldn't quite shake even as she left the darkness of the restaurant and stepped into the brightness of the foyer.

The new girl was dangerous.

Rilke

They sat on the roof of the pavilion, eating crisps and bread and taking turns to tell their stories.

The tall ginger boy went first, stuttering through his tale involving a psychotic girlfriend and an attack in a nearby garage. He was the one who had found this place, Fursville, and he was reluctant to share it. That didn't come across so much in his words as in the pauses between his words, slight hesitations in which Rilke seemed to be able to peer inside that copper dome of his and get a sense of what he was really thinking. Of course it was probably a hallucination brought on by exhaustion – she'd been awake for well over twenty-four hours now. If that was the case, though, then what was it that made her lean forward when he had finished speaking and say:

'Your girlfriend, she's still here.'

The boy's mouth dropped open, his cheeks blazing, his fist crumpling up the slice of bread he was holding.

'Don't be stupid,' he muttered. 'Of course she's not.'

She didn't have to read his thoughts to know that was a lie.

The sun had hauled its lazy bulk up from the horizon and daylight splashed across the roof, giving the four of them long, thin shadows that spilled over the edge. It was filthy up here, the spaces between the ventilation stacks and air conditioning units and aerials covered in bird mess and rotting debris. But there were comfy moth-eaten director's chairs that the park's staff had long ago dragged up here and the view wasn't bad. If you looked to the left, that was, over the crests of the fake waves and across the flat, featureless land all the way to a distant factory. In the other direction lay the sea, the same one Rilke had spent all night on. She didn't want to look at it ever again.

Still, at least it was warm, and getting hotter by the minute. It occurred to her that they should fetch Schiller and leave him out in the sun, but it would be safer inside, at least until they knew what was going on. Out here the world seemed too big. Anything could happen.

'What's your story, anyway?' The ginger one asked, aggression in his voice.

'Hang on,' said the other kid, the one wearing track-suit trousers. He was conventionally good looking, but beneath his messy hair his face was featureless and bland. *He's soft*, thought Rilke. *He's a pushover.* He wiped crisp crumbs from his lips, saying, 'Let's stay friendly, okay? My name is Cal, Callum. This is Daisy. She's, what, eleven?'

'Nearly thirteen,' corrected Daisy. 'I just look young-er, that's all.' The girl offered a nervous smile and Rilke returned it.

'And that's Brick,' Cal went on, nodding at the ginger kid.

'Why Brick?' Rilke asked. She took another piece of bread from the open bag, tearing off a sliver and putting it in her mouth. She felt like she was literally starving, but she didn't want to show weakness by scoffing down half a loaf.

'Because my dad's motto is never hit anyone with your fist when you've got a brick,' he growled.

'Nice,' she said. *Neanderthal.*

'What's your name?' asked Daisy.

'Rilke,' she said. 'Rilke Bastion. The boy in there is my brother, Schiller.'

'Your parents liked poetry, then,' said Brick, which threw her. How did a caveman like him know that they were both named after German poets? He smiled smugly. A smile that said, *Didn't expect that now, did you?* Daisy coughed politely, diffusing the tension.

'My parents, they . . .' the smaller girl started, and in that pause Rilke's brain filled in the gaps. She didn't see it so much as just feel it, the weight, the awful gravity, of two dead people in a bed. Daisy's face had crumpled like a paper bag left out in the rain and Rilke had an urge to go to her, to wrap her arms around her. Girls had to look after one another. But Cal beat her to it, and she seemed to find strength in his arms.

'My mum, she didn't want to hurt me,' Daisy went on. 'She was ill anyway, she had . . . cancer in her head. It made her act strange. She . . . she took my dad, then herself, so they wouldn't hurt me. Then the ambulance people tried to kill me, pushed me out the window.' The girl looked at the boy who held her.

'Cal found me. He saved me.'

'Nearly didn't, though,' said Cal, giving Daisy a squeeze then letting her go. He told his story more smoothly than the others, as if he'd rehearsed it in his head. When he'd finished he looked at Rilke. They all did. 'Now you.'

What could she say? She didn't have a clue what had happened. The only reason she was so calm about it all, so logical, was that the full force of it hadn't sunk in yet. None of it felt real. Maybe none of it *was* real. Maybe they'd got to the party and someone had slipped her some acid, ecstasy. Maybe all this was just a bad trip. She finished her bread then shrugged, more to herself than to the others.

'We got attacked at a party, a rave. Then suddenly we moved, we were in another . . . I don't know. Anyway, we managed to get away. I heard . . . no, *felt* you guys speaking to me so I brought my brother here. I thought you would know what was happening. I thought you'd have answers. I thought you'd be able to help us.'

Out of nowhere it hit her, a tidal wave of panic and fear and utter helplessness that sluiced through her brain. She clamped her teeth together until the feeling washed away. She couldn't afford to look weak in front of these people. Not now, not ever. *It's too late*, she realised, seeing the way Daisy stared at her, as though her thoughts were flashing across her forehead. She got to her feet, turning her back on them. It was starting to get hot, ridiculously so.

'We know what you know,' said Cal behind her,

and for a second she thought he was admitting to the ridiculous notion that they could read minds. 'That people are going crazy. That they're filled with . . .'

'The Fury,' Rilke finished for him, the word not hers. She wondered if maybe it went both ways, if she could steal their thoughts too.

'Yeah, the Fury. It doesn't seem to affect them unless one of us is close. Then they just go mental, try and kill us. They seriously try and rip us to pieces.'

'But afterwards they just go back to doing whatever they were doing,' said Brick. 'They go back to their lives, like nothing has happened. They totally forget that they went psycho. If you can get away from them, if you get out of their radar, then they'll leave you alone. I think so, anyway.'

A couple of squabbling gulls flapped onto the roof, ogling the strangers warily before taking off again. Rilke turned back to the others.

'What about Schill?' she asked. 'Why is he so cold? What's happened to him?'

They looked at each other, and she could sense the vast, black gulfs in each of their thoughts. They didn't have a clue. She shook her head, disgusted.

'So why bring me here?'

'Because we're safer when we're together,' said Daisy.

That's it? She had to bite her tongue to stop from saying it out loud.

'It's the only way we'll find out what's going on,' said Cal. 'The more of us there are, the quicker we'll find answers.'

'Well I'm here now,' Rilke snapped back. 'There are five of us, where are the answers?'

A memory from the previous night swam back into her thoughts, the image of somebody driving a car, somebody else running through the woods. She shook her head, knocking them loose.

'It's not just us, is it?' she said. 'There are others coming.'

Brick smiled without humour, leaning forward in his chair and resting his head in his hands.

'You have no idea.'

Cal

'There's a gap,' said Cal. He pointed at a battered stretch of fence in the front right-hand corner of the park, almost hidden behind the bulk of the log flume. There were piles and piles of scaffolding back here, rusted poles propped up against the wilting barricade. It reminded him of a bamboo forest, like in all the old martial arts movies, and he could even see a scraggly bird's nest sitting precariously on the top of one.

'Where?' Brick asked. The two of them had been scouting the perimeter for the past few hours to make sure the park was secure. It had been Cal's idea, and when he'd suggested it to Brick the boy had seemed to take it as a personal insult, as though Cal had said, *Hey, man, you're ugly, shall we see what we can do about it?* Daisy and the new girl, Rilke, were keeping an eye on Schiller.

'There,' Cal said, stamping down a clutch of vicious-looking brambles in order to take a step closer to the fence. One corner had come loose from the ground leaving a flap of steel. Behind it was the towering bulk of the laurel hedge which shielded the park from the street. Brick snorted.

'That's not a gap, who's going to get through there? A midget?'

'It's still a problem,' said Cal. 'This place needs to

be as tight as we can make it. You never know what's gonna happen.'

'Fine, put it on the list,' Brick said, waving him away like a bad smell. Cal lifted his notebook – a restaurant order pad – and added 'log flume, loose panel' to the two other breaches they'd found.

'I don't know what your problem is, mate,' Cal said, running to catch up with the bigger boy. 'Haven't you ever seen zombie films? Once one gets in, they all get in, and if you're overrun then you're finished, dead meat.'

'These aren't zombies,' Brick replied. 'They're not dead for one thing.'

'I know they're not real zombies,' Cal said as they walked past a couple of carnival stalls, both of which had rotted in the sea air. 'Duh. But you know what I mean. They swarm. If one comes after you, they all do.'

Brick grunted, shrugging his shoulders.

'Anyway, at least we're doing something, right?' Cal went on as they walked up to the small, squat ticket office. 'Better this than sitting around in the dark twiddling our thumbs.'

'Specially with that girl in there,' Brick added, whispering even though there was no way she could have heard them. 'She scares me more than the ferals out there.'

Cal laughed, the sound floating on the warm air, seeming to fill the whole park for a second, bringing it to life the way laughter had once kept its heart beating.

'You're not kidding,' he said, keeping his own voice low and casting a secretive look back at the pavilion.

'I'm not going to sleep in the same room as her, she might kill me in the middle of the night.'

Then they were both sniggering into their hands. It felt good. It seemed like years since he'd laughed. *It wasn't years, though, it was yesterday, remember? Yesterday when things were still almost normal.* But yesterday was gone. There was just before and after, and before was a million years ago.

'So how well do you know this place?' Cal asked, walking to the window of the ticket office and peering through the filthy glass. There was light inside, spilling through the massive hole in the roof and revealing a cash register with its tray open and empty, a couple of waterlogged magazines and a lot of dust.

'Like the back of my hand,' Brick replied. Cal could see him reflected in the window, his hair like fire. He was picking his nose. 'Spent more time here than I have at home this year. I've pretty much been in every building. There's nothing left but junk.'

Cal walked down the side of the office, the main gates towering over him. A chain the size of a fire hose was looped around the ornate ironwork and they'd been boarded up to hide the park from the street. There was a brick tower on each side, maybe ten metres tall. A turquoise ladder ran up the left-hand one to the massive sign that straddled the entrance. There were half a dozen more nests lodged in the back-to-front letters.

'That's a good lookout post,' Cal said. 'You can probably see half a mile inland from up there.'

'Yeah, if you want to sit around all day in bird crap,'

Brick said. 'What do we need a lookout for, anyway? Nobody ever comes out here, I told you.'

Cal didn't reply, just jotted it down in his notepad. Brick had a way of talking that instantly got your hackles up, but surely it was because of the situation they were in. There was a chance the guy might have always been an asshole, but Cal was willing to give him the benefit of the doubt. It was important that they got on – God only knew how long they'd be living here together.

'Gift shop,' said Brick, nodding towards the building on the other side of the gate. 'Lost property too. It's empty, pretty much.'

Cal walked to it. The windows were boarded over, but one sheet of plywood had been pulled off to reveal a single square, glassless eye. He checked the gap between the building and the fence to make sure it was secure.

'So, you used to work out here or something?' he asked as he joined Brick again.

'Me? Hell no, this place was in ruins when I was, like, seven or something. How old you think I am?'

'I just thought, with you being so tall and everything . . .' Cal said, shrugging. 'Twenty-one maybe?'

Brick snorted out a laugh. 'I'm eighteen,' he said. 'Same as you, I wouldn't be surprised. Just had to grow up a bit faster, that's all.'

Cal studied him properly for the first time, seeing the freckles, the loose covering of fine ginger stubble. And his eyes – they were squinty and unwelcoming but they were still those of a kid.

'You want to kiss me or something?' Brick said, taking a step back and holding out his hands. 'You're giving me a weird look.'

'Gross,' said Cal, his cheeks heating. 'You wish. Plus, I'm seventeen.'

There was an awkward moment, then they both started laughing again.

'I'm glad we got *that* out the way,' Brick said. They walked along the side of the gift shop, entering a pool of jagged shadow thrown by the huge roller coaster on the south-east side of the park. 'There's another way in just here. It's the one I usually use. There's a gap in the fence that's hidden by the hedge, easy to sneak in and out of. It's—'

Cal froze, grabbing hold of Brick's arm. The bigger boy carried on speaking for a few more seconds before the words dried up in his throat. Then they both stared in silence at the path that led down between the toilets and the Boo Boo Station, peering into the gloom at the blond-haired, bloodstained boy who stood there.

He was young, he looked even younger than Daisy. He was wearing a pair of Adidas tracksuit trousers and a Batman T-shirt, both of which were coated with plum-coloured grime. His feet were bare and filthy. His near-white hair had been stained pink in places, his face too – the dried blood making his skin look like parchment. He had no expression whatsoever. He looked like a shop-window dummy, his eyes empty pockets.

'It's one of *them*,' Brick hissed, taking a step back. Cal

still had him by the arm, refusing to let go when Brick tried to pull away. 'Cal, come on!'

'Wait,' Cal said. 'I think he's okay. Don't you feel it?'

There was something in Cal's head, that same deafening silence as before. It reminded him of the ocean on a calm day, when the sea was as flat as glass but you could still sense the vast, churning weight of water beneath the surface. Brick relaxed and Cal let him go.

'Hey,' Cal said, talking to the boy. He took a step towards him, his hands held up to show he didn't mean any harm. 'You okay? You hurt?'

How had he got here? The boy didn't look like he could punch his way out of a wet paper bag, let alone travel to the armpit of Norfolk. Something definitely wasn't right with this picture.

'We're not going to hurt you,' Cal said, edging closer. He got down on one knee beside him. 'Just let us know your name, or anything. Just say something so we know you're not one of them. Yeah?'

'You won't get the little git to talk.' The voice came from the hedge, followed by the snapping of branches and the hammer of footsteps. Cal felt his skin grow cold as a double-barrelled shotgun emerged through the broken fence. The guy who was holding it was in his late teens, maybe early twenties, his thin face concealed by a scraggly beard. He was wearing a green farmer's jacket over a white shirt. He lifted the gun to his shoulder, aiming it right at Cal. 'Don't move, or I'll blow your head off.'

Cal lifted his hands, backing away. At his side, Brick

looked ready to bolt, his body tensing up, then he obviously thought better of it. The man approached, swinging the gun from side to side. He drew level with the young boy, giving him a look that sent him scuttling away.

'Get in here,' the gunman shouted. There was more rustling, then a girl appeared, her hair almost as red as the rings around her eyes. She stepped out and another boy squeezed through the fence. He looked the same age as Cal, tall but slightly overweight. They both wore the same expression: *Help us*.

'You better tell me what I'm doing here,' the man said, jabbing the gun like it was a spear. 'Why everybody in the goddamned world is trying to kill me. Why you're inside my head screwing with my thoughts.'

Cal held up his hands and took a step back, slipping on the rubble-strewn ground.

'I said, *DON'T MOVE!*' the man barked. His finger was on the trigger, and it was tense. Even from here Cal could see where the joint had blanched. If the guy so much as sneezed then their brains would be splattered all over the Boo Boo Station.

'There's no need for that, mate,' said Cal, more tremor than voice. 'We're not going to do anything.'

'Got that right,' said the man, still walking towards them. The barrel of the shotgun was like two dark, unblinking eyes. 'How many of you are here?'

Brick and Cal glanced at each other.

'How many?' the man demanded.

'Five,' blurted Cal. 'One of us is injured.'

'Where?'

'Back there,' said Cal, tilting his head over his shoulder. 'In the pavilion. We're just kids.'

'Fatty, go check they're not armed.' The big kid didn't budge. 'Do it!' the man yelled, making the boy jump so hard his flesh wobbled beneath his shirt. He trotted over, apologising beneath his breath as he patted down Cal then Brick. His eyes didn't rise above their kneecaps. He scampered out of the way as soon as he'd finished.

'Nothing,' he whispered.

'Right, turn and start walking,' said the gunman. 'Take me to where the others are, hands on your heads.'

'What do you want?' asked Cal, obeying. He didn't really want his back to the guy but he didn't see how he had a choice.

'I want answers,' said the man. 'Shift, or I swear you'll be dead before you hit the floor.'

Cal started back the way they'd come, his hands clamped in his hair. Brick walked by his side, his face pale and downturned.

This is going to get nasty. The thought hit Cal hard. It wasn't just a fear, it was a premonition. *Someone is going to get hurt*.

And those words were still ringing in his mind when he stepped out of the shadows and the gun went off.

Rilke

'Something's wrong.'

Rilke looked up from her brother when Daisy spoke. The younger girl was sitting on a chair beside the sofa, huddled into herself and shivering. They'd been here for hours now, throwing more blankets on cold, un-responsive Schiller and sorting out the food into piles. Daisy had tried to start a few conversations but Rilke had been too tired to throw back more than a couple of words. This time, though, there was an urgency in her voice.

'What?' Rilke asked. There were plenty of things wrong, Schiller for one, his skin like marble, radiating cold. And the world. Right now the whole world was wrong.

'It's Cal,' said Daisy, getting to her feet and standing there trembling. In the flickering candlelight there was something not quite real about her, something fairy-like in her saucer-shaped eyes and her ghosted skin. 'He's going to die.'

'What?' Rilke said again, frowning. 'Cal? Why?'

'I don't know *why*. I . . . I just know.'

Rilke used the sofa to pull herself up off her knees, brushing the dust from her skirt. Her pulse was fast, and in its rhythm she understood that Daisy wasn't

302

being hysterical, she wasn't making it up. Cal was in danger.

'Is it Brick?' she asked. There was something about the tall boy Rilke didn't trust, something in his face, and in the way he'd avoided answering her when she'd asked about his girlfriend. He'd looked guilty. Daisy shook her head, her eyes on the floor and yet also somewhere else, somewhere far away.

'It's not Brick, he's in danger too. We all are.'

'Come on,' said Rilke, holding out her hand. Daisy took it, her skin fever-hot compared to Schiller's. They began to walk towards the door but Daisy stopped, shaking herself free and running to the far side of the restaurant. She slid a carrier bag out from beneath a table, rummaging inside it and pulling out something big. She ran back across the room and held it out to Rilke.

It was a gun.

'Where did you get this?' Rilke asked as she took the weapon. It was heavier than it looked. She'd used guns before, shotguns mainly. Schiller loved to shoot the pigeons and the rats for target practice and she'd often gone out with him, mainly because there wasn't much else to do.

'It's Cal's,' Daisy said, her tone more urgent now. She kept glancing at the door. 'Brick hid it, but I found it when we were going through the bags. Come on, please.'

They linked hands again, Daisy practically dragging her out of the restaurant, down the stairs and out through the chained-up fire exit.

'Wait,' said Rilke. 'Daisy, hang on.'

Daisy's only response was to increase her speed, racing past the pavilion's main doors towards the front of the park. Rilke trotted to keep up, and she was about to call out again when she saw them at the other end of the overgrown path.

Cal and Brick emerged first, their hands on their heads like prisoners of war. Then came the long, steel barrel of a shotgun, followed by a man, a teenager maybe, in a green jacket.

'Do it,' Daisy said, skidding to a halt. *Do what?* Rilke thought, *shoot him?* And, incredibly, Daisy screamed: 'Yes! Shoot him now!'

There was no time to question it. Rilke lifted the pistol, using both thumbs to pull back the stubborn hammer. She aimed past the notch on the barrel until she found the man's face. He had a dark beard, his eyes squinting against the morning sun. She pressed both her forefingers against the trigger, a storm of thoughts all shrieking at once inside her head – *You can't do this, you can't shoot a man!* Then, as if they had been vacuumed up, they vanished, leaving only one, leaving only Daisy:

Do it.

She squeezed. The gun resisted, then the trigger clicked. The shot was deafening, almost jolting the pistol out of her hands. She managed to cling on to it, peering through the smoke to see that Brick and Cal were on the ground.

Oh God, I hit one of them, she thought. Then she saw them both squirming in the dirt, trying to crawl away. The guy with the shotgun was still standing, but there was a crimson tear down the left side of his face, stretching from his cheek to his ear. She'd grazed him. His expression of shock was so extreme it was almost comical. It seemed to take him an age to see Rilke, and as he started to swing his shotgun round she took a step forward, aiming her weapon at his head.

'The next one won't miss,' she said, staring him dead on. 'I swear to God.'

The shotgun stayed down, pointed at Cal's back. Both boys looked up at her, their faces distorted by fear. The gunman's shock was fast becoming anger; even from where she was standing Rilke could feel it burning off him. But there was something else, too, the same weird, clanging silence she'd felt just before meeting Daisy and the others. This guy was one of them.

He is, but he's a bad man. Please Rilke, do it, I don't want Cal to die.

Had Daisy said that or was it just in her head? Either way the little girl's voice blasted everything else away.

'Drop it,' she shouted, her finger tensing. Was she supposed to cock the gun again? 'Do it right now. *Right now.*'

Blood was trickling from the man's wound, but he still wasn't letting go of his weapon. She thumbed back the hammer, the click barely audible over the feedback-like whine in her ears.

Please Rilke, Daisy's voice again, right in the flesh of

her brain. *I know you don't believe me but—*

'He's going to kill him,' Daisy said out loud, the switch making Rilke reel. The little girl was sobbing now, her words fractured. 'He's going to die.'

The gunman tensed, his face screwed into a wicked grimace. He raised the gun slightly, so that the barrel was pointing right at Cal's head. Cal was on his back now, his arms up in front of him, frozen like one of the sculptures in the White Witch's palace. The bearded guy never took his eyes from Rilke.

'Yeah?' he sneered. 'What if I—'

Rilke pulled the trigger, bracing herself this time. The gun barked but she let her arms absorb the recoil, watching as the man staggered back, a perfectly round hole punched into his forehead. Even though he was dead – he *had* to be dead – he still stared at her, something keeping his body rigid, upright, something stopping him from crashing to the—

White heat, burning bright as phosphorous.

The man exploded, like a nuclear bomb detonating in the middle of the park. A shock wave tore outwards, crumpling the food booths on either side of the path. Rilke didn't even have time to scream as she saw it hurricane towards her, ripping her from the ground and sending her spinning backwards into the wall of the pavilion.

It could have been a fraction of a second or a million years later that she remembered how to open her eyes. Debris still flew from the impact of the shock, moving in slow motion as if time had been knocked off its axis.

Metal poles were falling ridiculously slowly from the big wheel, thudding into the ground like giant javelins. Brick and Cal were in mid-air, rolling like rag dolls as they were hurled away from the source of the detonation.

The man, the gunman, was suspended over the path, his arms out to his sides like he was being crucified. His whole body shimmered, red hot. Suddenly his head snapped back, his spine arching, and his body seemed to split, like two ropes on either side had just been pulled taut. Inside him was an inferno, almost too bright to look at, but Rilke didn't turn away, she didn't blink. She *couldn't*.

Because something was coming out of the man. It could have been *another* man except this one was too big, and this one was made of fire – ferocious blue-white flames. Its distended jaw hung open in a silent scream, and the fire stretched outwards from its back, unfurling like twin sails. Its eyes blazed, and in those broken seconds the thing looked at Rilke, burning right into the fabric of her soul. Then another shock wave ripped outwards, atomising the man's body and the thing which clawed its way out of it, blowing the hotdog stand to ash before slamming into her.

She dropped into darkness.

Daisy

Daisy was burning.

She sat up, noticing that her skirt was smouldering gently, slapping at it until the dull embers died out. Smoke hung in the air all around her, a silvery gauze that looked more like morning mist. It smelled bad, like when her mum sometimes pulled hair from the brush and threw it on the fire. She was lying in the middle of the weed-littered path that led past the pavilion up to the sea. What was she doing here? She clambered to her feet, staring through the smoke to see that one of the food places, the one with the big soft drink on the roof, was on fire.

The whole place was a mess. The little shack on the other side of the path, the one with the hot dog, was totally gone. Further down was a huge crater in the concrete, so charred that it looked like a vast hole in the ground. The kind a giant spider might suddenly crawl out of.

There was a man standing there, a man with a gun. And with that thought the memories returned, fighting each other to be first in line. She'd seen something in her head, like a badly filmed home movie of Cal being shot. It had been horrible. She'd told Rilke, and they'd come out here with the gun.

Rilke. Daisy couldn't sense her, the way she'd been sensing people recently, those little ice cubes in her mind. She couldn't see Cal or Brick up there in her head either. There *was* an ice cube, though, one with a room that looked like a dentist's place, with the big chair. She could see a poster with a kitten on the ceiling, but there were no people in the ice cube.

What had happened? Rilke had shot the man, hadn't she? And it was okay, because he had been a nasty man, a really nasty man. He was the one who had been going to kill Cal. It hadn't been very nice, watching the man die, even though he'd deserved it. But then what? Daisy had seen something inside the man, a fire that howled, that tried to pull itself loose. She must have passed out and seen those things in a dream.

So why the smoke? And where was everybody? She started down the path, feeling woozy. Great big metal needles stuck out of the ground, like hedgehog bristles. Daisy looked up, wondering if they'd fallen from the big wheel. It was lucky nobody had been spiked. There was a pile of rags up against the pavilion doors, and she almost dismissed it until she realised who it was.

'Rilke!' Daisy yelled, stumbling over the cracked ground. The girl's face was covered with soot, and there was no sign of life. 'Help!' Daisy yelled. 'Somebody please help!'

What were you supposed to do if someone wasn't alive? Breathe into their mouth or something. They'd done it at school with a plastic dummy, the ABC rule. 'A' was for . . . *A heartbeat?* It didn't sound right, but

Daisy pressed her fingers against Rilke's neck, praying to feel something there. *Pulse-pulse-pulse-pulse*, rapid, like a rabbit's. Daisy almost cried with relief, stroking Rilke's long, dark hair away from her face.

'Is anyone here?' she called out again. Then, more softly, 'I'll be right back, Rilke, I'm going to find help. It's going to be okay.'

She set off again, heading for the front of the park, towards that gaping crater. *Please don't let anything come out of it.*

'Hello? Cal? I need you!'

'Daisy?' It wasn't so much a shout as a groan, uttered from somewhere to her right. She walked towards the splintered remains of the hot-dog stand, treading carefully over the rubble. There were a few crates beyond, and half a breeze-block wall that was covered in scribbled writing. Past it she could see a pair of feet, one in a trainer and the other in just a sock. They were moving.

'Cal?' She ran round the wall to see Cal sitting on the path. He was a mess too, and some of his hair was missing, giving him a funny bald patch just above his right ear. He saw her coming and tried to get up, collapsing onto his bum. Daisy crouched down beside him, putting a hand on his shoulder. There was a big rip across the front of his T-shirt. 'Are you okay?'

'I think so,' he said, patting his hands over his body. 'Seem to be all there, anyway.' He smiled, but it obviously caused him quite a bit of pain. 'Help me up, yeah?'

Daisy grabbed his arm and he used it to pull himself to his feet. He stood for a moment, his hands on his knees, his eyes scrunched shut.

'What the hell happened?' he asked. 'I feel like I was hit by a lorry.'

'Guys?' Daisy turned to see Brick limping towards them down the same path. He had coal-dark rings around his eyes, like a raccoon, and there was blood dripping from his left arm. Daisy was glad to see him, especially when he gave her a weak smile. 'You alright?'

'I'm okay, but Rilke is hurt. She's not waking up. She needs help.'

'She breathing?' Brick asked. Daisy nodded. If she had a heartbeat then she had to be breathing, didn't she? Brick coughed, hacking up a rust-coloured gob of spit. 'Got to get the fire out first. If people see it they'll call the fire brigade or send for the police.'

'Got any water?' Cal said. Brick shook his head, jogging towards the burning stall. Cal ran after him, hobbling in his one shoe.

Daisy followed, still not wanting to get too close to the crater. By the time she had skirted around the edge Brick and Cal were pulling the front wall of the drinks stand free, releasing a fresh plume of smoke. The fire flared up as it gorged on the fresh supply of air but Brick didn't hesitate, stamping and kicking on the flames until the plume of smoke began to wither and die. He stumbled away, coughing so much that Daisy didn't know how he could manage a breath.

'Where are the rest of them?' he said when he had finished, clutching his wounded arm. Tears painted black stripes down his face. 'You see them?'

The rest of who? she thought as Brick and Cal set off again. She ran after them as they wove through the spikes in the ground, trying to keep up, not wanting to be left on her own.

'There,' she heard Brick yell. He turned the corner by the carousel, vanishing behind more debris by the side of the path. Daisy heard a voice, a panicked shout, and suddenly there were more ice cubes sliding around in her brain. Even before she turned the corner she knew she was going to see three people there, two boys and a girl.

'We weren't with him!' the girl was shouting, holding her hands up in surrender as Brick stormed towards her. Her hair was red, almost the same colour as his, and her face was streaked with dirt and smoke. 'We didn't know him!'

'Brick, hold up,' said Cal. 'I think they're telling the truth.'

Brick stopped, taking a deep, rattling breath. The little boy in the Batman T-shirt edged cautiously around him, sidestepping towards Cal and casting quick glances at Daisy. The dentist ice cube was his, she realised, and she could see more now – a man in a white suit screaming through a face mask and reaching for him over the chair.

'Adam,' she said, seeing his name in the ice. He turned at the sound of it, his bloodstained brow creasing. She held out her hand. 'Come on, it's okay, you're safe here now.'

He walked to her straight away, not looking back,

and she took his hand.

'Do you want to come inside? We've got some food and some fizzy drinks.'

He didn't smile, but he didn't let go either. Daisy looked back at Brick, who was pacing from one side of the path to the other like a caged tiger. Cal was just behind him. The girl and the other boy were terrified. Daisy could feel their fear inside her, like the ice cubes were melting, bleeding their emotions into hers. She didn't like it.

'Who was he?' Brick said. 'Christ, he must have been carrying a bomb or something.'

'I picked him up,' the overweight boy was saying. 'The same way as the others, only he had the gun and he . . .'

'It's okay,' said Cal. 'Right, Brick? It's okay. We can trust them. Everyone just calm down.'

Brick snapped his hands up in an angry shrug. More blood dripped over his fingers, pattering on the ground.

'It's just the three of you?' he asked. 'Nobody else?'

The boy and the girl looked at each other, but it was the little kid by her side, Adam, who gave it away. Daisy saw a silver car inside his ice cube, a big one, and something thumping and shrieking in the boot, something with blood on its breath.

'There's one more,' said the girl, looking up the path that led out of the park. The plump boy finished for her.

'But it isn't one of us.'

Brick

The redhead's name was Jade. The fat kid was Chris. They told Brick this as they walked back down the side of the Boo Boo Station and out through the gap in the laurel hedge. Daisy had taken the little boy inside and Cal had gone to check on Rilke. Brick kind of wished he had their job and they had his, but he didn't trust them to be able to deal with the situation.

He certainly didn't trust the boy and the girl beside him. Whatever they said, they'd brought the gunman here, they'd led him to the park. He looked at his arm, an ugly gash across his bicep. At least the blood had slowed to a trickle, he wasn't going to bleed out. He'd been lucky. They all had. Who the hell carried a bomb on them?

And yet there was something at the back of his head that told him it wasn't a bomb, a memory scratching against his skull. He'd been looking right at the man when he'd exploded; hadn't there been something there, something crawling out of him with a body of fire?

Don't be an idiot, Brick. It's the adrenalin talking.

'It's just there,' said Chris. He nodded towards a silver car parked at an angle on the kerb. It was a snob's car, a Jag or something, huge. There were bloodstains on

314

the bonnet. Brick could already hear thumps from the boot, and a weak, groaning cry.

'We didn't have a choice,' said Jade. She had an accent that Brick couldn't quite place. Something northern. 'That guy, the one with the gun, he knocked him out and stuck him in the boot. Woke up, I don't know, half an hour before we got here and he's been trying to beat his way out ever since.'

'Weird thing is, when we're not anywhere near him he acts normal,' said Chris. 'Like now, shout something to him and he'll probably shout back.'

They both looked at Brick expectantly. He nodded his head.

'I know. They're all doing that.' He sighed, swearing under his breath. They couldn't leave the car out here, the first person who saw it would call the police. They couldn't bring it into Fursville either, there was nowhere big enough to get it through the fence. They could take it to the car park where he'd met Cal and Daisy last night, but he didn't fancy a ten-minute drive with a feral in the boot. Fursville had a car park of its own. It was locked up but they could probably find a way in.

Whoever was inside must have heard them, because the voice got louder, still muffled but now audible.

'*Please, let me out, I promise I won't tell.*'

And suddenly it was *Lisa* inside that car, clawing for oxygen in the heat, scraping at the lock with her nails. Brick clamped his eyes shut until the image disappeared.

'You got the keys?' he asked.

'They're in the ignition,' Chris said.

'We can park it in there,' he said, pointing at the Fursville lot. 'You'll have to ram the fence. We'll hide the car, work out what to do with him later.'

Chris nodded. He wobbled over to it, taking a deep breath before sliding into the driver's seat. Jade stayed by Brick's side.

'Ain't getting back in there,' she said when he looked at her. She didn't offer an explanation, just folded her hands over her chest as if she were cold.

Brick walked down the pavement, the boot-man's voice now a series of howling barks. The thumps got louder, the metal boot lid shaking as he pounded it from inside. Fifty metres down was the entrance to the Fursville car park, the main gates bolted shut. The fence here wasn't so big, though.

Chris swung the car out then lurched back onto the kerb, ploughing into the fence with a sound like fingernails running down a blackboard. The engine growled but he didn't let up, revving hard until the wire snapped and the car jolted through.

'Over there,' Brick shouted, pointing towards the huge hedge which separated the car park from Fursville. There was a small wooden office – a garden shed, really – where you'd once had to pay a quid. 'Drive in as far as you can, the other side of that building.'

Chris obeyed, steering the car over the rough dirt until the bonnet disappeared into the hedge. It penetrated as far as the middle of the roof before hitting something and crunching to a halt. There was a cacophony of rustling snaps and grunts before Chris appeared, batting branches away from his face. He stepped gingerly away, looking forlornly at the battered Jag.

'Dude, my dad's gonna murder me when he sees his car,' he said, blanching when he realised what he'd said. He bared his teeth in a bitter, humourless smile. 'Again.'

The voice from the boot was even louder now, the snarls of a caged animal. But the car was pretty well hidden, Brick thought, the small office concealing it from the road. He'd grab some boards from the park and cover it up properly once they'd decided what to do about the man inside.

'Come on,' he said, turning and heading towards the ruined fence. 'Let's get back. Something tells me we need to talk.'

Cal

Cal laced up his spare trainers, grateful that he'd thought to pack some before leaving the house. He removed his smoke-blackened T-shirt and tracksuit bottoms and pulled on clean ones before joining the others.

They all sat in the restaurant, huddled around a table on the far side of the room to where Schiller still lay like an ice sculpture on the sofa. Outside it was thirty degrees and golden; inside, behind the boarded-over windows, it was half that even with the dozen candles that sputtered and spat. But it felt safe here. It felt quiet. It felt hidden.

Cal cast another look at Rilke. He'd checked her pulse and her breathing outside the pavilion, where she'd been lying, then he'd carried her here. She was curled up on the floor in the corner, covered with a tablecloth, her head resting on a bundle of clothes which he'd taken from his duffel bag. She'd had a pretty bad thump to the head, the lump there like someone had sewn an egg beneath her skin. He didn't think it was too serious, though. He'd got lumps like that before playing footy and they went away after a day or two.

'What's wrong with him?' Jade said, nodding at

Schiller. 'Why is he so cold?'

'Tell us about you first,' Brick said. 'I want to—'

'Do you want some crisps?' Daisy interrupted, earning a glare from Brick. 'Or some chocolate, or a drink?'

'We haven't got much,' Brick said. 'We should be conserving it.'

Daisy looked at the table, obviously contemplating something. Then she scraped back her chair and pulled two packets of crisps from the carrier bag behind her. She walked to the new kids and handed them over, flicking a defiant look at Brick that clearly said, *Too bad, you big meanie*. Cal smiled, everybody waiting for Daisy to pour some Fanta into a couple of glasses they'd found in the kitchen. The big bottle was too heavy for her and quite a bit of it fizzed out onto the tablecloth, hissing like acid.

'Thank you,' said Jade, downing the drink in one, then burping into her hand. 'God that's good. I haven't had anything to eat or drink since yesterday.'

'So what happened, then?' Brick snapped. 'Why are you here?'

'You told us to come here, didn't you?' Chris answered, speaking through a mouthful of crisps. 'Who was it that left the message online?'

Brick pulled a face, shrugging. He glanced at Cal as if it were his fault.

'I saw it,' Chris went on. 'Look, this is what happened. I was at home, playing Fallout, was about nine maybe, half nine. Next thing I know my mum has snapped, she's coming at me with a knife.' He paused, frowning, like he'd only just realised what had happened. He sat back in his chair, pulling on his shirt so it wasn't moulded to the rings of fat around his belly. 'And she trips, right, she's so . . . I don't know, so savage, so mad, that she doesn't look where she's going.' He stopped again, holding up his hands, his eyes a million miles away. The only sound in the room was the splutter of the candles and the chattering of Daisy's teeth. 'So I called an ambulance, right? But before they arrive someone comes into the house, some guy I've never seen before, and he starts punching me, strangling me. Only he trips over my mum, smashing his head on the table. I swear, it was like something from a *Monty Python* sketch.'

'Then what?' asked Brick when the boy didn't continue.

'To be honest, I don't properly remember,' Chris said. 'I left the house, got in the car. My dad's car. He came after me in the garage, but he's like on crutches because of a toe operation, and he falls. So the ambulance people arrive and even before they get up the road I know what they're going to do. They start tearing at the car along with my dad. They looked like animals. I just drove, somewhere quiet, used my phone to check the internet, which is where I found your message.'

'You still got your phone?' Brick asked. Chris fished it from his pocket.

'No signal,' he said, putting it back.

'What about the others?' Brick said. 'What about that man?'

'Well, that's the strange thing,' said Chris. He grunted out a laugh. 'Well, *one* of them. I . . .' He looked at Jade, and for some reason his cheeks flushed. 'I . . . we . . . just knew where they were.'

'I'm from Whitehaven,' said Jade, filling the pause before it got awkward. 'But I was staying with my friend Heather who's moved down to Grantham, yeah? Anyway, we were in the taxi on the way to a gig in town, and I didn't even want to go 'cos of my head, it was really bad.' She felt her temples, as if trying to find the pain that had been there. *We had that too*, thought Cal, sharing a look with Brick, *the headache, it's part of this*. 'And the night's just getting worse and worse because Heather isn't even talking to me and I don't know why and then the taxi driver crashes the bloody thing into a tree. Like, a proper crash and everything and we rolled over onto the side in this ditch.' She wrapped her arms around herself again, pulling her legs up onto the chair for a moment before lowering them again. 'And Heather is kicking me and scratching, but I just think she's trying to get out because she's underneath me, yeah? So I pull myself out the window then lean back in but she takes a *bite* out of me. I mean really.' She held out her hand, a purple half-moon on her wrist. 'And the next thing I know the taxi driver is going at me, even though . . .'

She stopped, looking like she was going to barf.

'His arm,' she said, her eyes filling. She put her hand

to her mouth. 'His wrist was broken, his hand almost coming off, but he was still . . .'

She looked at Chris. He lifted an arm as if to comfort her then chickened out, resting it back on his knee.

'I got there a while later,' he said. 'I didn't even know where I was going, I just *had* to go that way. And I see the taxi on its side and an ambulance and a police car, and I know she's not there, but she's somewhere close, so I park further up and go into the woods and she's just sitting by a tree. And it's like we've known each other forever, you know?'

Cal did know. He was feeling it now, as if he'd grown up with these guys, spent every waking hour of his life with them.

'So we get into the car and drive a bit further until I'm just too tired to go any more, and we sleep in the car in this clearing. Then the next morning we both start feeling this thing in our heads, like . . . Like I can't even explain it.'

'Like a silence,' said Cal. 'But a silence you can hear.'

'Yeah, that's just like it. So we both had that silence and we know we only have to drive and we'll get to where we need to be.'

'Him,' said Jade, nodding at Adam. The boy wasn't listening. He was chewing crisps but the slow, mechanical movements of his jaw were the only sign he was alive. 'Man, we almost died. He was at the dentist's, yeah? In this house on this normal kind of street. Where was it? Peterborough?'

'Ely,' said Chris. 'Well, near there, anyway.'

'He'd managed to hide in the attic, God knows how long he'd been there. This dentist, he went for us, but . . .'

She looked at Chris again and in that look Cal saw what they'd done. What they'd had to do.

'He doesn't talk,' she went on. 'We got his name from the label in his shirt. Poor little chicken.'

'And the guy with the gun,' said Brick. 'What about him?'

'He was the last,' said Chris. 'We were on the way here, following your message to come to the sea. Not that we'd have needed it, I mean something was pulling us out this way anyway, that same . . . *thing* that led me to Jade, then to Adam, then to that guy.'

'Never told us his name,' said Jade. 'We show up at this farm, it's not even that far from here, an hour maybe. And I knew it was a bad idea, 'cos there was blood everywhere, like *loads* of it.' She shuddered. 'So this guy comes up to the car and he's just insane. Not like the others, not like the *feral* people. He was with it, just *crazy* with it, you know?'

'He dumps an unconscious man in the boot, gets in and says he'll shoot us unless we do what he says,' said Chris. 'So we drive up here, all of us, and we didn't even need the satnav. We just knew you were in the park.'

There was silence when he finished. Cal took a sip of his own Fanta, ignoring the dirt on the glass. It felt good, crackling on his tongue.

'I'm glad you killed him,' spat Jade.

'You see any explosives?' Brick asked. Both Chris and Jade shrugged. 'He had to have been wired with something, an explosion like that. Sounds like he was crazy, so he had to have wired himself, yeah?'

'I guess so,' said Chris, although he didn't look sure.

It had to have been that, didn't it? Whatever had happened had knocked Cal off his feet and into a dark dream that he didn't think he'd ever wake up from. He'd come round eventually feeling like he'd been run over. Maybe the guy had had a grenade or something, one left over from the war that his grandad had brought home.

Or maybe it wasn't that. He thought back to the exploding car on the dual carriageway, the shape that had risen from it on wings of fire, screaming.

'We'll never know now, I guess,' Chris went on. 'Guy's splattered all over the place.'

'You said your head hurt,' said Cal. 'Right before everything happened.'

Chris and Jade nodded.

'And mine,' said Daisy. 'It was really sore for days. And I could hear it too, like a pulse.'

'*Thump-thump*, *thump-thump*,' said Brick. Daisy nodded, her eyes widening.

'That's it,' she said, sitting up straight in her chair. 'It was just like that, *just* like that!'

Cal's skin tightened into knots of goosebumps, his scalp tickling like someone was breathing on it.

'Things went bad right after my headache stopped,' said Chris. 'Like, *right* afterwards, within seconds.'

'Yeah, me too,' said Jade. 'I even remember thinking *Maybe this night isn't gonna be so bad* because my head-ache had gone, and then three seconds later or whatever we were in the ditch.'

It had been exactly like that, hadn't it? Cal thought back, remembering the football pitch, the sunlight. The pounding ache between his temples had gone, like it had just been switched off. Then the whole world had come after him.

'My headache was definitely gone when the ambu-lance man came,' said Daisy.

More silence. They all looked at each other, and in their eyes they saw themselves, they saw their own confusion and fear.

'What does it mean?' asked Jade.

'It was like something banging on my skull,' said Brick. '*Thump-thump, thump-thump, thump-thump, thump-thump.*'

The sound seemed to shake Adam from his trance. The kid looked up at Brick, his jaw frozen mid-chew. He looked frightened.

'*Thump-thump, thump-thump,*' Brick was slapping himself on the head now. 'It's like something was trying to get in there, trying to break down the door. *Thump-thump.*'

'Brick, that's enough,' said Cal. 'You're scaring him.'

Brick wasn't listening, still rapping on his skull and uttering that one word like a madman. Adam was fully awake now, his eyes like saucers.

'*Thump-thump,*' Brick went on. '*Thump-thump,* just

like that. *Thump-thump, thump-thump.*'

'Brick,' said Cal. 'Just—'

And that's when Adam opened his mouth, uttering a cry so shrill and so loud that Cal had to slap his hands to his ears, a cry that caused his glass to shatter into shrapnel, which swept across the room and extinguished every single one of the candles, plunging them into night.

Brick

Brick fumbled for the matches, sparking one up and thinking, *That scream can't have come out of that little boy.* It had been deafening, it had shattered glass.

'Give him some air,' said Daisy, who had her arm round Adam's shoulder. 'He's scared.'

'We're all scared,' said Jade. 'What the hell was that?'

'He just didn't like the noise,' said Daisy, glowering at Brick. He felt a perverse impulse to do it again, to start shouting *thump-thump* at the top of his voice, but he resisted it. 'He's fine, he just needs to get out of this place, it's too dark and scary in here.'

'Yeah,' said Cal as he walked to the restaurant door, holding it open and letting faint, dusty light into the room. 'Come on, it's too cold anyway.'

Rilke was still unconscious beside her brother. Brick left her there and followed the others down the corridor – grateful that there was no noise from the basement – and out through the fire exit. The heat held him like a golden hug and he wished it was possible to pull yourself out of your skin and soar up over the tin-foil brilliance of the ocean, to just follow the sun around the world for the rest of time and never have to be imprisoned by flesh and gravity and darkness ever again.

'What's going on?' He recognised his own tone –

aggressive, like he thought they were all hiding something. But he couldn't help it. When he was angry, hell when he was *any* kind of emotional, he just acted like an idiot. It was who he was. Everybody hated Brick Thomas.

'How should I know?' Cal snapped back. 'We don't know any more than you.'

Brick opened his mouth, ready to fire off some more accusations. He stopped himself, taking a deep breath and counting to five. When he finally spoke his voice was softer.

'This isn't normal.'

'You think?' said Cal.

Brick bit back his first response and went with his second.

'We need to work out what's happening,' he said. 'We need to really think about this. Because it's seriously messed up, Cal. And . . .' *I'm scared*, he wanted to say, but something stopped him. He coughed, looking out across the crazy golf course. The one-eyed giant squirrel stared back, grinning insanely.

'I'm scared too,' said Daisy, as though she'd read his mind. She had sat down between Jade and Adam on the low wall that surrounded the crazy golf. The little boy seemed to have calmed down, but his doll-like expression creeped the hell out of Brick.

'We need to work out exactly what we know,' said Cal. 'Everything. Like, logically.'

'People are trying to kill us,' said Chris.

'It's not just that, though, is it?' Cal pushed himself

up from the wall, pacing. 'They only want to kill us when we're close to them, when we're, what did you say, in their radar?'

'Yeah,' said Jade. 'It's like they sense us and they go mental, like a dog senses another dog.'

'And if we get away, get far enough away, they go back to normal,' Cal went on. 'They totally forget what they've done. But why? What would make them do that?'

The only answer was the lapping of the waves.

'Okay, we need to start from the beginning,' said Cal. 'The headache, the thumping. Maybe it was some kind of, I don't know . . . some kind of psychological change.'

'Physiological,' corrected Jade. 'It would have to be chemical. Maybe we're producing a new kind of pheromone, some kind of mutant gene that makes people hate us.'

'Makes sense,' said Cal, his trainers scuffing the dry ground as he walked back and forth. Each step was treading on Brick's temper but he swallowed it back down, the anger boiling in his stomach. 'Until you think about Schiller. And Adam. I've never heard a scream like that before in my life.'

'Daisy too,' said Brick. Cal stopped, and Daisy looked up, frowning.

'What about me?'

'You knew that kid's name,' he said. 'After the explosion. I heard you call it out, before anyone said anything. How did you know that?'

Daisy just shrugged.

'You wanna hear something weird?' Cal said, running his hands through his hair. 'I've been doing it too, like I can sometimes see things that you guys are thinking. It's nothing bad or anything. It's probably nothing at all. All it is, is that some of the thoughts in my head aren't mine, you know?'

Brick hawked up a ball of spit and launched it towards the crazy golf. It tasted of ash. 'You serious?'

'And what about the explosion?' Cal said, nodding. 'Brick, me and you were lying right next to that guy, I mean just feet away. We get thrown halfway across the park, but we're *okay*? That blast demolished the hot-dog stand, it cut loose bits of metal from the big wheel, but we're *okay*? You think about that?'

Brick hadn't thought about it, not until now. But Cal was right, if the man had been carrying explosives then they'd have been blown to pulp, bits of them would still be raining down on Fursville. He'd just assumed that they'd been lucky, but that in itself was a long stretch. Luck, after all, was used to giving Brick a wide, wide berth. So maybe the man hadn't been carrying a bomb, maybe it was something else . . .

But it was, remember, you saw it, something crawling from his belly.

Brick shook his head, the image dissolving like salt in water, forgotten. They'd been lucky, that's all, lucky, lucky, lucky. *Keep saying it, Brick, and you'll believe it eventually.*

'What does that mean, that we're invincible?' asked

Chris, leaning against the wall, his expression a portrait of desperation.

'I have no idea,' Cal went on. 'We have absolutely no idea.'

Brick felt the sun on his face, burning his fair, freckled skin. And suddenly something hit him.

'Not yet, we don't,' he said. 'But I think I might know how to find out.'

☹

'Dude, this is a *seriously* bad idea.'

They were in the car park, close enough to the boot of the Jag to hear the feeble moans from inside – 'Please let me out, I don't want to die' – but far enough away not to trigger the guy inside, not to make him feral. It was about twenty metres, Brick had worked out, give or take a few. That's how far their radar stretched, whether they could see or not. He held a hessian sack in his hands, a big one he'd found inside the kitchen next door to the restaurant. It was filthy, but hopefully it would do the job. Cal, Jade and Chris were beside him. Daisy had volunteered to look after Adam back in Fursville – it was better that they didn't see this.

'Seriously, dude,' Chris said again. 'This won't end well.'

'Gotta say I agree with him, mate,' said Cal. He was holding several long strips of fabric they'd torn from another sack. 'You don't know who's in there or what he's capable of.'

'We never saw him,' said Jade. 'He was unconscious when that farmer guy put him in. Could be anyone.'

'Doesn't matter who it is,' said Brick, gripping the bag. The material was rough and the feel of it against his fingertips made his skin crawl. 'Right now he's the only one who can help us, he's the one who can explain what's going on.'

And Lisa, right? She's down there, in the basement, you could always tell them about her?

No. Not yet. He didn't know what to do about Lisa, he needed more time to work out how to help her.

'Everybody set on what they have to do?' he asked, psyching himself up – not that the adrenalin needed much help as it cut through his heart. 'Remember, he's been in there for a day, in the sun, with nothing to eat or drink. He's going to be weak. Just remember that.'

'Christ,' muttered Chris. 'This is insane.'

'Pop it,' said Brick, opening the sack in front of him. Nothing happened. 'I said *pop it*, do it now.'

Chris held out the remote lock and thumbed the boot key. There was a soft click as the metal lid popped up an inch. The moans inside stopped, as if in disbelief.

'Go!' Brick yelled, charging forward, hearing Cal's feet thundering along beside him.

The lid was lifting, darkness peeling away from a pale face. The man saw them coming, his frightened pleas lasting maybe five or six words before they got close enough to do whatever it was they did. His face creased up like someone having an electric shock – his lips pulled back, his eyes bulging – and he started to scramble out of the boot.

Brick screamed, plunging the hessian bag over the man's head. The guy was fast, swiping his hand across Brick's cheek. He ignored the pain, yanking the bag down hard until it covered the guy down to his waist.

'Quick!' he panted. The man crunched into Brick and butted him to the floor. He hit hard, forgetting to tuck in his head, fireworks gouging chunks out of his sight. The feral landed on him, knees working into his ribs. Savage, guttural howls blasted out from behind the hessian, the man's jaw flexing in the cloth, like he was trying to chew his way through it and straight into Brick.

There was a crunch as Cal kicked out, sending the feral rolling to the side. The man managed to find his feet, just a pair of legs and a sack that ran in wild circles. Cal lashed out, an impressive punch that knocked the man on his backside. He pinned him to the floor, calling out for help as he tried to wrap the canvas strips around him.

Chris got there first, sitting on the man's legs. Jade was quick to follow, pressing both her hands on his head until Cal had looped the first strip round and tied it tight. He wrapped another round the guy's waist, then used the last one to bind his feet. When he was done he fell backwards, wiping the sweat from his brow and spitting out a couple of choice swears. Chris and Jade retreated too, leaving a hessian mummy squirming on the grass.

'Yeah, *real* weak,' Cal said, his chest heaving, his heartbeat making his words flutter.

'Now what?' asked Jade.

'We get him inside,' said Brick. 'Then we make him spill his guts.'

Rilke

Rilke swam up from fire into ice, the inferno of her dream extinguished by the immense cold of the room.

She curled into herself, shivering, knowing that Schiller was close by because nothing else could be pumping out that chill. She lay there, trying to hang on to her nightmare, remembering only that she had been falling through a storm of fire, a tornado of heat and light and noise; falling towards a churning ocean made up not of water but of long limbs and twisted jaws and eyes of burning pitch. The image was so real that she was sweating despite the temperature in the restaurant, her skin burning.

Maybe she was coming down with a fever? It didn't seem unlikely, given what she'd been through in the last day or so. She'd had one before, a bad one when she was a kid, a temperature of almost 40 degrees but massive chills that had made the bed rattle. She remembered what the doctor had told her, that fevers were a good thing, it meant your body was fighting.

But this was different. This was worse. Because she knew this had nothing to do with being ill. Her body was fighting something, but it wasn't anything the doctors could fix.

Rilke was suddenly aware of how quiet the room

was. She couldn't even hear the sea any more, just her brother's soft, rapid breathing, no louder than a heart-beat. Where was everybody?

Outside, she knew. She could almost see them there, an image that hung in the corner of her vision, something she could sense but couldn't quite make sense of.

'You okay, Schill?' she asked, not expecting a re-sponse. The pattern of his breathing remained un-broken. She shuffled across the room, remembering the layout, only banging her hip once before finding the table with the candles. She sparked up a match and lit one, the dancing flame bringing back more memories from her dream – a man on fire, something clawing its way free from his skin.

She shivered, and this time it had nothing to do with the cold.

That hadn't been a dream. That had been *real*.

She collapsed into a chair. What had happened out there, before she blacked out?

An explosion, a shock wave, from the guy you shot in the head.

She had *killed* somebody. She'd pulled the trigger and taken his life. She rested her elbows on the table, cradling her head in her hands. The knowledge of what she'd done was overwhelming, pulling her to-wards madness. It had been Daisy, it had been the little girl's fault. She'd made her do it, she'd whined and cried and screamed until Rilke hadn't been able to think straight. Had the man been about to kill Cal?

There was no way of knowing; she'd shot him before he even had a chance. And worse still, it hadn't even been one of the ferals, it had been one of *them*.

Her thoughts blazed and guttered like the candle. She'd killed a man, but it wasn't just that, she'd killed something else too. She closed her eyes, dragging herself back, seeing the thing that had unzipped the man's body like a sleeping bag, like a fancy-dress costume, which had torn and ripped and raged its way free, which had opened the abyss of its mouth and howled at her, spread impossible wings of fire. It couldn't have been real, and yet this thing, this creature, was more real than anything she'd ever known.

Her body shook, her teeth chattering.

Think, you stupid girl, she shouted at herself, slapping her forehead. What had it been, this thing? What was it doing disguised as a man?

Or maybe it hadn't been disguised. Maybe it had been *hiding*.

She pictured its face, those eyes that blazed – not with emotion, but with power. The heat from them seemed to burrow into her mind, leaving blackened traces there. What was it? And more importantly, if it had been hiding inside the man then was something like that hiding inside her too? Was there one inside all of them? Was this what made them different? Had they all been . . .

The word 'chosen' was what popped into Rilke's head. *That's right, isn't it? We're special, we've been chosen.*

She curled up against the table, shivering, feverish,

wondering what was wrong with her, wondering what it was that her body was fighting. She was strong, like all the Bastion women. When she put her mind to something then she always got it done, whatever the cost. It was no surprise that she'd been chosen.

But chosen for what? She wiped a hand over her brow, the skin hot and damp with sweat. It was as cold as a church in here, and the thought brought back memories of St Peter's in the village. She'd been forced there for mass every week for as long as she could remember. But maybe all those hours hadn't been wasted. Because in the stories she heard in church people were always being chosen.

For good things, and for bad.

'Why are we here, little brother?' she asked Schiller. 'Can you see it, from where you are? Are there answers there?'

Maybe it was some kind of test. Maybe she'd been supposed to shoot that guy, proof that she was strong enough to do whatever it was that she was here to do. Maybe his role in all this was a sacrificial one, a pawn to be slaughtered so that she could be pointed in the right direction. There were plenty of slaughtered pawns in those church stories too.

She had killed. But was it really a bad thing? Was it truly any different from the times she'd gone out with Schiller and taken pot shots at the rats in the grain barrels? Or sniped the pigeons on the telephone wires and the guttering? She'd shot a cat once, too, although it had been about to die anyway, stuck in a fox trap for

God knew how long. Dead rat, dead cat, dead bird, dead human. What did it matter to her?

Because she was none of those things.

The restaurant reeled, vertigo making her grip the table before she lost her balance. Her body shook, gripped by fever, the truth suddenly as bright and as golden as sunrise. It was almost too much to take in, too much to think about. She closed her eyes, her lips peeling open into a shuddering grin.

And just like that, she knew exactly what she had to do.

Daisy

'Do you miss your mum and dad?' Daisy asked.

She sat on the carousel, on one of the three horses that remained. It had lost most of its paint, but she didn't mind – its plain grey coat made it look more like a real pony. It still had parts of its face, its frightened eyes and its big teeth. It reminded her a bit of the ambulance man but she tried not to think about him. This was Angie – her mum's name – Angie her beautiful white Lipizzaner. She leant against the pole, swinging her legs absently, gazing at the horse beside hers. Adam was sitting on it, his arms wrapped around its neck, his cheek resting on the colourless plastic mane. His eyes blinked every few seconds, but that was about all he seemed capable of. She'd had to lift him up there because he was so limp.

Truth be told, she was a little scared of him now. The noise he'd made, back in the restaurant, that scream. It had come from the little boy's mouth, but it hadn't been him. She was sure of it.

'I miss my mum and dad,' she went on, then stopped because it was making her heart hurt. 'What shall we call your horse?'

The ice cubes in her head clinked. She was learning to make sense of them, of the different layers they formed. The ones down deep were always dark, cloudy. She could see things in them but she couldn't see what those things were exactly. The middle ones were better, they had some sounds too, muffled voices or piano music, things like that. But every now and then one would bobble to the surface and it would be just like she was living inside it, as though she were really there. She didn't always like these ones because sometimes they were too real. And sometimes, very occasionally, they were full of fire. She saw things in the flames, things with burning faces, things that scared her.

'Geoffrey,' she said, reading an ice cube, seeing a dog there, a small one with big ears and a goofy dog grin. The boy's eyes met hers as she said the word, and she thought she saw a smile in them, gone before she could be sure. 'Was that your dog? Geoffrey? That's a funny name. Wolfie would be better, or . . .' She couldn't think of any other dog names and shrugged. 'Okay, we'll call your horse Geoffrey. Mine is Angie, and we need a name for that one too or it will feel left out.'

She pointed at the horse further along the carousel. It was the one that had weathered the best, and she could still make out its bridle and the reins over its shoulders, even splotches of brown left on the saddle.

'How about Fishy?' she asked. Adam's eyes met hers again and he shook his head, just once. Daisy's face broke open into a grin. 'No, you're right, that's a silly name. How about Ploppy?' This time Adam's smile stretched to his lips. It seemed to make the whole park light up. He shook his head again. 'Wonky-Butt,' said Daisy, giggling. 'Wonky-Butt the Wonder Horse.'

Adam opened his mouth and Daisy leant towards him, almost sliding off her horse. He was going to speak! He never got the chance, though, as more voices bubbled up from close by, angry, panicked shouts.

Daisy turned to see the others traipsing into Fursville. Then she noticed what they were carrying, and she didn't need the ice cubes to tell her that there was someone inside the sack. It wriggled and shook and screamed and bucked, the four of them struggling to hold it. Cal was at the front, his arms locked around the man's head. Brick had the middle and Chris and Jade the legs.

The sack lurched hard and Cal dropped it, the man's head thumping to the floor where it continued to shake wildly. She heard Cal swear. He hefted the man's head up again and they all waddled off towards the pavilion like some weird caterpillar. Daisy sat up straight, wondering what to do. She had an idea where they were taking the man, and what they were going to do with him.

'Do you want to have a walk?' she said. Adam shook his head and hugged his horse even tighter than before. Daisy nodded. It was probably better that he didn't see. 'Well, shall I leave you here for five minutes? Will you be okay?'

Adam didn't reply. His eyes had taken on that glassy, lifeless sheen. Daisy didn't like it, it made him look not quite real. Once again she thought of that scream, of another mouth inside Adam's own, howling like a banshee. She grabbed the pole and swung herself carefully off the horse, walking over to him.

'I won't be long,' she said, stretching up on her tiptoes so she could run her hand up and down his back. 'Don't move, okay? You're safe here, but stay on your horse. And if you need me, just call out in your head, okay? I'll hear you.'

It seemed a strange thing to say, and yet perfectly natural at the same time. He didn't respond. Daisy stood there for a moment more, then clambered off the carousel and ran after the others. By the time she caught up with them they were shoving the frenzied sack-man through the chained fire exit. He was writhing so much that it seemed likely he'd pull the doors off their hinges.

'Just keep his legs still,' shouted Cal from inside. 'For God's sake, he's gonna kill himself at this rate.'

The man howled. There was no pain in that noise though, or fear. There was nothing but fury. Jade threw herself down onto the man's feet, hugging them as Cal pulled him into the pavilion.

'Little help?' yelled Cal. Brick muttered as he ducked through, reeling back as the man kicked out then crawling awkwardly inside. Chris followed, struggling to get his bulk into the gap.

Daisy waited until the shouts had faded a little before entering. When her eyes had adjusted to the gloom she saw that Cal and Brick were dragging the man up the shadowed corridor.

'In here,' Brick said, kicking open a door halfway down. Daisy followed them as they hurled the man inside, dumping him roughly against the far wall.

'Go!' yelled Cal, everyone stampeding from the room, almost tripping over one another. The sackman was already clambering up, looking like a headless, limbless torso in the dark room. He bounced off a hatch in the wall and lumbered towards the corridor. Brick waited for everyone to scramble out before pulling the door shut. The man thumped against it, hard enough to shake the dust from the ceiling. His savage growls were barely muffled by the wood.

'Now what?' said Jade, panting. 'How do we lock it?'

Brick glared at her, but he didn't answer.

'We can use more sack,' said Cal, digging in his pockets. 'Move.'

The others stood to one side as he tied a strip of something round the door handle, then looped the other end round a pipe that ran down the side of the door, knotting it twice. It didn't look particularly secure to Daisy, but it seemed to make the others relax. They stood back, collapsing against the walls.

'You ready to tell us what your plan is yet?' Cal said, panting. 'How're we supposed to get anything out of him when he's like that?'

'You see the hatch in there?' said Brick, wiping his hand over his face. 'Dumb waiter. There's a shaft leading from it right up to the kitchen. Come on.'

He led the way through the lobby, up the stairs and

past the entrance to the restaurant. It was freezing here, an icy draught blowing through the crack between the double doors of Waves like it was the middle of winter. Daisy shivered, pressing herself against Cal as they walked past the restaurant.

'You wanna check on the twins?' asked Cal.

'No,' Brick grunted. The corridor up here was a small one, with only one other door. Brick pushed through it into another dark hallway, then took the first opening on the right. Daisy had to squint against the blade of sunlight which cut through a broken board on the window, her eyes gradually adjusting.

The kitchen was huge, the metal surfaces and industrial ovens covered in grime – feathers and bird droppings everywhere. The tiled floor was cracked and, incredibly, little clusters of sea grass had planted themselves in the dirt, stretching tiny green fingers up towards the window. In a decade or so the whole park would probably be lost in a forest of green, like a fairy tale.

'Like *Sleeping Beauty*', she whispered to herself.

Brick made his way over to the far wall, to a small, square door that sat right in the middle of it – the other end of the dumb waiter.

'You ready?' he asked nobody in particular. He opened the hatch, the rusted hinges putting up a fight but finally giving in. Inside was nothing but darkness, and Brick stuck his head into it. Daisy expected to see a frenzied face emerging from the shaft below, jaws snapping shut around the boy's throat. He cleared his throat, speaking into the bottomless gloom of the dumb waiter. 'Hello? Can you hear me?'

A noise rose up from the room directly below, a rattling clank. Daisy guessed it was probably the guy trying to break out of the storeroom. Sound travelled perfectly up the dumb waiter, as though the man were in this very kitchen.

'Hello?' Brick said again. 'I know you can hear me, jackass, so say something.'

'You want me to do this?' said Cal.

'Why? 'Cos you're the nice guy?' Brick snapped back. He held his ground for a second then stepped away, holding his hands up. 'All yours.'

'Listen,' Cal called out, sticking his head through the door. Daisy leant in to better hear what he was saying. 'We're not going to hurt you, we just want to talk.'

More clattering, then the squeal of a door opening. At first Daisy thought the man had managed to get out. Then the sound of deep, rasping breaths ghosted up the shaft.

'Hello?' The voice was weak, and old. 'Who's there? Why are you doing this?'

'There's water in the tap,' said Cal, turning back to Brick. 'Isn't there?'

Brick nodded. The rasping faded, replaced by the distant sound of pipes rattling. The man returned after a minute or so, panting hard as if he'd just downed six pints in one go.

'Thank you,' he wheezed. 'Look, please, whoever you are, I don't have anything, I'm not rich, I just have a farm, nothing else.'

'We don't want anything from you,' Cal shouted. 'We only want to know why you tried to kill us.'

Silence, even his breathing faded.

'What?' he said eventually. 'I never tried to kill you, I don't even know who you are.'

'You don't remember what just happened?' Cal went on. 'You don't remember us locking you in the room.'

'I . . . I . . .' Daisy imagined him taking a good look around him, trying to work out where he was. 'I don't know how I got here,' he stuttered.

'What's the last thing you remember?' asked Cal.

'Being in the car,' he answered hesitantly. 'In the boot.'

'And before that?'

'Um, I was at home, working. It's Friday, isn't it?'

'Dude, he doesn't even know what day it is,' said Chris. Cal hushed him with a hand.

'Then what?'

'I, er, I don't know. I don't know.' He was sobbing now – big, gulping, metallic cries. 'It's just black. You've drugged me.'

'Ask him his name,' said Daisy quietly. She couldn't read anything from this man, there was nothing of his life in the ice cubes in her head. *Because he isn't one of us*, she thought. 'Tell him your name too.'

'We haven't drugged you,' said Cal. 'We're trying to help you. I'm Cal, by the way. What's your name?'

'Maltby,' said the man. 'Edward Maltby. Ted.'

'OK, Ted. I need you to *really* think,' said Cal, and

there was something calming about his voice. 'Who is the last person you remember seeing?'

More thumps, but this time they came from behind them, from the restaurant. Daisy glanced at the kitchen door, expecting to see Rilke stroll in. Instead she heard the girl walking down the stairs. At least she was okay, back on her feet after the explosion. Daisy was relieved.

'I don't know,' the man repeated, the shaft giving his voice a robotic quality. 'Please just let me go, I have a son, he . . .'

Silence, everyone crowding round the dumb waiter door to see what came next.

'Wait, I remember him, my son, coming back to the house. Is he okay? Is he here? He hasn't been well, he's had this headache . . .' Another pause. 'That's right, he was shouting about how it had gone, and . . . And then I don't know, then there was nothing.'

'So the douchebag with the gun was his son,' muttered Brick. 'Makes sense.'

'You're sure there's nothing else, Ted?' asked Cal. 'Nothing you can remember?'

'I . . . I think I must have been dreaming,' said Maltby, still weeping. 'I saw something, in the darkness. There was something bad there, I can't remember, but . . . It was just bad, it needed to . . . I don't know, why are you doing this?'

'What was it?' asked Cal. 'What did you see?'

The man replied but his words were garbled. Brick leant in, shoulder to shoulder with Cal, both of them peering down into the darkness.

'What did he say?' Brick asked.

'Sssh,' hissed Cal. Sure enough the man spoke again, his whimper like a dog's, curling up at the end into a snarl.

'What the hell?' said Jade. 'Is he going feral again?'

'It's Rilke,' said Daisy, seeing a flash of something red and horrid inside an ice cube. 'She's with him.'

The eerie haunted-house squeal of a door rose up the dumb waiter. The man roared, a scream of rage that sent everyone skittering back from the wall. It was just as well, because the noise that followed would have deafened them – the unmistakable crack of a gunshot.

Brick

Brick and Cal looked at each other as the gunshot echoed around the room. Then they turned and ran.

Brick took the lead, his long legs giving him the advantage as he thundered down the stairs and across the lobby. He smashed through the door marked 'Staff Only', skidding to a halt when he saw Rilke in the corridor. Her eyes were gleaming, the brightest thing in the dusk.

She was holding the gun.

'What the hell have you done?' he yelled. She stared back, not blinking. The barrel of the pistol was smoking, the air thick with the bitter scent of cordite. Brick started forward again, reaching the stockroom door and looking inside. He felt his stomach churn, his legs shaking so much he had to lean against the door jamb or fall face-first onto the corpse that lay inside. A ragged hole had been sunk into the old man's chest and blood had pooled there.

Clattering feet, then Cal was by his side again. He made a noise that was halfway between a gulp and a dry heave, then whipped round.

'Don't look, Daisy,' he said. 'Stay there, stay there.'

Chris barged between Cal and Brick.

'You *killed* him,' he said.

Brick looked at Rilke again, the girl's face set in stone.

'I said *what the hell have you done?*' he shouted. He took a step towards her, stopping only when she lifted the gun, pointing that smoking barrel right at his forehead.

'That's enough, Rilke,' said Cal. 'Christ, what do you think you're doing? Put that thing down.'

'Answer, dammit,' said Brick, the emotions stewing in his gut, ready to make him do something stupid. 'Why did you do that? He was talking to us, he was about to tell us something.'

'No,' said Rilke. 'He wasn't.'

'How do you know?' Brick went on. 'You weren't even there.'

He felt a hand on his arm, Cal's fingers squeezing. He shrugged him away, taking another step towards Rilke. *How many shots have been fired?* He tried to work it out. *One on the beach, two outside, I think, then another one now. Two bullets left?* She'd only need one, though, to put a hole where his brain once sat.

'I reloaded,' she answered his unspoken question for him, offering him a smile as sharp and as dangerous as a scalpel blade. 'Cal was kind enough to bring a big, big box of bullets with him.'

'Rilke, I know you've been through a lot,' said Cal in that infuriatingly calm tone of his. 'I know how you must be feeling. We all feel it. But he was safe in there, we'd locked him in. He couldn't hurt us.'

'I know,' said Rilke, her entire body motionless

except for her eyes, which slid round towards Cal. 'That isn't why I did it.'

'Why, then?' asked Cal.

'Because he wasn't one of us,' she said. 'And anyone who isn't one of us doesn't deserve to live.'

'You don't know what you're talking about,' said Jade.

'But I do,' she said, lowering the gun but keeping her finger on the trigger. 'I know exactly what I'm talking about. And you do too, Daisy.'

Brick glanced back to where Daisy stood, wreathed in darkness, by the door. He could see her silhouetted head shaking.

'Leave her out of this,' said Cal. 'Just give me the gun, okay, then we can talk about it.'

He moved towards her, his hand out, but Rilke took a step back, her trigger finger twitching.

'None of you understand what's going on,' she said. 'It's pathetic. But we know, don't we, Daisy? We know the truth.'

'I don't know what you're talking about, Rilke,' said Daisy. 'I don't know anything.'

'You *do* know,' Rilke went on, still retreating down the corridor. 'You've seen it. The fire inside them, inside *us*.'

'Fire?' said Brick. 'You're off your head.'

'Please, Rilke,' sobbed Daisy. 'Please give Cal the gun, please. I don't want anyone to get hurt.'

'We can't have them here,' Rilke said. *Them?* Brick felt a finger of ice run up his back, settling at the base of his skull. 'They'll try to stop us.'

She was still retreating, stopping at the door that led down to the basement. She reached out and turned the handle. Brick's entire body tensed, ready to fly at her.

'Don't you dare,' he growled. 'I'll kill you.'

'Dare what?' asked Cal. 'What's in there?'

Brick tuned him out, tuned them all out. His head was a furnace, nothing but white heat and noise. He started forward, not even stopping when Rilke raised the gun again, that unblinking black eye staring right at him. She was crazy but there was no way she'd shoot him, no way she'd pull that trigger.

The corridor flashed, the shot making his eardrums ring. It was like a cannon had gone off. He crashed to his knees, his hands up to his face, expecting blood. But everything was there, where it should be.

'The next one won't miss,' said Rilke, the same thing she'd said right before blowing that guy's face off. She had pushed open the door and was now treading carefully down the stairs, never taking her eyes off him.

'Please,' Brick said, his voice breaking. He crawled to the top of the stairs on his hands and knees, hearing Lisa's panicked cries below, becoming less and less human as Rilke closed in. 'Please don't do this, don't hurt her, she didn't do anything to you.'

'Not yet,' Rilke said. 'But she will, if she gets the chance. They all will. It's us against them, now, but we're so much better than them.' She laughed, a lunatic chuckle that rose from the darkness of the steps. 'We're creatures of fire, now. And what does fire do best? It *purges.*'

Brick was crying, everything that had been boiling inside him now escaping like steam. The tears dropped onto his hands, impossibly hot, and through the blur he saw Rilke kick away the pole he'd used to wedge the basement door closed. Lisa was thumping herself against it, howling, screeching.

They couldn't be the last sounds she'd ever make, they *couldn't* be. He wanted to hear her speak again, even if it was just to insult him; he wanted to hear that laugh, the one he'd always found so annoying but which made him smile when she wasn't looking; he wanted to feel her lips on his, the warmth of her body.

'Rilke,' he sobbed. 'I'm begging you.'

'Don't,' she called back up the stairs. 'You're better than that now. You're *more* than that.'

And with that she opened the basement door. Brick watched as a shape flew out of it on all fours, thumping head first into the wall. He watched as Rilke levelled the gun at Lisa's head. He watched as she pulled the trigger. Then he closed his eyes and let the grief consume him.

Past the wracking sobs, past the thunder in his ears, he heard Rilke walk back up the stairs. She put a hand on his shoulder.

'You'll thank me for this,' she said.

Then she was gone.

Daisy

Daisy couldn't remember how to move. It was as though her body had been carved from stone, chipped away a piece at a time, given only the illusion of life. She watched as Rilke came back up the stairs and patted Brick's shoulder; watched as she walked calmly down the corridor towards her. Daisy wanted to run away, to flee before Rilke tried to shoot her as well, but those stone legs of hers wouldn't let her. She was fixed there, in that dark corridor that stank of bullets and meat.

'Don't be scared, Daisy,' said Rilke. She leant in, her eyes catching the light that seeped through from the foyer. They looked like alien eyes, as if they were radioactive or something. 'You may not know it yet, but I had to do that,' she said. 'We're the same, you and me. Look into your head, you'll see the truth soon enough.'

Rilke straightened up and walked through the door. Brick's sobs filled the space where she had been, the noise so much worse because it was coming from him, coming from someone so strong. Bricks weren't supposed to cry, they could weather anything.

'Brick?' Cal was stooped over the bigger boy, his hand where Rilke's had been. Chris and Jade looked on like they were in the audience at the theatre, their jaws

355

unhinged. 'Brick, mate, what just happened? Who was that?'

His girlfriend, of course. Lisa, thought Daisy. She'd been locked down there, that's why the stairs had given Daisy the creeps. Her head was full of ice cubes, all smashing against each other. She could see her, a pretty girl who maybe wore a little too much make-up, who swore a lot and who didn't always *get it.* Daisy wasn't sure exactly *what* she didn't get, it was just what she could see, and sense, from those little transparent movies. He'd loved her, though, had Brick. He'd loved her with everything he had, and now she was gone. Now he wouldn't be able to fix her. Not ever.

Those ice cubes were melting, and with them came anger – not hers, she understood, but his. She took a step towards Brick and Cal, then thought better of it, bolting through the door and chasing after Rilke.

'Daisy, wait!' Cal called out behind her. She ignored him, almost tripping up the sweeping stairs. Rilke was walking into Waves but she must have heard Daisy's clattering footsteps because she turned round, a weird, false smile imprinted on her lips. The gun hung by her side, little wisps of smoke curling up from it. Daisy opened her mouth, ready to shout at her, to *swear* if she had to, but she couldn't get the words out.

'We don't have a choice,' said Rilke. 'This is happening for a reason.'

'What reason can you . . . can there . . . You can't just *kill* people.'

'There are more important things at stake here,'

Rilke said. 'Don't you see that? We have to survive. We *have* to. If we don't . . .'

For the first time the expression on Rilke's face wavered, her smile fading. It was like watching a ventriloquist's dummy, thought Daisy, as though she was speaking not for herself but was a mouthpiece for someone else; some*thing* else. The older girl looked down at the gun in her hands and swallowed hard, but when she looked back at Daisy the smile flickered on again – uncertain on her lips but bright and unshaken in her eyes.

'I need you to trust me,' she said. 'To trust that I'm telling you the truth. Those two down there, they would have killed us without a second thought. Don't you see? It's us against them, now, but there's more to it than that, it's . . .' She seemed to struggle again, her eyes darting left and right. 'Just trust me,' she said, trance-like. 'You'll understand it, soon enough.'

More ice cubes, the ones with fire in this time. Daisy saw a tide of people, ferals, surging into the park on a wave of blood, crashing against something that burned, something wonderful. It didn't make any sense, the images were so fast and so disconnected that they were making her sick.

'And trust *them*,' said Rilke. 'They won't lie to you.'

'*Who?*'

'*Them*,' Rilke repeated, her eyes seeming to pierce Daisy's forehead, like she could see what was happening inside. 'Trust the ice. Trust the fire.'

Daisy heard the 'staff only' door creak below, then

the stomp of feet coming up the stairs. Rilke retreated further into the darkness of the restaurant until only her eyes, her teeth and the glinting barrel of the gun could be seen. Cal appeared by Daisy's side. His eyes were red, the dirt on his face tear-streaked.

'You shouldn't have done that,' he croaked. 'That was his girlfriend. He's going to kill you.'

'No,' said the shadow in the doorway. 'He's not. He's going to do exactly what I tell him.'

'What?' Cal spat. 'What are you talking about, Rilke?'

'*Exactly* what I tell him,' she said again, sinking deeper into the tar-pit dark. It didn't sound like Rilke speaking any more, it sounded like something much older. 'He doesn't have a choice.'

Cal looked at Daisy. He was scared, it seemed to ooze from his every pore. Daisy reached out and took hold of his hand and he squeezed back, so hard she felt one of her finger joints pop. Rilke retreated even further, letting the door swing shut.

'You'll come to me when you're ready,' said Rilke, her voice muffled. 'You all will.'

There was a click, a heavy thump, and it took Daisy a moment to realise she'd locked the door. Rilke laughed, a soft chuckle that set Daisy's teeth on edge.

'Because you'll die if you don't.'

The Other: III

Your enemy the devil prowls around like a roaring lion
looking for someone to devour.
   1 Peter 5:8

Murdoch

The convoy was made up of nineteen vehicles. Four police bikes took the lead, sweeping other cars out of the way, blocking the entrances onto the dual carriageway and letting the first three black government limousines move at a constant seventy miles per hour. Smack bang in the middle was a private ambulance, long, black and windowless, which looked more like a hearse. Two more police bikes flanked it, their riders equipped with machine guns and dark-visored helmets. Another three limos rode in their wake.

Detective Inspector Alan Murdoch sat in the second of these, sandwiched between Dr Sven Jorgensen, the Scotland Yard pathologist, and one of his assistants from the morgue. He glanced through the tinted glass of the rear window to see the two squad cars and four bikes that formed the tail of the convoy. Their blue lights turned the city around them into a constantly shifting ocean, the illusion so strong that Murdoch suddenly felt like he was drowning, like there was no oxygen left in the car.

He sat forward, sucking in air, the seat belt tight around his neck. The convoy thundered onto a roundabout, hardly slowing, then pulled onto the M1. Wide-eyed people watched them go from inside their cars.

If only they knew, he thought, peering through the vehicles in front to see the ambulance. Its single patient lay in a bed in the back. Not alive. Not dead either. Breathing in that one endless, howling breath. *If only they could see.*

He wanted to signal back at them. He wanted their help. He wanted them to know that he was a prisoner. Of course they'd never actually said that, the soldiers who had escorted him out of his Thames House cell. They'd invited him to come with them, but there had only been one answer he could give. This was MI5, this was national security. He may have been one of the top ranking detectives in the capital, but if he'd made a break for it — as he'd so desperately wanted to — they'd probably have shot him dead on the spot.

Murdoch was so tired that he wasn't sure if the muscles in his face worked any more. His eyelids felt as though they were being pushed down, like those of a corpse that somebody was trying to close for the last time. His skin broke into painful goosebumps at the thought and he had to sit forward in his seat again, fists clenched, to stop the world from spinning. The guy to his left, one of Jorgensen's assistants, sat with his face against the window, sobbing gently. He'd been like that since they'd left MI5.

A police bike accelerated past them, its siren squealing, vanishing past the side of the ambulance. *Please let us stop*, Murdoch prayed. *Let something distract them so I can get out of here.* But the convoy continued, blasting through the heavy evening air like a freight train. They were heading out of London, he realised, going north-west. The only place he could think of that lay out this way was Northwood, the military base.

He looked to his side, past Jorgensen's weary face, through the shaded window which turned the sunlight to toffee. He lived close to here, over in Finchley. Right now Alice would be putting John in the bath, maybe feeding him, trying to stay calm for the baby. She'd have called his work by now, his friends. She'd be desperate. Maybe the security service would already have spoken to her, told her he had been detained, but that would only make her more frantic. He wished he could put his hand to the glass, somehow beam out a message to her. *It's going to be okay*. He realised he was doing it anyway. *I'll be back soon, I won't let them keep us apart. I promise. Please don't worry*.

It was as he was directing those words out of the car, willing them to fly home, that he heard the squeal of brakes in front. Then the back door of the ambulance opened and the unravelling of his world began.

'Mick, what the hell is it doing?'

Mick Rosen jumped at the sound of his partner's voice. He felt like he was lying on a knife-edge, the slightest movement or sound ready to slice him in two. He'd never been this scared in his life, even though he'd been a medic in Iraq and Afghanistan, even though he'd ridden in ambulances across battlegrounds and minefields and through enemy camps with bullets punching through the windows. He thought he'd seen just about everything there was to see, every horror that man was capable of inflicting.

He'd thought wrong.

He glanced at the trolley that lay in the centre of the private ambulance. There were no machines there, no wires or drips. Why would there be? The man that lay on it, a sheet pulled up to his neck, was dead. He had no pulse, his blood wasn't flowing, he stank of rot the way any day-old corpse does in the middle of summer.

Yet his mouth hung open, too wide, a snake's just before it devours its prey. And it was still inhaling that single, unending breath, that hellish wheeze which had already made Mick throw up once that afternoon and which was close to making it happen again. He was wearing a biohazard suit, though, so he didn't have a choice but to hold it back. He swallowed a mouthful of bile, groaning without even knowing he was doing it.

Nobody knew for sure what this thing was, but there were rumours. They'd had a priest come in to look at it – not a doctor, not a surgeon but a *priest*. That had spooked Mick more than the corpse itself, that and the fact that he'd heard a few people whispering words like 'Antichrist' and 'Defiler'. It was absurd, ludicrous – until he looked back at the body, heard that awful, guttering breath.

'What do you mean?' he managed after a moment or two. His partner, sitting next to him at the back of the ambulance, was Alik Garro. They'd been working

together for a couple of years now for SIS, mostly dis-
posing of the bodies of terrorist suspects who had been
subjected to over-enthusiastic interrogation. They wer-
en't exactly friends, but they got on okay, united by the
knowledge that what they were doing was keeping the
country safe, was keeping the bad guys out.

'I thought . . .' Alik started. He was staring at the
corpse, and most of the colour had drained from his
face, leaven it ashen behind the plastic of his visor. He
shook his head, sitting back. 'Nothing. It's nothing.
That thing's just giving me the heebie-jeebies.'

The ambulance swung round a corner, hard enough
to throw Mick against Alik. His seat wobbled, and for
a second he thought he was going to end up face-first
on the corpse. This time a wad of something he'd had
for lunch made it up his throat, sitting on his tongue.
He swallowed again, drenched in cold sweat.

Hurry up, he screamed at the driver. They were only
going to Northwood, why hadn't they arrived yet? He
would give practically anything to get out of this metal
coffin. He felt the ambulance slow, pulling left then
accelerating again. Was the driver *trying* to make him
chunder?

'Mick, there it was again!'

Alik was on his feet this time, gripping the door
handle. He was staring right at the corpse, the look
on his face one of a man who's just seen his kid get
hit by a lorry. Mick's heart lurched, palpitating, as if it
couldn't quite remember how it was supposed to work.
He massaged the pain from his chest, still watching

Alik. He didn't want to see what the other man was seeing.

But something dragged his head round, forcing him to look. The corpse lay there, those eyes so dead and so alive at the same time. He'd tried to close them, as had Alik, but they kept springing open. There was a darkness in those milky, lifeless pupils, a heavy black weight which seemed to fly back and forth, invisible but unmissable. It was like there was something in there that wanted out.

'Wha—' Mick started, then he saw it himself.

The corpse's mouth was widening. It wasn't *opening*, it was just getting bigger. Mick realised he was on his feet as well, his back pressed against the door of the ambulance. *Open it*, his brain screamed. *Open it and jump, because better to be dead on the motorway than to see this*. But he could no more turn the handle than he could force a cry up the constricted passage of his throat.

A tooth dropped from the corpse's gums, vanishing into its throat with a dry click. Another followed, sucked in like it had been hoovered up. And that noise, that relentless breath, was getting louder, increasing in pitch like a jet engine before take-off.

'No,' Mick said, shaking his head, the fear like a suit of razor wire beneath his skin. 'No.' *Keep saying it and it will stop, it has to.* 'No, please no.'

Those gums were crumbling, dissolving into its expanding maw. It reminded Mick of a sandcastle at the beach when the tide rises, the water lapping away at the foundations, pulling it in slowly but inexorably.

The dead man's lips, too, were coming apart, breaking into a million particles which defied gravity, circling the chasm of its mouth.

'Jesus, stop the ambulance!' Alik was screaming, the words misting up his visor. He was clawing at the door, now, thumping on it, his eyes so wide they didn't look real. 'Stop the ambulance! Let us out!'

The ambulance didn't slow, the screams lost in the turbine-howl of the corpse's breath. Its eyes had changed, too. That spark of life inside them was brighter, full of rancid glee. Mick reached out and grabbed Alik's arm, holding it tight.

'Where's your radio?' he asked. Alik stared back like he didn't recognise him. 'Your radio, Alik?'

Alik didn't reply, and Mick realised he'd lost him. He'd seen what fear could do to a man. It could strip his mind in seconds and leave him nothing but a collection of broken, unconnected parts. Mick swore, scouring the ambulance for the radio. It was the only way of getting through to the driver. The cabin back here was sound-proofed.

Don't look at it, his brain told him. He knew that his own mind was on the verge of cracking. He could feel the madness there, like an unscratchable itch right at the base of his brain. *Don't look, Mick.* And yet how could he not? His head seemed to swivel round by itself, his eyes focusing on the nightmare in the middle of the ambulance.

The corpse's face was a whirlwind of particles which circled a throat of utter darkness. That throat wasn't just lightless, it was devoid of *everything*. It was pure, absolute absence. It was still growing, too, the flesh of the man's cheeks and nose crumbling into dust, circling that pool like debris around a black hole.

And those eyes. Those dead, all-seeing eyes. They were alive with laughter, a sick delight that seemed to scoop out Mick's insides. He collapsed against the door, the radio forgotten, all things forgotten. Nothing mattered any more. How could it, when something like this existed?

The ambulance slowed and Mick felt himself being pulled towards the centre of it. He managed to grab the door handle, to root himself in place, but Alik wasn't so lucky. His partner slid across the floor without a sound, hitting the end of the trolley and doubling over it.

That whirlwind breath seemed to double in volume, an inwards howl that detonated inside Mick's head, making him clamp his hands to his ears. Alik's face was dissolving into the whirlwind. His eyes were the first to go, melting into sherbet and spiralling down the churning hole. The rest followed, erased like an oil painting drenched in turpentine. Alik's body juddered and shook, suspended off the ground as if by invisible ropes.

There was something else, too, something else coming out of Alik. Mick couldn't see it so much as feel it, an energy seeping from his partner, being pulled from every pore, sucked into the madness.

The corpse was eating Alik's soul.

The Antichrist, Mick thought. *The Defiler, the Beast.*

Only he knew that this thing was older than the Bible; ageless, and infinitely evil.

The itch inside his skull expanded, obliterating everything in a single, devastating short-circuit. Mick no longer knew he had a wife, he couldn't remember the names of his children. Every moment of his past was erased in that one fraction of a second.

The last few flecks of Alik circled the mouth, disappearing. The vortex growled, bigger now, hungrier. It wanted more. Mick could feel it reaching for him, invisible fingers seeking to pull him close, wanting to devour his soul too. But he wouldn't let it have him.

He turned away, opened the door of the speeding ambulance, and stepped into the evening.

A man flew from the back of the ambulance into the bonnet of the car in front, smashing the windscreen and rolling over the roof. He dropped under the wheels of the limo in which Murdoch was riding, making it lurch so hard that everyone inside was jolted from their seats. Murdoch's head cracked against the ceiling but he didn't even notice. He watched the other car veer off into the hard shoulder of the motorway, striking the barrier and cartwheeling into the field beyond.

'What the—' said Murdoch, looking out the rear window as they passed the wreckage, the air behind them already full of smoke. 'What the hell are you doing? They need help.'

'Convoy doesn't stop until we get to our destination,' said the driver. And he said something else but the words tailed off, becoming a gasp as he looked at the ambulance.

'What *is* that?' Dr Jorgensen said, pressing himself against Murdoch, pointing past the front seats. Murdoch followed his finger, and at first he couldn't work out what he was seeing. Something was happening inside the ambulance, a raging tornado of objects which surged and spiralled through the air. The lights were flashing on and off, the doors flapping, making it impossible to see clearly what was going on.

'Get in touch with lead,' said the driver. The front-seat passenger – another MI5 agent in a black suit – put his hand to his ear.

'Convoy 1 this is Convoy 5,' he said. 'Convoy 4 is down and we have a problem inside the ambulance.'

Nobody spoke. Murdoch squinted, peering into the flickering chaos. A noise had risen up over the thrum of tyres on tarmac, a sound that grated down his spine. *It can't be*, he thought, but it was. It was the corpse, that same breath only louder now. Much louder.

'Pull over,' he said again, his voice a hiss. 'Do it now.'

'No, sir,' said the driver. 'Our orders—'

'Screw your orders,' said Murdoch. 'Stop the car *now*.'

'I need you to calm down, sir,' said the man in the passenger seat, turning. His right hand had strayed under his suit jacket and Murdoch knew what he had holstered there – a government-issue 9mm. It didn't matter. Whatever was happening inside that ambulance was a million times worse than any gun. 'Sit back in your seat and do not speak.'

Murdoch didn't obey. He reached to his side, past Jorgensen, grabbing the door handle and wrenching hard. It was locked. He tried the other side, the morgue assistant next to him no longer crying, just staring through the windscreen making choking noises.

'Sir, if you do not sit back in your seat and calm down then I will be forced to subdue you.'

The door didn't budge, and Murdoch leaned forward, ready to shout back at the man, ready to take a swing at him if he had to.

He never got the chance.

In front, the ambulance exploded – not into fire, but darkness. It seemed to happen in slow motion, a whip-crack of black lightning that buckled the metal walls, opening them like a flower; which lifted the wheels off the road, making the whole vehicle fly. A lightless wave pulsed from the ruined ambulance, so dark that it hurt Murdoch's eyes to look at it. It was as if that patch of existence had been erased, as if substance had been inverted, turned to absence. Through that gap, past that hole in reality, was something so vast, so infinite, so empty that his heart broke the moment he saw it. *That's the real universe*, he understood. *The truth behind the mask. That's all there is, and it's nothing.*

Another blast ripped the ambulance apart, sending pieces of wheel and engine and flesh in every direction – still in slow motion, like time had no power here.

Its exhaust javelined backwards, punching through the windscreen of the car, impaling the driver, not stopping until it had passed right through Jorgensen in the back seat. Murdoch could hear the sizzle of blood on the hot metal, the air suddenly heavy with the stench of cooked meat. Jorgensen's hand gripped his arm, flexing once before falling still. The car smashed into the centre divide, sparks cascading from the doors as it ground to a halt.

The corpse was suspended above the road in a pocket of absolute night. Its mouth was a churning void, one that seemed to suck up all the light and goodness of the world. Its eyes blazed into the car, right into Murdoch's head.

It lifted its hands, and as it did so another rippling wave of shadow expanded across the motorway. Murdoch saw a motorbike lifted into the air and pulled into pieces, its rider atomised into a sparkling crimson cloud which was sucked towards the corpse's raging mouth. He saw one of the limos in front peel apart like a kit model, its passengers disintegrating as they were dragged into the chasm. A storm of metal and emptied flesh ground around the living corpse like a tornado, more blinding black lightning firing wildly in the maelstrom.

There was another crack of thunder. Murdoch glanced round to see two young girls on the road, holding each other as a hail of burning embers drifted down around them. They stared at the monster hanging there.

I'm sorry. One of the girls spoke, a voice that seemed to be whispered right into his ear. *I can't save you.*

He reached out to them, his fingers pressed into the glass.

Don't be sorry, he thought. *It will devour you too. It will devour us all.*

'Alice,' he said, thinking of his wife, of his son, knowing that he would never see them again – not in this life, not in any other.

The corpse gestured again with its fingers and more of the world disappeared beneath a blanket of darkness. Murdoch felt his car rise off the ground, then that shadow reached him and it was as if everyone he knew and loved had died – a grief so heavy, so impossible, that it literally pulled him apart. He lifted his hands to his face, seeing his fingers begin to fragment into particles the size of sand grains. They funnelled towards the dead man, his hands vanishing, then his arms, his vision sparking as his brain turned to dust. And it was almost worse that there was no pain, because at least pain would be one final reminder that he had once lived.

But there was only the vast, roiling, infinite, silent darkness.

Then nothing.

The Fury

Brick felt it. He was drenched in sweat from toiling in the unforgiving sun, every muscle aching. He laid down the shovel, straightening his back, feeling as if night had fallen suddenly and without warning, even though the sun was still warm on his back. Lisa lay beside him, on a patch of light-drenched grass close to the back fence, covered with a tablecloth. He had carried her out here himself, her dead weight making her a hundred times heavier than she had been before. He hadn't yet looked at her face, because he knew that once he did there could be no more doubt, no more fooling himself that she'd be coming back. He blinked, the sunshine gradually returning. But that chill remained, keeping the gooseflesh on his arms. He picked up the shovel, stepped into her grave, and carried on digging.

Cal and Daisy felt it. They were watching Brick from a distance, her hands wrapped tight around his arm the way she had always clung on to her mum. They turned to each other, both feeling that same sudden, crushing sadness, the knowledge that something in the world

374

had gone terribly, irreversibly wrong. It was like animals sensing an earthquake, Cal thought, not knowing why they are scared, just understanding that they have to escape. *It's the Fury*, he realised. *Things are changing.* And even as the words crossed his mind Daisy hugged him tighter. He looked into her pale eyes and saw her voice there. *It's going to get bad, Cal. It's going to get a lot worse.* He gripped her tight, the same way he would grip a float if he was drowning. He didn't ever want to let go.

☹

Jade felt it. She sat slumped in the hallway inside the pavilion, a dead man within spitting distance. She felt it as a pressure, one that grated down the corridor and forced itself into her head, blocking her ears like that time she'd dived too deep into the swimming pool. It sat there, an unwanted guest, making even the sadness seem obsolete, futile. It was so dreadful that she opened her mouth to scream, but she couldn't get the noise out. She sat there, silently howling, knowing that nothing would ever be the same, nothing could ever be *good* again.

☹

Chris felt it. He stood on the beach, throwing stones into the sea. He watched one hurtle through the hot air, thinking that despite the Fury, despite the shootings, things weren't all that bad – at least the sun was shining. Then, in an instant, it was as if the ocean rose up, a solid wall of darkness which towered over him, which blocked out the light and which dragged itself over the world, burying everything in silt and saltwater. He dropped to his knees, fighting to remember how to breathe, blinking reality back to life. But even with the sun on his face again he knew that the darkness was still there. It had been born.

☹

Adam felt it. He slept deeply in the pavilion foyer. His dreams of horses and fairgrounds were abruptly tainted, like ink spreading through a bowl of water. Dark, bulging clouds mushroomed outwards, their blue-black surface as dense as granite, polluting everything and leaving him alone inside a bottomless cavern. He cried out for his mum, and for the girl, Daisy, but all that existed in the night was him and a shapeless creature of boundless sorrow. His sleeping body shook, but he did not wake.

☹

Rilke felt it. She shivered in the candlelit restaurant, still holding the revolver. She'd killed for a reason, because she had to, because they all had a more important job to do and they couldn't let anything stand in their way. But the faces of the man and the girl she had murdered hung before her, ghost-like against the gloom, not speaking, not moving, just watching her. They'd be there forever, she realised. They'd be there until she died. And the thought seemed like the worst possible thing she could imagine, until *it* hit her, a depthless, hopeless wave of utter nothingness. She dropped the gun, clamping her hands to her head, screaming, *Go away go away go away go away*.

☹

Even Schiller felt it, locked inside the cold casket of his body. He groaned, twitching, shedding sparkling flakes of ice on the floor. Rilke shot up, running over to where he lay and collapsing to her knees beside him. She called his name, holding his head, stroking his cheek, waiting for his eyes to open. He moaned again, a nightmare noise, then he lay still. But she knew he'd sensed the same thing as her, even from deep inside whatever fathomless sleep he was lost in. He understood what was happening.

'You have to get better soon, Schill,' Rilke said, brushing back strands of thin, dark hair from his eyes. 'We need you. We all do.'

She put her head on his chest, trying to ignore the bone-numbing chill, focusing on the shadow that had pulled itself over her mind, which had pulled itself over everything.

'Because it's here, little brother,' she said. 'It's here.'

Sunday

And where two raging fires meet together
They do consume the thing that feeds their fury.
William Shakespeare, *The Taming of the Shrew*

Brick

He woke to the sensation of needles in his back, moving rapidly up and down his spine. It wasn't painful, it was almost relaxing, until something else began to jab into the flesh of his shoulder.

'Ow!' he said, rolling over, the world a blur. There was a flurry of noise, wings beating and a coarse caw. He blinked hard until he made out a seagull on the ground a few feet away. It stared at him with black-eyed curiosity, skipping closer as if about to begin another attack. Brick grabbed a handful of soil and lobbed it at the bird, watching it waddle clumsily then soar with perfect grace into the burgeoning dawn. 'Yeah, you better run,' he called after it, and he almost managed a smile before remembering where he was.

The sandy soil was from a mound next to him, a five-foot-five by three-foot outline in the grass. It had taken hours to dig, but only minutes to fill in – he'd desperately swept earth over the corpse and its chequered tablecloth shroud until no trace of it remained. She had been cold when he'd touched her, stiff. She hadn't felt real. Brick wasn't sure if that had made it easier or harder.

He'd walked onto the moonlit beach when he'd finished. There he'd found a starfish, a dead one. He'd

381

placed it on the head of her grave and told himself he was doing it as a mark of respect, so he wouldn't forget. In reality, though, he'd done it because he worried that if he didn't weigh down the grave with something then her body would crawl free in the night. It would come after him. He'd followed the starfish with about a hundred stones.

And then he'd fallen asleep next to her. She had been cold, but the earth had been warm. It had spent the day soaking up the heat, and the touch of it on his skin was almost human. It could have been her lying next to him, keeping the night at bay.

But it wasn't, of course. He'd killed her. He hadn't pulled the trigger, but he hadn't stopped it from happening, and that made him as guilty as Rilke.

Rilke.

Brick struggled to his feet, his whole body aching. The effort made his head spin, a blood rush that caused the morning light to prickle like static. It brought back something else, a feeling he'd had when he was digging, a sensation that something really bad had happened. *It did, you moron*, his brain told him. *Lisa died*. Only it was more than that. He couldn't explain it, just that it had felt as if the entire world had lost someone it loved.

Had he seen something too? A shape amidst the chaos? A man whose mouth was a storm and who bled endless darkness onto the world?

He snorted, feeling ridiculous for even thinking it. The shovel was lying on the other side of the mound and he picked it up. The dirt-encrusted wood cut into the blisters on his palm, making him wince.

Rilke. She'd shot Lisa dead. She'd pay for that, she and her comatose brother. She had the gun, but that wouldn't help her, not forever. Sooner or later she'd let her guard down. Brick gripped the handle, sweeping the shovel through the air. The blade caught the amber light of the morning, making him smile. Yeah, she'd pay.

Lisa's grave wouldn't be the last to be dug in Fursville.

Daisy

Daisy didn't recognise the voice, and it was this uncertainty that pulled her from her dream. By the time
she'd opened her eyes she'd already forgotten what had
been in her head, only that it had been bad, an echo of
what she'd felt the previous evening with Cal.

She was lying in the staff room of the pavilion, on a
bundle of cushions she had pulled off the stinky, damp
sofa. They hadn't been very comfortable, but she'd still
slept okay, considering everything that had happened
yesterday. She sat up, looking around. Adam was curled
up next to her. Chris was still bundled in the far corner
of the room, his face pressed against the dirty wall like
he was trying to smooch with it. Jade and Cal were
gone. Brick had never been there.

Silky yellow light crept in through a crack in the
boarded window. It seemed to shine through the ice
in her head, and she could see another boy, skeleton-
thin. She clambered off her makeshift bed, careful not
to disturb Adam, then walked to the door. Her hand
was on it before she remembered that there was a dead
man outside, down the corridor.

Just don't look and it won't be there.

She opened it and turned left, walking purposefully
towards the fire door, speeding up only when she

thought she heard Edward Maltby's feet tap-tapping after her, his soft groans as he reached out with bloody fingers. She dived under the chains, squealing, kicking out at the illusion. When she stood, brushing herself down, she realised she wasn't alone.

'And that's Daisy,' said Cal. He was talking to the boy she'd just seen in her thoughts, another teenager, maybe a year or two older than her. He was very skinny, his T-shirt fluttering like a sail on a mast. He smiled gently from beneath a mop of curly hair, then stretched out a hand. Daisy noticed that it had been wrapped with cloth, like a white boxing glove tinged with pink. He seemed to remember the bandage and slapped his hand to his side.

'Sorry,' he said. 'Hi.'

'Marcus,' said Daisy, plucking his name from her head. The boy frowned, looking at Cal for an explanation. Cal just shrugged.

'I told you things were weird here,' he said. 'Marcus saw the message we left, on the internet.'

'Would have come anyway,' said the boy. 'You guys got this psychic brain pull thing going on. Couldn't have stayed away if I'd wanted to.'

'Did you just arrive?' Daisy asked. 'Would you like some food?'

As soon as she said it she remembered Rilke, and the fact that the girl had locked herself in the restaurant with all their supplies. Luckily, Marcus shook his head.

'Been in the old car showroom, over the road,' he said. 'Found a box of something that used to be crunchy in the office. Got there this morning, 'bout three or four, maybe. Didn't want to come over until I knew who was about, even though it felt safe, y'know?' He tapped his temple then paused, squinting at the brightening horizon over Daisy's shoulder. 'Wasn't just me. There were four of us, 'til we got to a place called King's Lynn.'

He looked at his hand, and more ice cubes bobbled to the surface of Daisy's head. She saw two girls and an older boy, floundering in a sea of raking fingers and blunt teeth and bulging eyes. Their screams filled her mind, and for a terrible instant pain flared all over her. She gasped like she'd fallen into a frozen pond, forcing the ice cubes down where she couldn't feel them any more.

'We got ambushed trying to steal some petrol,' he went on, the words catching in his throat. 'I had to leave them. I . . . They would have killed me too.' He held up his bandaged hand like a half-hearted excuse. 'Nicked a bike and cycled the rest of the way. Knackered now. Could do with a kip, yeah?'

'You want to show him to the staff room?' asked Cal. Daisy shook her head. She didn't want to go back inside, back to where the dead man lay. Better to stay in the sunshine where ghosts couldn't get you. Cal gestured towards the fire door and he and Marcus ducked under the chain, vanishing into the gloom.

Daisy looked left, towards the front of the park. She didn't want to go that way, either. That way was the tail of the night, still sweeping over the land. That way was whatever she'd seen in her head last night. She set off to her right. It was brighter here, the sun already creeping over the fence, and she could hear the soft whisper of the waves. She slowed when she turned the corner, seeing the mound of soil that lay halfway across the patch of overgrown grass next to the crazy golf. She and Cal had watched Brick for what seemed like an eternity last night. He'd still been digging when they'd gone inside. The poor thing.

She approached the grave, her thoughts turning to her own parents. Would they be underground now? She wiped tears away furiously, but they kept coming. How could people do that to their loved ones? How could they put them in a hole in the ground, cover them up with dirt and just leave them there for all the worms to eat? She couldn't imagine anything worse than being trapped in the cold ground, in the dark, all alone with nothing to do, forever and ever and ever.

She hurried away from the grave. There was a banging noise coming from somewhere nearby, and when she walked down the back of Fursville she real-ised it was coming from one of the small metal sheds against the fence. She passed 'Utility' then 'Sanitation' then 'Danger: Do Not Enter' before coming to an open door marked 'Caretaker'. She peeked around it to see Brick inside, rummaging through piles of junk.

'What are you doing?' she asked. He glanced at her, then went back to whatever the answer was, throwing sheets of corrugated iron against the wall of the shed. The clatter was deafening. Eventually he reached down and grabbed something, holding it up.

'Bingo,' he said, tripping out of the shed into the light. He held up a hammer that was so rusted it looked like it had been dipped in bright orange gunk. It didn't have a handle any more, just a short metal nubbin. He set off back the way Daisy had just walked. He didn't even look at the grave as he passed it, using the little hammer to hack through the jungle of the crazy golf. Daisy followed, careful not to get scratched by the jaggies that pinged back after him.

When she caught up she saw that he was hammering a big nail into the fence. It was awkward because he couldn't really get any strength behind it, but he was taking his time and making sure he hit the nail squarely on the head. Gradually, millimetre by millimetre, it disappeared into the soft wood.

'This bit was loose,' Brick said, running his thumb over the sunken nail. 'Whole fence could open up. No good if we want to keep the ferals out.'

He pulled another nail from the pocket of his jeans.

'I'm sorry about Lisa,' Daisy spluttered, the words out of her mouth before she could stop them. Brick tensed up, studying the nail in his hand as if it had the answer to everything written on it. Daisy stood there, hoping he wouldn't be mad. After a moment or two he looked at her through red-rimmed, exhausted eyes. He nodded, and she understood that it was a thank you. He placed the nail against the flapping fence panel and began to hammer again.

'There's another boy here,' she said. He paused, then

carried on. 'He's very thin. He said there were others but . . . but they didn't make it.'

He finished the nail and started on a third. Daisy hopped from one foot to the other. She was hungry, thirsty too. She didn't want to ask Brick about food, though. She didn't want to give him any reason to go inside and see Rilke. Only bad things could come from that. But there was another matter she wanted to talk to him about.

'Brick,' she started, talking over the hammer blows. 'Did you feel it too? Yesterday.'

He didn't even pause this time, tapping away at the nail until it vanished. He gave the fence a shake, the panel still flapping at the bottom, before reaching into his pocket again and squatting down.

'It was really horrible,' she said. 'Just this . . . a kind of feeling, like being numb, but being really sad too.' He still didn't reply. Daisy chewed her thumbnail, wishing she was better at finding the right words. 'It was like something had gone wrong with . . . with life.'

Tap. Tap. Tap. Brick hammered away, the nail going in at an angle. Daisy waited a moment more then turned to go. She didn't really need him to answer. She could see it in his head, in his thoughts. He *had* felt it, he knew exactly what she meant. Only there was more there, in his mind. She focused, pulling an ice cube free, trying to work out what was inside it. It didn't make any sense, there was only chaos, like a whirlwind, and a constant, gasping noise that made her flesh crawl. Something awful, something evil, something . . .

She glanced back at Brick to try and fine-tune the image. He was looking at her, and as their eyes met an understanding clicked home.

This storm, this whirlwind, this bad thing, it wasn't a something, it was a *nothing*. It was the absence of something, and that absence was spreading – deleting, erasing, cancelling everything it touched. That's why it felt so sad, so horrible, because this thing was the very opposite of life, the opposite of death too, it was the opposite of everything.

Antimatter, the word that floated to the top of her thoughts belonged to Brick, not her; she didn't even know what it meant. She knew that he was thinking the same thing as her, though. They both knew what it wanted, this *other*. It wanted to take everything and turn it into nothing, to devour it, to wipe it from existence.

And when it was done, reality would be nothing but an empty hole in time.

Rilke

'Please, Rilke, I just need to talk to you.'

Rilke stood by the restaurant doors listening to Cal rant and rave. He'd been out there for a while now, pacing back and forth like a wolf, first pleading, then threatening, then fuming.

'Rilke, we need our food, our drink. It's not fair, that's *our stuff*.'

He banged on the door, flakes of ice drifting loose. Rilke's silent laugh came out as little puffs of breath. She clutched the gun, her hand so numb from the cold that she couldn't feel it, only its weight.

'Look, you don't have to speak to me, you don't have to see the others. Just let me in for five seconds and I'll get what I need. You can keep some of the rations, okay?'

The door rocked on its hinges, making her take a step back. Cal kicked it again, hard, the wood creaking.

'I wouldn't do that if I were you,' said Rilke.

'Then let me in,' Cal said. 'We need food. I'm coming through these doors one way or the other, Rilke.'

She didn't answer, happy to let him stew in his own anger. He was so predictable, thinking he could do what he wanted because he was a boy, because he was strong. Rilke knew why she had been chosen, but why

Cal? Why the others? They were pathetic.

'Rilke!' he snapped. 'I mean it, you have to let me in.'

'No. I don't.'

Her smile widened. She was in charge because she had all the food. Cal and the others couldn't just stroll down to the nearest Tesco's and do their grocery shopping.

'Open the door!' Cal yelled. 'Seriously, I'm getting really pissed off. Are you gonna shoot us all? Tell me what you want or I swear to God I'm gonna break this door down and give you a slap, girl or no girl.'

Rilke uttered a brittle chuckle that seemed colder than the breeze.

'I only want one thing,' she said. 'I want to talk to Daisy.'

Cal protested, but after a while he gave up. She listened to him retreat down the stairs, his curses eventually fading into the immense quiet of the pavilion. She pressed her forehead against the frozen wood of the doors, wondering if he would give her what she had asked for.

He will. He has to if he wants to eat.

She straightened and walked over to the nearest table, laying the gun down beside a flickering candle. She had to peel her fingers from the cold metal. It was incredible, really, that something so small could be so deadly. That simply squeezing your finger could result in the end of a life.

But the two people she had killed, the two *humans*,

they hadn't deserved to live. None of them did. That's why she was here, why she had been chosen. And very soon she'd have weapons which would make this gun look like a plastic toy. Isn't that what she'd felt last night? The knowledge that there was something out there, something terrible and yet wonderful. A force of pure destructive power.

Schiller lay in his pocket of ice, his body still radiating cold like an inverse sun. He hadn't so much as twitched since the previous evening, but she knew he wouldn't stay like that forever. She wasn't sure how she knew, she just did. He wasn't dying, he was changing, like a caterpillar in a cocoon.

'But into what, Schill?' she whispered. 'What are you becoming?'

Daisy had the answers. The little girl didn't realise it, but they were locked away somewhere inside that pretty little head of hers. She just needed a little bit of encouragement to get them out.

The candle was struggling, as if the darkness had weight, snuffing out the solitary flame. Rilke took another one from the pile she'd collected, lighting it from the first and planting it in a socket of melted wax. It, too, began to stutter against the heavy gloom. She smiled at the blatant metaphor. *We few are the flames*, she thought to herself, mesmerised by the dancing colours. *We are the light in the darkness.*

And what could the darkness be, other than humanity? This crushing, heaving mass of people who had no legitimate right to life. How many souls lived on earth now? Six billion? Seven? All of them like in-sects, crawling around on their hands and knees or slaughtering one another in pursuit of scraps. They were ignorant, they were cruel, they were the night that smothered the day. They did not deserve their ex-istence.

That's why all this was happening. That's why she and Schiller had been attacked – why they'd *all* been attacked. The people sensed something different in them, something special. And they hated it, because it was *better* than them. She remembered the men and women back at the rave, the way they had turned into beasts – biting, clawing, scratching, howling. They had acted like animals because that's all they were, because they had sensed that Rilke and Schiller were more than them, that she and her brother were dangerous, that they were . . .

She paused, unable to think of the right word. The twin flames fluttered but they didn't go out. They wouldn't go out, they wouldn't succumb to the dark-ness.

And what about the thing she had sensed last night? That wave of utter nothingness, that awful knowledge that what lay beneath the skin of the world was an infinite abyss of absence. She wasn't sure, but this creature, this force – whatever it was – might be here to show them the way. As dark as its image had been, it might be the light they needed to follow. Why else would she have seen it?

Footsteps, more than one set. Rilke cocked her

head, feeling Daisy's presence outside even before Cal's voice came through the doors.

'She's here,' he said. 'She says she'll talk to you, but only if you let us have some food.'

Rilke walked to the doors, then doubled back and picked up the gun. Cal was too pathetic to try anything, she was pretty sure about that, but she couldn't afford to take any chances, not when the truth was so close. She slid back the lock, then pulled open the door with her free hand. Daisy stood there, squinting. Cal was beside her.

'You don't have to go in,' he said. 'Whatever she has to say, she can say it right here.'

'It's okay,' said Daisy. 'She isn't going to hurt me.'

Daisy gave Cal a hug, then walked into the restaurant. Cal watched her go, then glared at Rilke.

'You'd better not,' he hissed. 'You'd better not lay a finger on her. I'll be right here, Rilke, I'm not going anywhere.'

Rilke laughed at him, then let the door swing shut in his face.

Daisy

Daisy walked to the table with the candles and sat down, putting her trembling hands between her knees so that Rilke wouldn't notice she was scared. She had lied to Cal, she didn't know if Rilke was going to hurt her or not. But she had to do something to get some food or they'd all starve. She glanced around as innocently as she could, but she couldn't see the carrier bags anywhere.

'I've put them somewhere safe,' said Rilke, her eyes gleaming. She walked over, placing the gun in the middle of the table before sitting opposite Daisy. Her face had the same crazy look as yesterday. It was dangerous. 'Just until we've had a little talk.'

'About what?' said Daisy, shivering. It was colder than ever in here, Schiller entombed in ice on the sofa.

'You *know* what,' said Rilke, planting her elbows and stretching her hands across the table. The way her forearms uncurled made Daisy think of a praying mantis. She didn't offer her own hands. 'About this, about everything.'

'But I don't know anything,' said Daisy. Where would the food be? In a corner, somewhere. Or under a table.

'I think you do,' said Rilke, her face splitting into a

grin, her eyes burning. 'I think it's all there, in your head, you just don't know how to read it.'

Daisy didn't answer. Maybe Rilke was right. There had been all kinds of things happening in her brain that she couldn't make any sense of. The ice cubes, rattling and clinking around, showing her things she couldn't possibly know. They were doing it right now, but they were moving too fast, the way they seemed to do when she was frightened.

'I don't want you to be scared of me, Daisy,' said Rilke, gentler now. 'We're the same, you and I.'

Except I don't murder people, she thought but didn't say.

'I had no choice,' Rilke went on. 'You know how dangerous the ferals are. You can't have forgotten what happened to you already?'

Daisy shook her head, thinking of the ambulance man and his horse's teeth.

'Things are changing, Daisy. The world is changing. You felt it too, didn't you? Yesterday evening. All I want is to know what it was. Because I think something is trying to tell us what to do. It's trying to guide us, only we don't know how to listen.'

That made a strange kind of sense. It did feel a bit like when she was at school sometimes and she didn't really understand what the teacher was saying.

Rilke stretched her hands out a bit further, opening them to Daisy.

'I know things have been really bad. I've lost people too, I'm worried I'm going to lose my brother. The whole world has turned against us, we have to be there for each other. We're different now, different to the rest of them, all of us – me, you, Schill, Cal, Brick and the others. We're a family, we have to trust each other.'

Daisy liked the idea of a family. Cal already felt like her brother. In fact it was as if she'd been friends with all of them forever, even the new boy Marcus who, she knew without being told, liked loud music and hated football – she hoped Cal wouldn't mind this last fact. Rilke, too, was not a stranger. She never had been. She relaxed a little, her hands creeping towards Rilke's.

'Do you trust me?' Rilke asked. Daisy chewed her lip, then nodded. Rilke's smile widened even further, revealing a row of perfect, small teeth. 'Then take my hands.'

This time, Daisy didn't hesitate. She threaded her fingers through Rilke's, the girl's skin as cold as marble. Rilke held her tight – not so hard that it was painful, though. The contact felt nice. She smiled back at her, forgetting why she'd been so worried before.

'You're a special girl, Daisy,' said Rilke, her voice barely louder than the flutter of the candles. 'You can do amazing things. I think we all can. Not yet, maybe, but soon. I think we all have a gift.'

'What kind of gift?' Daisy asked. Her ice cubes didn't feel anything like a Christmas present. She wasn't sure she even wanted them when they made her feel sad and frightened. Rilke squeezed her.

'Think about it, Daisy. Why would the whole world turn against us? Why would they try to kill us?'

'Because they hate us, I suppose,' Daisy replied, shrugging. Rilke shook her head.

'*Think*, why would they hate us? What would make them behave that way?'

Daisy frowned, wishing that Rilke would just tell her. She hated being asked questions that she didn't know the answer to. Then, out of nowhere, she said:

'Because they're *scared* of us.'

Rilke nodded, obviously delighted, and Daisy felt some of the stress drain from her chest. It made a certain kind of sense, she realised. People did do silly things when they were really scared. Even so, they didn't usually start trying to pull your arms and legs and head off. They—

Don't they? said Rilke, interrupting her thoughts, and Daisy couldn't tell whether the other girl had spoken or not. 'It's happened before, throughout history. The ones that are different, who rise above just being human. People get scared of them, they kill them. What if they are supposed to be scared of us, Daisy? What if they're *right* to be scared of us?'

'Why?' Daisy said, struggling. Rilke eased her grip, but she didn't let go.

'Don't be frightened. I'm not going to hurt you. I could never hurt you. Don't you see? Don't you remember that feeling from yesterday?'

Daisy shivered just thinking about it, that wave of utter sadness that had washed over her when she was standing outside. No, it hadn't been sadness exactly, it had been worse than that. It had been as if all emotion had gone, as if there was nothing left. She couldn't explain it, only that it had felt like standing alone in an endless dark room and knowing that there was nobody else anywhere in the whole universe.

'It's a sign,' Rilke said. 'A sign that everything is going to change.'

'But why?' Daisy asked, feeling her throat tighten. 'People will get hurt, I don't want that. People are nice.'

'Are they, Daisy?' Rilke said. 'Think about it, *really* think about it.'

She didn't want to but she did — thoughts of the times she'd been bullied, back in her old school when she'd had eczema on her arms and everyone had called her names; the little boy in her town who'd been murdered by the creep who'd delivered leaflets, whose body had never been found; all the riots on telly, people beating each other up for stupid things they didn't even need; and even her own mum, when the cancer had been bad, when it had made her say things that were really cruel. There was another memory too, but this one was Rilke's, a man with rough fingers and long, dirty nails and breath that smelled of coffee and alcohol, his huge face looming in. Daisy squirmed, pushing the thoughts away, so sick of having other people's hate and fear and confusion inside her head, ready to scream, *Leave me alone!*

'No,' she said instead, choking on the word. 'People are good, Rilke, they're nice, most of them. I don't want things to change.'

Rilke's smile vanished, replaced by a look of sympathy and compassion that was heart-breaking.

'It's too late. I'm sorry, Daisy, but it is. What's happening to the world . . . It has already begun.'

'But what *is* happening?' Daisy asked, catching her breath. Rilke squeezed her hands, pulling them closer to her.

'*We* are,' she said. 'We're happening. Don't you see? Isn't it clear what we have to do? We've been sent here to make things different. To clean things up. Look inside your head, Daisy, and tell me I'm wrong.'

She didn't want to, not again. If she peered into those ice cubes then who knew what she might see? It would be bad, though, and there would be fire.

'Please, Daisy,' Rilke said. 'I can't do this without you. I need you, Schiller needs you, we all do. Just see for yourself.'

Daisy glanced again at the boy in the corner. He would be so hungry now, and thirsty. He might die if they couldn't wake him up. As horrible as it might be, what if she could help? She tightened her grip on Rilke's hands, grateful at least that she wasn't on her own. Then she closed her eyes and let the images float to the surface . . .

☹

It was like taking off a big coat in the middle of winter, one that was drenched with snow and water and which weighed a ton. She became as light as the dust that rose in the candlelight, free of everything and anything that could hold her down.

Even with her eyes closed she could see the others as if they were all standing in the same room. Only they weren't, they were scattered over the park – Adam and Chris and the new boy Marcus, still sleeping (they were sharing a dream, she realised, one involving tortoises), Jade sitting on the log flume thinking about a boy who had tried to kill her, Brick still mending the fence, his thoughts full of revenge, and Cal just outside the restaurant door, his ear against it, shivering as he tried to work out what was happening.

There were loads more, boys and girls she didn't yet know but who she seemed to recognise. They were everywhere, maybe twenty of them, more even, and they were all flowing this way. The sight of them – although it wasn't quite sight, it was more than that, a *vision* – was dizzying, but it was comforting. These were members of her family. They were all welcome.

The same feeling from yesterday was there too, though, and this was certainly not welcome. It tainted everything, the way the world turns the colour of old bruises when a storm is about to start, and it made her feel like crying even though it had been so good to soar through her thoughts. She wanted to be away from this thing, whatever it was, and she fought to claw her way back into her body.

It's okay, nothing can hurt us here. The voice was Rilke's, emanating from everywhere. *Just a little longer, Daisy. Just so we can see it.*

Why did she want to see it? It was horrid. But Rilke was right, it couldn't hurt them. Even though it felt like she was a million miles away in a million different places she knew she was still inside the restaurant in the little park by the sea. She focused on the dark cloud, trying to work out what it was and why it felt so un-kind.

A picture began to emerge: a wide road, with fields on either side of it. There were several big black cars there, and men in suits holding guns. Some of those men were shrieking, others were pointing at . . .

What *was* that?

It was a man, but he was floating inside a whirlwind of chaos, and his mouth . . . Daisy groaned. *It isn't real, it isn't real*, she told herself. But it was; this was the thing they had all sensed last night, the lord of ab-sence. She tried to close her eyes but the pictures were in her head, the sounds coming from inside her. She could smell blood, and burning meat, and smoke, she could taste the thick, oily air on her tongue. None of it mattered, though, because the man in the storm had left her empty. There was nothing left of her. She had never, ever felt this alone.

I want to go, she said, feeling Rilke's hands over her own. *Please, Rilke, I want to—*

A blast of light, like an old-fashioned photographer's flash, then a raging fire bit into her skin, making her scream. It was as if the floor had given way, her stom-ach lurching up into her throat. She opened her eyes and the air was full of flames, flickering blue and yellow and red. Just as quickly they were extinguished, leaving the same wide road as before, only this time it was completely and utterly real. Rilke was there, her mouth open in a rictus of shock, her hair billowing around her shoulders. Both of them were standing now, their hands linked together, the wind roaring past them like a train. Hundreds of bright embers had been caught up in the gale, all being pulled in the same direction.

Daisy watched them go, seeing them dragged towards the man in the storm. He was raised over the ground like he'd been crucified, his eyes blazing black light, his face like a drain, sucking in clouds of darkness. The noise was terrible, an inward howl like someone with asthma taking their last, desperate breath. It went on forever. All around him the air was in upheaval, like a tornado, like the one in the Wizard of Oz film. *He's a sorcerer*, she had time to think. *Or something worse*.

One of the cars was in the air, and Daisy looked through the windows to see five men inside, two of them dead, speared by a shaft of metal, the rest screaming. One – the man sitting in the middle of the back seat – glanced at her, and she could read the horror in his bulging eyes, his bared teeth.

I'm sorry, she said to him. *I can't save you*. And somewhere in the chaos she realised that although she was here, actually *here* on this road, these events had already happened. She could almost hear the vast, groaning weight of broken time.

The man in the storm hurled out another whip-crack of black lightning, more of the world disintegrating. The car exploded into a million pieces, the bodies inside turning into sand and spiralling into the corpse's mouth.

Daisy screamed, even her breath stolen by the wind. The man's lifeless eyes rolled towards her, the sensation like she'd been punched in the gut. And it knew who she was, because the raging storm seemed to call out her name – only, it *wasn't* her name. It wasn't even a word. The dead man flexed his fingers and Daisy felt herself rise from the ground. She gripped Rilke with everything she had, both of them swept up towards the vortex. And she knew that if they didn't get away, get away *right now*, then they'd be pulled inside it, that they would become nothing.

Even Rilke seemed to understand this.

Daisy screwed her eyes shut and suddenly she was falling again, the sensation so real that her whole body flailed. Another flash, more flames. She lurched backwards, the chair spilling over behind her, making her topple. She scrabbled on the cold ground, expecting to see the storm man there, ready to suck her up. But there was just the restaurant and a blizzard of glowing embers which drifted lazily to the ground.

Daisy waited for the real world to feel solid again before sitting up. Rilke sat on the other side of the table, wearing that same lunatic grin. She looked at Daisy, then she started to laugh.

'I told you,' she said. 'I told you that things were about to change.'

Daisy got to her feet, half running, half tripping towards the doors, knowing she should be looking for food but desperate to get away. She flew into them, fumbling for the lock, spilling out into Cal's arms. He held her tight in the warm glow from the foyer, stroking her hair as the tears came.

'Are you okay? What happened? What did she do to you?'

Daisy clung to him, hearing the sound of footsteps then the crunch of the doors closing behind her, the snap of the lock.

'Rilke, what did you do? Daisy, Daisy look at me.'

She tilted back her head and he ran his fingers over her cheek. They came away covered in fine, red sand.

'What is this?' he asked, and there were tears in his eyes too. 'Tell me.'

Daisy hugged him again, his shirt soon stained red with powdered blood. It wasn't hers, though. It wasn't Rilke's either. No, it belonged to a man whose body had disintegrated miles and miles from here, in another place and time, who had been dragged into the vortex. He had been real, it had all been real.

And so had the man in the storm.

Cal

Cal lugged the heavy pan of water out the kitchen door, careful not to trip over dead Edward Maltby, who still lay there covered by a tablecloth. Steam rose from the water that slopped inside it, welcome against his face. He'd heated it on one of the industrial gas hobs, which, incredibly, still worked. Chris was standing down the corridor, outside the toilets.

'Want me to take that for you?' he asked. Cal shook his head, even though his arms were trembling with the weight of the pan. He pushed into the left-hand toilet, laying the pan down beside the small shower unit that sat beside the single cubicle. Then he ducked into the staff room next door. Daisy was sitting on the sofa, wrapped in Jade's arms. The other girl had wiped most of the weird red sand from Daisy's face but it was still stained pink, like she was sunburned.

'Sorry it took so long,' Cal said as Chris walked in after him. 'Took ages to heat up.'

'Thanks,' said Jade. Daisy glanced up, but she was looking at something far beyond Cal, something distant. He smiled at her, and she imitated him robotically. She hadn't said any more about what Rilke had done to her. She hadn't said much of anything at all since coming out of the restaurant.

'No worries,' he said. 'It's not exactly nice through there, but it doesn't look too bad. I've seen worse bathrooms in my time. Just pretend you're at Glastonbury.'

'Come on, Daisy,' said Jade, gently tugging on her hand and easing her from the sofa. 'Let's get you cleaned up.'

Cal waited until they'd walked from the room before turning to Chris.

'Brick?' he asked.

'Won't come, says he's fixing up the fence. That guy . . .' He scowled, but he didn't finish. Cal was glad. Brick was a douche, yeah, but he *had* just seen his girlfriend get murdered. Cal walked past the sleeping figure of Adam and over to Marcus, shaking him gently. The new kid snorted, but it took another couple of attempts before his eyes opened. He flinched when he saw Cal, struggling inside his cocoon of tablecloths before remembering where he was.

'Sorry,' said Cal. 'I didn't want to wake you, but we need to know about Soapy's.'

'The car place?' Marcus said, groaning as he sat up. 'What about it?'

'Is there more food over there?'

He wiped the sleep from his eyes.

'Um . . . Yeah, I think so. Not much, mind, a few cans, a couple of boxes of cereal maybe, that's what I had. Tasted like turd. Thought you had stuff here?'

'Long story,' said Cal. 'We don't. You up for a return trip?'

'Over the road?' said Marcus. 'Sure, just gimme a minute, yeah?'

'Meet us outside,' said Cal. He turned to Chris. 'We should take weapons, just in case.'

Cal walked out into the corridor and through the fire door, blinking against the glaring sunshine. There wasn't a single cloud up there, the sky a vast, perfect blue. Any other weekend he'd be heading up the park with his mates, or into town to sit outside the library, maybe even hopping the school fence to use the pitches for a kickaround. It seemed so long ago. He was already forgetting what they looked like, all of them except Georgia. But even when he thought of her he could only see her eyes, the rest of her face hidden behind a book.

What's the point? Why bother trying to find food, trying to survive, when everything you had is gone?

He sighed, the sunlight no longer quite as bright, the sky no longer quite as blue. Chris appeared beside him, scouring the ground then waddling to a waist-high clutch of sea grass and wrestling something from it. He swung the wooden plank like it was a sword and it snapped in two with a soft, rotten puff.

'Guess not,' he said, throwing it to the floor and wiping his hand down his trousers. 'Ew, woodlice.'

There was a rattle of chains and Marcus crawled through the fire door. He shot Cal a grin, holding his hand up to shield his eyes.

'Ready when you are,' he said.

Cal set off again, heading for the front of the park.

The big wheel towered overhead, creaking as it absorbed the morning heat. He gave it a wide berth, not wanting to be skewered if anything else decided to break free. The main path from the pavilion to the gates was strewn with rubble and debris, the earth still ruptured and black from the explosion. He spotted a rusted iron bar poking from the mess where the hot-dog stand had been and pulled it free. It was half a metre long and heavy. It wasn't exactly a gun, but it felt good when he swung it from side to side.

'There's nobody over there,' said Marcus. His arms were so skinny Cal didn't think he'd be able to hold a knife and fork, let alone a club. He bounced when he walked, his gangly body flapping. The kid could have been a scarecrow.

'Better safe than sorry,' said Cal, swinging the bar again, imagining it was caving in the side of Rilke's head. The image made his stomach curdle. There was no sign of Brick as they wove through the metal struts and turned left, heading for the Boo Boo Station. He was there, though. He was watching them. Cal could feel it.

He walked to the fence and squeezed through, laurel leaves cool and waxy against his skin. It took him a little while to find his way past the thick hedge, but eventually he popped free of the foliage and found himself on a wide road that stretched right and left for as far as he could see. He felt weirdly exposed out here. Fursville wasn't exactly a fortress, but he'd come to think that as long as they stayed there the ferals couldn't get them. The dealership was directly opposite, the box-shaped showroom drenched in the long shadow of the big wheel.

'Coast looks clear,' said Chris. 'Place is deserted.'

'Like I said,' added Marcus. 'Didn't see a soul when I was cycling up.'

'Well, don't let your guard down,' said Cal. 'Stay sharp.'

'Yessir, Colonel sir!' said Chris, snapping off a salute. Marcus laughed. Cal gave them both a look, then set off over the road. Their footsteps seemed like the loudest thing in the world, like gunfire. If there was a feral anywhere nearby then surely it would hear them and come running.

He bolted over the empty parking bays and slammed into the boarded-up showroom window. Marcus was next to him in a flash, Chris taking a few seconds longer, already out of breath.

'Way in's round the back,' said Marcus, taking the lead around the side of the building. They passed a caged propane tank and the empty skeleton of a vending machine before reaching a door. It was open, nothing inside but darkness. Marcus slapped a hand to his head. 'Oh yeah, I meant to say we should probably bring a torch.'

'Use this,' said Chris, fishing his phone from his pocket and holding it out. Cal didn't take it and Chris got the hint. 'You want me to go first? I don't know the way.'

'I'll do it,' said Marcus, pulling out his own phone

and stepping through the door. He vanished immediately, like he'd been swallowed up. Cal followed him, hoping the others couldn't hear his racing pulse. Chris came in last, holding the phone over his head. They didn't do much to light the way, covering everything in a silver moon sheen and making the shadows twice as deep. They stuck close, almost touching, as they scuffled down a short corridor.

'Where you from, anyway?' Chris said, his whisper as loud as a hurricane.

'West,' Marcus said. 'On the border, really. Go out the front door I'm Welsh, go out the back I'm English.'

'I know which one I'd rather be,' said Chris. Marcus laughed, and Cal hushed them both. 'I think we're okay,' said Chris. 'If there was a bad guy in here they'd have sensed us by now, right?'

He had a point, but all the same Cal didn't feel comfortable creeping through the dark making small talk. There were two doors at the end of the corridor, one leading into the main showroom. Marcus went through the other into a large office, the floor covered in rubbish. There were rats in here, Cal could hear their faint chatter inside the walls. He opened his mouth to comment when a noise cut through the quiet, the 'screech screech screech' sound from *Psycho*. He almost screamed.

'Sorry,' said Marcus, holding up his phone. 'Should probably change my ringtone given what's going on.'

'Think I can find some new underwear in here?' said Chris. 'I need it after that.'

'My brother,' Marcus explained, sliding the phone into his pocket. After a while the noise ended. 'Keeps calling to ask where I am. Doesn't seem to remember trying to stamp on my face with his steel caps.'

Cal thought about his own phone. He couldn't get a signal out here, but what would have happened if he could? Would Megan have called again? Eddie? Georgia maybe?

Or his mum. Would she ask him where he was? Why he'd run away? The thought made his heart feel like a deflated balloon and he was grateful for the darkness as he rubbed a tear away.

'Anyway,' said Marcus, 'look around. There isn't much but there are bits and pieces.'

Cal got down onto his hands and knees, trying not to notice the soft, wet pellets that littered the ground. The first couple of boxes he lifted up – one that might have been Frosties, another faded beyond recognition – were empty. The third had something living which scuttled over his fingers into the gloom. He shuddered, resisting the urge to get up and bolt, instead crawling across the floor, feeling for anything that might be useful.

'Got something,' said Chris. 'Oh, damn, cake candles. Is it anyone's birthday?'

Nobody replied. Cal shuffled forward a little more, finding another box. This one rattled when he shook it, and he peeled open the flap to discover a sealed bag inside. He lifted the box up, squinting.

'Anyone like old Weetabix?'

'Got any milk?' said Marcus.

'Got Fanta,' said Cal.

'Mmmm, old Weetabix and Fanta, my favourite,' the new kid said.

It was another couple of minutes before Cal's knuckles hit a small jar, making it roll in a circle. He snatched it up, not realising how hungry he was until he read 'Peanut Butter' on the label.

'Jackpot,' he said, telling the others what he'd found. They both groaned, Marcus making puking noises. *Weirdos*, how could they not like peanut butter?

They worked for a while in silence, the occasional whoop letting them know that more treasure had been discovered. Cal wasn't sure how much later it was that Marcus spoke.

'You guys really not know what's going on, then?'

'No more than you,' Cal answered. He found a packet of biscuits that pretty much dissolved into mush the moment he touched them. Now the air stank of digestives and mould.

'I don't know anything,' said the new kid.

'Exactly,' Cal muttered.

'Guess they're not zombies, though,' Marcus went on. 'They're alive, for one thing. They go back to normal too when you're not around them. Well, the ones that haven't injured themselves. But even those ones don't remember how they got hurt. You noticed that?'

'Uh huh.'

'Sponges!' said Chris. 'Oh wait, they're the kind you wash with, not the kind you eat.'

'I got hit at home, right,' Marcus said. 'Like I said, my brothers. Man, isn't like we really got on all that well, but the way they turned on me. It's like they were . . . I don't know . . .'

Cal gave up looking. Everything was gone, even the plug sockets had been stripped from the walls. This was pointless.

'. . . possessed. It's like they were possessed,' Marcus said. 'You know, like in *The Exorcist* or something. You ever seen that film?'

'Bit of it,' Cal said. 'Got bored.'

'Well my brothers, they had this look on their faces like they were possessed. I guess that's my theory.'

'Demonic possession?' said Chris. It sounded like he had a mouthful of something. They were supposed to be stockpiling. 'You reckon?'

'Well, what's your suggestion?' Marcus said. They could all sense Chris's shrug even though they couldn't see it.

'What happened with your brothers?' Cal asked.

'What do you think happened? I legged it. They were always bigger than me, and stronger, but they were like a couple of carthorses. I legged it from them, I legged it from my mum, I legged it from every one of them. Pays to be skinny and fast sometimes.'

'Like me, you mean,' said Chris.

'Yeah, just like you,' Marcus laughed back. His tone was light, but Cal could hear a terrible sadness lying just beneath the surface. It made him want to be back in the light, in the fresh air. He moved towards the pile of food, squatting down beside it. Pile was a big over-statement, he realised. There were maybe seven things there.

'You guys ready?' he asked.

'Yeah,' said Chris. 'Nothing over here but dust.'

'Could have sworn there was more,' said Marcus. 'Sorry.'

'It'll keep us going,' said Cal, picking up what he could and walking back down the corridor and out into the light, looking down at what he carried. Weetabix, a cracked jar of PB that looked runny and green, a box of marshmallow snowballs which had been half eaten by rats. Chris strolled out holding a can without its label and a box of Alpen which had lost most of its colouring. He pulled out the bag from in-side and a trickle of flakes drifted out, leaving it empty.

'Oh,' he said.

Marcus followed, cradling a big bag of something that turned out to be dog biscuits.

'Dammit,' he said. 'I thought they were Oreos.'

'That it?' asked Cal, a knot of dread forming in his stomach. This wouldn't be enough to feed them for a morning, let alone for however long it took for things to go right again. The truth was that even if they did manage to get their supplies back from Rilke they wouldn't last forever on Haribo and Dr Pepper. He looked around, seeing the road, the dunes, the distant factory. There was nothing else. 'We should get back.'

'The mighty hunters return with their spoils,' said Chris.

They sprinted over the road, their shadows elastic, held back by the garage. Two words resounded in Cal's head with each set of pounded footsteps: *We're dead, we're dead, we're dead.*

Brick

Brick watched them run back across the road from his lookout post above the main gates. Everything looked different from up here, like he'd literally risen above it, like he could just watch the world go by and no longer be a part of it. Up here he was halfway to the sun, halfway to oblivion. It felt good.

It was bloody uncomfortable, though. He shuffled, holding on to the big plastic exclamation mark of FURSVILLE! to stop himself toppling off. It was only about six metres or so to the ground, but he'd probably still snap a leg or an arm or maybe a vertebra. Cal and the two new kids disappeared into the hedge in completely the wrong place, and he could hear them rustling about in there, whispering urgently, trying to find the opening in the fence.

They hadn't found much food, that was pretty clear. It didn't bother Brick too much. They had water and that was the main thing. They'd think of something.

He took a deep breath of salted air then swung off the top of the pillar onto the small access platform that ran beneath the park banner. It creaked under his weight but the rusted bolts held fast in the worn brick. When he'd been rooting around in the caretaker's shed he'd found a can of paint and a couple of brushes that

418

had seen better days. The paint was black, for iron-work, but it would do the job.

He walked carefully down the ledge, stopping at the giant green 'S'. Using the handle to pop open the can, he gave the gloopy liquid inside a stir and slapped the dripping brush against the plastic. A few big strokes did the trick, and he stood back to admire his handiwork.

'Furyville,' he read, nodding. 'That works.'

He started back, then changed his mind and edged all the way to the end of the platform where a big, goofy animal smiled down at the world. It was another squirrel, the park mascot.

'Don't know what you're grinning at,' Brick said, dunking the brush again and giving the creature a drooping, unhappy line for its mouth. He added two giant x's for its eyes, with sweeping angry brows – the same picture he'd drawn back in the restaurant when Cal and Daisy had first arrived. 'Not so happy now, are you?'

He left the paint there, wiping his hands down his jeans. The fumes were making him light-headed, and he retreated to the ladder, clambering carefully back to solid ground. He could hear laughter from nearby and he trudged towards it, curious.

Daisy, Jade and Adam were sitting on the carousel. Daisy was the one who was giggling, the sound like birdsong. She was pretending to ride her horse, as were the other two, like they were racing the Grand National. Cal, Marcus and Chris were standing beside them, holding whatever they'd got from the garage and grinning as they watched the race. Brick turned to go. It was better for everyone if he wasn't around at the moment. He'd only taken a couple of steps, however, before Daisy called out his name.

He looked back to see her waving at him. Her face was spotless and glowing and seemed too tiny to hold that giant smile. She looked like an angel. The others glanced over as well, Cal holding up a hand. Brick hovered for a second, unsure, then swallowed his protests and joined them.

'We're having a race,' said Daisy, jiggling up and down and kicking her legs. Adam was shaking an invisible pair of reins so hard he was in danger of falling off. Jade was going along with it, her head down and butt up like a jockey. None of their horses was actually moving, of course, although the whole carousel was rattling alarmingly.

'Yeah?' he said. 'Who's winning?'

'It's not that sort of race, silly,' Daisy said. 'We're all winning.'

Brick considered telling her the definition of 'race' then decided better of it. He turned to Cal.

'Any luck?'

'What you see is what you get,' Cal said, holding out a box of cereal. 'It's these and some dog biscuits, I'm afraid.'

'We can feed the dog biscuits to the horses!' exclaimed Daisy, breathless. 'They'll need something after all this running.'

'That's a deal,' said Cal. 'Biscuits for the horses,

Weetabix for the jockeys.'

'Think I'd rather be a horse,' said Chris. 'Weetabix taste like crispy crap.'

The new boy, a skinny runt of a kid, waved a bandaged hand.

'I'm Marcus.'

'Brick,' said Brick.

'Brick? Kind of a name is that?'

'Because I'm built like a brick outhouse, obviously,' he said. Marcus laughed.

'No you're not, you're almost as skinny as I am.'

'Bollocks,' said Brick, but the new kid's good humour was kind of contagious. He stuck his middle finger up at him, doing his best to scowl. 'Welcome to Furyville anyway.'

'*Fury*-ville?' said Cal. Brick held up his paint-stained hands but he couldn't be bothered to explain. The others looked at each other, perplexed, but nobody pressed it. Brick turned back to the carousel, the three people there even more animated than before.

'Come on, Angie, we're nearly there!' cried Daisy. 'Adam, you have to talk to your horse to make it feel good.'

The little boy shook his head, glancing nervously at his audience but still tugging on those imaginary reins.

'You have to talk to it, Jade,' Daisy screamed. 'Remember it's called Wonky-Butt the Wonder Horse!'

'It's called Samson,' Jade said. '*You're* called Wonky-Butt.'

The three of them rode hard, their horses wild eyed

and nostril-flared, so real despite the fact they were obviously plastic. And for an instant Brick was tearing over the ground, the wind rushing past his ears, the bulk of the animal beneath him – the sensation of movement so powerful that he was gripped by vertigo. He closed his eyes, staggering, thinking *that's what she's seeing, that's what's going through Daisy's head*. And it was so good to be moving. Then, just like that, the moment passed. He opened his eyes, grateful for the fact that nobody was watching him.

'So, anybody want one of these?' Cal asked, rummaging in the cereal box. 'They're out of date, but . . .' He opened the bag and pulled out one of the blocks, sniffing it cautiously and shrugging. 'I don't think they're too bad.'

'Long as you try it first,' said Chris. 'In case they're poisonous.'

Cal nibbled the Weetabix. He pulled a face as he swallowed, then took a bigger bite.

'Gross,' he said through a mouthful of mush. 'But it's better than nothing.'

He handed one to Chris, then another to Marcus. Brick shook his head when he was offered, then took one anyway. He didn't know when he'd get to eat again. He bit off half of it in one go, the biscuit like cardboard. It took him an age of chewing before it was small enough to force down his throat. Cal was up on the carousel handing out Weetabix to the others.

'Are they made by Nestlé? If they are, I'm not supposed to eat them,' said Daisy, looking at the box. 'My mum said Nestlé are evil.'

'Don't worry, they're not,' said Marcus, smiling. 'Hey, maybe that's what's causing all this. Maybe Nestlé have put something in their food that turns people into crazy zombies?'

'I thought you were all for the demonic possession argument,' said Chris.

'The *what*?' asked Brick, almost choking on the last of his biscuit.

'Demonic possession,' said Chris. 'Possession by demons.'

'*Duh*, I know what it means. I meant why did you think it?'

Marcus waved it away, then realised everyone was looking at him. 'Oh, I don't know, was just a thought. 'Cos the, what do you call them, *ferals*? The ferals act like they're possessed, like they've got demons in them or something.'

Brick spat out a humourless laugh.

'You've got more chance of being right with the Nestlé thing,' he said.

'Least I'm trying to think of things,' Marcus said with a gangly shrug. 'Don't see you guys coming up with anything.'

'What are demons?' asked Daisy. She'd stopped riding now and was looking at Marcus with an intense curiosity. 'Are they the same as bad ghosts?'

'Kind of,' said Marcus. 'They're like evil spirits or something, they can go inside you and take over your body, like you're a puppet or something.'

'In films,' Cal butted in. 'That's all, in films. They're not real.'

'Okay,' Daisy said, starting to bounce on her horse again. Adam was imitating her, and at least the little kid was kind of smiling. Jade was climbing down from her faded saddle. She looked exhausted.

'No, Jade!' Daisy yelled. 'Not until the race is over.'

'It's a relay,' the other girl said. 'I'm passing the baton. Who wants it?'

'Brick does,' Daisy said. 'Let him have a go.'

'Uh uh,' he said, backing away. 'No chance, give it to someone else.'

'It's yours, Brick,' said Jade, hopping down from the carousel and approaching him. 'Come and get it.'

She broke into a run, grinning, and a wild excitement rose in Brick's chest, one that made him swirl round and start to run too. He tripped, his arms wheeling, and Jade slapped him on the back.

'It! Brick's it!'

And before he even knew what he was doing he was tearing after Cal, the other boy kicking up dust as he spun out of the way, too fast to catch. Brick changed direction, darting after Chris, the bigger boy wobbling as he bolted.

'No fair, you can't get me, I'm big boned!'

Brick tagged him, spinning off in a different direction as Chris jumped onto the carousel and chased Daisy and Adam from their horses. They ran in circles around the central joist, everyone overcome with laughter. Even Brick, sprinting as Daisy gave chase,

424

laughing so hard he couldn't run straight, tears streaming, the wind roaring in his ears just like before, so good to be moving, moving, always moving.

Rilke

Even though she couldn't see them, Rilke knew what they were doing.

She could feel it, a warmth that crept through the chilled air of the restaurant, a light that robbed the shadows of their strength. They were letting themselves laugh, they were letting themselves forget.

And it was *wrong*.

She was so cold now that she could no longer feel anything. Even the chills had subsided, her body too frozen to shake. There was no light to see her skin by, but she knew it would be the colour of ivory, maybe even gunmetal blue, like the time she'd been locked out of the house for three hours in the middle of a blizzard. She could feel the dusting of ice on her but it no longer burned. She was beyond pain.

Schiller lay where he had lain since they arrived, his breathing as steady and as slow and as constant as the ocean outside. He emanated the winter wind, and it was because of this that Rilke wasn't scared of it. Why would she be frightened of her brother? He had never hurt her, he idolised her.

More to the point, why should she be frightened of what he was *becoming*? If they had been chosen for a reason then surely they wouldn't be harmed in the process. After all, you didn't kill soldiers during training.

Rilke pulled her legs against her chest. The last candle had gone out a while ago – exactly how long she had no idea – and she couldn't quite make herself get up to light another. There were jumpers and other clothes strewn around the room, mainly Cal's. She wouldn't wear any extra layers, though. Whatever was doing this to them, maybe it was *testing* them. She didn't want to look weak.

Unlike the others. Their weakness rode into her head on a wave of light and warmth, nauseatingly pathetic. The world was changing, something incredible was happening, and yet all they could do for the past hour or more was run around outside like children, laughing. They had no idea, they had no respect for what they had become. And they would pay for it, they would be punished.

Her eyes were sore and she tried to blink, but her skin was too cold and her eyelids wouldn't obey. This didn't matter either. She got the feeling that soon she wouldn't need them. She wouldn't need any part of her body. She would never feel the cold again. Neither would Schiller, when he broke out of his icy chrysalis. That's why she had kept him in here rather than take him out in the sun to thaw. It had all been part of his test, and surely he had passed.

She sat and she shivered and she thought. What had happened, when Daisy had been in the room? Rilke remembered the creature they had witnessed. It had towered over the world, a vortex of strength. It had been terrifying, yes, the same way death was terrifying. Because it was something pure, something ultimate. It was a force of good not because of any artificial sense of morality, but because it would strip away everything ugly, the tainted, the impure, the rotten, the broken. It promised oblivion, a beautiful, flawless nothing into which all the world would fall.

And she had been chosen to help it.

Are you sure? something inside her asked, a voice locked in the core of her mind. *Are you really sure, Rilke? Because it doesn't seem right.*

But it *was* right. How could there be any other explanation? The human race had turned against her and Schiller, and the rest of them too. It had hunted them down the same way villagers hunt down a lion or a wolf that has been feeding on their livestock. People had turned on them because they were scared. *And they should be*, she thought, trying to work her frozen face into a smile. *They should be terrified.*

It had run its course, humankind. That much was clear. It had *always* been clear. Rilke despised church, and yet there had been a truth in the stories she heard while sitting on those cushionless pews. Warnings that humanity's place here was not to be taken for granted, and stories of a terrible vengeance that could be wreaked upon those who did. It had happened before, and now it would happen again – a flood of fire and wind and blood that would wipe the world clean.

And had they learned? No. Every day war and famine and pestilence and disease; every day murder and greed and fear and stupidity. Worse things, too, things that had happened to her that she never, ever let herself think about. Yes, every day the human race became sicker, and this thing was the cure.

Antichrist, she thought. Yet this thing, this man in a storm that she had seen, was older than anything written in the Bible. It was as old as time. *How can you know that?* she asked, the tiny part of her that still doubted. But she *did* know it. Just as she understood that there was something in her too, something like this creature only different. There was one in each of them.

There were still so many questions, but Rilke had faith that answers would come in time. For now, she knew enough. Something had called on her and her brother to try and make the world right. Something had called upon them both to fight. They had all been chosen, even the idiots outside. If Cal and Brick and Daisy and the rest of them decided not to accept then they'd be punished just like the vermin who scurried through the streets in every single corner of this planet. Yes, everything was about to change, Rilke understood that better than she'd understood anything else in her life.

She was a soldier, now. And there was a war coming.

Daisy

'You okay?'

Daisy looked up, shaken from a weird sensation. Cal was looking at her, his face still flushed from their games. It had been so much fun. More fun than Daisy could remember having in *ages*. Even back at school people didn't really play tag or hide and seek any more, they were considered baby games. But they'd spent ages running round the park chasing each other and hiding and laughing so much she'd thought her lungs were going to stop working.

Now she and Cal and Adam were sitting on the wooden walkway that led up to the log flume. It was absolutely baking, the sun even fiercer than the one time she'd been abroad, to Majorca. She couldn't bear to go back inside, though, not after what had happened with Rilke. Even the shade made her feel scared. Out here in the sun there was only chasing and games and fun and laughter.

'I'm okay,' she said. 'Just tired.'

'You must be,' Cal replied. 'I don't think I've ever seen anyone run so fast for so long. You even managed to catch Brick, and his legs are like three metres long.'

Daisy giggled, her sides still protesting from the stitches they'd had earlier. Brick had gone off somewhere with Marcus and Jade, and Chris had staggered off to the toilet a while back saying that all the running around had 'knocked something loose'. Daisy didn't like to think about what he meant. She shifted on her uncomfortable seat, putting an arm round Adam's shoulders.

'Are you thirsty?' she asked. He shook his head. Cal had brought out another saucepan full of tap water, cold this time, and they'd taken turns drinking from it. 'Hungry? Would you like another Weetabix?'

Adam pulled a face. Daisy didn't blame him. They tasted horrible without milk and loads of sugar. It was like eating a piece of wood. She'd had to force two down because she was starving, but it hadn't done much to fill her up. Right now she'd give just about anything for a cheese and ham panini or one of those Margarita pizzas from Tesco's that her dad always used to buy. She wished Rilke would stop being so cruel and let them have some of their supplies. There had been chocolate up there, and jelly sweets, and there was no way that Rilke could eat them all by herself.

Rilke. The funny feeling she'd just had was about her, but she couldn't quite work out what it was. Being out in the sunshine seemed to have melted the ice cubes in her head, blurring them all into a big, squidgy mess that didn't make sense. It was nice, she was tired of seeing the world through other people's thoughts. She hoped they would never come back.

'Earth to Daisy,' said Cal, waving his hand. 'Sure you're okay?'

She nodded, but there was something else niggling at her, the thing that Marcus had said. Demons and possession. She didn't really understand what possessed meant, only that you weren't yourself. What had Marcus said, that it was something inside your body controlling you like you were a puppet? That was a pretty good explanation of what was going on, wasn't it? She thought about Mrs Baird, the lovely old lady next door who'd always brought round pots of yummy marmalade and disgusting chutney. Why would she suddenly try to attack her unless something was making her do it? The same with the ambulance man and all the others. If there was a nasty ghost or whatever living in their bodies, making them do things, that would explain everything.

But how were they supposed to make themselves better?

'Adam,' she said. 'Do you like flowers?'

The boy looked up at her, frowning. Daisy pointed to a little cluster of purple blooms that poked up from the sea grass.

'I do, do you think you could pick me some?'

He nodded, then ran over to the patch. When he was out of earshot, Daisy turned to Cal.

'How do you get rid of demons?'

'Huh?' he said. 'You mean what Marcus said? Just ignore him, Dais, he was being silly.'

'I'm not scared,' she lied. 'I just think, what if he was right?'

'He's not, demons aren't real. People just made them

up hundreds of years ago, thousands maybe, because they didn't know how to explain all the bad stuff in the world. They thought people did horrible things because they were possessed.'

'But maybe that *is* why people are doing horrible things,' she said. 'That would explain why everyone tried to kill us, because they're possessed and we're not.'

Cal took a deep breath, gazing out towards the silver strip of sea that hung over the back fence. Sunlight caught in his hair. He was very handsome, Daisy thought. He was the kind of boy who might be on a Disney Channel show.

'I don't know,' he said. 'I don't know if we'll ever know for sure.' He looked back at her. 'But please don't worry, okay? We're safe here. Demons or no demons, they can't hurt you.'

'I know,' she said, another lie. Adam was running back with a handful of scraggly flowers. He dropped one, spilling most of the rest when he bent down to pick it up. Daisy got up to help, but by the time she'd reached him he'd recovered them all. He thrust out the blooms with a bashful grin and she took them, their sweet scent making her feel slightly woozy. 'They're so beautiful, Adam, thank you.'

He didn't reply, just ran back to where he'd been picking them and lifted a stick from the dusty ground. He began to whack the sea grass like he was a swashbuckling pirate attacking a ship.

Boys will be boys, she thought. She picked one of the small buds and tucked it behind her ear the way her mum sometimes did when she was out in the garden, then she looked back at Cal.

'We should put these in some water.'

'No probs,' he said, getting up and stretching. 'Come on, there are jugs and things in the kitchen.'

They wandered slowly back towards the pavilion, Adam following and taking wild swipes at everything he passed. When they reached the fire door, however, Daisy heard a scuffling coming from the back of the park.

'What is that?' she asked.

'Wait here,' said Cal. 'I'll go and check.'

He set off, but she didn't wait, chasing after him as he disappeared round the corner of the pavilion. When she peeked she saw him standing outside one of the little buildings, the one that said 'Danger: Do Not Enter'. The voices inside reverberated with an eerie metal twang.

'I think that's it. No, wait, that one.'

'This one?'

'Aw, hell, I don't know, try it.'

'Bugger off, you try it.'

Daisy pressed up against Cal, looking into the shed to see Marcus and Chris there. The walls were covered in weird boxes and wires and big yellow stickers that had skulls and crossbones on them.

'What are they doing?' she asked Cal.

'I have no idea. Hey, guys, what are you doing?'

Chris turned and flashed them a grin from the dark.

'Marcus here is an electrician, he reckons he can get

the park up and running. We'll have lights and air con, arcade games, maybe even a telly if we can find one.'

'No,' Marcus said. 'One, I'm not an electrician, I've just started my apprenticeship in plumbing, and we cover a bit of electrics too, for bathrooms and stuff. Two, this place hasn't had a feed in years, so there's maybe a zero point one per cent chance that anything will work ever again.'

'Like I said,' Chris went on. 'He's going to fix it.'

Marcus sighed and turned back to whatever he was doing.

'Are you sure that's a good idea?' Cal asked. 'If it does work, and we start using electricity, won't people notice?'

But neither of the boys was listening; they were fighting over something that Chris was holding, which didn't seem like a great idea, given all the warning stickers.

'Come on,' said Cal. 'Let's leave them to blow themselves up.'

They walked back the way they'd come, crawling in through the fire doors. Almost as soon as the cold darkness of the corridor gripped her Daisy felt the ice cubes start to return, clinking their way back to the surface of her brain. She tried to push them down again but they kept slipping loose and rising. She followed Cal into the kitchen, telling herself not to look at the dead man. He wasn't there, and at first she thought that maybe he'd got up and walked off. Then she saw the tracks, oil-black in the gloom, which led off towards the basement. Somebody finally must have moved him.

'Here you go,' said Cal, picking a cracked, filthy tumbler from one of the shelves and filling it from the tap. 'This should do it.'

He handed it to her, and she placed the flowers inside. They were wilting already, as if the darkness of the building had weight. She could feel it too, like a pressure pushing her down, squashing her.

'Can we go back outside?' she asked. Cal nodded, and she could see by his expression that he was scared in here. Scared of the dark, scared of Rilke. They retreated up the corridor, stopping only when they heard Brick behind them, slamming through the door from the foyer.

'She still isn't letting us in,' he said. 'I swear I'm going to light this whole place on fire and smoke her out.'

'Calm down, Brick,' said Cal as they waited for him to catch up. 'We'll think of something else.'

'See if she's so smug when she's burning,' he said. 'Her and her brother. See if she's so smug when she has to watch *him* die.'

Daisy squeezed under the chains, holding them up so that Cal and then Brick could follow. Out in the sun the bigger boy seemed to lose some of his anger, but his fists were still clenched so hard that Daisy could see where his long nails dug into the flesh of his palms. It was so sad, because just an hour ago he'd been running around with the rest of them, his laugh a high-pitched giggle that had made him seem like an entirely different person.

'She wouldn't even answer me,' he said. 'After everything, after what she did, she wouldn't even answer me.'

'Come on,' said Cal, putting a hand on the other boy's shoulder. 'Let's go and find the others. I think we need to make a plan.'

Cal

'We have to deal with the food situation first,' said Cal. 'We can't do anything if we're starving to death.'

They were back at the carousel, although nobody was sitting on the horses. Daisy and Adam were walking between Angie, Geoffrey and Wonky-Butt the Wonder Horse with piles of dog biscuits cupped in their hands. The rest of them − apart from Marcus, who was still messing around at the back of the park − were perched on the rusted metal steps, enjoying the shade of the half-disintegrated canopy. The air smelled of sea salt and sweat.

'Amen to that,' said Chris. 'I'm gonna waste away if we don't get something soon.'

'Yeah, somehow I don't see that happening,' spat Brick, nodding at the fold visible beneath Chris's T-shirt.

'It's water retention,' he replied, blushing. 'No, actually it's in my genes. Hang on, wait, it's *none of your bloody business*.'

'Seriously, guys,' said Cal, feeling an uncomfortable tickle of impatience in the vast emptiness of his stomach. The Weetabix he'd eaten had done nothing to fill him up and the prospect of going all night without eating was making him nervous. 'We need to think of something. Any ideas?'

'Yeah, I think maybe not running around like crazy people using up all our energy might be sensible,' said Jade. Her eyes were red again, like she'd been crying, but she managed a gentle smile.

'Fair point,' said Cal.

'We need to find a way to get Rilke out of her rat hole,' said Brick. 'I'm serious, we could light a fire outside the restaurant. She'd have to come out.'

'Look, forget about her,' said Cal. 'You really don't want to make her angry. She's still got the gun.'

'And who brought the gun, genius?'

'I'm not saying you can't get back at her, Brick,' Cal said. 'But we need to think about food first or none of us are going to be able to do anything.'

Cal's gut gurgled, loud enough for Daisy to turn and laugh.

She held out the dog biscuits. 'Do you want to try these?'

It might come to that, he thought, saying: 'No thanks, Dais, they might make me grow a tail.'

She laughed and went back to her game, Adam following her around the carousel like a shadow.

'You leave any food in your car?' Brick asked. Cal shook his head.

'No, we brought it all. We've got to think of something else. You know the area, Brick, can you think of anywhere we might be able to get supplies?'

'Well there's an ocean right there,' he said. 'If anyone knows how to fish.'

Nobody responded, which was answer enough. Even if they managed to catch anything, Cal wouldn't have a clue how to take its scales off and pull its guts out or whatever you had to do to make sure they weren't poisonous.

'And Hemsby's about a mile off. Plenty of chip shops, probably won't be more than, I don't know, a couple of thousand people there at this time of year.'

A couple of thousand feral, screaming, punching, biting, stomping people. They wouldn't last five seconds in a place like that. Cal sighed, kicking out at the steps hard enough to make the entire platform rattle.

'Come on, guys, this is serious. If we can't get food then we're going to die here.'

'We could always eat fatty,' Brick said, looking at Chris. Cal had to stop himself leaping up the steps and thumping the guy square in the mouth. He waited for the anger to fizzle away before speaking.

'Is there a supermarket or anything nearby? A shop we could break into after dark?'

'There's another garage about a mile inland,' Brick mumbled, almost reluctantly. 'But it's open twenty-four hours. That's where I nearly got it the first time. There's a Sainsbo's, too, but there are always people in there. They stack the shelves at night; my brother used to work at the one in Norwich, before he joined up.'

'That it?'

'That's it. This isn't London, *Callum*, this is the arse end of Norfolk, what did you expect?'

Cal shook his head. He wasn't sure what he'd expected. It wasn't like he'd ever been in this situation before. He tried to remember the ride up, with Daisy in the car. They had to have passed something.

'Hang on,' he said. 'What about the factory, the one you can see from here?'

'That place? They make fertiliser or something. You gonna eat that?'

'They might have a café there,' said Chris, shrugging.

'Yeah, they'll have a canteen, if it's a big place,' Jade added. 'My old man worked in a car plant, took me for lunch there sometimes if I wasn't at school. Chips and beans, still my favourite meal in the world.'

Someone else's stomach rumbled.

'But there's no way we're getting in,' said Brick. 'There's a security guard, probably more than one.'

Cal swore, dropping his head into his hands.

'I'm telling you,' Brick went on. 'We have to force Rilke to come outside then we can get our supplies back.'

'What, a few bags of sour mix and crisps?' Cal snapped back. 'That will keep us going for a couple of months, yeah?'

'I really think the factory could work,' said Jade. 'Think about it, if there's, what, a couple of guys looking after the place at night then we could distract them while somebody goes in to look for food.'

'Distract them?' said Chris. 'How do we do that?'

'We just have to get close,' said Cal. 'Then we'll trigger them. They'll chase us.'

'That does *not* sound like fun,' said Chris.

'But we could take the car,' said Cal, standing up, already excited. 'Stop outside the gates until we hook them, then drive fast enough to stay away but slow enough to pull them along. We could be in and out in a few minutes, if we can find the café or whatever.'

He looked at Jade and she shrugged. Chris was shaking his head but he was licking his lips, too. Brick's face was as hard as his name, his eyes glowering.

'Brick?'

'Don't know. It's too dangerous. We should give it a few days, think about it.'

'We don't have a few days,' said Cal. 'Tomorrow, we should do it then. It's Sunday tomorrow, there will be nobody there.'

'I hate to break it to you, Cal,' said Jade. 'But tomorrow is Monday. If we're going to do this, we need to do it now.'

'Now?' he said, and suddenly the idea of leaving Fursville and breaking into a factory seemed utterly ridiculous, completely impossible. 'Maybe you're right, Brick, maybe we should think about it some more.'

'You think?' said Brick, flapping his arms and making chicken noises. 'Not such a tough guy now, are you?'

Cal took a step towards the bigger boy, his fist bunched.

'Go fu—'

He never got the chance to finish as the top of the carousel exploded, sparks flying from the rows of broken bulbs. He ducked down, shrapnel slicing through the hot air, stinging his skin like mosquito bites. Daisy was screaming, crumpled in a heap as an electric rain dripped down on her. A screeching noise rose from the battered ride, winding up into an old-fashioned song that was so out of tune it sounded like something from a nightmare. The horses were moving, lurching forward then halting; all the while a deafening, grinding roar emanated from the machinery beneath them.

'Daisy!' Cal ran for the steps but Brick was already there, hoisting the girl in one arm and Adam in the other. He almost fell as he clattered back down, his face twisted into a grimace. Jade was legging it, her hands over her head.

There was a second explosion, this time from overhead. Cal looked up to see the big wheel shake, unleashing a monsoon of dirt and dust and metal shavings so thick that it turned day into twilight. One of the few remaining carriages tore loose, crashing into the booth that sat below it and firing out another deadly barrage of broken glass. The structure juddered, squealing so loudly that Cal slammed his hands to his ears. Daisy squirmed free of Brick's grip and ran over to him, hugging him tight.

'What is it? What is it?' she sobbed.

From the other side of the park there was an almighty crunch, wood splintering. An ugly fist of smoke thrust up towards the sky. Cal could hear more music now, coming from everywhere, a hundred different tunes that clashed with each other. It was so loud, so confusing, that it was making him feel seasick. And there was laughter too, laughter and applause like in a game show, like there was a crowd watching them. This was what terrified him the most, because it was an impossible sound. It had no right to be here.

Chris was yelling at him, pointing at the pavilion, but the hurricane of noise swept his words away. The carousel was spinning faster now. The horses looked wild, like they were about to leap right off the platform and stampede through the park. They looked as if they were coming alive.

The whole park was coming alive.

Cal suddenly understood what Chris was yelling.

'Marcus,' Cal said. He saw Brick's confusion, and shouted, 'It's Marcus. He must have got the electrics working.'

'The *what*?' Brick called back, dropping Adam to the floor. He broke into a run, heading for the back of the park. 'Stupid, stupid idiot!'

The big wheel shuddered hard, another wave of dark matter spiralling down from its skeletal frame along with half a dozen metal spikes which thudded into the path. A siren rose up, a blaring air-raid noise that was coming from the pavilion.

'It's okay, Daisy,' Cal said. The girl was clinging on to him so hard it hurt. He could feel her whole body shaking. 'It's just the electricity, it's come back on.'

'They're going to hear it,' she said. 'They're going to hear it and come and kill us.'

'They're not, they won't, there's no one close enough.'

He prayed that he was right. If he wasn't, if people came to investigate, then they were all in serious trouble. Daisy looked up at him.

'But I can *see* it, Cal, in my head. They're going to come.'

The carousel lurched, the mirrors on the central post shattering. One of the horses jolted so much that its post snapped, the plastic animal bending out at an angle as it rotated. The pole caught on the pile of rubble next to it, peeling the horse from its mount and depositing it on the ground. Cal grabbed Daisy and pulled her away.

'It's going to be okay, Brick will sort it out.'

Another shower of sparks ripped from the top of the carousel, dropping like a curtain, then the machine ground to a halt. The tune got slower and deeper before dying out completely. Gradually, the rest of the chaos passed, leaving the park quieter than it had ever been. Cal straightened, breathing a sigh of relief like a tornado had just passed overhead. His heart felt like it had received a sudden surge of electricity too, palpitating. He put a hand to his chest to steady it.

Adam had run over and was gripping Daisy with the same force she was holding Cal.

'You alright?' he asked them. 'You didn't get hit by glass or anything?'

They both shook their heads. Daisy was looking at something that nobody else could see, her eyes flicking back and forth. Her skin had gone so pale that it was almost translucent.

'It's just in your head,' he said, stroking the hair away from her eyes. 'Don't let it scare you.'

'But I can *see* it,' she said. 'They're going to—'

And that's when the screaming started.

Daisy

They were coming from the pavilion – muffled screams that were somehow louder than the deafening chaos that had just faded. Daisy clung on to Cal's arm, her head a constantly churning madness of ice cubes.

'Who is that?' said Cal as another shriek tore through the air. Even the birds had stopped singing, as if they were afraid of what was to come.

The scream was nothing like the ones in the movies, it was desperate and broken and insane and weak and strong all at the same time. It made the inside of Daisy's skull tickle, the blood in her ears roaring like there was an ocean flowing through them. Adam was crying into her chest, his skinny arms locked around her. Cal swore, running his hands through his hair. Chris was beside them, ghost-like. Neither of them knew what to do.

'Wait here,' Cal said to him. 'Make sure they're safe.'

'No, man, we should stick together,' Chris said. 'If it's the ferals, we shouldn't split up.'

Cal nodded, prying Daisy loose.

'Okay, stay with me, yeah? Stay close, and keep hold of Adam.' He looked at Chris. 'Grab a weapon, mate, we might need them.'

Both the boys scrabbled in the rubble, picking up

447

metal poles of different lengths. Cal tucked his beneath his arm, taking Daisy's hand and leading her towards the pavilion just as another awful screech pierced the walls. They ran past the locked main entrance, almost bumping into Jade as they tore round the corner.

'You okay?' Cal asked her. 'You screaming?'

She shook her head, turning her wide eyes to the fire door. Daisy heard a scuffling of feet, then Brick appeared from the other direction. He was holding Marcus by the scruff of the neck and he looked angrier than Daisy had ever seen him. They marched down the side of the pavilion, Brick giving Marcus a shove. The younger kid fell, sprawling in the dirt.

'That's Rilke,' Brick said. The screams were louder here, squeezed from the fire door as if they were trying to escape whatever was inside. An ice cube clinked to the top of the pile: the restaurant, and a shape that moved inside it – bright and dark at the same time. *Don't go in, please don't go in.*

'What's happening in there?' Jade asked.

'Whatever it is,' Brick said, 'I hope she's screaming in pain.'

Marcus was on his feet again.

'It started when the electricity came on,' he said. 'Sorry, by the way. I didn't think all that would happen.'

'We should—' Cal had to stop as more screams tore the air in two. 'Come on.'

'You serious?' Brick asked, moving in front of the fire door. 'Let her suffer.'

'We don't know what it is,' Cal said, toe to toe with

the taller boy. 'For all we know it could be another one of us in there, someone who wandered in when we were out front. Rilke might be doing something to *them*. You think about that?'

Brick obviously hadn't, because after chewing on it for a second he stood to one side.

'We might even be able to grab some food while we're up there,' Cal went on. 'If she's distracted.'

He looked at Chris, nodding. Chris nodded back, his metal bar raised, then the two of them ducked into the darkness. Brick cursed, following them in on his hands and knees. Daisy looked down at Adam. He was shaking his head, still crying.

'Don't be scared,' she said. 'We're safer if we're all together. They'll look after us.'

He resisted for a second, then let her lead him to the door. She crouched down, squeezing through the gap. After the blazing sunlight the corridor was extraordinarily dark. She couldn't breathe under the weight of the shadows, but when she turned to try and escape Adam was in the way, Jade already pushing through from outside.

A shriek echoed down the corridor, so much louder now, so much more real. Daisy opened her mouth, a scream of her own rising fast, cut off when she felt a hand on her shoulder.

'Come on,' said Cal. 'Stay with me.'

They huddled together as they passed through the dust-thick light of the foyer and up the stairs. The restaurant was in sight when the next scream cannoned out, the doors rocking in their frames with the force of it, flakes of ice spiralling to the frozen floor.

'What the . . .' said Brick. 'We should get out.'

While we still can. Daisy realised they were all thinking it. There was a crunch from inside Waves. Something big slammed into the other side of the wall, a huge crack splitting the plasterwork and making them all stagger back – Marcus almost tumbling down the stairs. A cry, howled out with heart-breaking strength:

'*Schiller!*'

'Whatever's happening, she deserves it,' said Brick, retreating. 'She can go to hell for all I care.'

Crunch. Dust rained down from the ceiling. Rilke called out her brother's name again.

'Ah screw this,' Cal said, taking a step back. Daisy thought he was going to leave, but he was just getting a run-up. He threw himself at the doors, yelling as he kicked out. The wood splintered but they didn't open. He did it again, and this time they flew apart to reveal a world turned inside out.

There was light in the restaurant, a flickering glow that was definitely fire, but which was too cold and too bright for a candle. In its uncertain grip Daisy could see that the restaurant had been trashed, every single table and chair upturned, most splintered into pieces. There was barely a patch of floor that wasn't covered in rubbish.

Rilke knelt in the middle of the room as though she were praying, her legs folded beneath her. The flames were reflected in her wide, unblinking eyes, and in the rivulets that ran down her cheeks, making her look like someone burning up from the inside. Her mouth gaped open. Without warning the scream came again – not from Rilke but from something else. It was like a needle sliding into Daisy's brain. Adam let go of her, collapsing to his knees with his fingers in his ears, and it took all her strength not to do the same.

The source of the light was moving, fast, the shadows in the room sweeping in wide arcs. A shape flew across the restaurant, bathed in weak flames. It thumped into the far wall and dropped to the floor, struggling like a dying bird. It wouldn't stay still, launching itself into the air again before Daisy could make any sense of it. It ploughed through an upside-down table, blasting it into splinters before flailing out of sight.

'Rilke?' Cal yelled into the room. 'Get out of there!'

Her head swivelled round, staring right at them. Daisy understood that Rilke wasn't scared. There was something else in her expression: part fear yes, but part sick, gleeful excitement too. It was utterly insane. She smiled at them, a grin that belonged in a madhouse. All the while the fire moved, chasing shadows as it hurled itself from wall to wall.

'Rilke,' Cal said again, his voice an empty husk.

'Don't you see?' the girl called back. The shape dropped in front of her, the flames dulled now but still covering it like a flickering blue skin. It was a body, its arms wrapped around itself, its legs splayed out at unnatural angles, like they were broken. Its head was tucked into its chest, but Daisy had no difficulty working out who it was.

Schiller.

The boy arced his back, his mouth splitting open and unleashing another scream. The inferno raged, too bright to look at. He thrust himself from the ground so fast that he slammed into the ceiling. One of the panels snapped loose, crashing down beside Rilke. She didn't even notice it, her eyes locked on her brother as he flapped upside down against the top of the room, as if gravity had suddenly been reversed.

He slid out of sight, and Daisy found herself taking a step forward. Her terror was now so extreme that she could barely feel it, it could no longer register. She felt Cal's hand around hers, both of them walking through the door together because they had to see, they had to know what this thing was.

Schiller was rolling against the ceiling now, looking like he was trying to put out the flames which burned from his skin. That fire gave off no heat, and it didn't spread. It did the opposite, in fact, leaving sparkling crystals of ice wherever it touched. It was sucking the warmth from everything, feeding on heat and light, devouring it. He cried out again, ripped from left to right and slammed into the far wall.

Rilke's brother wasn't the only shape in the flames, Daisy realised. There was something else there, faint but unmistakable. Unmistakable but impossible. Impossible but real. It stretched out from Schiller's hunched shoulders, unfolding gracefully, longer than the boy's whole body. It swept down with incredible force, blasting debris from the floor and propelling him across the room. Schiller screamed again, the sound cut dead as he struck the other wall, hanging there like a rock climber as that shape beat frantically.

It was a wing. A single, flaming, beautiful, terrible wing.

'Don't you see?' Rilke said again, still looking at them.

The flames flickered, fading again, and Schiller collapsed to the floor. He cried out, trying to crawl towards his sister before disappearing inside another inferno, that same swan-like wing pushing from his back, hauling him into the air. Rilke laughed as she watched him go, a sound like cut glass.

'Isn't it obvious what we are?' the girl went on. 'What we're becoming? What we're meant to do?'

Nobody answered. How could they? Schiller flapped towards the window, tearing at the boards. Sunlight trickled in but it had no power here, cowering before the living flame. His single wing beat and he was hoisted up to the ceiling again, then slammed back to the floor with just as much force. Daisy didn't know how he could still be alive, but he was, his face knotted into a mask of pain, of confusion, as he tried to climb to the window again.

'You have to make a choice,' said Rilke. 'You have to embrace this, embrace our gift, or turn your back on it.'

She got to her feet, walking unsteadily towards the door. Her hands were held out in front of her, no gun in sight. But she was still dangerous, Daisy knew, more dangerous than ever. Her brother railed behind her, drowning in fire.

'We are all changing,' Rilke said. 'We have been chosen. Look at what Schiller is becoming. It will happen to all of us, don't you see that, Daisy?'

And Daisy *did* see it. It was suddenly clear. Marcus had been right all along, and yet he'd been so wrong too. She looked at Cal, feeling the last of the warmth drain from her, snuffed out. Rilke was telling the truth, they were all going to change.

'The ferals, they're not the ones who are possessed,' Daisy said, staggering back, wanting to cry but unable to remember how. Cal reached for her but she stepped out of the way, towards the stairs. 'They're not the ones with the demons inside them.'

Everyone but Schiller was looking at her, waiting for her to finish, to state what they all now knew.

'*We* are.'

Brick

Brick couldn't take his eyes off Rilke's burning brother.

The boy was quiet again, those blue flames simmering from every pore. He lay on the floor, his head turned up. Even his eyes had ignited, pockets of impossible light. Brick thought he would go mad if he stared into those eyes for too long, the same way you could go blind by looking right at the sun. They weren't Schiller's eyes, they belonged to something else – a form that Brick could almost make out in his shimmering, dancing second skin.

Daisy was right. Schiller was possessed.

'Daisy, wait!' Cal was yelling after the girl but she was gone, her footsteps fading. The rest of them stood there, paralysed by the cold fire from Schiller and the intensity of Rilke's gaze. Cal turned to her, his face grey. 'You're mad; you're off your goddamned head.'

But she wasn't. What she was saying made a terrible kind of sense. Brick doubled up, feeling the world begin to come apart. Reality was like a house of cards – strip away enough of what you know and the rest of it collapses.

'You don't have to listen to me, Cal,' said Rilke. She had to pause as Schiller erupted again, like somebody had flicked a gas hob from the lowest setting to the highest. The boy's faces – both his and the one in the flames – howled together as that hideous wing punched out and launched him into another lopsided flight. 'You just have to use your eyes. Look at what he is. Listen to your head and tell me you don't feel it too.'

Don't listen, Brick ordered himself. But it was there, lodged in his brain, an inescapable truth that seared through everything else. There was something inside him the same way there was something inside Schiller, inside all of them, fighting its way to the surface. It had started with the headache, that maddening *thump-thump thump-thump thump-thump*. The noise *had* been something trying to get in, something knocking at his door. And it had succeeded. It was here.

'I don't know why we were chosen,' Rilke went on, fixing her doll's eyes on them all in turn. 'But we were. Give it time and you'll see.'

'It can't be,' said Chris, crumpled against the banister.

The others too were shaking their heads. He could see it in their faces, though. He could see that they believed.

'Demons aren't real, Rilke,' Cal said without conviction. '*This* isn't real, it's a . . . a . . .'

Schiller was clawing at the window again. He ripped away the board, hurling it across the room so hard that it impaled itself in the far wall. Sunlight streamed in, seeming to funnel around the burning shape. The effect was dizzying, making it look as though he was burning inside a pocket of darkness.

Rilke smiled.

'These aren't demons,' she said. 'I don't know why we're here, but it isn't for something evil. It is for something good. Something incredible.'

'What?' asked Jade, her red-rimmed eyes swimming.

'Don't you see?' Rilke said. 'After everything that's happened to you, isn't it clear?'

Brick screwed his eyes shut, fighting the swell of emotion that churned up from his gut. He saw the people at the garage, grunting and howling and barking like mindless animals as they chased him. These were the people he had hated for so long, who had hated him. The idiotic, annoying masses who'd been making his life a misery since long before all this had started. Wasn't it right that they should be punished?

Not Lisa, though. Not her. She hadn't hated him.

'Don't fight it, Brick,' said Rilke. 'You know what we have to do.'

He could feel her thoughts in his own, planting a seed in the flesh of his brain. He knew what she wanted. And it felt so right, so pure. It felt more real than any other thought he'd had in his life. People were bad, people did terrible things. Humanity needed to be purged.

He recoiled at the thought, his mind fighting it. That couldn't be right, that *wasn't* right. Rilke had made a mistake.

'Don't resist it,' she said, her whisper detonating inside his head, a shock that swept away his reason. 'You can't say no, Brick. It's why we're here, it's what we have to do.'

He felt something warm and wet trickling from his nose, the taste of salt and copper on his tongue.

'Don't listen to me, listen to *them*,' Rilke said. 'Listen to what they're trying to tell you.'

It *was* trying to tell him something, whatever it was that sat inside his soul. There were no words, just an instinctive feeling which burrowed upwards. *We've been chosen, but not for this, for something else.*

'You're wrong,' he said, his voice faint and distant like a muffled recording of himself. 'That's not it.'

'It *is*,' she hissed. 'If you don't see it, then you're no better than the rest of them. If you don't understand, then you'll *die* with the rest of them.'

Schiller screamed, the flames fading like a broken jet engine. He collapsed, his second skin flickering on and off, only the fiery sockets of his eyes still fierce.

'What we are is a miracle,' Rilke said. 'What lives inside us is holy, it is right. Those of you who accept it will be saved. Those of you too blind and too scared to comprehend what is happening will perish. You have to make a choice, right now, or it will be too late.'

'But what *is* inside us, Rilke?' asked Jade, taking a step towards the other girl. Blood dripped from her nose, and her eyes were wide, innocent, trusting.

'Jade,' said Cal. 'Rilke, let her be.'

'I want to know,' Jade said. 'Don't you? Isn't that—' she gestured into the restaurant but she could find no words to describe what she saw. 'Isn't *that* proof enough?'

Cal wiped a hand across his face, smearing away crimson tears.

'What are they, these things inside us?' Jade asked again.

'You already know,' Rilke said. 'You all do.'

Jade smiled, like someone hypnotised. She glanced at Cal, then at Chris, and finally at Brick. He thought he could see right into her head, into the broken pieces of her mind. Then she walked into the restaurant, collapsing to her knees in the middle of the room.

'Come on,' yelled Cal. He grabbed Adam's arm, dragging the boy towards the stairs. 'Let's go.'

Brick didn't move. He wanted nothing more than to be outside, to be away from this madness. But still Rilke's voice clamoured inside his skull, utterly wrong and yet utterly convincing. He looked at Schiller, bathed in flames. Was this his fate too, if he stayed? Could he really walk away from such a gift?

'Last chance, Cal,' said Rilke, calling down the sweeping stairs.

'Screw you, Rilke,' he shouted back. 'Go to hell.'

Chris was already stumbling after him, but Marcus wasn't moving. His face wore the same look of rapture as Jade's.

'Last chance, Harry,' Rilke said to Brick, and the sound of his real name sent a surge of poisonous euphoria vomiting up his throat. He almost threw himself to his knees right there, ready to embrace her. 'Listen to their call, make your choice.'

He took a step towards her. Marcus was moving too, laughing softly to himself as he pushed into the restaurant and knelt down before Schiller.

'You know what they are,' Rilke said. 'How can you say no?'

Brick opened his mouth and let out a hoarse, desperate scream – a noise that seemed to come not from him but from the thing inside him. Then he turned, falling over himself and crawling backwards towards the stairs, tumbling down the first few before he recovered. He slid down them, never taking his eyes off Rilke. She shook her head, her expression drenched in a profound sadness.

'How could you say no?' she asked again, then she closed the restaurant door. He turned and ran, tearing through the foyer and down the corridor, pushing through the fire door so hard that the chains ripped out a lock of his hair.

He fell in the dirt, his whole body shivering in the blazing sun. And all the while the truth of it was a beacon inside his skull, burning with white heat, the thing inside him issuing a clarion call that he could not ignore.

No, not a *thing*. Not a ghost or a demon either.

It was an angel.

Cal

Cal caught up with Daisy by the carousel, calling out until she staggered to a halt. When she looked round it was as though she didn't see him, as though the burning boy had blinded her.

'Daisy,' he said, running over, wrapping his arms around her.

She blinked, her eyes swimming in and out of focus and eventually finding him. He held her tight. He didn't know what to say.

After a moment or two he heard heavy footsteps on the gravel. Chris walking down the path, Adam treading on his shadow. Daisy saw them too. She peeled away from Cal's grip and ran over to Adam, hugging him. He didn't react. He didn't even seem to notice she was there.

'Tell me Marcus and Brick didn't go in,' Cal said. Chris shook his head.

'Marcus, yeah. Brick's back there puking his guts up.'

Cal put his hands in his hair, clenching so hard it hurt. He wanted to rip the top of his head off, pull out the memories of everything that had just happened. It didn't even matter if it killed him. Better dead than this.

'What happened in there, Cal?' Chris said. 'What was wrong with that boy?'

461

He's not a boy, Cal thought. *Not any more. He's something else.*

But he wouldn't let himself say what, even though the word flashed up before him like a signal flare in the darkness of his thoughts. He didn't need to speak, because Chris plucked it right out of his head.

'Angels?' the boy said. 'That's insane, man.'

'Forget it,' spat Cal. *Ha, yeah, just forget it, forget that you saw a boy covered in fire flying around the restaurant, it's not important.*

He ran back the way he'd come, turning the corner to see Brick on his hands and knees outside the door. He wasn't being sick, he was sobbing, which was a million times worse. Cal went to him, putting a hand on his back. Brick glanced up, his face so pale that his freckles looked like pen marks. Neither of them spoke. They didn't need to – they saw in each other's eyes the truth of what Rilke had told them.

'Come on, mate,' Cal said eventually, holding out his hand. Brick took it, hauling himself to his feet. They had taken a dozen steps back towards the carousel before he let go.

Cal collapsed on the steps, the same place they'd been sitting only a few minutes ago but which was now on the other side of time. He put his head in his hands, trying not to think. Brick sat down next to him.

'What—'

'Don't,' Cal interrupted Chris before he could finish. If they didn't talk about it, then maybe it might not have been real. 'Don't say it, Chris, not now, not ever.'

'But we have to—'

'We *don't*,' Cal snapped, looking up. Chris was sitting on the path. Daisy and Adam were next to him, both of them staring at nothing. 'Look, there's something weird going on, sure, something we don't understand. But I can promise you this, Rilke doesn't have a clue what it is either, she's just guessing, like us. Which is why everything she says is total bull.'

Nobody argued, but nobody looked very convinced.

'Jade, Marcus, they'll see that soon enough. They'll be back. And we need to keep our heads screwed on straight, yeah? We can't afford to start falling apart now.'

'So what do we do?' Chris asked after a moment.

'We're all exhausted. We've all been through more in a few days than anyone should have to go through in their whole life. None of us has eaten much, we're probably all bordering on crazy anyway.'

'That was no hallucination,' said Brick.

'I'm not saying it was. But it was dark in there, yeah, and, I don't know . . . We just need to stick to the plan, we need to get some food. We'll be able to think of something when we've had a chance to eat.'

He looked around. Chris was nodding. Brick shrugged. The idea of going for food seemed alien to Cal. The idea of doing *anything* seemed alien to him now. Yet they had to do something or fall back into the madness of what they had just seen.

'Need to get the hell away from this place anyway,' Brick croaked. 'I never want to come back here again.'

'Daisy?' Cal asked. She seemed to stir, her eyes drifting up.

'I want to go home,' she said.

'I know. We all do. Just not yet. Not yet.'

They sat there, listening to the ocean running its ceaseless course against the shore. Even the gulls had fallen silent.

'So what is the plan?' Chris asked.

'We get the car,' Cal replied. 'Your car. We go to the factory. We'll work out the rest when we get there.'

They were out of the park in five minutes. As soon as Cal squeezed free from the laurel hedge he felt the warmth of the day settle back inside him. It was brighter out here, like the park had been drowned in shade, caught beneath the weight of a dirty big cloud. It was easier to forget.

He held up a branch so that the others could push through, Daisy and Adam first, then Chris and Brick. He could hear them all taking a sigh of relief when they stepped into the shimmering haze of the empty street.

'Maybe someone will have fixed it,' Daisy said as they started walking along the front of the park. 'Maybe people won't hate us any more.'

And it was tempting to believe it – something in the fresh sea breeze that curled over the fence, ruffling their hair, which made it seem like everything might be okay. It was an illusion, of course, a fantasy, but it still felt good.

'Maybe,' Cal said. 'I guess we'll find out soon enough.'

He looked up, seeing Brick's graffiti on the Fursville sign. The glaring face looked down at him with its dead 'x' eyes, making him shudder. What if they got to the factory and it was full of people? What if they got trapped? One mistake is all it would take for them all to die.

Yet the alternative was worse. The alternative was going back up to the restaurant and falling to their knees in front of Rilke and her burning brother.

They reached the car park and walked through the damaged section of fence. The Jag was rammed into the hedge behind the shed, its tail end glinting through a mask of branches, its boot still open. At least it would be fast, he thought. If they had to make a getaway in a Punto or a Fiesta they'd definitely be screwed. Brick jogged ahead, pulling away the foliage.

'Got the keys?' Brick asked. Chris patted his pockets, pulling a face. 'You *kidding* me?'

'Yeah, I'm kidding you,' said Chris, pulling out the fob and unlocking the car. 'Calm down.'

Brick's expression was so sour that Cal couldn't help but laugh. Daisy too, chuckling into her hand.

'Seriously?' Brick asked. 'You think this is *funny*?'

'Just your face, mate,' said Cal, and God did it feel good to smile again.

'Yeah? We'll see if you're still giggling when your face is under my backside,' Brick stuttered, the stupid insult making them all laugh harder. 'Just shut up,' he said, but his eyes showed a glimmer of light. 'You know what I mean.'

'Come on,' said Cal, pushing the boot shut. 'Before Brick sits on my face. Shall I drive?'

'Uh uh,' said Chris, jiggling towards the car and sliding behind the wheel. 'My car, my rules.'

'Shotgun!' Cal and Brick yelled together, both of them making a break for the passenger door. Brick got there first, ripping it open and diving in head first. He manoeuvred his gangly body round, extending two middle fingers towards Cal.

'Looks like all the babies are in the back,' he said with a grin as Cal kicked the door shut.

'Up yours,' he said. He held the rear door open so that Daisy and Adam could clamber inside, getting in after them and planting his knees into Brick's seat. The bigger boy's response was to slide his chair all the way back. 'Hey, no fair,' Cal yelled. 'Chris, tell him.'

'Behave,' he said, starting the engine. 'I'm not going anywhere until you stop messing around. And put your seat belts on.'

That did it, all of them doubled over with laughter – even Adam, caught up in the sudden surge, his eyes shining. It could go on forever, Cal thought, this golden light which melted up through each fibre of his body, which made every single particle in the car seem to glow. It wasn't coming from him, it was flowing from somewhere else, a current of warmth which spread from him to Daisy to Adam to Chris to Brick and back again. Whatever this thing was inside them, it was healing them. It would keep them strong and it would keep them safe.

Cal wiped the tears from his eyes, his cheeks aching. He looked at the others, and in that moment of quiet they seemed to know each other like they had been together for an eternity.

'You ready?' he asked.

They all nodded. Chris put the Jag in reverse, revving the engine.

'Then let's do this.'

Rilke

Rilke could hear the faint growl of a car engine, rising and then fading. She knew who it was, she could almost see it through Daisy's eyes — the five of them inside the big silver car, the fat boy driving. They were laughing. *Laughing*. The sound of it, echoing almost silently through her thoughts, made her blood boil.

She knew where they were going, too. She could pluck that thought out of the storm of emotions inside their minds, as easily as taking a sweet from a bag. It was a sign that whatever was inside her was growing in strength. It had to be. Soon she'd be like Schiller, gripped with a holy fire and ready to burn down the world.

He sat before her now, and even though he was no longer alight, even though he was slumped and loose-limbed like a marionette with its strings cut, she could feel the energy pulsating from him. He was still cold, the carpet beneath him a lake of ice. He stared at the floor with two sets of eyes — the old eyes she knew so well, and two pits of fire which sat over them, shimmering gently.

Marcus and Jade were there too. They were both on their knees, gazing at Schiller as though they had just seen the face of God. It wasn't too far from the truth, she guessed, except they both had this same gift. It just hadn't been opened yet. They all had it. She'd seen it inside the man with the shotgun, the one she'd killed – the creature of flame inside him which had died when he died. The ones who fled had it too. She was disappointed that so many had run from their responsibility. It was no surprise that Brick had gone, Cal too, blinded by his own self-righteousness. But she had wanted Daisy to stay. Of all of them – Schiller aside, of course – Daisy was closest to changing, to becoming what they were all destined to become.

Jade turned round. Her eyes were wide and wet, her copper-coloured hair like a pyre in the sunlight from the broken window. She was the kind of weak creature that Rilke would usually hate. But she had been chosen too. She was her sister now, as much as Schiller was her brother.

'What are we, Rilke?' Jade asked.

'Angels,' Rilke replied. Jade cocked her head, her mouth hanging open. It seemed an age before she spoke again.

'How can that be?'

'Because they have chosen us.'

Rilke could feel a force inside her stirring as she spoke. It was so small, now, but it would grow.

'But *how* can it be?' Jade said. 'How is it possible?'

'It doesn't matter. I don't think we're supposed to know. The only thing that's important is what we're being asked to do.'

Schiller groaned. His left arm was hanging at a

strange angle, it had been dislocated at the shoulder. *Don't fight it, little brother*, she told him, knowing that the words would get through. *You're going to be okay. Just don't fight it.*

'What are we being asked to do?' said Marcus. A trickle of blood was winding down from his ear and he wiped it away with the back of his hand. 'I saw it in my head, I think. I saw people, the ones that tried to kill me.'

'They tried to kill you for a reason,' said Rilke. 'Because they know how dangerous you are.'

'But why would angels want to hurt people?' Jade said. She was glancing towards the door, frowning like she was stirring from a deep sleep. Now that Schiller had stilled, she seemed to be changing her mind. 'They're supposed to be good, aren't they?'

Rilke spat out a laugh.

'What do you think they are? Little cherubs with harps and halos? No. They're soldiers. They are powerful, and they are cruel.' She knew that much from church. 'They can't exist here by themselves, they'd burn right through the skin of reality. They need a host, a vessel. They need *us.*'

Marcus and Jade looked at each other. If they bolted now, Rilke decided, she'd shoot them both dead before they reached the door. How could they be so ignorant?

'They're cruel?' said Marcus.

'No, that's the wrong word,' Rilke said. 'They're not cruel. But they're not kind either. They have no emotions. They are warriors. They have no love for us, they don't feel anything at all. They have been sent here before, to destroy cities. They've killed thousands. If I had a Bible I'd show you, there's proof. It says that the angels will cleanse the world of the wicked.'

Even as she spoke she knew the creature inside her was nothing to do with the Bible. It was much, much older than any human stories. Rilke could feel the weight of its age on her soul. But they must have been here before, they must have *inspired* those stories.

'That's our job?' Jade said, shaking her head. 'Killing people? It doesn't feel right.'

'Just the bad ones. Don't you see? The world is a horrible place. People do terrible things to each other all the time. Would it be such a bad thing to purge all that . . . that rot?'

As she said it, a sudden doubt took hold of her. She thought back to what she'd seen with Daisy, the man in the storm that hung over the street and howled, which sucked in all that was warm and light and which spat out only absence. If they were angels, then what had that thing been? One of them?

No, not one of us, it isn't one of us. That thing is the opposite of us, it's here to destroy everything. We have to fight it, we have to fight it. The words in her head were not hers, and she pushed them away. She had to believe that what she was doing was right. If she didn't believe it, then she was lost.

'You'll see,' she said. 'You won't doubt me for much longer.'

None of them would. Something incredible was going to happen – even more incredible than Schiller's transformation – she could feel it the same way she could feel the tickle of a sneeze. She didn't know what, but it would involve fire. She wasn't sure if that premonition had been hers or Daisy's, but it was inevitable. There would be fire, and they would see the truth.

And she knew what she had to do to make it happen.

'I need a phone,' she said. 'Do either of you have one?'

'Battery's dead,' said Jade. Marcus fished his from his jeans and examined it.

'Why d'you want it?' he said.

'Trust me.'

He obviously did because he handed it to her.

'They're going to the factory, aren't they?' Rilke asked. 'To look for food.'

Jade nodded, her expression uncertain.

Rilke dialled 999 and lifted it to her ear. Daisy and the others would soon understand exactly what they had to do – if they survived, that was. There was a click, then a voice asking her which emergency service she required.

'All of them,' she said, smiling. 'I think there's going to be a terrorist attack.'

Daisy

By the time Daisy had finally managed to clip in her seat belt they were already slowing down.

The factory loomed up from the horizon, a cluster of black buildings and half a dozen towering chimneys which pierced the brilliant blue sky. It looked like a dead fly with its legs in the air, Daisy thought. There was nothing else nearby apart from a sign on the side of the road that said 'Thank you for visiting Hemmingway and Fursville – Please Drive Safely!' The same bug-eyed squirrel grinned at them from it. Fursville itself now lay half a mile behind them.

'See anything?' Cal asked. The factory entrance was set just off the road, up a short, wide driveway. There was no gate, just a barrier. On either side of that were big walls topped with mean-looking spikes. There was a booth there too, a little one with a door and a window, attached to the main building.

'There's somebody in there,' Daisy said, seeing a blurred shape behind the sun-drenched glass. 'I think we should turn round.'

'It might just be one person,' Chris said, letting the engine idle.

'And he might have fifty mates out the back,' Brick said. 'A hundred.'

473

Daisy felt her stomach complain. It was partly fear but mostly hunger. She wished they could just phone the factory people and ask them to bring out some food. Wouldn't they do that for a car full of kids?

'Yeah, we should call them,' said Cal, scooping the thought out of her brain. 'Look, it's right there, Cavendish-Harbreit. We could one-one-eight it.'

'And say what?' Brick asked. 'Hi there, we're just wondering if there's anyone in today because we'd like to break in and steal some stuff?'

'No, idiot, we could just see if anyone answers.'

Chris tapped a button in the centre of the dashboard and a keypad appeared on the touch-screen there.

'Nice,' said Cal. 'Does it have a signal?'

'Let's find out,' he said, typing in 118 118. There was a hum, then a flurry of numbers, and a voice sounded from the car's speakers. Daisy tuned it out, gazing through the window and back towards Fursville. The whole park looked tiny, and shimmered in the baking heat. It didn't seem real, as though any minute now the view would just flicker and switch off. It was a crazy thought, but surely not anywhere near as crazy as having creatures *inside* them.

Angels.

And yet it felt so right, what Rilke had said. Well, *most* of what she'd said. What lived in them wasn't really angels, she didn't think. These weren't the same things her mum had pictures of in the house, the ones she'd become obsessed with when she was ill. Those had smiling faces and rosy cheeks and sat on fluffy clouds.

474

These . . . They were different. Daisy didn't have the right words to explain how, only that they weren't alive in the same sense that people were. They couldn't live here, in this world. That's why they'd chosen her and Cal and Brick and the others. They needed a body to ride around in, the same way that humans needed cars to get places.

Only these angels couldn't control you like a person controlled a car. It was more like they just rode around with you, giving you strength – fire, like Schiller's – but waiting for you to make the right decisions.

Was that right? Daisy wasn't sure.

They were good, though, these things. Not like nice people, more like a friendly animal, like a dog or a tiger. They wouldn't speak, but they would look after you. That's where the ice cubes in her head came from, those little glimpses of other people's lives. Only other people with angels in them, though, she realised. That's how they talked to each other.

'Shall I put you straight through?' said the voice.

'Yes, thanks,' said Chris. There was a soft click then more ringing.

The big question was why the angels were here. There was no way that angels would make them murder people. Rilke was wrong, *really* wrong. Daisy didn't blame her. It wasn't like they'd all been given a big instruction book or anything. None of them had any idea what they were supposed to do. But they weren't here to hurt people, Daisy was sure of it.

'Nobody's answering,' said Brick as the ring tone

continued to fill the car.

'Really?' said Cal. 'I thought somebody had picked up and was just making phone impressions.'

Brick had his mouth open to reply when a voice blasted out of the speakers.

'Welcome to Cavendish-Harbreit Agricultural Technologies. Our office hours are nine a.m. to five p.m., Monday to Friday. If you require emergency assistance or product advice outside office hours, please hold.'

Music, something classical that reminded Daisy of her drama class. The memory of it was like somebody had slapped her around the face. The play! They would have done it by now. Emily Horton would have played Juliet, she would have kissed Fred. It should have been *her*. The hunger in her tummy turned into something much worse, like she was being crushed. Tears ran down her cheek but she wiped them away before anyone could notice, taking a couple of deep, shuddering breaths until the weight lifted.

She couldn't worry about the play now. There were more important things. There had better be, anyway. There had to be a reason for this, something that made it all okay, otherwise she'd have lost everything – *everything* – for nothing.

It's the thing you saw, she thought. *The man in the storm. He's the reason you're here. You have to fight him.* And even though the memory of that creature was terrifying, the thought settled her.

They were here to stop him. Before he could eat the whole world.

That's what he wants to do. He wants to eat everything, until there's nothing left but darkness.

'Hello?' said a voice through the speakers, making Daisy jump.

'Oh, yeah, hello,' said Chris, looking urgently at the others and mouthing, *What do I say?* 'Um . . . How are you?'

Cal was pointing at the booth, and they all squinted through the glass to see that the person inside was on the phone.

'This is an emergency number,' the voice said. 'We're closed. If you just want a chat, call back tomorrow.'

'Wait,' said Cal, leaning between the front seats. 'We need to speak with somebody urgently.'

'Is it an emergency?'

'Yeah,' Cal went on. 'Er, we're outside and we think someone might be trying to break in.'

'*What?*' hissed Brick. 'You trying to get us caught?'

'Who is this?' the man repeated.

'Outside, on the road, a gang in a silver car. They look suspicious.'

There was a clunk, a squeak, shuffling noises, then the door of the booth opened. Daisy ducked down, peeking as a man in a security guard's uniform appeared. He cupped a hand over his forehead, looking towards the Jag.

'What the hell are you doing?' Brick said.

'Trust me,' said Cal. 'He's going to come over. Chris, as soon as he gets close enough, move off, okay? Drive slowly, make him follow you back up to Fursville.

There are plenty of places to turn round up there, just make sure you keep him hooked. And lock the doors, yeah?'

'Sure,' said Chris, his voice a tremor. 'No probs.'

The guard reached into his booth for a cap, putting it on then walking out into the sun. Daisy could hear his footsteps crunching on the sandy track as he approached the road. He wasn't far away. Any second now he'd sense them. She took Adam's hand, squeezing it.

'If he gets too close then you just floor it,' Cal went on, doing his best to smile at Daisy. 'Keep them safe, whatever happens.'

He popped open his door, the car rocking as he got out.

'Come on, Brick, you're up.'

'No way, man, I'm staying in here,' Brick said, snorting a laugh. 'Why doesn't Chris go?'

'Can you drive?' Cal asked. The guard was walking fast, shouting something at them. Brick swore, slamming a hand down on the glove box. 'Come on, mate, this is your chance to be a hero.'

Brick grabbed the handle and shouldered open the door, almost knocking Cal over.

'Hey, stay where you are,' the guard yelled. He was jogging now, a big belly swinging beneath his tight, grey shirt.

'Good luck,' said Daisy, putting her hand on the window. Cal pressed his against the other side as Brick slammed the door shut. 'Be safe, Cal, please be safe.'

'You too,' he said. 'We'll meet you at Soapy's, yeah?'

'Gotcha,' said Chris, pressing a button to make the doors lock. 'Good luck.'

'Who arrrrrrr ooooo?' the guard's mouth was drooping out of shape, his eyes filling with a depthless rage. Daisy pushed herself away from the door as his steps became lurches, then bounds, propelling him down the last section of path.

'Go!' yelled Cal, running into the ocean of sea grass that grew by the side of the road. Brick followed him, both boys ducking out of sight as the guard careened towards the car.

'Oh crap, should have thought about this,' said Chris. He spun the wheel, trying to turn round. The back of the Jaguar slammed against the verge as he reversed and the engine almost stalled. Daisy screamed as the guard threw himself against the window, thumping the glass. He butted his head against it, his nose bending at a weird angle. Blood gushed past his yellow teeth but he didn't notice. He didn't know anything now except the Fury.

Chris revved hard. The front of the car scuffed the verge at the other side of the road, bumping up and down, then they were clear. Remembering what he was supposed to be doing, he eased on the brakes. Daisy looked through the back window to see the guard tearing after them, his face a mask of cruelty and anger. Behind him, sneaking from their hiding place, Cal and Brick jogged across the road towards the factory.

'Be safe,' Daisy said to them. 'Good luck.'

But she had an awful feeling that luck wasn't going to be enough.

Cal

Brick reached the booth first, running through the open door so hard that he almost ripped it off its hinges. Cal skidded to a halt outside, casting a look back up the road. He could just about make out the glinting roof of the Jag, the guard's guttural shouts drifting back on the wind. His pulse was so fast and so hard in his throat that he felt like there were fingers there, squeezing.

'Cal, come on!' Brick was at the door, furiously waving his hand. Cal pushed past him into the small room. It was empty, just a desk, a control panel, a couple of security monitors and a phone with the receiver out of the cradle. He lifted it to hear the roar of a car.

'Hello? Chris, you still there?'

'Cal?' Chris's voice was laced with panic.

'Yeah, we just got in. There's nobody else here. You guys alright?'

A pause, then Daisy's voice:

'He's catching up!'

'We're okay,' Chris said. 'Go on, get it done.'

Cal dropped the phone back on the desk, keeping the line open. Brick was focusing on the monitors, clicking a switch that changed which camera was being shown.

'Looks dead,' he said.

Cal walked across the booth to the other door, opening it a crack to see a short corridor. He stepped through, stopping when he heard Brick's voice.

'This might come in handy,' the other boy said, pulling a sheet of paper from the wall and handing it to Cal. It was a plan of the factory, made up of fine lines and even smaller print. Cal recognised the booth in which they stood and, close by, a big rectangle marked 'Staff'.

'Gotta be it,' he said, pointing. 'Right?'

'One way to find out.'

They walked through the door, Brick doubling back to pick up a giant Maglite torch from the desk. He held it like a rounders bat as they ran down the corridor, past a big reception room and a toilet. There was another door at the far end, and Cal opened it up onto a sunlit courtyard. Two jeeps with the factory's logo sat there alongside a dented blue Rover. Cal glanced at the map, getting his bearings.

'That way,' he said, setting off. They jogged past the cars, their ragged breathing the only sound in the entire place. The factory loomed over them, giant chimneys casting finger-like shadows over the open ground. He increased his speed, making for a squat, low building dead ahead.

They'd almost reached it when another security guard appeared, a short woman who strolled out from between two huge, gleaming silos about thirty metres away, swinging a set of keys around her finger. She was whistling, the tune cutting out when she saw them. Cal skidded to a halt against the wall, Brick running into him, and for a second all three of them stood like statues.

'You Roger's kids?' the woman asked, dropping the keys into her pocket and reaching for her radio. 'You can't be playing back here.'

She walked briskly towards them, speaking into her handset. Her words dropped into a low, wet groan, the whine of a dying dog. Then she was running, her hat flying off. Cal ripped open the door, but Brick held his ground.

The woman reached him, her fingers hooked like talons, her teeth gnashing. Brick didn't hesitate, swinging the Maglite. It struck her in the jaw, the crack echoing between the buildings. The woman dropped, a gout of blood spurting from her broken mouth. She twitched, then lay still. Brick stumbled away, throwing the torch on top of her like it was a poisonous snake.

'Get her radio,' Cal yelled. Brick snatched it up from the ground, running to the door.

'Oh Christ,' he muttered. 'I didn't mean to hit her so hard.'

'She'll be okay,' said Cal, grabbing the walkie-talkie from Brick's trembling fingers. 'You didn't have a choice.'

They were in another corridor, this one longer and darker. The only light was coming from a door up ahead on the left. Cal lifted the radio and pressed the button.

'Is anyone there?' he whispered. There was only static. He repeated the question, still no response. 'If there were more guards here then someone would answer, wouldn't they?'

'I don't know,' said Brick. He was as white as a sheet, staring at his hands. Cal grabbed his arm, dragging him towards the door. A glance inside revealed a big room lined with lockers and empty coat hooks. They jogged a little further, past another toilet and a room packed with sofas. *Come on*, Cal thought. They were running out of corridor. *It has to be here.*

It was. The last door they reached led into a canteen with dozens of tables and chairs and a big silver counter. Cal ran past it, through a set of double doors, and he was grinning by the time Brick caught up.

'Whoa,' said Brick.

'Whoa indeed.'

They were in a kitchen similar to the one in Fursville, only this place was spotless. There was food everywhere, shelf after shelf of cans and jars and packets and tubs and bottles. Brick angled straight for a crate of bread, ripping open a wholemeal loaf and wolfing down three slices. Cal was tempted to do the same, a pressure in his gut almost dragging him towards the mountain of crisp boxes in the corner. But they might not have long. They had to take what they could.

'Bags,' he said, dropping the radio on the floor and pointing towards a pile of sacks. He upturned one, releasing an avalanche of potatoes. Brick did the same, both of them working in silence as they looted. Cal stopped when he could barely lift what he had, spinning the sack round to seal up the top. He dragged it towards the door. 'You nearly done?'

'Nearly,' Brick spat through a mouthful of something. He dropped a tin of spaghetti hoops into his sack then spun it closed, hefting it over his shoulder.

They were running out of the kitchen when the radio bleeped. The sound almost stopped Cal's heart dead and he lost his grip on the sack, a box of coconut wafers dropping to the floor. There was a burst of static, then a man's voice.

'Roger? Claire? You there?'

They tore through the double doors into the canteen, but even from here they could hear the radio bleep again, the amplified voice chasing them back out into the corridor:

'Guys, what's going on? The police are here.'

Daisy

The security guard was getting tired, but he wasn't slowing down. He chased after the car with that same ferocious expression, his bloody teeth bared, his fingers stretched out towards them. His feet scuffed the road, and at one point he even tripped, falling flat on his face. Chris slammed on the brakes, waiting for the man to push himself up. He teetered, looked for a second like he might be coming out of it, then caught scent of them again and stumbled forwards.

It was horrible. The guard didn't know what he was doing, and they were going to kill him at this rate. Couldn't they stop the car and put a sack over him, like they'd done with that other man? At least that way he couldn't hurt himself. She didn't suggest it, though, just in case *she* was the one who had to run out and do it.

Chris slowed as he reached the end of the road, Fursville almost directly opposite them now.

'Left or right?' he said, glancing at Daisy in the rear-view mirror. The guard almost caught them again, his fingers squeaking on the boot as Chris made a decision and swung left. Daisy heard the man utter a soft mewl as he scuffed his way along the road after them, his shirt hanging out over his big belly and one foot shoeless.

The poor guy. She wished there was something she

could do. Surely there was a way to switch off whatever was making them so angry. If the man knew what was inside them – that it was something good – then he wouldn't try to kill them. If Daisy was right, and the angels were here to fight the man in the storm, then they were helping people, not hurting them.

Chris pulled into the abandoned showroom across from the park, turning in a circle so they were pointing back the way they came. The man shuffled towards them in a pitiful, shambling run. He tripped, falling again, and this time Daisy heard the crack of a broken bone.

'That's enough!' she said, watching the guard try to push himself up. A red nub of bone was sticking out of his forearm but there was still nothing in his narrow eyes but rage. 'Please, Chris, he's going to die.'

'I don't know what else to do,' Chris said. 'We can't let him catch us, and we can't leave him here because he'll go back to the factory.'

The man had somehow made it back onto his feet. He stumble-ran across the forecourt, his good arm held out. He hit the window, slapping it with no real strength. Chris swore, moving the car out onto the road again.

The ambulance shot by so quickly that it made their car rock. Daisy screamed, watching in horror as the ambulance wobbled, clipping the high verge and spinning into a series of cartwheels. It disintegrated as it rolled, shedding glass and metal and plastic for what must have been fifty metres before lying still. The engine ignited with a soft puff, smoke drifting lazily into the flawless sky. Only the security guard was moving, still throwing weak punches at the side of the car.

'What the hell?' said Chris, his words drowned out by another siren. This one was a police car, catapulting past them and skidding to a halt beside the ruined ambulance. 'Oh no, oh no, this is really bad.'

Two policemen scrambled out of the car. One of them ran towards the ambulance, the other stared at the Jaguar. He shouted something to them but the wind snatched it away. Chris spun the wheel round, accelerating to the left away from the accident. The security guard toppled over behind them, but Daisy was no longer watching him. She was gazing across the flat land towards the factory, and the flickering blue haze which surrounded it.

Cal

It wasn't just the police. A fire engine was coming through the open barrier, its klaxon still blaring. There was already a cop car in the courtyard, and was that a bomb disposal van on the road?

Cal ducked back inside the door of the staff block.

'We've had it,' he said.

'What happened?' Brick asked. 'How'd they even get here so quickly? It's been, what, twenty minutes since we broke in?'

They looked at each other, and the answer seemed to dangle in front of them in the gloom.

'Rilke,' they both said together.

Brick threw his sack of food to the floor. 'I'm going to kill her.'

At this rate he wasn't going to get the chance. Cal could hear shouts amongst the sirens, dozens of them. Luckily nobody was close enough yet for the Fury to trigger. But it wouldn't be long. There were already people running this way through the shimmering blue light. He gently clicked the door closed, his thoughts wheeling.

'Is there another way out?' he asked.

'How would I know?' Brick said. 'Left the map back

489

there, didn't I.'

They set off, dragging their bags of food. There had to be a back exit, surely. For fires and stuff. Cal glanced up, seeing the familiar green emergency signs with the running stick man on them. He followed them inside the canteen, crashing through the double doors. It took him a second to spot the fire exit at the rear of the kitchen.

They were halfway there when they heard a voice from outside, distorted by a loudspeaker.

'This is the police. We know you're inside. Return to the front of the facility immediately.'

'Man, it's like a bank robbery or something,' Brick said. 'What are they worried about, that we're going to steal a big bag of horse manure?'

'It's fertiliser, isn't it,' said Cal. 'It's what terrorists make bombs out of.'

'Out of horse crap?' said Brick as they reached the door. 'Seriously?'

'Shut it, Brick, we need to be quiet.'

Cal pushed the bar in the centre of the door, nudging it open. There was a soft click, then the silence of the room was torn apart by a clanging alarm.

'Real quiet, Cal,' said Brick, punching open the door and legging it outside. Cal ran after him, a blanket of bells sitting over the whole factory. They were in another courtyard, smaller this time, with a squat, square building dead ahead and more massive industrial vats to the right. Right behind those was the wall, five metres high and crowned with black spikes.

'This is your last chance,' said the loudspeaker man, muffled but still painfully clear. Cal thought he heard a bark, the sound making his skin grow cold. Ferals he could outrun. Dogs he couldn't.

'What now?' he said. There were footsteps close by. He glanced over his shoulder, imagining fifty cops tearing round the corner of the staff block. Brick was moving towards the shining metal vats, each of them four, maybe five times as high as the wall. The giant silos were held in a nest of white scaffolding, and it didn't take him long to work out what Brick was planning.

The barks were louder now, heading their way. And there was another sound too, the distant *whump-whump-whump* of a helicopter. Why the hell did it have to be a fertiliser factory? He had to force himself to start moving again, panic making his body feel twice as heavy as it actually was, filling his bones with lead. The sack didn't help, and he nearly dropped it. But if they left here empty handed then they'd be right back where they started.

Brick was obviously thinking the same thing, because he was spinning his bag round like a hammer thrower at the Olympics. He let go of it, food spilling out in a tight circle as the sack rose up towards the top of the wall. It didn't quite make it, bouncing off the bricks and thumping back onto the dirt. He ran to it, picking up cans and cartons and lobbing them individually over the spikes. Cal tore open his own bag and started throwing too, a barrage of food sailing over the wall. He'd thrown seven or eight items when he heard voices, much closer now.

'That'll do,' he yelled, throwing over the now nearly empty sack. 'Let's go.'

They both ran to the nearest silo. Brick went first, jumping and grabbing one of the thick diagonal struts of the scaffolding. He grunted as he hauled himself up, his feet struggling for purchase on the smooth metal. He made it to the next one, and Cal followed. His fingers slipped on his first attempt, jarring his knee as he fell back onto the concrete. He ignored the pain, leaping up and grabbing hold just as the first policeman ran into sight.

The man started to call out, but the word never made it as the Fury took over. He threw himself across the courtyard, his mouth open too wide, his eyes black pebbles. Cal's heart almost juddered to a halt. He reached for the next pole, clutching it and pulling his feet up as the cop slammed into the bottom of the scaffold. Fingernails raked at his ankles, the man's mouth a dark, gnashing pit.

Cal climbed, not caring that he was overtaking Brick. They pushed against each other, their frantic movements almost knocking them both loose. Two more uniformed figures skidded past the side of the staff block, changing into ferals without missing a step. They clustered at the base of the silo, clawing upwards. A fourth appeared, slipping on a can and cracking his head open on the ground.

'Keep going!' Brick said, navigating his way up the

side of the silo. Cal looped his arm around the next strut, almost slipping into the ocean of hands and teeth that swelled beneath him. He hung there, the terror almost too much for him, leaving him faint. He nearly fell, then Brick's hand was on his arm. 'Don't you dare,' the other boy said. 'You're not leaving me on my own.'

His feet found something solid and he pushed himself up to the next level. More and more police were piling into the courtyard, howling as the Fury overwhelmed them, their eyes burning into Cal. There were dogs too, their tails between their legs as they watched their masters turn into beasts.

Brick was level with the wall now. He stretched out one arm, the spikes almost close enough to touch. But it was a long drop, and certain death lay in the surging, shrieking chaos below.

'Do it,' Cal said. 'You can make it.'

Brick swore, then with a choked cry he pushed off the scaffold and flapped towards the wall. He hit hard, grunting, but he managed to hook his hand over the top and pull himself up. The bass thump was louder now; a helicopter flew overhead like a bloated bluebottle. Cal could imagine the pilot's face as he looked down, seeing his police mates baying like wolves.

'You coming or what?' said Brick, moving carefully to the side. Cal eased up another couple of struts, trying and failing not to look down. The courtyard was now a heaving mass of black uniforms and hate-filled faces.

He took a deep breath then threw himself at the

wall, his stomach turning in wild circles as he reached out for one of the spikes. It sliced into his hand but he held on, hauling himself up until he was perched on the edge. A quick glance down the other side revealed a sheer drop into a patchy meadow, nothing but sand and sea grass and assorted items of food.

Together, they eased themselves round, hanging over the drop. The helicopter spun overhead, angling ever lower, battering them with a hurricane of wind and noise. Cal looked at Brick and smiled.

'This is insane. If we die, I just want you to know that you're an asshole,' he shouted.

Brick grinned back.

'I know.'

Then they both let go.

Rilke

Furyville, 6.14 p.m.

It was like watching a dozen different films at once on a television that flicked wildly and randomly between channels.

Rilke could make out snippets – a huge steel container that flashed brilliantly in the sun, a wall with spikes on it, a moving car, an ambulance in flames. But she couldn't make much sense of what she saw. All she knew was that her plan was working. The others, the ones who had turned their back on her, were now at the mercy of the Fury. They would either drown in an ocean of human rage, or they would be forced to take action, to do what it was they were here to do.

They would have to fight back.

She opened her eyes. Some of the madness outside was bleeding into the restaurant. Faint sirens faded in and out with the soft lull of the sea, plus the guttering roar of a fire. There was a helicopter too. She wondered how long it would hang in the sky before its pilot was consumed by the Fury.

'Shouldn't we go and help them?' whispered Jade. 'They'll die out there.'

'Not if they embrace their gift,' Rilke replied.

Schiller had been quiet for a while now, but he was starting to stir. He tilted his head up, looking at her with eyes of fire. His left arm still hung oddly, a lump beneath his skin where the joint had popped out. He didn't seem to be in any pain, though. If anything, he was stronger than she'd ever known him to be, his gaze so intense that she had to look away.

'But what happens when the others are caught, or killed?' Marcus asked. 'Won't the police come here? Won't they sense us?'

'Yes,' she said, glancing at her brother again. 'But we'll be ready for them. Won't we, Schill?'

Schiller lifted his good arm, studying his hand as if he'd never seen it before. It burst into flames, soft blue tongues which caressed his skin, darting between his fingers. He pressed the burning palm against his dislocated shoulder, those playful flames spreading. With a series of ugly, wet cracks his arm slotted back into place. He held both hands in front of him, radiating cold light. He was smiling.

'Oh yes,' Rilke said, grinning back. 'We'll be ready.'

Daisy

'Turn round, Chris, we can't leave them!'

Chris ignored her, the car accelerating hard, an invisible hand pushing her back into her seat. She cried out again, and this time he slammed on the brakes, tyres squealing as they shuddered to a halt. It wasn't her pleas that had stopped him, though. Up ahead, blocking the road, was a police car, its blue lights flashing.

'No!' Chris yelled, wrestling with the gear stick and reversing. He swung the car round, gouging a chunk of dirt from the verge as he drove back the way they'd come. The police gave chase, pulling up close behind them. Daisy twisted, looking at the policewoman driver, seeing the exact moment that her face went from normal-angry to feral-angry. She let go of the wheel, reaching over it. The man next to her was doing the same, leaning forward in his seat, his cries misting up the windscreen.

With nobody steering it, the police car slammed into the angled roadside verge, flopping up then down, the windows shattering and the airbags deploying. Chris was going too fast for her to see what happened to the people inside. The burning ambulance was up ahead and Chris jerked the wheel, Daisy sliding across the leather seat into Adam as they re-entered Soapy's car lot. Two policemen were waiting for them. One flashed past the window, too fast for the Fury to kick in. The other bounced off the bonnet, rolling over the car and hitting the floor limply.

'Chris, no!' Daisy wailed. 'You're killing them.'

He didn't answer her, his eyes bulging in the mirror. He kept his foot down as they ploughed towards the rusty fence at the back of the forecourt. Daisy wrapped her arms around Adam – the boy still as quiet as a mouse – the impact bumping her into the air and cracking her head against the roof.

She blinked away the pain, seeing that they were in a huge, open field. The factory sat at the other end of it, its ugly bulk filling up the cracked windscreen. She bit down on another cry as the car bounced over the uneven ground, her insides feeling like they were being shaken to pieces. At least they were going in the right direction again. They might be able to find Cal and Brick.

A fresh siren, another police car pushing through the loose flap of fence and giving chase. This one was bigger, one of those giant truck things. It hardly even seemed to notice the craters and hillocks of the field, looming up behind them like a shark in the ocean.

'Don't!' Daisy cried out to the policemen inside, her voice lost in the thunder of engines. 'You'll get hurt!'

But they had already turned feral, nothing but glinting eyes and half-moons of teeth in the darkness of the four-wheel drive. It shunted them, the back of their car jolting off the ground. The view through the windows lurched like a ship's wheelhouse in a stormy sea. She had time to see the ditch dead ahead of them, a deep scar that ran the width of the field.

Then the car plunged into it and her world flickered off.

Cal

Cal cried out as he landed, his legs sinking into the soft, beachy soil. This time the pain in his knee was like a poisoned knife twisting into the cartilage. There was a thud as Brick dropped beside him, rolling clumsily away from the wall. He scrabbled to his feet and picked up the sack Cal had thrown over, before running back and offering Cal a hand.

'You okay?' he asked, hauling him up. The pain flared as he pulled his foot free and he couldn't stop the moan tumbling from his lips.

'I'm fine,' he said, limping across the rough ground. Brick ran off, frantically foraging for food in the short grass and throwing anything he found into the sack. From behind them came a nerve-shredding chorus of banshee wails and the thunder of fists against the wall. The cops would go back to normal as soon as he and Brick were out of range, then they'd start the chase again. The helicopter roared above them, flattening the strands of sea grass and making the field ripple like water. It was pumping out so much noise that Cal didn't hear the growl of engines until there was an almighty crunch from the other side of the field.

He looked up to see a silver car flip end over end, its bonnet crumpled up like a fist, punching into the

500

dirt, then collapsing onto its roof. A police Land Rover somersaulted gracefully over it, losing momentum mid-air and tumbling sideways. Smoke spewed from the wrecks, but through the billowing black curtain Cal recognised the driver.

'It's Chris,' he said, pointing. He began to run, his twisted knee forgotten.

'Here they come,' yelled Brick, slinging the half-empty sack over his shoulder. Cal glanced back to see four or five cops charging from the main road, all of them shouting and pointing. They were a hundred metres away, maybe, but they'd soon catch up once the Fury had them.

We're going to die, Cal thought, and he was surprised by the lack of emotion. It was a statement of fact, one that seemed to carry no weight. If anything, it filled him with a trace of relief. *No more running, no more hiding, no more not knowing*. Just death.

And then he thought of Daisy, upside down in the car, clawing at the window as petrol fumes filled her lungs. He ran harder, putting his head down, overtaking Brick. In the distance, another Land Rover was emerging from Soapy's, the bulk of Fursville hanging over it like a dark cloud as it accelerated across the field. Incredibly, somebody was clambering out of the crashed one, too, a broken shape whose police uniform had all but been torn away. The man staggered onto his feet, then seemed to collapse on the upturned Jag, kicking at the windows.

'What do we do?' Brick said, wheezing.

They were halfway between the factory and the car now, the sound of shouting behind them rising up even over the thunder of the chopper. There were barks, too. It wouldn't be long before Cal felt needled teeth in his legs, dragging him to the ground. Then it would be game over.

'Cal? What do we do?'

He didn't have a plan, only his instinct. If they could just get to the car, if they could just reach Daisy, if they could just get back to the park, they'd be okay.

'Keep running,' he shouted as they closed the gap. The other Land Rover was going to beat them to it, but it didn't matter. 'Keep running, and trust me.'

Daisy

Somebody was shaking Daisy from a dream of fire. She was glad, because in her dream the whole world was burning, but instead of heat there was cold − bodies freezing and buildings collapsing while ash-coloured snow fell from the heavens.

She snapped open her eyes, thinking at first that her dream had come true. Everything was wrong, the world upside down, her head full of horrible, choking smoke. Her whole body ached, but there was a really bad slicing pain in her neck. When she reached up − no, *down* − she felt a noose there, digging into her skin. It took her a moment to understand it was her seat belt.

It took her another moment to realise that Adam was next to her, crouching on the ceiling which was now the floor. His small hands were on her shoulders, shaking her wildly, and his sooty face opened up like a flower when he saw that she had come round.

'Are you okay?' she wanted to ask, the words coming out as a hacking cough. Something was banging, a bare foot crunching against the window, the toes bruised and bent unnaturally. Daisy's memories shone in the smoke, the police car that had chased them, then Chris driving into a ditch.

Chris. He too was suspended the wrong way up, in

the driving seat. Blood dripped freely from his nose, forming a little pool on the ceiling. She called his name between more coughs but he didn't respond.

Adam was fiddling with something on the seat, and she followed his hands to her seat-belt clip. The button was jammed, not budging no matter how hard she pressed it. A powerful wave of claustrophobia ripped through her and she cried out, tugging the belt in an attempt to free it. There was a funny smell in the air, behind the smoke. It was the way her dad smelled every time he put the barbecue on in summer. It was the horrible fuel stink that came right before a fire.

'Go,' she said to Adam. 'Get out.'

She wasn't sure if they were words or just coughs. Either way Adam showed no sign of leaving. He pulled at her belt, making soft, scared whimpers, his face screwed up with the effort. She could hear another engine sound from outside, then their car rocked wildly as something thumped into it. The cramped space seemed to shrink and darken even further, like it was sinking into the ground. There was a soft *whumping* noise, and the air flickered and glowed.

'Please, Adam, you have to go or you'll die in here.'

He shook his head, still pulling at the belt. There was a shriek from outside, then the window right next to her shattered. A pair of rough, bloody hands reached in. She screamed, fingers like steel rods in her skull. Another crash, a cut-throat grin slithering in through the boot and bloodied fingernails around Adam's throat.

Daisy's vision was fading, the pain too much. And the worst of it was that as the shadows and the smoke crept into her head, turning everything to dusk, she could only hear Rilke's voice. *I told you*, it said. *Why didn't you listen?*

But if Rilke was right, and they were here to murder the world, then Daisy didn't really want to live any more anyway. She would rather be with her mum and her dad, wherever they were. At least this way she could go home.

She let go of the claws that ripped at her scalp, and reached out to Adam.

'It's going to be okay,' she said. 'We're going together, and I'll always look after you.'

Even though he was being dragged from the car, Adam seemed to hear. He stuck out his hand, stretching his fingers towards her. And incredibly, he was smiling.

It's not such a bad way to leave, Daisy thought. *Looking at a smile.*

And offering him one back, she grabbed hold of his hand.

Brick

Brick was only ten metres away when the car exploded.

The upturned Jag was surrounded, five policemen kicking and punching it, trying to get inside. One of them had his hands through the back window and Brick could make out a familiar face in the billowing smoke. Daisy. Rage boiled up from his stomach, howled from his mouth as a ragged scream.

'Leave her alone!'

There was a flash of pure, white light, a bubble which expanded from the car and blasted away the smoke. Brick threw himself to the ground, a hand over his face, waiting for the fire.

It never came.

He looked up to see that searing white light engulf the police, burning through them. They crumbled into ash like sticks of dry wood, filling the air with a snowstorm of burning embers. The blinding orb flickered, then was sucked back into the car with lightning speed. A shock wave blasted across the field, a crack of thunder that almost knocked Brick's head off. Then an impossible silence.

He worked his way unsteadily to his feet, swaying. Beside him Cal was doing the same, wiggling his fingers in his ears as though he'd gone deaf. They peered back through the infinite quiet to see the surging mass of police still stampeding towards them from the road, not yet close enough for the Fury. In the other direction the Jag sat inside its blizzard of incandescent ash, no sign of life anywhere near it.

'What happened?' Cal's voice sounded a mile away. Brick flexed his jaw, noises gradually easing their way back into the world. The helicopter had pulled back from the explosion, but it was hovering above them again, the downdraught making Cal's hair billow.

Brick didn't answer him, just started running again. It was only after a couple of steps that he realised he'd dropped the half-empty sack of food. Not that it mattered — as hungry as he was, it didn't look likely that any of them would live long enough to eat again. He reached the car in seconds and dropped to his knees beside it. Hot ash danced around his face, burning his skin where it landed. He brushed the falling flakes of dead people away, peering into the crushed darkness to see Chris there.

'Daisy?' Cal yelled, ducking down next to him. They both looked into the back seat. It was empty. 'He must have dropped them somewhere. Come on, help me get him out.'

'But I just saw her,' Brick started, wondering if he'd only imagined her face in the churning chaos.

Cal tried the door but it was crumpled into itself. He stood back and kicked the splintered glass of the window, reaching through the gap and calling Chris's name. Brick looked up, the mob of cops maybe thirty metres away, close enough to make the ground shudder. There was an army of them.

He pushed in beside Cal, both of them trying to loosen the seat belt. There was a pool of blood in the bottom of the car, still dripping off the tip of Chris's nose. He was unconscious, his motionless bulk making it impossible to free him. Brick glanced up again. Twenty metres, and the ones at the front were already turning. He grabbed Cal's shoulders, pulling him out of the window.

'We can't leave him!' Cal shouted, throwing himself back, wrenching at the boy inside.

'We have to,' Brick said. Fifteen metres, a line of witches' faces. 'Cal, come on!' He grabbed Cal's arms and ripped him free, hauling him up. '*Look!*'

They stared at the wave of uniforms, the grunts and howls and shrieks and growls almost too much to bear. Cal looked back at Chris.

'I'm so sorry, mate,' he said. Then they were both running again, bolting from the madness at their heels.

Daisy

Daisy felt like she'd been inside a tumble drier, her head spinning and her stomach churning. She doubled over, a jet of milky vomit erupting from her mouth. Flecks of fire settled in the mess, hissing as their heat was extinguished. The air was alive with fireflies, those same glowing embers that she'd seen back in the restaurant with Rilke.

She realised there was a hand in hers and she looked to see Adam there, a halo of ash circling his head, dropping onto his shoulders. He was still smiling.

Daisy stood up, reeling. She was standing in a field. The *same* field. But their upside–down silver car was all the way over *there*. She spun round to see the deserted showroom right next to her, and behind it the towering toothless grin of the big wheel inside Fursville.

We moved ourselves, she realised. *We touched hands and somehow got from over there to over here.*

Gradually pieces of reality were clicking back into place – the sound of sirens and the fat, black fly that hovered over the distant car. Squinting into the sun, she could make out a swarm of people stampeding across the other side of the field, and two more sprinting towards her.

'Cal!' she shouted, recognising them. 'Brick!'

She tightened her grip on Adam's hand and started

running, stumbling over the lumpy earth and through knotted traps of long grass until they were within earshot.

'Daisy?' Cal was calling. 'You okay?'

'I'm okay,' she said, skidding to a halt, panting. The two boys galloped up to her, both of them drenched in sweat. They all looked back across the field. The car was invisible beneath a mass of writhing, black-suited forms, the helicopter hanging over them and making the whole horrible scene swim in dust.

'Chris,' said Daisy, the tears bubbling up even though she didn't want them to. Whatever they'd done, her and Adam, they'd left him behind. She peered through the blur to see Cal shaking his head.

'I'm sorry, Daisy. We couldn't get him out.'

There's still time. She didn't say it, though, because it was a lie.

'We should go,' said Brick. 'We might be able to hide inside the park. It's our only shot.'

But none of them moved, watching as the horde tore its way into the upturned car. And they all felt it when Chris died, a sudden cold shadow in their heads as though something had been switched off. A burning shape seemed to claw its way out of the wreck, a flickering, insubstantial figure made of flame. It spread its huge, graceful wings, opened its mouth as if to howl, then evaporated into the heat and noise of the meadow.

That was Chris's angel, Daisy thought. *It died too.*

'Come on,' said Brick. 'We should go.'

Daisy looked for a moment more, seeing the police seem to snap out of a trance. Some of them had red, glistening hands. She hated them so much. It didn't matter that they hadn't known what they were doing, that it wasn't really their fault. They'd still murdered him. Some of them were already turning to face her, pointing and shouting. The helicopter banked, sweeping towards the park.

They clambered over the broken fence that led back into Soapy's, running past the bodies of the security guard and the policeman. The ambulance lay to their right, just a smoking shell. But there was nobody else in sight. Daisy looked up as they jogged across the road, seeing the sign that Brick had painted over. *Furyville*. Cal disappeared into the thick hedge and the rest of them followed. Only in the welcome coolness of the shade did Brick turn to her.

'What happened back there?' he asked. 'In the car? I saw you inside it, then you vanished.'

'It was the angels,' she said. 'Rilke was right. They moved us. They *saved* us.'

'And what happens now?'

'Something bad, I think,' she said, shaking her head. 'I don't know.'

She didn't know, yet hadn't she already seen it? The park drowning in flames, and Rilke standing in the middle of the inferno, laughing. What choice did they have, though? Outside there was only the Fury, there was only death. At least in here they were together.

Brick held her gaze for a moment more, then he took her hand and led her into the park.

Rilke

'They're here,' said Schiller.

Rilke straightened at the sound of her brother's voice, the first words he'd spoken since this all started. He sounded the same, and yet different. There was a hidden depth to that familiar, whining tone. Something ageless which resonated inside her skull.

She stared at him. His hands were still alight, painting the room in a shimmering glow. As she watched, the fire spread up his arms, engulfing his torso and his neck and finally his face. His eyes were two raging suns, their light overwhelming. Rilke gazed into them, and it was like she was looking through her twin into a realm of pure being, a place of terrifying, mesmerising power.

Schiller shrugged, and this time two translucent wings unfurled elegantly behind him, stretching over his head like twin sails. They seemed to shimmer in and out of being, as if they were made from nothing more than air, heat. He extended them, their tips almost bridging the gap between the restaurant walls, and when he folded them again they unleashed a hurricane of wind. It sent Marcus and Jade rolling across the room, tables and chairs crashing into the walls, but Rilke held her ground against the cold blast, kneeling before her brother like someone praying at an altar.

She had never loved him more.

'You know what you have to do,' Rilke said to him. He cocked his head, unsure.

'I think so.'

'You *know* so,' Rilke said, standing and taking a step towards him. 'Because I've told you why you're here, why this is happening. Don't disappoint me, Schiller. Don't disappoint *them*.'

Schiller's fire flared, and he smiled at her.

'I won't, sister. I promise.'

Jade was crawling frantically back, her eyes like saucers. She lay prostrate beside Rilke, laughing. Marcus huddled against the back wall, shaking his head. Schiller extended his wings again, and with a gentle effort he raised himself into the air. He began to move, not walking, just gliding a foot or so off the ground. Beneath him, things seemed to grow from the floor – tremulous shapes that looked like budding plants but which were made of flame, twisting and dissolving after a second or two.

'Where is he going?' asked Jade.

'To do what he was called here to do,' Rilke said, watching her brother float ghost-like towards the doors. He pushed through them, and the wood evaporated at his touch, blossoming into a cloud of dust and ash which defied gravity, buoyed up by the energy streaming from him. Rilke followed him as he descended the stairs, Jade huddled against her, Marcus too, all of them treading carefully over the carpet of glowing tendrils in Schiller's wake. He still gave off that subsonic hum, a sound that made the air tremble.

'To do what we were all called here to do,' Rilke said. She was giddy with excitement, a surge of insane glee which rattled up her throat and exploded from her grinning lips. 'He's going to start a war.'

Cal

Brick led the way down the side of the Boo Boo Station, his face a grimace of panic as the helicopter swept overhead. A tornado of rubbish swirled in the narrow alley, the world shaken by the helicopter's relentless thunder. Cal kept hold of Daisy's hand, screwing his eyes shut against the grit, trying to remember the way. He could hear Brick calling out:

'Where are we going?' At least that's what it sounded like. There was no air any more, just the howling dust.

He opened his eyes as much as he dared, pointing up the path.

'Pavilion,' he shouted. It wouldn't exactly be safe, but there was nowhere else to go. In seconds the park would be infested with police, all of them feral. If they could get inside then they might be able to barricade the doors, hold up until they thought of a plan. Brick shrugged, cupping a hand to his ear. 'Pavilion!' Cal repeated, as loud as he could manage.

He didn't wait to see if Brick had understood, just dragged Daisy to the end of the path then up past the carousel. The chopper banked round the big wheel, the wind easing up. In the sudden lull Cal could make out voices behind them. He looked back in time to see the main gates balloon inwards, spitting shrapnel.

There was the growl of an engine, and with a massive crunch the chains snapped. A Land Rover barrelled into the park, its bonnet smoking, and a river of police streamed after it.

'Do not move!' one of them shouted, pointing right at Cal. 'Or we will open fire.'

Open fire?

Three helmeted cops with sub-machine guns ran to the front of the pack. They crouched, aiming the weapons down the path. Even from here Cal could see that their fingers were on the triggers. Who could blame them? They'd just seen their mates get blown into ash. He slung his hands up, turning to the others, mouthing, *What do we do?*

But there was nothing they could do. If they ran, the chances were they'd be mown down. If they stayed, they'd be torn to pieces as soon as the cops got close enough.

'We're just kids,' Cal shouted. 'Don't shoot.'

'Stay where you are,' shouted the same man as before. Some of the cops were moving cautiously forward.

'Please don't,' Daisy said, sobbing. 'If you come near us then bad things will happen. Please stay away.'

'Yeah,' said Brick, his voice cracked in a hundred places. 'We've got a bomb.'

The police hesitated.

'A bomb?' hissed Cal, looking at Brick. 'They're definitely going to shoot us now.'

'We need you to put the device on the ground,' the

man shouted, his words almost drowned out by the helicopter that circled overhead. 'And step away. Do this now, or we will be forced to shoot.'

'Now what?' Cal said.

'Hell do I know?' Brick spat. He took a step backwards, his hands locked in his hair.

'Brick, stay still for God's sake,' Cal said. But the boy wasn't listening, taking another step, and another. His body was tense, like he was going to bolt. 'Brick, *don't!*'

As he spoke, he realised that the helicopter wasn't the loudest sound in the park any more. There was something else, a hum inside his head, soft but deafening. It was like the noise an amp makes when you stick an electric guitar in it but don't play any notes, a dull buzz which was making his skull vibrate. Brick could obviously hear it too, because he clamped his hands to his ears, crying out.

A howling shriek, one of the cops stepping past the invisible line of the Fury. His face shrivelled into something that was only just human, white rage driving him on. Someone else, a policewoman, chased after him, turning feral, both of them hurling themselves down the path.

There was nothing else to do. Cal turned and ran, they all did, as the air behind them was torn apart by gunfire.

Brick

Adrenalin made the world turn in slow motion. Something whistled past Brick's ear, sounding like a hornet, stinging his flesh. He ducked down, his arms and legs like pistons as he sprinted towards the pavilion, his brain screaming *Not me, not me, not me* in time with every pounding step. He didn't look back – not because of the fear but because of the guilt of leaving the others.

He made it halfway before he saw it, the sight stripping away every grain of strength and making him crash to his knees.

Schiller floated from the pavilion, bathed in flames, the building's walls literally peeling away from him like the edges of burning paper. His feet didn't touch the ground, an invisible force holding him up. Something extended from his back: a pair of wings made up of gossamer-thin flames. The boy's face wasn't his any more – his eyes were twin furnaces which blazed out across the park, devoid of all emotion. It was the most terrifying thing Brick had ever seen.

There was more gunfire, but distant now. It no longer seemed to matter. Brick heard cries, the cry of the Fury, but he couldn't quite remember how to be scared. He could only gaze at Schiller as the boy advanced. He would look at him forever, even if it burned his eyes from their sockets. Was it possible that a creature like this lived inside him too, dormant for now but ready to wake and embrace the same power? For the first time he believed it, he believed what Rilke had said.

Schiller reached him, making the path erupt into a forest of fiery plants which curled up and vanished as quickly as they appeared. The hum in the air was incredible, a current of pure energy. Brick shuffled round on his knees, watching the boy – the *angel* – as he glided towards the front of the park.

It was chaos over there. Cal was on the ground, pinned by two cops, his legs kicking out helplessly as they tore at him. Daisy and Adam were still running, both of them blinded by tears. Behind them was a seething wall of feral police. The three men with guns were still firing. A bullet punched through Daisy's shoulder, emerging from the other side and dragging a comet tail of dark red blood behind it. The impact threw her forward, rolling her over in the dirt until she slid to a halt, motionless.

'Daisy!' Brick shouted. He raced over, skidding down beside her and lifting her head. Her eyes were open, but they weren't seeing anything. Adam was there too, holding her hand in both of his, tugging on it like he was trying to wake her up. 'No!' Brick shouted, the word as weak and as useless as he was, drowned out by the gunfire and the roar of the helicopter and that endless, nightmare hum.

Brick lifted her up and pushed his hand against the wound, blood spilling through his fingers, so hot it felt like it was scalding him. He held her, wanting it to be over, wanting it all to end. It was just too much.

Schiller turned his head, surveying the park with those soulless pockets of light. The men with guns had turned their weapons on him – aside from one, who had ripped off his helmet and was gouging at his own face in a fit of insanity. The bullets seemed to freeze when they reached the boy, hanging in the air in front of him and forming a shimmering curtain of lead. With a swipe of his hand, Schiller scattered the bullets in all directions, a dozen cops thrown backwards as their heads and chests exploded.

Kill them, Brick screamed silently. And he wanted it more than anything. These pathetic, murderous humans who had broken into his home, who had attacked his friends. They had given up their right to life. He clutched Daisy to him, firing out the message to the boy who hung in his cradle of flame. *Kill them all, kill them now.*

A hand dropped onto his shoulder and he looked up to see Rilke there. Jade and Marcus were behind her, both of them transfixed by the creature before them. Rilke smiled at him.

'He will,' she said, turning her face up, bathed in her brother's golden glow. 'Watch.'

Schiller opened his arms, like he was about to hug someone. His eyes settled on the police. More and more of them were turning feral, running up the path towards the angel. Even the ones that had been stamping on Cal switched their target, throwing themselves at the floating boy.

They didn't even get close.

Without so much as touching them, Schiller lifted the two closest men into the air and turned them inside out – their bodies folding and refolding until they were nothing more than mangled meat. He flicked his hand and the ruined corpses sailed over the park, rising into the darkening sky as though launched by a catapult. The other ferals didn't notice and continued to charge mindlessly towards him with bared teeth and clawed fingers.

Schiller cocked his head and another dozen cops were scooped up by the same invisible force. This time they were thrown at each other, crushed into a giant sphere of flailing limbs. It spun wildly, growing smaller and smaller with a chorus of cracking bones until those twelve men and women were no bigger than a beach ball. The knotted lump of flesh slammed into the ground with enough force to shatter the concrete, a web of cracks stretching out from the crater.

This isn't right, something in Brick protested. He pushed it aside. He didn't want to hear it.

The helicopter was retreating, pulling up fast. Schiller pumped those vast wings and launched himself into the air. He rose alongside the machine, and even though he didn't lay a finger on it the rotors buckled and twisted, breaking free with an ear-shattering squeal. The rest of the chopper began to crumple, something red and wet blossoming behind the shattered windscreen. Then the wreck jolted to the side with incredible force, ploughing a hole through the pavilion and the fence beyond, carving a mile-long trench across the surface of the sea.

The ferals were still coming, but Schiller had only just started to experiment with his powers. He dropped back down, stopping just above the ground and stretching his arms out once again. The electrical hum grew louder, making Brick's eardrums feel like they were about to implode. The flames around the boy were as bright as magnesium flares, burning a hole in the very surface of reality. His mouth opened, a pocket of utter brilliance.

And he spoke.

His voice was wordless and world ending. It was a roar that ripped through the air and shook the ground to dust. Everything before it fractured and disintegrated – the concrete and the stone beneath, the Land Rover, the bricks in the walls, the metal gates, the flesh and blood and bones of the ferals, the mud and grass in the field beyond – a tidal wave of broken matter which rose into the air, blotting out every last scrap of sunlight.

Brick cried out, teetering on the brink of madness as that cloud rose and rose into an endless, lightless night.

Then Schiller's voice died and the night died with it, a million tons of debris falling back to its resting place. Brick curled into himself, the noise impossible, utterly terrifying. The world shook, and shook, and shook.

And finally fell silent.

Cal

Furyville, 7.05 p.m.

For as far as he could see, the world was an ocean of ruin; a landscape of rubble and plundered earth, rent and broken all the way to the distant factory. Even that hadn't escaped unscathed, pillars of smoke rising in front of the glowering sun like prison bars. Dust was still falling, a rain of dirt and blood and bone which pattered onto the vast grave that had once been Hemmingway.

Every part of Cal was in pain. He thought his nose might be broken, and there were welts over his face and neck where the ferals had torn at him. One of his fingers was bent at an odd angle, too sore to touch. He cradled it against his chest. He should be grateful, because he was alive. But he wasn't. The cost of his survival was too great. It wasn't just the town that was gone. Everything he knew had been irrevocably changed.

It took him a moment to find the courage to look round. The first thing he saw was Schiller. The boy sat on the path, his legs curled up to his chest, no trace of the flames or the wings or those star-burned eyes. He was shivering, and his sister crouched beside him, her arms locked around his shoulders. Jade and Marcus stood close by, holding each other.

Brick was on the other side of the path, next to Adam. He was holding something, and when Cal realised it was Daisy he pushed himself up, stumbling over to them. The girl was deathly pale, an ugly, gaping wound in her shoulder. But she was alive. Her soft, shallow breathing filled him with such an overwhelming sense of relief that he didn't notice the ice until he touched her.

She was freezing.

He pulled his hand away like he'd had an electric shock. Her skin was pearled with frost, and the chill that emanated from her was like a winter breeze.

'Daisy?' he whispered, stroking her cheek. 'Daisy? Can you hear me?'

'She isn't answering,' said Brick, his teeth chattering. The tears had frozen in the corners of his eyes and on his cheeks, hanging there like glass beads. 'It's just like Schiller.'

'She's changing,' said Rilke matter-of-factly.

'She didn't want this,' said Cal. 'Make it stop.'

Rilke shook her head.

'None of us can make it stop. Didn't you *see* him? Don't you understand what we're capable of?' She laughed, a chuckle of amazement. 'It was wonderful. Schiller saved you, Cal, he saved all of us.'

He had. There was no doubt about it. Without him, they would all have been trampled into the dirt. Rilke's twisted logic battered against his mind. Was she right? Was this really why they were here? To uproot all of humankind, to purge their species from the face of the earth. He looked out across the wasteland that Schiller had created. Only it wasn't a wasteland. It looked more like a field which had been ploughed and furrowed, which was ready for something new. And the peace that hung over it, free of shouts and screams and sirens. It was truly perfect.

And yet still that nagging doubt, the feeling that Rilke was wrong, that she was making an awful mistake.

'Daisy will be okay,' said Rilke. She got to her feet, hooking an arm under her brother and hoisting him up. Schiller smiled at her, just a boy again. But that power was still there, his to call on. Cal knew this the same way he knew that he too would someday go cold, and that something terrible would break through his soul. 'We'll all be okay. You'll see, Cal. It might take a day, it might take a week, but you'll see.'

'It doesn't hurt,' said Schiller, his voice weak and quiet, almost exactly the same pitch as his sister's. After seeing him burning through the sky, ravaging the earth, Cal could make no sense of the young boy before him. 'It's like . . . like there's something in your body, but it doesn't control you, it doesn't force you to do anything. It just makes you strong, it keeps you safe. Don't fight it, it's . . . it's . . .'

He obviously couldn't find the word, but his rapturous expression said everything.

'But it told you why we are here, didn't it,' said Rilke. 'To wage war with humanity.'

Schiller's eyes fell, scouring the ground for a truth he

couldn't quite find. Rilke's grip on him tightened, so hard that Cal saw the boy wince.

'Tell them, little brother.'

'Yes, that's why we're here,' he said, trying to break away. But for all his new-found power he couldn't find the strength to free himself from her. His eyes met Cal's and there was fear in them, fear and a heartbreaking sadness. 'That's why we're here.'

Rilke started walking, her brother taking small, cautious steps like someone using his legs for the first time. Marcus ran to the boy's other side, looping Schiller's arm around his shoulder and taking his weight. Jade finished the procession, brushing her hair from her eyes and glancing nervously at Cal.

'You don't have a choice,' said Rilke as she walked patiently by her stumbling brother's side. 'No matter where you go, no matter what you do, the same thing will happen. People will try to hurt you, and you will fight back. They won't leave you alone. They can't. It's in their nature. And that rotten, violent, corrupt nature is why we're here. We got it wrong; it isn't their Fury that will change the world, it's ours.'

She looked down at Brick, the warm, gentle smile never leaving her face.

'Just think about it. Try to imagine what this world will be like when our job is done.'

Cal *could* imagine it, nothing but sunshine and peace.

No no no no no, the protest railed, a drumbeat in his skull.

'Look after her,' Rilke said, stepping onto the ocean

of dirt, her feet kicking up clouds of black ash which had once been buildings and cars and people. 'It will be easier for you when she wakes.'

'Where are you going?' Cal asked.

'Nowhere, and everywhere,' was her answer. 'When you're ready, you'll know how to find us.'

Cal watched her walk into the reddening sky with her flock – Schiller, Jade and Marcus – the dust of the world raining down at their feet.

'We need to go too,' said Brick. 'This place will be swarming soon. We should find somewhere safe.'

Safe. Rilke was right. There was nowhere safe any more. They would be hunted wherever they went. Cal looked down at Daisy, radiating coldness, her eyes iced over, her small face expressionless. He wondered where she was, and what she could see there. He wondered if she knew what she would become when she woke.

'Yeah,' he said, getting up. 'You're right. Let's go. My mum's car's still down the beach, by the toilets. We can use that. You want me to carry her?'

'I'm okay,' Brick said, struggling to his feet with Daisy in his arms. He shuddered with the cold, his words billowing from blue lips. 'You take him.'

'Come on, little guy,' said Cal, scooping up Adam, wincing as pain lanced down his broken finger. The boy didn't react, staring at something only he could see. 'Don't worry, it's gonna be okay.'

'No it's not,' said Brick. 'Whole planet's going to hell.'

'Thanks. Way to make him feel better.'

'Up yours,' Brick said, but there was a glimmer of a smile in his eyes. It spread to Cal, and even though it had no place here it felt good.

'You really are an asshole,' he said through a grin as they staggered across the park. Brick looked around, sighing. Then he turned back to Cal.

'I know.'

Epilogue

Whoever battles with monsters had better see that it does not turn him into a monster. And if you gaze long into an abyss, the abyss will gaze back into you.

Friedrich Nietzsche

Daisy

She had always thought that death would be peaceful, a place of infinite calm and quiet.

But Daisy stood inside a kingdom of fire and ice, of relentless movement and noise. She was at the junction of a billion different lives, the joining place of worlds. From here, she could see everything.

She had been shot, she knew that much at least. They had been inside the park, Fursville, running from the police. Then she'd felt like she had been struck by a sledgehammer. She couldn't remember hitting the floor. It had been more like she'd fallen *through* it, through the skin of the real world and into what lay beyond. She'd been like Alice tumbling down the rabbit hole, only what she was looking at now was no Wonderland.

And there was no sign of her mum and dad. She'd hoped at the very least they'd be here waiting for her.

It's because you're not dead, something said. Was that her own voice? She couldn't be sure, everything was too chaotic.

'Who's there?' she called out. 'Where am I?'

No answer. She focused on the wheeling shapes around her, all inside ice cubes just like the ones in her head. They made no sense, countless flickering images and muddled sounds in each one.

'Daisy, can you hear me?'

The voice seemed to cut through the rest, and with it one of the ice cubes grew larger, groaning and cracking like an iceberg as it filled her vision. It was Brick, his copper hair glowing in the sun, his clothes ripped to tatters and covered in blood. It seemed like his chest was on fire, an orb of blue flame which sat where his heart should be. He was holding something in his arms, a tiny shape whose head lolled, whose eyes were open and unseeing. It was *her*, she realised. But she wasn't scared, because she too had a smokeless inferno inside her chest – one that burned even brighter.

It's them. That's where they live.

And with that thought the ice cube melted. Another rose in its place, and through it she saw more people she knew. Rilke was helping her brother, Schiller, walk across an endless field of dust and dirt. Marcus and Jade staggered alongside them, their shadows long in the setting sun. They all had flames in their chests too, except Schiller, whose whole body was alight. He seemed to have another shape laid over his own, a figure with blazing eyes and huge, Sphinx-like wings which left glowing trails where they dragged in the ground. Looking at it made Daisy feel scared and excited at the same time.

That's what they look like when they've . . . She paused until the word *hatched* popped into her head. *Yes, when they've hatched. They can't survive in our world, so they have to live inside us.*

The image changed again. Did that mean she was right? Was this a test, maybe? She swept towards Rilke, into the girl's head, the world unravelling and reforming. This time she saw people, hundreds of them, maybe thousands. Schiller stood amongst them, his face emotionless as he spread his hands and turned those men and women and children to dust. She could just about see Rilke there too, grinning insanely, before the scene was lost in a billowing cloud of ash.

So this is why we're here? Daisy said, her heart dropping to her toes. *But I don't want to hurt anyone. People do sometimes do bad things, and some of them aren't very nice, but most are kind and funny and peaceful. They don't deserve to die.*

The same scene again, Schiller slaughtering countless more innocents. Daisy seemed to understand what she was being shown.

That's what Rilke sees, she said. *But she's wrong, isn't she. We're not here to kill people, we're here to save them.*

The shadows of the last scene melted away, the ice cubes clinking. Even though she had no body in this place, no face, she still felt like she was grinning.

I knew it! she told the angel inside her. *I knew you weren't bad!*

Her happiness didn't last, though. Another image swelled, this one even worse than the last. Daisy knew what she was going to see there, but she could not close her eyes. She felt herself pulled into the scene, battered by a wind that stank of flesh and smoke. The man in the storm hung inside a nest of fractured darkness, his mouth a churning, grinding whirlwind. That same horrid, deafening sound — the endless inward breath — made her skin crawl.

Daisy screamed without sound, struggling to escape. But there was nowhere to go. She could do nothing but watch as the man in the storm opened his arms and more of the world shattered like glass, falling into a bottomless, lightless abyss. It was impossible not to notice how similar he was to Schiller. But this thing was utter evil, the opposite of life. The man in the storm turned his dead, scribble-black eyes towards her and somewhere in that awful sound was a sickening, gleeful laugh. He tilted his corpse hands and even from this distance, even though she was only seeing it inside her head, she could feel the light draining out of her, the happiness and the love. It was leaving her utterly empty.

He's why we're here, Daisy spat, squirming, praying that it was the right answer and that the scene would fade away like the others. *He's a bad man, and he's doing something terrible, and we have to stop him.*

Cracks began to appear in the view, a golden glow spilling through them until the man in the storm disappeared in the haze. Daisy walked into the heat, like she was stepping onto a beach in the middle of summer. There was nothing here but light.

Who are you? she asked. *Are you angels?*

No answer. The view didn't change. Did that mean she was right or wrong? Or maybe she was a little of both. Maybe they weren't angels, but something else — something that people had caught glimpses of over the centuries and which had been given that name. There were all sorts of things that people didn't know about yet. Who's to say that creatures like this couldn't exist?

Daisy realised that there was a face in the light, so faint that it almost wasn't there at all. It was devoid of all emotion and feeling, its eyes burning sockets. It seemed to constantly peel apart and repair itself, as though it couldn't hold its shape for longer than a few seconds. Those blazing eyes looked at Daisy, so much power there that she could hear it in the air like an endless roll of thunder.

This is my angel, she understood, her terror and her awe like a white heat inside her.

Then, just like that, the light fell apart, the face dissolving into the fading glow. Daisy felt herself pulled away, so fast she left her stomach behind. She landed somewhere dark and cold, but she could feel that creature in every cell of her body, its fire spreading.

Voices, ones she recognised, echoing in the shadows.

'Which way?'

'Any way, just get us out of here.'

She would wake up soon enough, and when she did she would be something different, something more. But Cal and Brick and Adam would still be there. They'd look after her. She'd look after them, too. That was her job now, at least until their angels hatched.

And when that happened, they'd all be ready.

Ready to fight the man in the storm.

THE STORM

The story concludes in *The Storm*, coming soon.